Max Blake,

Federal Marshal

Trail of
Revenge

Max Blake, Federal Marshal

Trail of Revenge

William Florence

Dally Press

Dally Press
12822 E Rialto, Sanger CA 93657
On the internet at
www.dallypress.com
email: editor@dallypress.com

ISBN 0-9718511-3-1

Max Blake, Federal Marshal
Trail of Revenge
© 2005 William Florence

This publication is a work of fiction. Any resemblance of any character within this work to an actual person, living or dead, is purely coincidental. The names, characters, locales, and incidents depicted in this book are either the product of the author's imagination or are used fictitiously; any resemblance to actual persons, living or dead, is entirely coincidental. The exception, of course, is Arizona, although the territories presented here continue to exist at least in the spirit of the Old West.

Cover: Ben Protasio and Jack Lee

ACKNOWLEDGMENTS:

Bob Leroy, for a thorough critique of the early manuscript; Floyd Strand, M.D., for valuable medical perspective on black powder gunshot wounds; Raphael Drouillard, who invented the instructions; Jack Lennox of the University College/Dublin, for his expertise on all things Irish; Stevie Purchase, for landscape research; Ben Protasio and Jack Lee, for cover art and design; and for all of you who lent a name to the cause, the author is both grateful and deeply indebted.

Trail of Revenge

A Max Blake Western

"Trail of Revenge" is the second book in the Max Blake Western series. If you enjoy this book, ask about "The Killing Trail" at your local bookstore, or visit www.dallypress.com for more information.

For Linda, for Will, and for Erin
... *Stelle brillanti nel cielo occidentale*

Prologue

Hunting Parties

Reno Walker was spitting mad.

The outlaw sheriff of the outlaw town of Aguante refused to tolerate bad luck, ineptitude, and men who didn't follow orders – and he was staring into the face of all three.

He didn't like what he saw.

"If I don't get some answers," he said, "I'm gonna bust up some thick heads. And I'm good at bustin' heads. Talk."

"Yes, sir. We lost 'em not more'n an hour out, sir," Amos McFadden said with a nervous, uncertain shrug.

McFadden was a tall, raw-boned deputy with dull eyes fastened to an otherwise eager face. His fingers curled in and out in rolling waves when he talked – a nervous habit made worse when he faced his quick-tempered boss – and McFadden and his partner, a deputy named Underhill, had plenty of reason to be nervous now. It was clear that the sheriff was ready to explode, and that was not a good thing for any living creature within a fifty-mile radius of the seedy border town.

"So where are they now?"

"We don't know, sir."

"Then what are you doing here? Why ain't you trying to find 'em?"

"Most of the boys are doing just that, sir. I came back with Hillie 'cause, well – 'cause we got a theory, I guess you'd call it, as to what these skunks might be up to."

"A theory? You have a theory, McFadden? I'm surprised you know the word."

The sheriff regularly carried a horse quirt, and he was thumping it into

8

his gloved left hand as he talked, staring holes into the two men who faced him. The steady beat of hard leather on rawhide was disquieting to McFadden, whose stellar qualifications for promotion to Aguante deputy rested on the fact that he had recently killed three men during a card game in El Paso; he was good with a gun and wasn't adverse to using it.

But his gun skills didn't make him feel any easier now as he stood rigid before the man who controlled Aguante. McFadden's fingers continued to roll in waves, and he nodded at the sheriff but said nothing.

Aguante was a haven for violent lawbreakers in the vast, empty lands that stretched across the bottom of the Arizona territory: Order was assured by the iron fists and fast guns of Reno Walker. But the order of things had changed six hours earlier, and Walker was searching for reasons and for answers – and for easy targets.

"Let me get this straight," he said, his right hand working the quirt with a steady motion. "Two jackals march into the saloon, kill two reliable men, burn the place to the ground, disappear in the night – and you have a theory?"

McFadden jumped when the smack of the quirt exploded like a gunshot.

"Yes, sir," he said, his eyes on his boots.

"All right, let's hear this theory," Walker said, his fingers fitting nicely around the quirt's black handle. "Seeing as how it's brought you here with no Hoss Johnson or that other back-shooter in tow, I trust you feel good about it."

"Yes, sir. Well, first off, we know they had help. We had signs of five sets of tracks heading out toward the border – due south as the crow flies. They was making a bee-line fer Mexico."

"Get to it, McFadden."

"Yes, sir. Five sets of tracks, though one or even two of 'em could have been pack horses – hard to say 'cause the wind was already starting to blow hard when we lit out. But we knew they had some help, and it likely come from here.

"So we got out there a ways, and I get to figuring that maybe them boys wouldn't be dumb enough to try and head into Mexico with us right on their heels. I mean, that's what everyone would expect 'em to do, and they had to know we'd come a-chasin' 'em, which is jest what we did."

McFadden worked his fingers doubly hard now, talking even faster when he saw the sheriff grow increasingly impatient.

"So I figured they used the wind to double back on us and likely are hiding right here in town while we chase 'em half way 'cross the desert.

"That's why I came back, sir – with Hillie here. The rest of the boys are out there, hunting for any sign of track. We jest wanted, me and Hillie, to make sure we had everything … covered is all."

Walker shook his head in disbelief.

He was a tall, muscular man with deep-set blue eyes that sparked with whatever emotion he felt at the time. He had a chiseled face with a day's growth of thick stubble and a nose that was bent at odd angles from too many fights with too many hard men. The top third of his left ear was missing, the result of a close call from a gunfight in Tucson. His black Stetson was cocked toward the left side of his face in an effort to cover a portion of the missing ear, though no one who knew him would dare stare at the damage or comment on it. He wore trademark buckskin trousers with a matching fawn-colored buckskin vest over a bright red flannel shirt. His gloves, blackened and hardened from wear, completed the image that the sheriff liked to convey: authority, meanness – and dangerous, deadly business.

He had used many names through the years; Reno Walker was only the most recent. He liked the sound of it, and he had once been lucky in the Nevada town.

"That's some story, McFadden," he said at last. "You came up with that?"

"Yes, sir. Well, me and Hillie, I guess – but mostly me, sir."

Underhill, who stood silently by, head bowed, snuck a quick glance at McFadden, his face betraying a hint of gratitude. It was a look that the sheriff picked up, however, and his eyes flashed with anger. "You must be dumb as a stump," he said.

McFadden blanched but didn't say anything – an omission that likely saved his life – as he cautiously held the sheriff's steady gaze.

"And how 'bout you, Underhill? You got anything to add to this tale?" the sheriff asked.

"No, sir. Other than we talked to Thompson and Culveyhouse a'fore we headed back. They seemed right with it, sir – something about looking in all the dark corners."

"They did, huh?"

"Yes, sir." Both deputies spoke in unison, shaking their heads emphatically.

Reno Walker scowled in turn.

"Let me explain something that's escaped you both: I control this town. I know every move made by every rooster and hen in it, and I know it quick. Do you really think for a minute I would somehow miss this Johnson fella and his idiot partner crawling back to town? You kin look me in the eye and say that?"

McFadden shuffled his feet, his fingers working hard now to keep up with his thoughts and nerves. He glanced at his partner again, but Underhill was staring at the floor, his mouth clamped tight.

"No sir, I guess not," McFadden said at last. "I don't see how it's possible, now that I think on it some – even if them boys had some help, which … ain't likely, I guess."

"I'm going to let you in on a secret, McFadden, because you might amount to something if you keep yer eyes open and yer mouth shut and yer thinking to yerself." The sheriff thumped his quirt once more, his gaze shifting from McFadden to Underhill and back to McFadden again.

"Hoss Johnson and this other fella had no help from no man who was in town a'fore they arrived. I figure they had help from the man thumped Gentry dead. And I figure that same fella is riding with 'em right now – somewhere out in the desert, not here in town. You follow?"

The deputies nodded vigorously but didn't venture a word.

"The lesson here, McFadden, is I do the thinking. You don't think. You do what I say and keep thinking out of it. Understand?"

"Yes, sir."

"Good. Now take that idiot with you and get out. And don't come back without them peckerwoods in tow. That clear enough?"

"Yes sir."

McFadden bolted and smacked into Underhill, who also was on the move. "For gawd's sake, Hillie," he said. "Ain't you got no brain in yer head a'tall?"

When the deputies were gone, Walker turned to Richard Nash, who was lurking in a dark corner. "You believe that?" he asked, his anger barely concealed. "Underhill I kin understand; he ain't got two sticks to rub together fer brains. But I had more hope for McFadden. We'd best keep an eye out – can't have thinking become contagious."

"Yes, sir," Nash said with a chuckle.

Richard Nash was the lone man in Aguante who could talk with the sheriff on equal terms. The two paired up years before in Denver and had covered each other's backs through hard times and harder miles. Nash was a smaller version of the sheriff: muscular, with grim, dark-brown eyes pinched into a natural squint, a trim black beard and mustache, and a face like tough leather from years in the sun and wind. Both of his ears were intact, but a long scar on his right cheek betrayed a penchant for knife fights.

"I don't like it," the sheriff said at last. "I'm troubled 'bout them back-shooters and whoever it was helped 'em. And I ain't liking we've had no sign of this killer who took out Gentry, though it could be the same man. So McFadden's talk of five sets of tracks might make some sense; how he stumbled into it is a mystery."

Nash remained silent, his eyes devoid of emotion.

"All right," Walker continued, "we'd best take a long look at sentries. We knew about Johnson and the one with him – Morgan? – not more'n a minute after they got here. But we sure didn't know 'bout the other two till they all a'sudden showed up. What happened to Baxter? He was supposed to be up on the hill all day."

"Yes, sir. Best I know, he was up there and keeping watch."

"That don't seem likely now," Walker said. "I find out different, I'm like to shoot him full of holes."

"You want me to have a chat with Rufus and that ridge-runner he's taken on?"

Walker thumped the quirt again. "I'll handle Baxter. What's Hicks says about the saloon."

"They salvaged the south end – maybe a bit more. Hicks kin have the whole thing replaced in four weeks if we freight in some decent lumber. The galoot he works with, Parker, is trying to figure out where to get it and save time."

"Somebody's gonna pay for torching the saloon."

Nash nodded. "I'll see to it right now."

Nash was about to leave when a harried young deputy ran, panting and nearly out of breath, into the office. Clyde Roberts was a short, compact man with a nervous smile and an anxious disposition that was exaggerated when he was in close proximity to Reno Walker. The sheriff scared the man, and try as he might, Roberts couldn't hide that fear.

"Something you need to know, sheriff," he said. He glanced at Nash for an instant, but his eyes nervously returned to Walker before shifting off in another direction.

"It'd better be good news then, Roberts. Talk."

"Yes, sir. I'm afraid not, sir – it's not good news, I mean." He paused, trying to catch his ragged breath, his eyes still shifting about the room. "We hadn't heard from Jim and Pete after they took that stranger from the jail out to the desert – the one you beat hell outta after we caught him – so we sent a couple'a boys out to scout their tracks.

"We found 'em a mile or so out, both of 'em tied to the wagon. Jim was thumped good on the head. This stranger got the drop on 'em somehow – caught 'em by surprise."

Walker whacked the horse quirt hard on his desk as his eyes smoldered. The sound made Roberts jump.

"Any sign of the stranger?" Walker asked after a minute.

"No, sir. Nothing yet."

"Dammit." He thumped the quirt again, this time in his hand.

"Any sign them two idiots was hitting the bottle?"

"The boys we sent told me a jug was empty and dumped at the side of the wagon when they found 'em."

Walker cursed again. "Where are they right now?"

"Pete's back to the hotel, sir. Jim's getting his head looked at. He took a fair thumpin' a'fore he was hog-tied."

Roberts continued to run his eyes around the room, at times finding Nash's gaze, at other times glancing for an instant at the sheriff before searching for a wall or a corner to ponder. He shifted his weight, giving the appearance of a man who would rather be elsewhere – anywhere, in fact – but directly in front of the Aguante sheriff.

Walker didn't like Clyde Roberts, and he found himself growing increasingly annoyed at the man's shuffling. *His day is coming, but it ain't today – and lucky for him,* he thought.

"All right, Roberts, go get both them idiots and bring 'em here. I'll deal with it right now."

"Yes, sir."

Roberts hurried out the door, leaving Walker and Nash alone once more.

"Well, that puts a cork in an ugly night," Walker said. "I got a feeling things might perk up, though. Somebody's gonna pay, and I got me two candidates."

The sheriff smacked the quirt viciously into the desk again.

"Give me yer thoughts on that stranger we entertained in the jail – the one these two are gonna answer for," he said after a minute.

Nash considered his reply carefully.

"We didn't hold him long enough to get good information, and the fire got in the way. But there was something about him you could … appreciate, maybe. He was tough; he stood up to that beating as well as any I've seen."

Walker's eyes flashed. "I don't like the thought of that one running loose. Might be he's nothing to us; maybe not. Might be he was in cahoots with Johnson and his partner. Ain't likely, but it might be."

The sheriff thumped his quirt again, his gaze drifting across the room. "There was something about the man – he was no cowpoke just passing through. I don't know what or who he was, but there was nothing I liked – and a lot more I didn't. I figure the man needs some attention. You get my meaning?"

Nash nodded, taking a moment to pull a thick cigar from his shirt pocket.

"Good. Saddle up and track him," the sheriff said. "I don't care how long it takes or where it takes you, so long as you get him. You right with that?"

"Yes, sir."

"Good. See to it."

"I'll leave now," Nash said, and he held Walker's gaze for a moment before he turned toward the door.

"Hey, one more thing," the sheriff added.

Nash stopped and turned. "Yes, sir?"

"Good hunting."

Chapter One

Chance Encounters

When the searing sun finally broke through the low-hanging clouds and haze that clung to the sides of the mountains like the billowing folds of a woman's skirt, it already was just shy of noon and Jack Sloan couldn't keep his mind on anything but a stiff drink of whiskey.

A whiskey and a beer, maybe – and a couple of both would be even better, he thought.

He laughed aloud at the idea – a barking, bellowing hoot that echoed off the flanks of the surrounding mountains and carried far off on the wind – and firmly nudged his horse forward. *I'll be in town in two hours and good and drunk in three,* he thought. *How can a man top that?*

Sloan had left his camp in the higher elevations at daybreak and wound his way steadily down a faint game trail, picking a path across the rocks and shale and scree that crumbled and splintered and cracked away beneath his horse's hooves. He was on a mission to drink and talk, in that order, and nothing short of sudden death would stop him.

Sloan was reed-thin with a rough-hewn, florid face that had fronted too much sun and too much wind through too many years of punching cows and pushing horses from points north to Canada and as far east as the Dakotas. He had tried many jobs at various times, some more savory than others. He had gone by many names, made and lost many friends, and acquired a fair share of enemies.

Frustrated that all he ever got from punching cattle was meaner and older, and with his skin turning into hard leather, he had quit a couple of years back and drifted farther south. He found his way to the Arizona high country, looking for color in the rocks that would lead to a vein of gold.

The life hadn't made him any meaner, but he was two years older and still no closer to a big strike – a thought that crossed his mind every day. It was a thought, in fact, that made him want to drink, and Sloan was an eager drinker. He also was a talkative drunk, but that just made him doubly happy: He enjoyed talking almost as much as he enjoyed drinking.

Sloan's destination was the bustling settlement of Adobe Flats: population fifty-five and growing. He had been to the town once before, about four months earlier when he left the mountains after his overpowering thirst overtook his lust for gold. He had stayed for three days, drank until he could no longer stand, and needed a full week to stop the dull throbbing in his head.

Even the crisp mountain air was of little help.

He had no idea how he made it back up the mountain. He also used every bit of gold dust he brought along for the binge, and that was most of the dust that he had collected during the better part of a year of working a clumsy sluice.

But the thought of that trip brought a smile to Sloan's dry lips, and he laughed aloud once more. *A whiskey and a beer and another whiskey at the same time,* he thought, looking ahead to his first request at the bar. *I can just about taste it.*

He understood full well the reason why he drank to excess, of course. But he chose not to dwell on it – or at least not on this day.

His dusty black Stetson was as rough as his thickly bearded face, pulled low across his eyebrows to cut the angle of the sun. He wore dirty denim trousers better suited to a trail drive than to working a claim, but they were the only pair he owned. He carried a revolver and knew how to use it as well as any cowhand, which was at least adequate for shooting snakes at close range. But his skill was useless against a determined man who could pull a gun and fire it rapidly and accurately from the opposite side of a dusty street, and he knew that, too.

Still, Jack Sloan feared no man save one. He was good with his fists, willing enough to pull his gun in a fight – even though he had run from such fight in his younger days – and he was afraid now only of dying alone without a bottle in his hand.

He was closing in on Adobe Flats, whistling softly to himself, when two strangers – the town's judge and undertaker, as it turned out – rode toward him in a billowing cloud of dust that was unsettling to a man intent on drinking and enjoying the company of talkative strangers.

"Murderers," one of the approaching riders shouted as he bounced past, slowing only momentarily so that he could yell out his warning. "There's murderers. Run if you want to live."

The second man also slowed his horse and called out as best he could: "Don't go ... heading into town ... if you value your life, or ... it'll be the last place ... you ever go." The man seemed to be out of breath, as though he had run all the way from Adobe Flats on foot instead of riding on the back of a sleek, hard-galloping horse.

This was more than enough to get Sloan's full interest, and he turned his horse quickly about and hailed the two as they hurried past. "Hold on there a second," he called.

When the galloping riders refused to stop, either because they didn't hear him or wouldn't comply, Sloan carefully and deliberately pulled out his long-barreled Remington .58 caliber revolver, a weapon he had won in a card game with a former Union Army officer who had once served in the Great War Between the States, and fired off a single noisy round into the air.

As the gunshot thundered off the heavy pines and rattled farther up the walls of the swiftly rising mountain sides, the two men riding in earnest in the opposite direction skidded their horses to a halt. They turned the animals about and looked angrily into the face of Jack Sloan.

"You'll pardon our caution, but you'll get the three of us killed by firing that gun of yours. And I for one take exception to that, sir. Can't you see ..."

"Didn't you hear ... what was said here ... a second ago, mister?" the other man broke in, glancing sternly at his riding partner. "Good lord ... man, but there's ... murderers afoot in Adobe Flats: honest-to-God ... murderers, I tell you. We only escaped within an inch of our ... lives. You have no right to ... detain us – no right at all."

The man was regaining his breath again, giving Sloan the impression that he could take the time to have a thorough conversation.

"Just hold on," Sloan said, his right hand firmly wrapped around the Remington. "Slow down and tell me what's going on, you two. I'm thirsty and a touch on the talky side, and I aim to bring my business to town and do something about both, murderers or no."

"You'd better pick another spot, mister, because Adobe Flats is sure death," the taller of the two men said. "There'll be business in spades when it's over, but it'll be the dubious business of burying men, not serving them drink. I'm an undertaker by trade, and it grieves me deeply to say that – if for no other reason than I won't be there to ply my considerable skills."

"Exactly what kinds of murderers are we talking about here?" Sloan asked.

"Why, renegades. Where have you been?"

"Renegades? What renegades?" Sloan asked. "The Apaches aren't ..."

"Apaches?" one of the men interrupted in disbelief. "Who said anything about Apaches?"

"Yer the one mentioned renegades," Sloan replied casually, noticing the way the pair continued to glance nervously at each other and down the trail they had just covered, expecting the devil at any moment. *Something has them spooked, all right,* he thought – *good and worried.*

The undertaker looked Sloan up and down, clearly not pleased with what he saw. "I don't know what rock you crawled out from under, sir, but it must've been a large one. Considering the bleakness of our situation, I don't know why I take the time to even talk with you."

"It might have something to do with this," Sloan said with a half-smile, holding the Remington higher in his hand.

"Yes, you are quite right, sir," the man said with a nod, his eyes glued to the revolver. "I'll tell you what I know, but the discussion will be brief."

Sloan nodded agreeably, and the man forged ahead. "We have in our midst what appears to be the very Confederate renegades who have stirred up trouble for days – or so we've been told. There's been hell to pay in the territory, sir. We've heard talk of raids and of killings – lots of killings, in fact – and even of torture and … and worse things. Where the dickens have you been through all of this?"

"Prospecting," Sloan said with a slow drawl, wiping his mouth with the back of his hand. "I've been up in the mountains to the other side of the rim and ain't seen hide nor hair of another living man till this very morning, and he was the first in weeks. He didn't say anything about renegades, though. So if you tell me about Confederates on the prowl, it surely is some piece of interesting news to me, what with the war being over for some years now."

"We are most happy to oblige your curiosity, sir, the status of the late war being of no concern whatsoever," the second man said. "And now that we have courteously performed our civic duty, allow us to offer a cheerful good-bye and continue on our way before those murdering gray-coats catch up with us and God only knows ..."

"What is it that you do in Adobe Flats?" Sloan interrupted, the trace of a smile working its way across his rugged face.

"I was the judge," the man replied. "Note the past tense: was. I am no longer the judge. I am leaving – quickly leaving, in fact, if you would only let me do so. We both would like to leave at this very instant, if only you would let us, sir."

"First things first," Sloan said with another waggle of his revolver. "What's a band of Confederate renegades doing in Adobe Flats?"

"We only heard the rumors."

"What rumors?"

"About the gold, man – rumors about the gold."

"What gold?" Sloan asked, his interest immediately quickening.

"Nobody seems to know," the undertaker said. "There's talk of a missing Army gold shipment, but no one knows a thing beyond that. And now the renegades are here, and all hell's come down on us. So let us pass. They may be on our trail as we speak, ready to murder us, too."

"They were chasing you two then?" Sloan asked. "How many of 'em are there, all told?"

"Not exactly chasing us," the man replied uneasily. "But they might as well have been. And there were many of them: ten, a dozen, two dozen – maybe more. More than enough to kill us all, I can assure you of that."

"How's that again?" Sloan asked, his tone remaining warm and friendly as he enjoyed the pair's uneasiness. "Why would any renegade worth his salt want to kill the likes of you – or me, comes to that? Unless they thought you two know something about this gold shipment. Is that it? You fellas have the gold and they want to get it from you?"

"Haven't you been listening to what we've said?" the undertaker jumped in again. "These renegades are shooting up the town. They are murdering our friends and neighbors in the street. And you want to pass the time with silly, meaningless questions? We know nothing about gold shipments or anything else. And I'm sorry if we fail to impress upon you the true nature of the emergency at hand, but we clearly have no more time for this.

"Good day to you now, sir – with your leave or without it. We are off, and there is little you can do or say to stop us without firing that ancient revolver of yours again."

The pair turned to ride when Sloan called out: "You boys can head on down the trail if you like. But there's no way of telling if you'll run into something even worse in that direction than what you saw down the other."

"And what exactly do you mean by that?" the undertaker asked, again pulling his horse to a halt. Both men turned once more to face Jack Sloan, who couldn't hide a broad grin.

"Well, you know exactly what yer dealing with back there – a handful of renegades, as you call 'em, who may even be gone by now," Sloan said casually. "Hell, I can't hear any shooting – can you? But it's just possible that things might get worse for you both by going the other way.

"That's all I meant to say, really."

"Well if that doesn't top everything I've ever heard in my life," the undertaker said incredulously, finding his voice once more. "We meet the Devil himself in Adobe Flats in the form of murdering renegades, and you would have us believe that we could encounter an even worse fate by riding as hard away from that direction as possible."

"Yep, that about sums it up," Sloan said. "You recall that stranger I told you about earlier, the one I met up with this morning near the three-pointed peak? He was in a might of a hurry, too; told me to watch out for the Morgan brothers. Thing of it was, he was heading in this direction" – Sloan pointed back over his shoulder – "riding hard to the town you boys just left behind."

He grinned and shrugged, as though nothing more remained to be said.

"The Morgans?" the judge asked, adding genuine puzzlement to his frightened, angry face.

"The very ones," Sloan said, his full grin returning once more. "The Morgan brothers – that's exactly what the man told me: Freeman and Weasel. Such were his very words.

"So you boys just be my guest and head off in that direction. As for me" – and at this, Jack Sloan turned his horse about and started off once more in the direction of Adobe Flats, calling over his shoulder – "I'll take my chances with a handful of renegades, Confederates or otherwise."

"I don't know what you saw or heard earlier today," the judge called back, "but I know for certain fact that Max Blake killed the Morgan brothers not more than two weeks ago. Surely you've heard of Max Blake – the federal marshal out of Twin Forks?

"So you head where you like and do what you want, and good luck to you. But I have every reason to believe that we will run into far less resistance going in this direction" – and he pointed with a long arm – "than you will in yours. A good day to you, sir – and a good day forever."

As the judge and undertaker turned and bolted down the trail heading away from Adobe Flats once more, Jack Sloan was halted in his tracks with a frozen half-smile on his face, wondering for the first time in a long time exactly what he should do next.

"Max Blake killed the Morgans?" he said aloud after a full minute had passed and a distant trace of trail dust was all that remained of the two galloping strangers. "Gawd a'mighty, but is anyone safe from that man?"

Chapter Two

A Minor Detail

A cool chill began to blanket the sand and sage and mesquite and thistle that covered the ground for miles in every direction between Aguante and the border. It was always surprising, even to those who had spent their lives in the great expanse of desert in the Arizona Territory, how quickly the air turned frosty and then downright cold once the baking sun finally ground its way deep into the edge of the earth.

Deputies David Doucette and Jay Silverbird were silent as they left the border town in a wagon pulled by two draft horses of considerable girth. The animals that Silverbird selected for the task were larger and stronger than the job required of them – a fact that had gnawed at Doucette for some time.

The two were more than a mile outside of town and well off the trail leading directly to the border when Doucette looked hard at Silverbird, opened his mouth to talk, and then thought better of it and instead tossed a pebble at the rump of the horse in front of him.

"You know how I get tied up in details?" Doucette blurted out at last, his voice cutting like a sharp knife through the crisp desert air.

Silverbird, a tall, thin man who shared Apache, Cherokee, French, Canadian, and Irish blood, looked at Doucette and nodded. "Sure," he said with a shrug of his muscular shoulders. "What's bothering you now?"

Doucette tossed another pebble. He was a patient man, tall and fair-skinned, with a trademark wide-brimmed Stetson that he wore to keep the sun off his pale skin. He tugged at it now and rubbed a dark red welt on the side of his cheek.

"I got to git me a better hat. The sun jest burns up my face something awful."

"That's what you wanted to tell me?" Silverbird asked, his soft, melodic voice indicating mild irritation. "That's the detail you want to share with me and that cargo riding in the back?"

"Naw, hell, it ain't that; it ain't got nothing to do with that," Doucette said, still rubbing his cheek. "It's jest, well, I need to work harder at staying out of the sun, is all."

"Good. You do that." Silverbird shook his head as he looked hard at Doucette. "I'm glad you find that important right now, considering what's going on around us and back in town and what we're about to do and all."

"Aw, it ain't that, you dumb – "

"You'd better watch what you say next," Silverbird cut in. "For a man who pays attention to small details, you are close to forgetting an important one."

"Calm down, Bird – no need to be ornery. It's jest that I've been thinking about, well, why you picked the two biggest horses in the livery when we ain't got us but two dead bodies in back of this rig. That's the detail I been thinking about."

Silverbird stared at his partner, disbelief etched on his gaunt face. "This is what's been eating at you since we left town? Why I picked these two horses to do this job?"

"Well, yeah – it's been on my mind some, sure," Doucette said. "I mean, ol' Jim and Pete didn't weigh much in life, and they is far beyond caring now. And these horses here are – well, look at the size of 'em, Bird. You'd think the sheriff had shot up a dozen men and told us to dump the bodies, from the size of these two critters you picked. What the hell was you thinking about when you picked 'em? That's what I meant."

"Whoah. Hold up there!"

Silverbird pulled the team to a stop and turned halfway around on the buckboard seat so that he could look squarely at Doucette. "This has been bothering you?"

Doucette nodded. "Yeah, it has."

"Since we left town?" Silverbird asked, as though he couldn't quite grasp the concept and had to clarify it in his mind. "All this time?"

"Well, hell, yeah – it's bothered me some. That's why I brought it up. You gonna git this rig moving, or you thinking we maybe should dump them boys here?"

Silverbird arched an eyebrow and shook his head again. "If that don't beat all," he said at last. "I take the time to pick Jim and Pete the best draft horses we got to carry 'em to their final rest, such as it is, and this turns into some great concern for you?

22

"I swear, Davey, that you ain't right in the head sometimes. I think the desert sun has somehow cooked yer brain into some kind of damned stew, and what's left up there ain't nothing but – hell, I don't know, scrambled eggs or something."

"Scrambled eggs? In a stew? Why, yer crazier'n me if'n you think that scrambled eggs ever end up – "

"Let it go," Silverbird cut in sharply. "Yer missing the point, and one more time at that. For a detail man, you sure don't spot too many of 'em – even when they's staring you right in the face. What's wrong with you anyways?

"The point I'm making is I liked them two boys we got loaded in the back. I liked playing cards with Jim, and I always thought Pete was good in a fight. I'm damn sad them two is back there dead as stumps – and, hell, you ought to be, too."

"Well, I am," Doucette said after a minute of consideration. "I ain't happy the sheriff saw fit to kill 'em dead. It weren't their fault that drifter got away from 'em, you ask me. Sure, they might've took a pull from the jug time to time, but so would any man. What's all that got to do with them two big horses?"

Silverbird laughed out loud at the question – a deep, throaty bellow that carried far out into the night. He nudged the horses forward again and looked at Doucette, who sat on the buckboard with a wry smile on his face, as though he had missed the punch line to his own joke and was trying to replay the conversation in his head again to figure out where he went wrong.

"For a man who prides himself ... hell, Davey"– and Silverbird broke out in laughter once more.

"I liked them boys is all," he said after a minute, "and I wanted to see 'em off on their last ride with the best we had. How's that for a detail you can get your arms around, you dumb silly bastard?"

"Hey – I ain't dumb, and I sure as hell ain't silly," Doucette said indignantly, crossing his arms in front of his chest and staring straight ahead again as the wagon lurched across the broken terrain. "And I guess what you say makes sense, wanting to see them two off in style after the sheriff shot 'em both full of holes.

"But that's the thing of it, Bird: The sheriff is starting to act ..."

Doucette let the words hang in the air, and Silverbird set the reins in his lap for a moment and pulled his collar tight to ward off the growing chill.

"You'd best be careful what you say 'bout the sheriff," he said at last.

"A whispered word gets back to Reno Walker, and I'll be hauling your sorry carcass out into the desert. Don't want that detail – no sir."

"You don't feel like talking to the sheriff – "

"Let it go, pardner; I know what you mean. Truth is, we work for a man who's slightly more'n crazy – and he's getting crazier by the minute, you ask me. And I ain't sure what we kin do about it, exactly."

"We kin always quit," Doucette said with a shrug.

"As if he'd let us jest git up and walk away. I don't rightly see that. Even if he did – or even if we managed to git out – then what?" Silverbird countered. "What would we do? Where would we even go?"

"We could make our way down to Mexico, I reckon. We might find us a couple of little Mexican gals with long dark hair and – "

"Ain't no Mexican gal gonna settle down with you. Hell, that face of yers is a damn sight even I kin hardly stand. No sir, I'd say we're stuck right here, marking time and keeping our heads down and out of the line of fire – and sure as hell out of the sheriff's crosshairs."

"But I'm telling you, Bird, the sheriff is getting – "

"We need to let it go if we want to stay living. That man is hell on two legs and the Devil hisself, and we both of us know it, and that's all that needs saying.

"Whoah there. Hold up now." He pulled suddenly on the reins, bringing the horses to a halt once again. "I guess this is as good a place as any. Come on."

The two climbed from the wagon and headed to the back, where the bodies of two Aguante deputies, killed unceremoniously by Reno Walker, had been tossed an hour earlier.

"Look at 'em," Doucette said, shaking his head. "The sheriff worked 'em over good the last two days a'fore he finally got 'round to killing 'em off. Damn shame, you ask me. Damn waste of good men."

"Letting that stranger get away and getting hog-tied the way they did weren't no good, but this weren't necessary. I mean, look at Jim here. The sheriff must have put – what? – six or more bullets into him."

"More like a dozen maybe. Come on, let's git this done and head on back."

"Wait. I brought along a little help," Silverbird said, reaching under a heavy wool blanket and pulling out two long-handled shovels. "I don't care what the sheriff told us. I ain't gonna leave these two out in the night for the coyotes or buzzards to tear apart."

"Good. We ought to bury 'em and not leave 'em out for the critters to pick at."

24

"Let's get to it then. What the sheriff don't know won't trouble him."

"I ain't worried what troubles the sheriff," Doucette said. "It's our hides I worry about. I'm a detail man, you understand."

"Then let's get this detail done and head back to town."

Chapter Three

A Gathering of Flies

Jack Sloan rode slowly through the littered main street of Adobe Flats, taking in the carnage on all sides. He pulled the big Remington from the battered holster strapped to his leg and held it expectantly in his calloused right hand, waiting for the slightest sign of trouble.

My gawd, he thought. *What in the Sam Hill happened here?*

He counted a half-dozen bodies in the dust and another three on the boardwalk that fronted the saloon, the general store, and the trading post off to his left as he rode through the silent street.

Three dead horses, still saddled, were lying in the dirt near the front of the saloon; another horse was tied to the hitching post, nervously twitching its tail in a losing effort against the already-gathering flies.

Them two down the trail was right to be in such an all-fired hurry getting the hell away from here, Sloan thought, thinking back to his earlier conversation with the town's judge and undertaker as they raced out of Adobe Flats. *I feel bad holding 'em back on a lark.*

That conversation had seemed almost comical to him at the time, in fact; but all that had changed as soon as he rode into the town and looked around.

Right now a man's got to wonder where everyone's gone off to, or if anyone's left alive a'tall.

As he drew nearer, Sloan could see that the horse tied to the hitching post had been hit by stray gunfire, and he climbed down to check the damage. A bullet had grazed the animal's flank, but Sloan decided that the wound looked worse than it actually was after he steadied the

26

frightened beast with some soothing words and a gentle hand.

A rain barrel, peppered with bullet holes, was trickling water into the dirt at the side of the saloon. He cautiously holstered his Remington as he walked over to the barrel and shook it back and forth, splashing more water onto the thirsty ground. He mixed a thick paste of mud with his fingers and took a handful back to carefully spread over the horse's wound.

"Easy there, big fella," Sloan whispered as he worked, scratching the animal's head with one hand at the same time that he covered the wound with the mud. "This won't hurt you none."

He made a second trip back to the barrel, gathered another handful of mud, and again gently covered the horse's wound before wiping his hands on the sides of his pants and pulling out his revolver once more. Looking up and down the street and seeing nothing else moving, he stepped onto the boardwalk and cautiously walked through the batwing doors leading into the saloon.

He was thinking again of a whiskey and a beer – for the first time since he rode into Adobe Flats.

But the blast of a single gunshot suddenly shattered the stillness of the high desert air and sent Jack Sloan crashing to the floor of the saloon.

Chapter Four

Calls in the Night

The voice carried softly on the night air, stirring the solitary figure from a restless sleep.

In the man's sluggish, dream-filled mind, the call was a bellow that rolled in from the distance – a wounded range cow, perhaps. He reluctantly focused his attention, slowly but steadily, until the images of an injured animal gave way to a human voice.

"Hellllllllooooooo the camp."

The man was in no hurry to reply, choosing instead to watch and listen and wait. When the silence of a few seconds drifted into half a minute or more, the voice again called out from the darkness; it was gruff and persistent this time and had a nervous edge to it.

"Helllllllllooooooooooo, you at the camp: We're coming in, so you best git ready. This here's a warning. Our intentions are mostly peaceable, and nothing more's intended."

The words lingered in the quiet of the night air, and the now wide-awake man in the bedroll thought for a second that he recognized something about it.

Federal Marshal Max Blake had stopped close to sundown near a clump of cottonwood trees, establishing a cautious camp and building a low fire. He had boiled a half-pot of coffee and warmed a ration of prairie stew before seeing to his horse a final time and settling in for the night. He had been on Judge Thomas Radford's business for three long days and longer nights, covering miles of hard ground with hard traveling and no sleep at all to this point, which explained why he had finally dozed off – for exactly how long, he wasn't quite sure.

Max's Colt revolver was in his right hand, the hammer cocked, his taut index finger on the well-used trigger. He smiled grimly and murmured under his breath, "We start the game again."

But he felt something – sensed something, really – that he didn't like. It was lurking in the darkness, well beyond the hailing voice, something he had been vaguely aware of, on and off, from the moment he had halted for the night. And so he took his time and called out in a low, steely voice, "State your intentions before you move a foot."

"We mean no harm, mister; no need to git yer back up. Smelled the coffee's all, my partner'n me, and the night's already got some chill on it, yes sir."

"Keep talking," Max called, still trying to place the voice. "Let's hear something from your partner, too."

"He ... well, I guess he don't talk much these days, no sir."

"He'd better start," Max said, finally connecting the voice to a face and a name. *One way to make sure, though:* "Let me hear you both before I get a look at your ugly face."

"Now jest what do you mean by that, mister? It surely ain't what I call being friendly – no sir it ain't, and I don't much like it none."

The high-pitched inflection and the quick indignation confirmed Max's deduction. *It's Jasper Perkins all right.*

Still, Max could sense an undercurrent beyond the mournful call and the subsequent chatter from a lone man who had stated with a trace of trepidation that he was coming in with a partner – a partner who had said nothing to this point.

Jasper's never traveled with a partner. Something's wrong out there, Max thought.

"Hey in there – you ain't answered me yet. What'd you mean by that last call-out anyhow? I'm a'mind to come and teach you different'n calling me ugly, yes sir."

"You heard me, Jasper Perkins," Max called. "With your face, I'd as soon you kept your distance."

"Hey, jest who's in there calling me by name? Come on and talk so's I kin figger it out."

"You're getting downright slow, Jasper. The years are starting to tell."

"Max Blake? Hey, Max, is that you?"

"Took you long enough, you old goat," Max called back, his voice remaining as soft and low-pitched as possible. "No need to shout about it."

"Why didn't you jest say so in the first place?" Jasper called as he started forward. "What's wrong with you, keeping an old man waiting out here in the dark? Didn't that no-account judge of yers teach you any manners?

"And hold still with that exceptional hog-leg of yers, Max. I don't want to git plugged by the likes of you – and nobody else, neither."

"Where's your partner?"

"You know I ain't never yet had me no partner, no sir," Jasper said as he emerged from the trees and approached the camp. He was wearing his familiar deeply soiled deerskin trousers with a thick, often-stained flannel shirt and a heavy buffalo coat; his battered hat was made from an odd assortment of animal skins, with heads and tails still attached that stuck out at a variety of angles on the top of his head. His beard was a dingy gray that hung past the second button of his coat, and his face was like weathered leather.

"Jest me and the old mule here, that's it – like always," Jasper said, holding up the reins. "I only tell people I got me a partner so's they think twice a'fore sendin' lead my way."

"You're right talkative, Jasper," Max said, his fingers still wrapped around the Colt. "You all right?"

"I'm fine Max – fine as a frog hair split in two. Only ..." Jasper hesitated a moment, unsure of what to say next.

"What is it?" Max asked, breaking the silence. He noticed again that the old man's voice had taken on the uneasy edge he had detected earlier.

"Cain't say as how I rightly know myself, Max, though I'm right glad to see you and feel better right now'n I did a might ago, yes sir," Jasper said, looking directly into the federal marshal's haunting gray eyes. "There's something ain't quite right out there, if you git my meaning. I been uneasy now the better part of an hour. And the mule is close to being spooked. I cain't put my finger on it, but it's there – a'brewin fer some time, Max."

"I feel it, too – on and off. It's not an easy thing to get hold of," Max said.

"I hear ya, all right. All the way in I'm looking back, waiting to see something lurking close by or moving in the shadows – almost stayed shut of yer camp. But the coffee smelt right good.

"I don't like it though, Max. Not a bit. I'm still up fer looking to my backside, even if I can't get a handle on what's giving me the jitters."

"You've sure taken to jabbering." Max's eyes smiled as the prospector flared his nostrils and thrashed at his beard. "It's good to see you, though."

Jasper snorted. "Don't know why I bother. But it's good to be seen, even by a man with a sharp tongue. Been a spell now, ain't it?"

Max nodded, although his mind was elsewhere. He was looking out into the night again, his eyes peering into the blackness, every sense within him alert. He shifted his weight from one side of his muscular frame to the other, almost impatiently, trying to determine what he felt and sensed but couldn't yet hear or see or identify.

"Yes sir, the last time I saw you was by the San Juan," Jasper said, anxious to talk again. "You was jest about to step into the street with some no-account horse thief, as I recall."

"Your memory must be better than mine," Max said, paying little attention to Jasper's chit-chat. "I don't recall that."

"Yer to the point you braced so many men now, you don't recollect one from the next," Jasper said. "As I remember it, the horse thief in question was jest about to ..."

"Quiet!"

Max held up his hand at the same time that he snapped out the one-word command, bringing Jasper up short. The old man halted in mid-sentence, looked about, and then joined Max in sorting through the night sounds, trying to determine exactly what was out of place in the still, chilly air.

"What is it?" Jasper murmured after a minute went by. His beard was poking out in odd angles around his creased face, and he rubbed it gently as he spoke.

Max shook his head from side to side but said nothing, his attention directed at the darkness. Jasper followed Max's gaze. "I don't see nor hear a thing. But I rightly know what you mean, Max. It's something," he whispered. "Something or someone."

"My guess is someone, and more likely a lot of someones," Max said softly at last, staring into the blackness past the trail that Jasper and his mule had crossed minutes before. "Quick, Jasper, douse what's left of that fire."

"What do you think, Max? Apaches?"

"Doubtful, unless they don't care about being seen or heard. More likely it's a roving pack, a dozen men or more, close enough now to warrant attention."

Max quickly checked his Colt Peacemaker, a .45 caliber model with pearl-handled grips, and slipped into the shadows, crouching low to the ground.

"Stay there – and stay down," he whispered. "Keep your head low till you know it's me."

And then he was gone.

31

Jasper Perkins, his body slowed by tough years in the high country, dropped to his knees and filled his hands with soil, tossing the dirt onto the fire. A dull hiss of protest seethed from the embers as the flames sputtered and died.

Jasper flopped to the ground and crawled to his mule. Rising momentarily, he grabbed the Sharps carbine that he kept in a deerskin sheath on the mule's side and pulled the weapon free. Then he hit the ground with a muted thump, crawled behind the nearest tree, and waited.

An hour crawled by as the prospector remained still and silent, watching for any sign from the federal marshal. But Jasper heard only the faint murmur of the wind in the trees, the distant gurgle of a trickling stream, and the brush and flight of insects on the cool air.

The stillness, the deep blackness, of the night shut out everything else around him.

Jasper's body was bowed and gnarled from hard years of working a harsh and unforgiving land. But his mind was as agile as it had been when he was a hell-raising mountain man, wandering in search of gold and silver throughout the great ranges of the West: the rugged, snow-capped Rockies of Wyoming and Montana, the Black Hills in the Dakota Territory, the Sierras in far-off California, and finally the craggy, crumbling desert peaks of the Southwest.

It was here, in the Arizona Territory, that he first set eyes on Max Blake.

It was a long time ago, he thought. *But I recall it fresh – like it was yesterday.*

Jasper could count that yesterday on the fingers of both hands. Max Blake was a boy of twelve and already the fastest hand with a Colt .45 that folks in the territory had ever seen. Jasper had witnessed his share of hard men with hard eyes and the uncanny ability to pull a holstered revolver with efficiency and deadly precision. But he had never seen anything quite like the young Max Blake. *He had the look, all right, especially his eyes, even then –* and a lightning-quick right hand that could pull a six-gun and dispatch a man to a receptive hell with remarkable urgency.

I been around some time now, Jasper thought, settling in to a flood of memories, his back propped against a thick ironwood. *But I ain't seen since, nor ever before, the likes of that boy.*

Even then, Max Blake had haunting, deep-set gray eyes and a dark shock of wavy black hair that curled softly beneath his trim Stetson. His body already was lean and well-muscled, his face just shy of handsome, and he walked with a ghost-like economy of motion that wasted no effort and that somehow seemed both essential and effortless.

Jasper had been in town less than an hour, collecting supplies for another futile trip to the mountains in search of a trace of color in the rocks, when a ruckus at the jail caught his attention. The sheriff had just captured a notorious outlaw – a killer called Tom "T-Bone" DePue – and was tying his horse to the hitching post outside of the jail, his hands looped around the reins of the outlaw's animal, when DePue spurred his mount and tried to make a run out of town.

The surprised sheriff turned as the outlaw's horse bucked, and the lawman was pulled to the ground and dragged through the dirt, his grip tight on the reins of DePue's horse. Forced to let go or risk being trampled or dragged to his death, the sheriff finally managed to shake the reins loose and get back on his feet. He quickly pulled his revolver and leveled it for a shot; but the outlaw already was three-hundred yards or more down the dusty street and well out of range, oblivious to everything but the wind in his face, as the sheriff and the startled men around him called to onlookers down the line.

Jasper was both annoyed and amused by the incident. He didn't like towns to begin with, and he wasn't used to noisy crowds; he far preferred the mountains and the peace of the tall grasses and the snow in season and a stain of color in the rocks and the long distances from civilization and other human souls.

But he also recognized a good time when he saw one, and this event had potential. Jasper ignored the hollering and watched with a casual smile as T-Bone DePue raced toward freedom, his hands strapped tight together, his knees and legs clinching the sides of his horse, the reins still trailing behind him, bouncing along on the hardpan.

Jasper was even pulling for the outlaw's escape when a young boy emerged from the bank just as T-Bone made his gallant but foolhardy charge. The sheriff and a half-dozen other men were yelling as they rambled in pursuit, the outlaw was riding as hard as he dared in a wild effort to escape certain hanging, and Jasper couldn't remember anything quite so funny – right up to the moment when he saw the boy.

Mostly, Jasper remembered his eyes.

They were cold and pale gray in the sun, like hardened chunks of granite in the distant hills of the Superstitions or the far-off, snow-capped peaks of the Cascades in the Oregon Territory to the north.

Even more than the escaping outlaw, Jasper remembered watching the boy, mesmerized by his presence from the moment he stepped onto the rough-hewn planks of the boardwalk that fronted the bank.

Even now, two mules later, Jasper remembered exactly how the young Max Blake instantly reacted. He could still picture the way the boy looked up as he walked from the bank, spotted the escaping rider, glanced at the frantic sheriff running hard down the street – the lawman's six-gun waving in the air, his arms flailing, his voice high-pitched and anxious – and took in the men on either side of the town's dusty main thoroughfare as they sprinted out of the way and the rider passed them by.

The boy then pulled a Colt revolver from a tightly strapped holster and snapped off a single shot at the fleeing outlaw – a shot that, to this day, Jasper Perkins could only marvel at and describe in awe around a campfire with other story-telling mountain men.

It was a thing of beauty and precision, Jasper considered, even now.

Jasper figured that the distance between the boy and the fleeing man on the bounding horse was well over a hundred yards, although it seemed to grow ever greater as the years went on. He recalled the almost casual way that the boy suddenly had the Colt in his hand and fired – instinctively, without taking the time to consciously cock the hammer, or even to aim.

Mostly, though, Jasper remembered the immediate result. The bullet knocked T-Bone DePue off his horse with a noisy thud, shattering the bone on his upper arm. The surprised outlaw, shocked at the suddenness of his departure from his mount, banged the dusty heels of his boots onto the ground and tried to get up as his now-free horse continued running without him. He managed only a few steps before a group of running men arrived and the sheriff puffed up and grabbed the outlaw again, tugging hard on T-Bone's already secured wrists.

"Who shot me?" DePue screamed out. "Who was it shot me, damn his dirty hide? I'd a'been long gone had some yella coward not shot me off my horse. It ain't fair."

Once the outlaw was safely tucked behind bars in the town's rickety jail, the sheriff returned to thank Max Blake. A crowd had gathered around the boy – a crowd that included Jasper Perkins. The mountain man, like many in the surrounding territory, had heard stories about Max Blake and was curious. *How can a pup like that shoot a hog-leg at a moving target from that distance with that much precision and so little effort?* he wondered.

The sheriff wasn't surprised at all.

"Nice shooting, Max, and my thanks," he had said. "Lucky you happened by. I rightly think that no-account T-Bone would've got clean away, and we'd be chasing him down this very minute. Might've missed my dinner on account of him."

"I had some business in the bank is all," the boy said quietly. "Nothing more to it than that, sir."

"But what a shot, boy!" a man in the back of the crowd called out, his voice sharply pitched in excitement. "How in the world did you do that?"

"Why, this here boy is Max Blake," the sheriff said matter-of-factly, as if that explanation were sufficient for everyone.

The sheriff moved along, thanking Max once more, and the boy self-consciously started to walk away, clearly uncomfortable with the attention. Jasper Perkins, fascinated by what he had seen, couldn't help himself.

"That was some piece of shooting, son," he said. "I been around a bit and seen a bunch more, and that was as good as I ever seen it. I'd 've needed a Sharps carbine and a tree limb to set the barrel on to match me a shot like that, yes sir."

Max looked up at the old man, his expression unchanged. He nodded at the prospector but said nothing.

"My name's Perkins, son – Jasper Perkins. I git around some."

"Yes, sir. I'm Max Blake," the boy said simply. He tipped his hat and moved on.

God, but it all seems so long ago, Jasper thought, pulling his mind back to the present.

Even then, Max Blake already had the ability to pull a six-gun faster and shoot it straighter than any man or boy he had ever seen – before or since.

The boy's skill was uncanny.

It was unnerving.

It was deadly.

A decade and more had passed – years in which Jasper came to know Max Blake, first as a boy possessing a man's skill with a revolver, and later as a federal marshal and a friend who possessed an even deadlier ability – and a reputation for dispensing justice with speed and unerring certainty.

I never saw anything quite like that young stallion, Jasper thought as he peered out into the darkness – his eyes watching, his senses attuned to whatever the chill air would float his way. *That kind comes around but once a lifetime. And that might be a good thing.*

But I sure wish he'd git on back, Jasper thought after another minute passed. *I must be getting a might skittish in my old age.*

And so he watched and waited, his Sharps carbine in his hands, his ears tuned to the many sounds of the night.

Chapter 5

A Bottle of Collateral

Jack Sloan instinctively ducked to the floor when he heard the single shot from a small-caliber revolver bark and then echo around the battered walls of the saloon in the otherwise silent village of Adobe Flats.

He hit the floor with a thud, grunted once and waited, listening carefully, but he detected no other sound and saw no other movement. He took off his dusty Stetson, placed it next to the edge of an overturned card table that provided some cover, and almost as an afterthought pulled his revolver before he chanced a look around.

Keeping his head low, his eyes darting about, he counted three bodies. He sensed that others were lying about that he could not see.

Sloan picked up an overturned beer glass within inches of his hand, looked at it wistfully for a few seconds, and tossed it high in the air in a long arc toward the bar at the opposite end of the room.

Another gunshot rang out as the glass crashed into the wall.

"Hey, hold your fire," Sloan called out. "You are like to kill someone."

"That's the general idea," a voice called back. "Better you than me."

"No need to shoot a'tall," Sloan replied. "I didn't start this mess and won't finish it. I just rode in and ain't yet straight on what's happened. Maybe you can fill me in."

"How do I know yer a pilgrim on this?" the voice called back.

"Well, I ain't no pilgrim, but I'm new to this ruckus. I been trying to figure what in hell went on here, and now you take a shot at me. That ain't friendly."

When there was no immediate reply, he added: "I ran into your

37

undertaker and judge on the way in. But they were in such an all-fired hurry to scat, I didn't get much of a story from 'em."

"What'd you say yer name was, pardner?"

"Didn't say, but it's Jack Sloan. Yours?"

The man behind the bar ignored the question but had another of his own.

"Where d'ya hail from, Jack Sloan?"

"I been prospecting up north for some months," Sloan replied, trying to sound casual but failing, even in his own mind. "I was here maybe four months back, give or take, and had a few drinks of some potency in this very spot, which is why I'm here now. Living in the hills don't let me get at the bottle near as much as I'd like."

When his words were met with silence, Sloan tried another approach.

"Look, I'm gonna stick my head up now, and I'd appreciate yer not taking a shot at it. I'm tired, I'm thirsty, I'm downright curious, and I ain't much for lying on the floor while a man with a gun wants to shoot my ears off."

Sloan holstered his revolver and slowly pulled himself up, his hands held high over his head, his eyes searching in all directions for the man with the revolver.

"I didn't catch your name," Sloan called.

"Name's Corn – Cliff Corn," the bartender replied, his face rising above the jangle of broken glasses and shattered bottles that lined the long bar. "What do you think of the place?"

The destruction was surprising. Sloan could see six bodies now, sprawled in various forms of grisly death on the floor; every card table and most of the chairs were tipped over and broken, bullet holes were in every wall and through every window and door, glass was shattered and strewn about, cards and poker chips and a handful of coins were haphazardly tossed aside like tiny leaves after a hard forest rain.

"Seems to be going downhill since last I was here. That's not a criticism, mind you – just an honest observation. You look familiar, though. Am I right on that count, Mr. Corn?"

"I'm the barkeep here, and I recognize yer face now that I see it, Jack Sloan. Wouldn't have placed a name with it, to be sure, but I'm a man kin always recognize a face. You was here all right – some time back and a man with a right-powerful thirst, as I recall."

"That's the truth of it," Sloan said. "Thanks for holding your fire. Wouldn't take kindly to getting shot."

Sloan walked slowly toward the bar, his hands still raised above his head, his eyes taking in the remnants of the shattered room.

"I could use a drink," he said simply.

"I'd say we both could," Corn replied. "Let me see what I kin find. And Sloan, put yer hands down, for gawd's sake. You think I'm gonna plug ya even yet?"

"Truth be told, I didn't realize I still had 'em up in the air," he said, lowering his arms to the top of the bar. "You gonna tell me what took place here, Mr. Corn?"

"Call me Col. Corn," the bartender said, rummaging to locate an unbroken bottle.

"Col. Corn? You were in the war?"

"Nah, nothing like that. It's jest a joke – a play on words."

"I'm afraid I don't quite capture it," Sloan said, "but I confess that I'm not thinking straight at the moment."

"Well, this might help you out some," Corn said, his face appearing above the bar again, his smile grim, a dusty bottle of whiskey in his hand. He produced two shot glasses, filled each to the brim, and set the bottle down with some finality.

Hoisting one of the glasses, Corn offered a toast: "To living another day."

"I'll drink to that, though I'd drink to most anything," Sloan answered, and both men downed the whiskey in a single gulp.

Corn was a clean-shaven man who had been around the mountain a time or two, Sloan judged. He had a thick head of salt-and-pepper hair, a slightly crooked nose, and eyes that were deep brown and searching, offset by wire-framed reading glasses. His dress was immaculate and included a black-ribboned bowtie which even now was set in perfect position beneath his jutting chin.

"I am not a drinking man, but that helped," Corn said, smacking his lips.

"I am a drinking man, and that was as righteous as a day in church, Mr. Corn. With your permission, sir, I'll have another, if you please."

"I'll join you then, Jack Sloan, though one is normally my limit. But on a day like today…"

Corn poured a second round of drinks – "you've a steady hand, sir," Sloan told him as he watched the whiskey stream gently into the shot glasses – and then a third before he spoke again

"The bastards came from nowhere," Corn said at last. "One minute everything was normal, peaceful – jest what you'd expect. The next, well, all hell had busted loose in here and on the street. Guns were blazin' in every direction, three men walked in here a'fore we could even determine what was happening, and the next thing you know I was on the floor behind the bar" – he pointed with a long finger – "and stayed right there till the smoke cleared. Truth to tell, nobody fired so much as a single round in return, so far as I know.

"I eventually poked my head up long enough to see the place all shot to hell and everyone in here dead 'cepting me. But the gunplay seemed to be jest getting started out on the street, so I stayed down and said nothing and was extra quiet till you showed up."

He stopped to draw a breath. "You want another?"

"Sir, you needn't bother to ask. I'll drink whatever you set before me for as long as you care to serve me. I'm happy to pay my way, of course, and I'm delighted for your company and the story that's unfolding. Please continue," he said with a flourish, already feeling the effects of the whiskey.

"Well, I don't know what else to say 'cause I don't rightly know much more'n that. We heard talk only yesterday 'bout some reckless band of renegades traveling in the area – the word had come in from a Whiskey Bend freighter who passes through once a month – but it weren't the kind of thing to get a man rattled or on edge, you understand.

"I guess we should've paid more attention, but how kin you figger something like this happening?"

"I recognize the problem all right," Sloan said. "I run into it all the time myself, I'm sad to say. What are you planning now?"

"Haven't thought about it none, or leastwise till you just mentioned it," Corn said, scratching at his chin with thick fingers used to tapping kegs and pulling corks. "Guess I'll have to take stock and see if anyone else is alive and hiding out somewheres. After that? Well, you tell me. Yer as much an expert as I am about now."

"An expert? No, not in matters like this," Sloan said with a vigorous shake of his head. "This is a matter for the law to determine, and I stay clear of the law. Or at least I do when I'm able." His glass was empty, and when Corn didn't notice quickly enough, Sloan took the bottle and poured himself another shot.

"It's not that I have anything against the law," he added. "It's just, well – a man can't be too careful in … uncertain times."

"Yep. I understand, Mr. Sloan. Still, the law needs to know about – well, how would you put it? – about jest what the hell happened here, I guess you'd say; ain't no plainer way to say it. And I cain't do it. Aside from everything else, I've got bodies to bury – which I don't look forward to in the heat – and a saloon to put back together as best I can. Plus, I'd best scout around and see if anyone else is still kickin' – friends or neighbors and such.

"So I reckon it's up to you to notify the authorities, Mr. Sloan. What do you say?"

"What of your sheriff? Surely it's his job to…"

"That body in the corner is what's left of Sheriff Ford. Cain't say I ever liked the man much – he was a bully at times and had a mean streak in him – but not even a snake deserves gettin' back-shot like he got. No sir, it's up to you."

"But I've already told you…"

"I'd pay, of course, for yer trouble. The town, or what's left of it, can pick up the freight. I reckon Twisted Junction is the nearest place with a reliable telegraph line, and that's a day's ride south. It's too far to Twin Forks, where the judge sits with his federal marshals, but Twisted Junction will do, I'd wager."

"It's not a matter of money, sir. It's…"

"I'd pay you in whiskey, you understand."

"How's that?"

"Whiskey. I'd pay you in whiskey," Corn said. "You said you work a claim in the hills north of here, right?"

Sloan shook his head, pouring himself yet another drink.

"Fine. I'm guessing this town is the closest thing to civilization you know, which means yer drinkin' gits done here. Am I right? It's why I recognized you right off and didn't shoot you full of holes."

"Close enough, Mr. Corn." Sloan's eyes wavered, but his ability to function after consuming large capacities of alcohol of varying types and quality could not be underestimated; his attention was still directed at the Adobe Flats bartender, and he still had his mind wrapped around the problem.

"What I'm proposing is that fer as long as you want, or as long as you're able, when you come in here, the drinks are on the house – so long as you notify the law as to what's happened here. Someone's got to be told, likely the Army, and you are the only man available."

"Let me think on it some," Sloan said. "And I'll have another drink while I'm thinking – if you are able, of course."

"If you don't mind my saying, Mr. Sloan, you are a hard-drinkin' man."

"I take that as a compliment, Mr. Corn."

"It's colonel – Col. Corn."

"I still don't understand it, but I'll drink to it regardless," Sloan said as a long, languid smile eased the length of the day and the horrors of the barroom and the streets off his face. "If you don't mind, of course, Mr. Corn, ah, Col. Corn" – and he pushed his empty glass forward again – "just so long as you don't mind."

Jack Sloan was reaching for the bottle again when his face suddenly lit up, and he slapped his hands together in glee.

"Col. Corn: Of course; I get it now – very good. Col. Corn? I think that calls for a drink."

Chapter Six

Paths and Identities

Richard Nash was following a twisting trail of revenge. He was a tenacious man and a persistent tracker, and the heat and the miles and the hostile terrain and the shifting winds and sand did not deter or discourage him.

The trail he initially found lead south from Aguante toward the border, where he spent two full days searching for tracks and asking questions that had few if any answers.

On little more than a hunch, he abandoned this pursuit and slowly backtracked, widening his search with each passing mile, heading north. He finally picked up a faint boot print in a patch of dried mud a day's ride west of the outlaw town. He located a full set of tracks two days later and once more began the process of criss-crossing the wind-swept desert floor, trusting that he was at last heading in the right direction.

Where that would take him was anyone's guess. The identity of the man he was tracking was an even greater mystery – and he thought a great deal about both questions as he pushed toward the mountains.

After another two days of tedious tracking, he stumbled on a dead body, as much by accident and the gathering of big-boned buzzards as by either luck or skill. Three well-placed rifle shots drove the raptors temporarily away, and he wetted a kerchief, covered his mouth and nose, and took ample time to carefully examine the carcass that was being picked apart on the desert floor.

Nash considered the quality and condition of the tattered clothing, soiled boots, and the black Stetson half-covered by sand; he also considered the volume of scavengers, which numbered close to fifty birds in the immediate vicinity. The carcass, he decided, was all that remained of one of the three outlaws who days earlier had terrorized Aguante before escaping into the night and the empty miles.

At least I'm on the right track, he thought.

It was clear at a glance that the dead man had been shot once in the head; a large bullet hole in the exposed skull was proof enough of that. Nash also could tell from his examination that this was not the body of Hoss Johnson, the big man who had shot up the town saloon, killing a deputy in the process.

Too small for Johnson. This one must be Morgan, he thought. *The sheriff will be glad this bushwhacker's dead, but he won't like it that somebody else pulled the trigger.*

Nash shook his head as he stood over the body, thinking about one scenario after another, considering a variety of options as to why the man died – and at whose hand.

Might be his partner, the big fella, did him in – who knows why or cares? Nash thought. *Might be the one that got Gentry killed this one, too. Then again, the stranger I'm chasing might be the cause of this mess.*

He thought about that, picturing again his quarry's face and holding the image in his mind. He could see the stranger's steely gray eyes – alert, unafraid, issuing a constant challenge with every glance – and he shuddered inwardly.

Jest give me a name for this phantom I been tracking across all these miles of nothing, he thought. *It would help if I just had me a name.*

He paused to let some sand run through his fingers as he stooped near the body once more. *Not that it matters much to this fella, I guess. And the sheriff ain't gonna like it none regardless.*

Nash left the carcass to the buzzards and continued his pursuit of the solitary stranger who had slipped through the fingers of the Aguante sheriff and a passel of deputies. He still had no idea what the man was doing in Aguante when he was first apprehended near the livery stables. Even after he was badly beaten by Aguante Sheriff Reno Walker, the man had refused to provide his name – *not a real name anyways* – or offer a satisfactory explanation.

Once again, the litany of what had transpired in Aguante scant days before ran through Nash's mind: killings, shootings, the burning of the town saloon, the appearance of the mysterious stranger, the escape of Hoss Johnson and Freeman Morgan, the possibility that the outlaw pair had help within the town – *and the flat-out disappearance of this bastard I'm tracking now.*

I'll get him, though: no matter how long it takes, he thought.

Sure hope it don't take long in this heat. It's like following a trail straight to hell.

Richard Nash was on that trail for two more days before his luck turned. It took him across the flat of the desert and straight up to the foothills of a low-slung mountain range riddled with streams and fertile volcanic ground. Eventually the tracks lead him to the tiny settlement of Indian Wells.

What he found there surprised him: the end of the trail for the big man responsible for the saloon killings, and the death of another man who was traveling with him.

The big man's name was Hoss Johnson, according to the peaceful farmers and ranchers who spoke with Nash in a dingy cantina. The second man was called Grant, in one form or another.

And the man responsible for the death of these outlaws was a federal marshal named Max Blake.

"Well, that's a might interesting development and explains a lot," Nash had said when he digested this news and examined two unmarked graves near the edge of town. But his remark was lost on the inhabitants of the sleepy little village, most of whom spoke little or no English, and he was soon on the trail again.

Nash was now following a path that he hoped would lead to the federal marshal by instinct as much as by track or hoof-print. Every living person in the territory – and certainly every outlaw – knew full well that the hanging judge in Twin Forks, Thomas Raymond Radford, controlled both the law and the law-dispensers there.

And somewhere in the back of his mind, Richard Nash recognized the name of Max Blake.

To git at this Blake, all I gotta do is head on in to Twin Forks, Nash thought. *Hell, a man don't have to be much of a tracker a'tall to follow that trail.*

He just can't be afraid to ride into the belly of the beast.

Chapter 7

Departures and Disappearances

Max Blake slid into the deep underbelly of the forest and disappeared into the night. He could sense the danger lurking nearby, and he moved directly toward it, slipping his index finger over the well-worn, familiar trigger of his Colt revolver.

Detecting a slight disturbance off to his left, he paused, cocked his ear, and picked up another faint noise from the same area. He listened carefully for a minute or more and this time heard the distinct snap of a small branch, dry and brittle.

No animal's that clumsy, Max thought. *Most likely it's men – a lot of men – and trouble.*

Max slipped silently along an old game trail, heading north from the spot where he left Jasper Perkins. He moved efficiently, without sound, much as a hunting cat slinks through the night, until he detected the low murmur of distant voices. He stopped to precisely locate the sounds as they drifted through the spaces left by struggling trees and the underbrush of the forest. Satisfied that he was moving in the right direction, he cautiously edged forward once more, sliding to his left, until he came to the edge of a clearing.

Max could see the outline of a dozen men gathered around a bright fire. *It's clear these boys don't care about being cautious or found. They're almost inviting trouble,* he thought.

Two men were breaking inch-thick limbs and tossing them into the hungry flames. The others were sitting quietly by, ignoring each other and the flickering fire. One man was cleaning a revolver. Another seemed to be whittling on a fat stick, his long knife picking up the glint of the flames as the steel blade flashed back and forth in a steady rhythm against the soft wood.

46

In the darkness behind the men, Max detected the outline of tethered horses. He also sensed that other men were moving about near the animals, behind the clearing and out of the firelight. Dropping softly to the ground, Max slithered noiselessly along until he reached a clump of aspens and some low-slung brush, which provided excellent cover and a filtered view ahead. He held the Colt, watching and listening, as silent as death itself.

"Hey. How far do ya reckon we come today?" one of the men asked, seemingly directing the question to no one in particular.

"Nigh on to twenty miles and maybe more," another man answered, although he didn't seem interested in either the question or his own response. His head was tucked between his knees, which were propped up near his chest, and he neither looked up nor moved as he spoke.

"I sure thought somebody was hereabouts when we first come in to camp," the first man said after a minute. "Smelled somethin' – like coffee or such."

"The way I figure it, yer always smelling something, Slim. You should do less smelling and more eating, less'n you blow away in a good breeze."

"I'd be obliged to eat, were anyone inclined to bring me a thick beefsteak or something like it," Slim answered. "I'm tired of eating turkey and wild pigs and dawg and such. And we ain't had none too much of that these past days, neither."

The man stood, and Max could see immediately why he was called Slim. Although he was tall – several inches above six feet, Max figured as he judged the man's narrow frame against the flickering firelight – Slim likely weighed no more than a hefty sack of grocer's flour. His arms, his legs – even his fingers and hands and face and neck – were stick-thin.

A dusty, beat-up Stetson looked awkward and out of place on his head, and his gun belt was pinched so tightly on his hips that the excess leather was looped a couple of times around the inside of the belt to keep it out of the way.

"I could eat something all right," Slim said after another minute. "Maybe I'm a tad on the thin side, but that don't mean I don't like to sit down and eat, ya know."

When no one answered, Slim moved closer to the fire and stuck out his hands as if warming them. "That's why I thought I smelled something when we first pulled in," he said, again directing his conversation to no one in particular. "I was hungry then, and I'm hungry now, comes to that."

47

"Then cut on out and rope yerself a big ol' steer and tote it on back in," one of the men said with a laugh. "You got so much spark left in you, jest you go on out and git us all some grub, I say. But you'd best be sure to bring back plenty. I'd say we all is a might on the gnarly side."

"Yeah, well, I'm with Slim here. I could eat something, too," yet another man said as he stood and joined Slim by the fire. "Ya think ol' Johnny and the rest of them boys'll bring something back in yet tonight?"

"Ain't likely, it being this dark and they ain't already back," Slim said. "We're more'n like to end up with nothing tonight – not even a turkey or a bit of deer. Hell, I'd eat me a possum right about now, I swear, if'n we had one to sample."

"Johnny and them others got started too late is all," the man standing next to Slim said. "We rode hard today, and maybe too hard, I'd say. We might've stopped sooner – given them boys a better chance to hunt up some grub and not run the horses half-way to ground. Now we'll likely go hungry again. God knows we're all of us hungry."

"You boys complain too much."

A distinct silence followed as a large man with a hard, grim face appeared out of the darkness. He wore a dusty black Stetson that was set back on his head, exposing eyes that were like dark coals. He carried a shiny Colt revolver, and his fingers hovered at holster level as he eyed Slim and the second man by the fire. It was clear that the newcomer didn't like the talk he had just heard; it also was clear that the men in the camp feared him.

I'd wager this fella's in charge, Max thought as he hunkered down in the brush, careful to remain still and to keep his head low. The only sounds he could hear were the nickering and blowing of the horses in the distance and the snap and spark of the fire.

"We rode hard today 'cause we had to," the big man said after a minute. "We ain't had time to hunt food nor chase after whiskey and women. Chances are good we'll ride hard tomorrow, with not much more than we got right now.

"When we git shut of the Army boys on our tails, then we kin lead the easy life you boys prefer. Meantime, this is the hand we got."

"What Iron Mike says is right enough for me," a voice called out from behind the clearing where the horses were tethered. But there was no other agreement from the rest of the men.

Iron Mike Truax waited, letting his words linger in the night air. He casually edged close to the fire, standing immediately next to Slim and his partner. Max could now see that Iron Mike was even larger than he had first thought: tall and muscular, with broad shoulders and a massive chest. He also saw a look of meanness in the man's eyes, even from a distance.

"Till then," Iron Mike added, "I suggest you two do less jabbering and staring at that fire and try on a little more work 'round here. You might even hunt up something yerselves sometime, seeing as how you both are so damned good at talking about it."

"Meant no harm, Mike," Slim said. "Jest feelin' a might hungry – that's all."

"How many men you reckon are following after us now?" the man with Slim asked, directing the question Iron Mike's way but hesitating to look into the big man's eyes.

"Might be one; might be a hundred or more – who kin say fer sure?" Iron Mike replied.

"Well, how far you reckon they're behind us?" the man asked.

"What do I look like, Dirk – a damn gypsy? You think I'm maybe some kind of fortune teller in one of them tent shows?" Mike snarled. "All I know is we didn't see 'em today, but that don't mean we won't see 'em tomorrow or the day after, or even tonight.

"And jest 'cause we ain't yet run into 'em sure as hell don't mean they ain't back there, riding hard right now, 'cause they is back there – and every man-jack of you knows it."

"Then why don't we jest stop and fight 'em?" Dirk asked. "There's a good thirty of us, give or take. We kin all fight and shoot – and better'n most men, too."

"And there's like to be a good two hundred of them," Iron Mike said. "We got the whole U.S. Army on our tails. That ain't like picking a fight with some runt of a sheriff's posse."

When no one spoke, Mike said, "I take it, then, we got no more arguments."

Iron Mike took a step or two toward the fire and kicked some wood shavings at his feet into the glowing flames. "You boys ain't been too well-trained, I kin see," he said. "You ought to speak yer minds to my face instead of waiting till my back's turned all the time."

"That ain't it, Mike," Slim said, although he was careful not to appear confrontational.

"Like hell it ain't. Ain't a man here's not a'feared to say his peace directly to me." Mike's eyes swept the men around the fire but quickly landed on Dirk again.

"What? You callin' us cowards?" Dirk asked suddenly, turning to face Iron Mike as he spoke.

"Jest you, Dirk. The only coward I see here is you."

"Well, I ain't afraid of speaking my mind," Dirk said. "I'm getting tired of running, and that's my feeling on the matter. We've done too much running and too little eating fer too damn long now and nothing to show fer it. I say enough – and I want me a look at the gold, too."

"Jest what the hell is that supposed to mean?" Iron Mike asked, a decided menace growing in his voice.

"It means I don't like what we're doing or where we're going. And I don't like you taking me there, neither," Dirk said, paying little heed to the growing swarm of black clouds that Iron Mike attracted.

Max Blake could clearly see them, however, and he settled in for the storm that was clearly coming.

Mike Truax took the time to measure the mood of the men gathered nearby, subtly gauging Dirk's support. Satisfied, he turned and said, "So what are you gonna do about it?"

Dirk thought for a minute, taking his own assessment. "Well, I say we put it to a vote," he offered, finally sensing the danger and recognizing that safety in numbers might come to his aid.

"Then here's my vote," Iron Mike said without hesitation.

He deftly pulled the holstered six-gun at his right side and fired a single, well-placed shot that struck Dirk in the belly from no more than ten feet away. The bullet drove the man backward to the ground, and he groaned loudly as he held both of his hands over the wound in a futile attempt to stop the bleeding.

Even from where he was hidden, more than thirty yards from the clearing, Max Blake could see the surprised look on Dirk's face – and on the faces of the other men in the camp. Surprise, in fact – even more than pain – continued to register in Dirk's eyes as he twisted in the dirt.

A half-dozen men rushed into the clearing at the sound of the gunshot, pulling their holstered revolvers. But when they saw Dirk on the ground and Iron Mike, gun in hand, standing over him, they drew up quickly, holstered their weapons, and were silent.

"Anybody else wanna vote?" Mike asked casually.

When there was no reply, Mike looked down at the wounded man for a second or two, holding his eyes, before he slowly cocked the revolver and fired it once more.

"One less mouth to feed – a bit more to go around when the food comes in," he said simply.

Iron Mike turned to face the men. "I'm leading this pack, and don't none of you ferget it, now or ever." He waited for a moment to let the words sink in. "Now, is there another man here got something to say to me?"

No one said a word.

"Anybody else want to vote on something? Anything?" he asked.

Again there was no answer, and Iron Mike watched the men closely for a time before he turned toward Slim. "Get rid of that mess," Mike said, pointing at Dirk's motionless body. "I ain't fussy how you do it, but be certain nobody finds him till we're gone. That clear?"

Slim nodded dumbly and shuffled the few feet over to where the body was sprawled. "It only come up 'cause we was hungry, ya know," he muttered.

But Iron Mike Truax already had moved off into the darkness, away from the fire and the men who had gathered around it.

And when the man was clearly out of earshot, Slim said, just loud enough for his words to drift toward the spot where Max Blake was hiding, "That man is gonna be the death of us all; he most surely is."

Max watched silently as Slim and a second cowboy who got up to give him a hand grabbed the dead man's arms and boots and carted him off, slowly lurching away from the fire until Max could no longer see or hear them.

The sudden turn of events was surprising, and Max could hear the men now talking in low murmurs about what had happened, their voices softly carrying on the thin night air.

"It sure don't pay none to rile up ol' Mike," one of them said.

"Thing is, I don't think Dirk was much outta line with what he done or said," another man answered, although he was cautious in offering the opinion. He had taken the time to look behind him before he spoke, no doubt searching for a sign of Iron Mike's presence nearby.

"Well, this business with the Army is troubling ol' Mike some, and well it should," the first man said. "It's bad enough to git chased by a sheriff and posse. But when Army boys start the chasing – well, that ain't good fer none of us. We got to live with it till we git shut of them bluecoats."

"It ain't reason enough to git shot in the gut," one of the men said. "But I ain't about to offer that thought to Iron Mike. He surely has been in a foul mood of late, I swear."

"Well, what'd you expect?" a man said. "When you steal gold from the Union Army, you gotta figure on getting chased by 'em. It only makes sense. The reason we don't like it none is there's more of them than there is of us, I reckon."

"Yeah, and now there's one less of us than there was a minute ago."

The men were quiet for a time after that, each of them lost in some private thought.

"I'd jest like to see some of that gold," a short, squat man with long, greasy hair and a scraggly blond beard finally said, breaking the silence in a thinly pitched voice that seemed to gasp for air as he talked. "I mean, we stole it all right. But who was there to see it stored? I reckon I'd like to see that much gold again, and we're a long ways off from where we started."

"You'll see it again, and soon enough."

The surprised men turned to see Iron Mike Truax emerge from the shadows behind them once more. The edge to his voice was as hard as a blacksmith's anvil, and the men quickly dropped their eyes or stared into the fire.

"Well, that's soon enough fer me then. Whatever you say, Mike," the blond-haired man quickly offered.

"Yeah," Mike said. "Whatever I say. Don't forget that. Never. We clear?"

Max Blake waited for more than an hour, counting the minutes off in his head, before he slipped away from the clearing and silently worked his way back toward his campsite.

Gold – apparently a lot of it. That explains a lot, Max thought as he moved silently along, pondering what he had heard and the deadly actions of the man called Iron Mike. But another thought quickly crossed his mind. *Outlaws on the hunt this late mean more trouble. No telling where they might be, and they could stumble on Buck and Jasper and the mule.*

Max picked up his pace, listening carefully for tell-tale sounds or stray noises that might indicate the presence of the late-night hunting party, but he saw and heard nothing unusual or disconcerting.

When he crept silently into the camp where he had left Jasper Perkins, however, there was no sign of the old man.

It was almost as if he had never existed at all.

Chapter 8

A Chill in the Air

The disappearance of Jasper Perkins was a puzzle, and Max Blake wrestled with it as he meticulously inspected the area around the camp where he last saw the old man.

Everything looks normal, he thought. *That's the strangest thing of all.*

Max knew that Jasper wasn't the kind of man to be caught unawares or to leave a friend behind without a word of explanation – unless, of course, he was in serious trouble.

Max examined the ground for signs of a struggle or other telltale marks that might explain what had happened. But he was certain of only one thing as he looked at the tracks around him in the filtered light of the crescent moon: The gabby prospector and all of his possessions were gone from the camp that Max had put down for the night – his mule included.

It's almost as if the earth swallowed him whole, Max thought. *It just doesn't track; there's no signs of a struggle, no indication that anything's ... wrong here.*

He cursed softly as his thoughts returned to the nearby gang of outlaws. *Their arrival and Jasper's vanishing act are somehow connected, at least by coincidence,* Max thought. But he reminded himself again that the old man could take care of himself and had done just that for years. *In fact, I pity those boys if they tangle with Jasper with no more help than they've got now.*

Max smiled a bit at that – a tight, grim smile devoid of mirth. But try as he might, he could not put a good face on the events that he had witnessed in the woods. He scratched around in the dirt by the campfire instead, looking for answers that were not readily apparent.

That's a force to be reckoned with, he thought. *And that big fella is downright unsettling.* Max kicked at a rock as he rolled the problem around in his head. *If this Iron Mike had hooked up with Hoss Johnson or the two Morgans, this territory would have been in for a long period of pure hell.*

He puzzled over a stray track for a moment, collecting his thoughts, and he knelt down and carefully examined the lone boot print. *I just hope old Jasper is a long way off and heading in the opposite direction,* he thought.

If a couple of them snuck up on the old man – got the jump on him somehow – that would explain it. Or that hunting party looking for fresh meat might've moved in close, and Jasper simply bolted before he was spotted.

But that didn't explain why the old man hadn't yet resurfaced. It also didn't explain why Buck, Max's chestnut gelding, and the rest of Max's trail possessions had been left untouched – and seemingly unnoticed – unless ...

... unless Jasper drew them away from the camp to keep them clear of Buck – and me. And for the first time since he returned to the camp to find Jasper Perkins missing, Max thought that he might have an explanation that made some sense.

I'll need to find Jasper and warn him about how deep this trouble runs, he thought.

Max hurried over to Buck. The big horse was cropping contentedly at the scattering of oats that Max had spread on the ground when he first pitched camp. He patted Buck a time or two, then saddled up and started off into the brush of the thin forest once more, looking for any sign at all of Jasper Perkins or the outlaw hunting party.

But he heard nothing unusual, and he saw no other living thing for the rest of the night.

And for reasons that Max Blake couldn't immediately understand, his thoughts turned from Jasper Perkins to Thomas Radford, the hanging judge of Twin Forks, and the events of the past few weeks.

Only days earlier – and already he had lost track of time spent on the trail – Max had returned to Judge Radford's courthouse, tired and dirty, trailing the horses of four dead men behind him.

Under normal circumstances, he would have taken the time to bathe, get at least one good night's sleep, thoroughly check the condition of his horse, and look after his personal affairs before tending to the paperwork of his last assignment. But these were not normal circumstances for Max Blake; these were not ordinary times in the territory.

Was it days or weeks since the judge had sent Max out to the edge of civilization in search of Hoss Johnson and the Morgan boys? Max was no longer sure. He only knew for certain that Hoss Johnson was dead; the two Morgan brothers, Freeman and Weasel, were equally dead; and a handful of good men who didn't deserve their fate also were lying in rough-hewn graves scratched out of the endless desert because their paths had crossed the killing trail.

He thought of Pedro Ruiz, the village leader of Indian Wells, who was gunned down for reasons that made no sense to anyone who remained alive.

He thought of Larry Nelson, who was leading his wife and two small sons away from the violence of the Texas range wars to California and a new life. But instead of finding a land of promise and opportunity for his family, Nelson found sudden death at the hands of the outlaws.

He also thought about Henry Grant, a soulless predator who sought revenge for his brother's death. Grant had tracked Max across the miles, even as Max himself had tracked Hoss Johnson and the Morgans. And now Grant, too, was dead, killed in the dust of a sleepy village street. Like the brother he was avenging, Grant had been a ruthless killer; no one in the territory would mourn his passing.

Mostly, however, Max thought of Judge Thomas Radford – still very much alive. Imposing, cantankerous, formidable, educated, aggressive businessman, steeped in the traditions of the law and the ways of a hostile land in a hard-scrabble territory, certain of his power and of his cause, a showman as well as a dispenser of justice at the end of a knotted rope, Judge Radford was a man who commanded – and demanded – respect at every level.

The citizens of Twin Forks were well acquainted with the judge; he loved to move boldly through the streets, smiling broadly and shaking hands and loudly calling out names and favors. Few sought him out, however; fewer called him friend; and most secretly feared or despised the man.

The judge, oblivious, was happy only so long as he was the center of attention. He could not abide being taken for granted or ignored. He also could not abide lawlessness in any form or disguise.

The judge, in fact, preferred to settle the accounts of the territory in his own fashion and in his own quick time. A hanging brought steady business to the hungry merchants of his town, and Thomas Radford was among the hungriest of all: He had substantial financial interests in a saloon, the hotel, the laundry service, the general store and mercantile establishment, and at least two of the town's public eating houses.

The source of the judge's power was his ability to dispatch the three federal marshals who served under his jurisdiction, including Max Blake, into the territory. Their assignments were straightforward: capture their quarries alive and bring them back to Twin Forks for trial and a prompt hanging.

The more notorious the outlaw, of course, the better it was for business.

If the marshals who worked for him complied with his rules, the judge would find no quarrel with them, regardless of their methods. If they left more men in shallow graves in the desert than they returned alive to the town, however, the judge could become a hard case, indeed – as hard as any of the outlaws he was so anxious to hang.

When Max Blake rode into Twin Forks after attending to Hoss Johnson, Henry Grant, and the Morgan brothers, leading three horses instead of living men, Max knew that a difficult discussion with the judge would follow.

But Max had no interest in the judge's personal financial stakes, particularly where his own life was concerned. He was not opposed to returning a man who deserved to hang back to Twin Forks to dangle at the end of a rope. But when the bullets started flying on the trail, he refused to consider what the judge might say after the fact – as troubling as that always seemed to be to the judge himself.

Besides, other issues were occupying his thoughts this day as he left the stables and headed toward the courthouse. Chief among them was settling a score with the sheriff of Aguante, the small border town notorious for harboring all manner of dangerous outlaws. Max had been captured and badly beaten there only days before, and he was anxious to return under different circumstances – a trip that first had to be approved by Judge Thomas Radford.

"I'll require a word with you, Marshal Blake," the judge had said as Max sat at a small wooden desk in the outer offices of the courthouse's upper floor, sorting through the appropriate paperwork that was required of a federal marshal after a killing. "Please don't keep me waiting," the judge added gruffly and turned instantly, heading into the darkness of his office.

Max took his time, finishing his task before walking into the judge's chambers. He didn't bother to knock but went directly to the judge's desk, where the big man was reading a law book.

"You wanted to see me?"

"Please be seated, marshal. I'll be with you shortly." The judge didn't bother to look up, waving his hand instead in the general direction of a chair in a dark corner. He continued to read as Max kicked the chair toward the center of the desk and sat down, his back ramrod straight against the dark oak slats.

A full minute passed.

At the end of a second minute, Max stood again and started to walk out of the office. "You're busy," he said, "and I've got a lot to catch up on."

"I'm not finished with you, marshal."

"Then I suggest you get to it, your honor," Max replied evenly. He continued standing as the judge set his book down and looked up for the first time since Max had entered the room.

"I am disappointed in you, Marshal Blake," Judge Radford said. "Please be seated again."

"No thanks," Max said. He paused for a moment and then added: "Why?"

"Why? Why, indeed?"

Max paused. "You just said you were disappointed. Why?"

"You can't guess, sir?"

"You sent me out to stop a killing spree. I put a stop to it," Max said simply.

"You didn't return those responsible to my courtroom."

"They were in no hurry to come in," Max said, shrugging his shoulders slightly.

"You may find this amusing or of little consequence, Marshal Blake, but I fail to see the humor. You seem to make a habit these days of leaving more men in graves in the wilderness than you do in filling my courtroom. It's a trend that I find most … disturbing. I want it stopped."

Max's impatience was clear in his reply. "I'm more interested in my life than I am in your courthouse or your gallows," he said. "I bring them back when I can. When I can't, I bring in their horses instead. Either way, justice is served."

"In my town and in my territory, justice is only served at the end of a rope, Marshal Blake."

"Then you'd best find yourself another man," Max said, rising from the chair.

"I see. It's come to this, has it?"

"Put it any way you want, your honor," Max said. He pulled the tin star from his vest and let it clatter onto the small wooden desk in the outer office as he walked past.

Max left the courthouse with his mind at ease for the first time in months. *That's something I should have done a long time ago,* he thought.

He left the town's most imposing structure and walked briskly down the dusty main thoroughfare, heading for Mad Dog's Steakhouse. Jim Madden was a trail cook who had managed, after years on the open range in the back of a chuck wagon, to pull together a sufficient grubstake and buy a small wooden building a block from the courthouse that he had turned into a decent eating establishment.

Mad Dog's wasn't owned or otherwise financially supported by Judge Radford, and that fact alone made it popular with many Twin Forks citizens, Max Blake included.

The specialty of the house was a steak dinner that required a sharp knife and only a moderate portion of sauce to keep the meat edible.

Most of the cowhands who ate there regularly brought their own knives. Mad Dog, as the proprietor was commonly called, supplied the steak and the sauce – a concoction he maintained was a special blend he had learned in the finest cooking schools in New Orleans. In fact, Mad Dog had never been east of Amarillo. His sauce was a mixture of whatever he had on hand, laced with burnt sugar and a large dollop of cheap whiskey.

Max walked into the kitchen area, nodding as he passed the handful of customers who had looked up, surprised and wide-eyed, when he entered; most either carefully nodded in return, or they averted their eyes entirely. Max didn't seem to notice.

He spotted Jim Madden crouched over a stove in the corner and hailed the man. "Hey Dog, you old horse thief," Max called.

Mad Dog looked up in surprise. "Hey yourself, Marshal Blake. I ain't never stole a horse in my life. Cooked a couple, though.

"Where you been these past weeks? Ain't seen Colt nor Winchester of you in a dawg's age, seems like. You've come for a meal, I trust, 'cause my steaks are so damn good, they make you wish you had a neck as long as a pole."

"Maybe later," Max said. "I've got some errands to run. But I'll take a couple of steak bones if you can spare them."

"Sure thing, marshal: anything you want. Used to be good at carving on bones – made all kinds of trinkets and such. Course, that was back in my drinking days," he said. "That's how I got my name, ya know ..."

When Max didn't offer more, Mad Dog considered other paths to engage the marshal in some casual conversation while he busily poked at large hunks of smoking beef.

Jim Madden didn't consider himself to be an actual friend of Max Blake's; it was unlikely that the marshal had a real friend anywhere in the world, outside of his horse and the stable boy, as he saw it. But Mad Dog prided himself on being a sparkling conversationalist who could talk with any man – especially the town's most famous federal marshal.

"I used to drink some, ya know," he said. "I used to be quick with a hog-leg, too, in my younger days, and kin still shoot a touch when I have to. You remember the time that old galoot came in and wanted to know if the place was called Mad Dog's 'cause I served up dog meat? Why, I was like to – "

Mad Dog paused to see if Max was interested in the story. But it became clear after an uncomfortable moment of silence and a stony gaze that the federal marshal wasn't, and so Madden shrugged instead.

"You are taking a bone to that fat old lazy stable dog, I see. Well, good for you, though it's a damn good thing that beast helps keep them horses calm, else he wouldn't be worth keeping around a'tall, you ask me."

"Easy there, Mad Dog. Buck is partial to the old boy. So am I."

"I know that, marshal; I'm just funning ya some is all. Anything else I can get you?"

"The bones will suit me fine – better yet if they have a little meat left on them." Max paused before adding as an afterthought, as though it were expected, "How have you been, anyway?"

"I manage, as always, though it's been a might slow, I gotta admit. We ain't seen a neck stretched in some time around here, you know, and that tends to cut down on business. I considered having me a talk with the judge, though he never seems to be in much of a talkin' mood when I happen by.

"So how 'bout you, marshal? You keeping outlaws outta the territory and such, are ya?"

"I've been busy," Max said. "I'll come back for that steak later."

"Then I'll save you a good one fer when I see you next."

Max took the steak bones, which Mad Dog wrapped in thin butcher paper, and headed to the livery. He hailed Joey Gray when he saw the boy grooming Buck, his chestnut gelding.

"How is he, Joey?" Max asked as he took a moment to scratch around the horse's ears.

"Hey, Max. Buck's great, the best horse in the territory – you know that. You aren't really worried about him, though, are you? I mean, well, is there something I should know about? Should I be looking for anything special or …"

"I'm just checking is all, Joey. You know how partial I am to Buck. Where's old Buddy? I didn't see him when I came in earlier."

"Oh, he's just lazin' about somewheres, Max – like always. You want I should fetch him out for you?"

"I'll hunt him up, Joey. He's got some gnawing to do."

Lon Barbers, the livery owner, walked in from the back room and nodded at Max. "I don't think that old dog would make it to the front part of the next week if you didn't bring him a bone from time to time, marshal," he said before calling loudly, "Hey, Buddy – come on, boy."

"No need to bother, Lon," Max said. "I'll find him all right."

Max headed to the back of the stables, where the dog was known to sleep the day away in the shade. "Buck looks fine, Joey," he called over his shoulder. "Just keep doing what you're doing. I'll check him over with you in a bit."

But even as he found Buddy and bent over to rub his belly before unwrapping the paper and handing him one of the steak bones, smiling as the dog's tail thumped on the ground in anticipation, Max's mind already was on other things and other places in the territory.

Thoughts of Judge Radford and Twin Forks drifted out of Max's mind as morning broke, and he was snapped back to the present by the sound of a single gunshot. He hadn't slept since Jasper Perkins first hailed his camp and then disappeared; he already was on the move when the echo of the gun – most likely from a big-bore rifle – thundered dully in from the hills to the east.

Max was leading Buck through a rough stretch of game trail that he had followed for an hour or more. He stopped abruptly when he heard the shot, which sounded like the low rumbling of a distant storm, and cocked his ear in the direction of the gunfire. But there was no answering volley or any other sound.

Max paused for a minute, holding Buck still, waiting patiently. But he heard nothing more and eventually urged Buck forward again.

I wonder if that's a call from ol' Jasper, Max thought. *I surely expected to see him by now.*

It was a full two days later, however, before Max Blake again picked up the faint trail of Jasper Perkins. He could tell that the old man was in trouble even then. Patches of dried blood spotted the ground, and the tracks that Jasper left in the forested path were unsteady and ungainly, at times looking as though a drunken man had stumbled through the woods.

Of Jasper's mule, Max could detect no sign at all.

Chapter 9

Staying Even

The faint, plaintive cry of a distant owl echoed eerily on the thin mountain air and brought Max Blake to a sudden stop. He pulled on the reins of his chestnut gelding and sat perfectly still, his ears – like the ears of his horse – attuned to the sounds that drifted through the depths of the surrounding forest.

Max nudged Buck into the deep shadows of the woods, selected a well-sheltered spot, and waited. Without consciously thinking about it, he pulled his familiar Colt and cradled the revolver in his right hand.

A full minute passed, then another. Max concentrated on a twinkling, distant star, fixing it in his mind, listening for the cry that had stopped him so suddenly.

He was about to move on when he heard it again – far away through the gnarled junipers, stubby pines, and the handful of swaying aspens that were sprinkled throughout the forest floor. It seemed to carry up the slope of the mountain to his left, although he knew that noises could be deceiving at this elevation, particularly when they floated on the soft winds of the night.

The mournful owl's murmured plea seemed to hang in the wind for a second or two, drifting away, and then he heard the same call again.

Only one man I know makes that call, and it's been some time since I heard it last. Max chuckled and playfully scratched Buck's right ear before turning the horse to the south.

"Figured he was too tough for that outlaw pack," Max whispered to the horse. "Let's head over and see if he's too proud for some help."

Buck carefully picked his way through the trees, mindful of the low-slung branches. Max let the horse choose his own path to the source of the owl-like hoots that occasionally sounded through the forest; it allowed him to concentrate on the shadows around them. But the closer Max got to the source of the sounds, the clearer it became that the calls were less like an owl's and more like the tired wheezings of a lonesome, worn-out old man.

Buck edged into a small clearing at the top of a rise that offered a view of the trail in the distance. Max snapped his head toward the rasp of a faint cough and smiled when he heard the growl of Jasper Perkins.

"Well, it sure took you long enough to find me, dammit. I was about to give up on you, I was – yes sir."

"Nice to see you, too, Jasper," Max replied, looking for the old man but spotting only his mule at the base of a weathered aspen.

"Well, you ain't quite found me yet. Best look up this tree aways 'fore I fall clean out and hurt myself worse'n I'm already hurt," Jasper said, taking a deep breath to force some fresh air back into his lungs.

"Thought you'd never get here," he added. "No need to doubt you, though. I apologize, Max."

"If that's a thanks, it's accepted but not necessary," Max said as he swung off Buck and holstered his Colt. "How'd you get up there? You must be half goat – or something else entirely."

"Most all goat anymore. Used up the something parts long ago – probably got hungry one night and ate 'em," Jasper huffed. He paused, catching his breath. "Had to keep an eye on the trail for that pack of rascals I was up against after we got split up."

"So they did force you out of the camp," Max said. "I got off the track some looking for you and trying to steer clear of them. Heard your owl plain enough, though."

"Kind of you, Max – given the nature of yer work and all," Jasper said. "Help me outta this tree now and I'll be more obliged than I kin make clear, yes sir."

The old man was in pain and doing his best to mask it as Max took a firm hold on Jasper's legs and helped ease him out of the split in the trunk of the old juniper that held his frail frame a good seven feet above the ground.

"Got you now, Jasper," Max said, easing the prospector down so that his back rested against the juniper's trunk. "What happened with you and that pack of bandits?"

Max stood, waiting for a reply, but Jasper had passed out from pain and exhaustion. It was only then that Max noticed the patch of dried blood staining the right shoulder of the old man's shirt and the deep loss of color in Jasper's haggard face.

As Jasper's breathing turned from ragged to steady to an occasional loud snore during the course of several hours, Max's thoughts drifted like the passing clouds that framed the moon. He thought of Aguante and its black-hearted sheriff. He thought of Paul Reyelts, the man who had helped murder his uncle so many years before. He thought of Joey Gray and his pretty widowed mother, Rebecca.

Mostly, however, Max thought about the hanging judge of Twin Forks, Thomas Radford.

Days earlier, Max had pulled the marshal's star from his shirt and tossed it onto the desk in the judge's courthouse. He was exhausted from a tough assignment that took him to Aguante, the territory's toughest town, and he was tired of arguing with the judge; walking away had been easy.

He had bumped into Doc Strand that day, and the town's lone physician and dentist quickly sized up the battered eye and badly bruised face that Max had collected in Aguante.

"Hold up a minute there, marshal. That's some shiner you've picked up," Doc said. "What nasty bit of business did you walk into, pray tell?"

"A disagreement with some boys by the border is all, Doc. How've you been?"

"From the looks of things, a lot better than you. You'd best let me have a look at that."

"No need, Doc. It seems to be healing fine – no trouble to speak of," Max replied.

"Let me be the judge of that. Come on, let's head over to my office for a minute and I'll take a closer look."

"It's not necessary, Doc. Besides, I'm in something of a hurry…"

"Look, Max, how long have I known you? Four years now? Maybe five?"

Max nodded as Doc Strand flashed an easy smile. "I won't give you a lecture or pull you away from important marshal's duties; I won't even tell you to duck when a man throws a haymaker. Let's just make sure nothing's broken. Whoever hit you knew what he was doing."

He paused for a moment and added with a wink: "It *was* a man who hit you – right?"

Max liked Doc Strand, and with good reason. He had been in Twin

Forks for years, working mostly for Judge Radford ("a man must be fit to hang, and Doc Strand makes sure of it," the judge liked to say with a chuckle), although Doc did a brisk business with the rest of the town's population when the mood was upon him. He had obtained the bulk of his medical experience on the battlefield during the bloodiest engagements of the Civil War, heading west when the fighting stopped. He enjoyed an occasional drink, although he didn't make a habit of marking time in the saloon. He could pull a festering tooth as easily as he could set a broken bone, and he appreciated the value of a whiskey bottle in both instances.

Doc also carried a Remington .41-caliber derringer tucked behind his belt and a pearl-handled Colt .44 single-action revolver with a seven-inch barrel strapped to his side.

Max recalled asking about the Colt one day. "What is with you, Doc?" he had said. "You work hard to keep men alive – I've seen you do it a time or two – but you won't hesitate to pull that big Colt and plug a man, and I've seen that, too."

Doc had laughed at the observation. "It's a question of staying even in all things, Marshal Blake," he replied. "You laugh, you cry; you get sick, you get better; you eat, you drink. And, of course, you save a life so that you can take a life away. Staying even – and living in moderation – is what life is all about, I guess. Death, too, comes to that."

"Did you learn that in Sawbones school?"

"No sir. I learned it on the battlefield, where I learned lots of things. Some of them are worth remembering. Most of what I saw there, I try to forget. But that's staying even, too."

Doc had pulled Max into his office by this time and poked and prodded around the marshal's eye. "What did you say happened here?" he asked.

"I didn't."

"Leave it to Max Blake to offer no telling details." Doc stepped back and wiped his hands on a small white towel. "You took a fairly good blow there," he said. "You are fortunate – more so than you know. Had you been struck a smidge to the right, or even a little less than a smidge, you might have lost that eye entirely. As it is …"

"Thanks for the assessment, Doc," Max said. "Is *smidge* a medical term?" When Strand laughed aloud, Max added, "So what do I owe you for the look?"

"Why, not a thing, marshal. I'll simply add it to my fees on the next bill to the judge."

"I don't work for the judge anymore," Max said. "But I'm happy to pay my own way."

Doc Strand was not a man easily surprised, but he was taken aback by Max's casual comment. "You want to explain that remark to me?" he asked.

Max pulled a silver coin from his pocket and dropped it into the doctor's hand. "Nothing to be said. You keep staying even, Doc."

Strand remained silent and open-mouthed as Max left his office and walked briskly across to the hotel, where he kept a small room that he rented from the judge. He took a long bath in hot water that helped to soak some of the saddle kinks out of his tired muscles before falling into the first real sleep he had managed in weeks.

His Colt .45 was tucked under his pillow, but it was doubtful that Max would have heard a gunfight had it taken place inside the very walls of his room.

He slept for seventeen hours straight.

By noon the next day, he had dressed in clean clothes after taking a second long bath, eaten a good meal at Mad Dog's Steakhouse, and made his way to the stables to again check on Buck, his big chestnut gelding.

Joey Gray, the stable boy, greeted Max with a concerned look on his face as he neared the front gate. "Is it true, Max? You can tell me. Is it?"

"Hey, Joey. Is what true?"

"That you quit – that you aren't a marshal any more?"

"Yes, I guess it is true," Max replied. He had given little thought to his decision to leave his tin star at the courthouse the previous day. "Where did you hear this?"

"Gee, Max, it's all over town. Everybody's talking about it. I went over to the hotel twice this morning to ask you about it, but they wouldn't let me go upstairs. Mr. Tovar behind the counter told me I'd have to find you later. But then he said I'd better be quick about it 'cause now that you weren't a marshal, you'd likely be leaving town for good.

"Is that true, Max? Is that what you're planning to do?"

"I'm in no hurry to leave anywhere, Joey – regardless of what Tino Tovar thinks."

"I don't want you to go, Max. I like you as a federal marshal better'n as just another cowboy. Cowboys have a way of dying that marshals don't have, you know. And I don't want you to die, Max – any more'n I want you to leave town."

Max smiled at Joey but said nothing. The boy's questions would need some answers sometime soon, however, and Max knew that he would be forced at some point to sit down and think about his future for the first time in a long while.

"How's Buck?" Max asked after a time.

"Why heck, Max, Buck's the greatest horse in the territory – and maybe in the whole wide world," Joey said proudly, smiling for the first time that morning. "I took extra good care of him, Max – made sure he got the best grain, a good rubdown, lots of brushing. I checked out his teeth, his shoes, his legs. He's just fine.

"He could go a hard two weeks out there even leaving today. But I'd rather see you rest him another couple of days or so to be safe."

"You never know, Joey," Max said, pulling a five-dollar gold piece from his pocket and flipping it end over end, watching the boy's eyes grow wide when he caught and then examined the coin. "You can keep that if Buck looks as good as you say. Let's go and see."

Max scratched at the stable dog's ears for a minute before he thoroughly examined his horse. *Joey's right*, Max thought as he checked the gelding. *Buck could head for the toughest parts of the territory right now, if he had to.*

"It's like I told you, Max: Buck's the greatest horse there is – not another one like him anywhere around."

"I'd say you're right, Joey," Max said, turning his attention toward the side door. "You've done a fine job with him. Keep it up for another day or so, all right?"

"You bet, Max. But I'm worried about you. I want you to be a marshal again. Why don't you go over to the courthouse and see the judge?"

"That won't be necessary, son. It seems that the mountain has come to the man instead."

Max had spotted Judge Radford the instant the big man tentatively entered the stables and moved slowly from the door when he spotted Max and Joey with the horse. Joey had paid no attention; he was caught by surprise and jumped when the judge spoke.

"Are you in the mood for a discussion about your future, Marshal Blake?" the judge asked.

"Make that Mr. Blake," Max said. "I turned in my star yesterday."

"It seems you somehow dropped your badge on the way out of my office, Marshal Blake. I've come to return it, with a reminder to make sure it's fastened more tightly the next time."

"Do you think it's that easy?"

"I think this is something we had best discuss in depth, Marshal Blake. I would like to take the time to do just that right now."

"I can spare a minute," Max said. "I'll be riding out tomorrow or the next day, so we'd best settle up soon."

"And where exactly are you riding to, Marshal Blake?"

"Aguante," Max said simply, letting the single word hang in the air.

"Then all the more reason for us to talk – and talk now."

"Fair enough."

"My office?"

"Right here's good," Max said.

"I would prefer the courthouse and more, ah, familiar surroundings."

"I'm comfortable here with my horse."

"As you wish, Marshal Blake. As you wish."

The judge turned his attention to Joey. "Son, you'd best run along now and let the marshal and me have our discussion. Please don't allow anyone to disturb us. Do you think that you can handle that all right?"

Joey didn't move until Max nodded in his direction. Then he walked out of the stables without saying a word, keeping a wary eye on Judge Thomas Radford all the while.

"It's time you made it back to the living," Max said hours later when Jasper Perkins stirred from a fitful sleep and opened his eyes to find a small but warm fire and the comforting presence of the federal marshal from Twin Forks.

Even though he smelled the coffee and a kettle of rabbit stew, it took the old man a moment to get his bearings and pull himself into a sitting position. He felt his shoulder and saw that it had been properly bandaged; the filthy dust kerchief he had used to stem the flow of blood from a single bullet wound had been replaced by a clean dressing from Max Blake's saddlebags.

"Don't git yerself worked into no frazzle on my account," Jasper said at last, doing his best to put some bark into his voice. "I'll be jest fine in a day or so. Am a might hungry, though, Max. I ain't had much of a chance to eat since them boys took to making sport of me, no sir."

"Just relax, Jasper. Let's be sure you're up to it."

"I felt better, I kin tell you that," Jasper replied. "Felt worse once or twice. Not for a while, though – been awhile since I felt worse'n this. How 'bout some of that stew yer boiling? It sure smells mighty good – yes sir."

"I thought you never ate anything but your own cooking," Max said with an easy shrug. "I can remember more than once ..."

"True enough – that's all true enough," Jasper said, cutting him off. "But the shoulder is a might on the sore side, I gotta admit, yes sir. Causes me to git hungry, I'd say."

Max spooned out a full plate of stew as Jasper leaned closer and said, "Can't rightly call to mind the last time I got shot. And I hate to ask it, Max, but could you look after my ..."

"It's already done," Max said matter-of-factly, setting the plate of stew in front of Jasper and handing him a tin spoon. "I took care of the mule along with Buck. The mule's doing better than you. He looks better, for sure; he even smells better."

"It's not that I ain't able to look after my own animal, mind you," Jasper said after chewing on a mouthful of the stew, ignoring Max's insults. He picked at his teeth with a dirty finger for a minute. "It's jest that it's been a time since I was last shot at and hit, you know."

"You're doing fine, Jasper. You can tell me what happened once you feel up to it."

"Well, you jest give me some time to eat, Max, and I'll fill you in fast enough 'bout them rascals. They had more on their minds than jest me, yes sir."

Within minutes, Jasper finished the stew and accepted another full plate. He smacked his lips aloud after digging into the second helping and looked up with satisfaction at Max.

"Mighty tasty, Max. Almost as good as I kin fix it myself," Jasper said. He brushed some of the stew off the side of his beard and forked another bite into his mouth. "It's been a time I had, and I want to tell you what those bastards are up to," he mumbled, his mouth full.

"There's no rush, Jasper," Max said, his back set straight against the trunk of a pine; the position allowed him to watch the surrounding area and the trail. "We've got all night, and there's been no close sign of that pack for a couple of days, at least."

"None you've seen, maybe," Jasper said, "but I ain't had such good luck, no sir. Them boys was in the woods when you left, scouting something – likely food, from the sound of it. I heard a passel of 'em coming near the camp and took the mule with me, trying to draw 'em away 'cause I knew you was none close by and couldn't help out none – and I knew Buck was tethered and didn't want 'em findin' yer horse, Max."

Jasper drew a breath, forked in another bite of stew, chewed thoughtfully for a bit, and started in again: "They heard me, jest like I planned it, but then they caught up with me too quick – a mile or less away, which is something I didn't plan on. And they took to makin' sport of me and the mule. It weren't nothing to git worked up about now it's over, though they did threaten to eat the mule at one point – and that riled me some, yes sir."

"How'd you get free?" Max asked.

"I snuck off when they was sleeping, though one of 'em managed a lucky shot and popped me here," he said, gingerly rubbing his shoulder. "I sent the mule round-about then and wiggy-waggled fer a bit a'fore I climbed the tree. They must'a got tired of looking after a time, though how long I was up there I cain't rightly say. And then the mule showed up again not long a'fore you did. A good thing, too. I ain't sure which I was glad to see more – you or the mule, Max."

Max offered a thin smile. "How many men did you see in all?" he asked.

"Hard to say. They seemed to move about in groups, and I kept trying to count faces but got confused. I'm guessin' there was maybe forty, more or less. I must be gettin' old, yes sir."

"Any idea what they were after?"

"Might've been me they was looking fer all this time, you know," he sniffed. "Truth be told, though, they was after something else entirely."

"Such as?"

"Gold, Max. Them boys is all of 'em chasing after Yankee gold dollars. Lots of it. A boxful of the stuff, to hear 'em tell it. No telling where it come from, but that's what they's after or already has, all right – or so I heard 'em say more'n once. What do ya say about that?"

"I'd say you're right."

Max's answer caught Jasper off guard; he had been certain that he was delivering big news to the federal marshal and was disappointed in Max's almost casual reaction.

"I heard them talking about it just before we lost track of each other," Max explained when he noted the surprise on Jasper's face. "Gold was on their minds then."

"If you heard 'em talking about gold, then we both heard the same thing," Jasper said. "They stole it somehow from the Army. And anyway you look at it, gold spells trouble. Big trouble, I'd say – yes sir."

"I'd say you're right again."

"Right as usual, you mean," Jasper added. "The question is, what are we gonna do about it? I'd like to git me a touch of that gold – and a little revenge fer what they did to me and the mule, you understand."

"We, meaning you and me, are going to do nothing," Max said. "I'm not even likely to do much about it – at least not right now. I'm on the judge's business, and that doesn't include chasing gold thieves. It's more likely the Army is after this bunch."

Jasper shook his head. "Yer judge friend surely wouldn't look poorly on you for bringing the hand of justice down on a pack of thieving varmints – would he now, Max?"

"Likely not," Max said, "especially if gold's involved. Most every man pays attention when talk turns to gold."

"Thought as much. Yer judge must like gold same as the next man – 'specially if he don't have to do none of the work to git it, I reckon," Jasper said smugly.

"But that still leaves you to consider, Jasper," Max said at last. "You're not up to it."

"Now you jest hold on there, Max Blake. Never thought I'd hear the day you'd say I cain't hold my own, no sir." Jasper tugged on his beard in anger and stared at Max with dark, accusing eyes.

"You won't hear me say it now," Max offered, picking up a handful of sandy dirt and throwing it into the fire to kill the flames. "You need some rest and a doctor's care. Twisted Junction is nearby. You know it yourself."

"Come on, Max. I cain't stand to lie on my back in no real bed in no real town."

"We'll talk in the morning."

"But ..."

"Give it up, Jasper. You're on the wrong side of the law."

"All right, Max. All right – have it yer way fer now. But you know I kin talk up a powerful storm, and I'm of a mind to do it right now, yes sir. I'll talk yer leg clean off and won't even git warmed up. I'll ..."

"Jasper?"

"What?"

"Did you run across Army tracks the past couple of days?"

"Not a thing, Max. Why?"

"Strange," Max said quietly, almost to himself, as he stared thoughtfully into the distance. "The night we ran into this bunch, they talked like an entire regiment was on their trail. But neither of us have seen any sign."

"What do you figure it means?" Jasper asked. "Maybe they want to..."

A sharp look from Max cut Jasper off in mid-thought, and the old prospector noticed that the forest was deadly quiet; the only sound he could hear was his own breathing. Max was holding his Colt .45, looking out into the darkness.

Jasper quietly pulled his own revolver. Max pointed off to the left, and Jasper peered out into the night, listening, his eyes moving back and forth between the still form of Max Blake and the patch of forest that had suddenly closed in around them. Max was almost flat on the ground, his head moving carefully, cautiously, from tree to tree, his gun hand swinging in the same careful, cautious arc.

A minute passed, and still the forest remained silent.

Jasper reached across with his left hand and gently tapped Max on the shoulder. "Whatcha think?" he whispered. But Max only shrugged, his eyes scanning the blackness.

The two men waited in silence.

Another minute passed, then another, and soon a half-hour had slipped by. But the forest remained quiet except for the soft, gentle breathing of Max Blake and the short, raspy breath of Jasper Perkins. And when Max at last turned his attention toward Jasper, he saw that the old man had passed out from exhaustion once more, his revolver in his hand, an empty stew plate on his lap.

It's just as well, Max thought. *I don't like the feel of this night, and ol' Jasper likes to play hero.*

Even though he stayed awake and alert throughout the long vigil of the night's slow passing, constantly watching Buck to see if the horse detected any movement in the blackness surrounding the camp, Max didn't see or hear another sound until Jasper Perkins began snoring loudly close to sun-up.

Chapter Ten

A Series of Disagreements

In a clearing in the woods miles from the camp that Max Blake shared with Jasper Perkins, Slim Berning was pacing beside a skimpy campfire. He was silently cursing to himself, oblivious to the hard men around him.

"Why don't you slow down some, Slim, and take a bite of this stew?" one of the men asked at last, tired of watching the scarecrow-like Berning move in constant circles around the fire. "The stew's good – leastways it is tonight."

When Slim ignored him, the man tried again. "Jest smell it some and you'll see what I mean."

"Why don't you jest shut up and leave me alone?" Slim snapped, not bothering to look up or slow down.

"You could stand to eat something," the man said casually, as though he hadn't heard Slim's angry response. "A few more pounds on your hide would do you a world of good."

"You don't hear none too good these days, Toad Wright. I wonder why that is," Slim said, stopping in his tracks to glare at Toad, who was sitting with his back to a tree near the fire, holding a tin plate full of the stew. "I got no intention of listening to you and no intention of eating yer cooking, neither. You probably up and shot some dawg – or maybe it were that old man's mule. You never was much good as a shot and even worse as a cook – especially with dawg meat."

"Well, don't say I didn't try to interest you none," Toad replied, shrugging off Slim's angry insults. "You'll be sorry, if'n you ever find out what yer missing."

"Then I'll never know, and a good thing," Slim said as he paced around the fire again, talking to no one in particular now. "You boys been sleeping too good and thinking too little fer some time now."

"What's that supposed to mean?" another man asked. Slim's outbursts were so common these days that most of the men in camp ignored him. But sometimes – when the mood was on him – he was hard to ignore.

"While you boys've been busy filling up yer bellies with Toad's dawg meat, Iron Mike has run off again, planning to split that gold money so it goes a long ways – meaning yer share."

"Thought we wanted the gold to go a long ways," the second man said. He was short and squat with long, dirty blond hair, a scraggly beard, and a hard-coiled face that couldn't disguise the dim eyes of a killer.

"You chunkheads don't know trouble till it drops you dead, and then it's too damn late," Slim said, pacing faster now. "That means you especially, Hersh. Iron Mike only wants the gold to go a long ways into his pockets. He don't care a short blade fer the rest of us. And he ain't gonna rest till he picks us off – every one of us – one by one till all the gold is his."

"What makes you say that?" Toad Wright asked, encouraged by the nods of several others who had perked up when the conversation turned from stew to gold.

"You all forgot so soon about Dirk Luehrs? And what about ol' Charlie a'fore him, huh?"

The men said nothing, and Slim let the words hang in the air.

"Dirk didn't mean no harm the night he got his," Slim said at last. "The way Iron Mike plugged him, just like he plugged Charlie, is a good map to read fer what's in store fer the rest of us, if we don't watch our backs – and by that I mean our own and each other's."

"Maybe yer friend Dirk had it comin' to him. Maybe Charlie did, too," Hersh said. "I don't take to being called no chunkhead by the likes of you, Slim Berning. Maybe yer the damn chunkhead. Maybe yer the one's got it comin', you ask me."

"Maybe. Then again …" Slim stopped his pacing once more and looking squarely at Hersh. Slim's fingers started twitching ever so slightly as his hand stretched down to the grips of his revolver, ready for the first sign of movement.

"Maybe you both better cool off some – git down to the stream and jump in," Toad said.

"Shut up, Toad," Slim said. "Nobody's askin' you."

"This is between me'n him," Hersh added without taking his eyes off Slim. "You keep the hell out of it, Toad – the rest of ya, too."

"Like hell I will," Toad said, standing up quickly and throwing his tin plate to the ground. "If what Slim says is true, and I think it might be, then this is between every man-jack of us. If we start to picking each other off now, we'll only be doing Iron Mike's work for him. And I fer one ain't liking that one damn bit."

The men around the campfire looked thoughtfully toward Toad, considering his logic, forgetting Slim and Hersh for the moment.

"So you agree with me?" Slim asked, his eyes shifting now between Hersh and Toad.

"I'd be real surprised to hear either Dirk or Charlie were the first men Iron Mike took a sudden dislike to," Toad said matter-of-factly, looking intently from man to man.

"And there's no doubt Mike wants as much of that gold as he kin carry off by himself," Slim added. "You've all seen it."

"Jest you make sure he don't hear none of us right now," Toad said in little more than a whisper, and every man in the camp glanced nervously about.

"He'll be gone a spell yet, I expect," Slim said. "Now's likely a safe time to bring this up, else I wouldn't have done it – that and Howry's off with Iron Mike and Townsend's riding guard herd. To my mind, them two can't be trusted, neither."

"Jest where did they git off to anyhow? You think they're trying to find that old man?"

"I can't see why. The prospector means nothing."

"But you know Mike don't like no loose ends; never has. The way we had that old fella and his mule and then the way they just plain disappeared after trying to slip the camp – well, it jest weren't natural somehow. You reckon?"

"I'm a damn sight more worried about the Army than the old man," Slim said. "What concerns me most is we ain't seen nary a bluecoat since we took the gold. If Iron Mike wants to run down anything out there in the dark, I hope he takes out the whole damn Army fer us all and forgets everything else."

"I'd say Mike Truax knows what he's doing out there," Hersh said. "The way we cleaned out that town north of here shows that plain enough."

"The way we cleaned out that town was downright stupid," Toad said, kicking at the dirt with his boot. "You think nobody's gonna notice? Hell, we kilt every living thing that moved and some things that didn't.

But kin we say for sure we got every man in the place – that no one a'tall was left alive or that someone didn't jest sneak out and get away?"

"Hard to say one way or t'other: maybe so, maybe not," Hersh said. "Maybe that's jest what Mike had in mind. I'd say it's why we ain't seen them Army boys yet. And if that's what's been keeping us shut from the bluelegs, then all the better fer us."

"Well, that still don't explain where Mike's off to right now."

"I'd say Mike's checkin' the gold," Slim said. "That's why he took Howry for company."

"You think he's looking at the gold right now?"

"What else would he be doing this time of night?" Slim asked. "He sure ain't tracking the prospector. And he don't seem worried near enough 'bout them bluecoats to suit me, though the rest of us damn well ought to be."

Slim paused for a few seconds, spitting toward the fire.

"Think about it," he said at last. "Iron Mike leaves and takes Howry. How come? He trusts Howry; he don't trust us. He's got us locked in here. Rand Townsend's on patrol, but I'd say it's as much to keep us in as to keep others out. Mike don't want us near the gold."

"What do you think, Toad?" a man asked.

"Slim's right – about some things anyways," Toad said, waiting for some grunts and nods. "Iron Mike's likely looking after the gold right now. Sure, Mike wants all the gold fer himself; hell, every man among us does, Mike especially. He's always said it was more his than the Army's."

"True enough."

"But Iron Mike needs to keep at least some of us in one piece, to fend off the Army boys on our tail and to haul the gold. So that buys us some time – or at least it buys time fer some of us."

Silence filled the night air as the men considered Toad's words.

"The question is, who's gonna be lucky enough to steer clear of Mike in the meantime?" Slim asked, looking around at the men gathered nearby, trying to assess those he could trust and those he could not. The ledger was evenly balanced, however, and he didn't like the odds.

"Well, if Mike don't git us," Toad said with a grim laugh, "we're like to git in the way of Slim and Hersh here and picked off in the cross fire."

"I kin think of worse ways to go," Slim said with some conviction.

"Yeah? Like what, exactly?" Toad asked.

"Like eatin' yer damned stew," Slim said with a shrug, his face a sullen, frozen mask as he began pacing again. He ignored the nervous laughter of the men around him.

"You jest call me a chunkhead one more time and you won't have to worry none 'bout eatin' again – Toad's stew included," Hersh said, his bearded face twitching slightly, his eyes flashing from side to side.

But Slim ignored Hersh, and Toad Wright cut off further discussion with a final warning.

"We'd all best be careful 'bout what's done or said around Iron Mike. He's right touchy these days, and gold is like to make a man act strange. You think I'm wrong? Dirk found out. So did Charlie. It won't pay fer none of us to do the same."

As Max Blake sat with his back to the fire and stared into the deep forest around him, his mind only dimly registering the sounds of Jasper Perkins' ragged breathing, he again thought about his meeting with Judge Radford in the Twin Forks stables days before. The judge was not pleased with Max's decision to turn in his tin star, and he had demanded a conversation with the fastest and deadliest of his marshals.

"There's no gentle way to put this, Marshal Blake," the judge said, "but your behavior was out of character and unappreciated in my courtroom yesterday. I'm sure you agree upon reflection."

When Max remained silent – his gaze unwavering, his mind resolute – the judge uneasily reassessed his position, realizing that he was suddenly far less comfortable than he had been at the start of the meeting. *It's funny how Max Blake can do that to a man without saying a word,* he considered.

"Nonetheless," he said after clearing his throat, "I have given the matter some thorough consideration and believe it is in our mutual interest to continue our working arrangement. As a result, I am returning your marshal's badge and will only dock you a single day of pay."

The judge took the tin star from his coat pocket and offered it to Max, but the marshal remained silent, his hands at his sides.

"Is there a problem, Marshal Blake?" the judge asked.

"No sir," Max said. "I quit yesterday. I'm a man of my word."

"Of course you are; so am I, as we both know. I'm certain you never intended to end our relationship. I'm certain it was all a misunderstanding of one kind or another. I'm willing to let the matter rest without other considerations. Let us both simply agree to move forward, shall we?"

Max's silence forced the judge to drop his hand to his side. "Come

now, Marshal Blake," he said at last. "Surely you don't expect me to beg
– do you?"

Max said nothing. The judge's thick fingers fiddled with the tin star.

"Surely you must know this is hard for me – to ask you to return like
this. There's not another man in the territory I would even consider
providing this concession to; not one. I think highly of you – and have
from the first day we met. You have been like a son to me.

"Come now, what do you say?"

Max shifted his weight from one foot to the other, looking the judge
directly in the eye.

"I'll reconsider the pay," the judge said at last. "I suppose you worked
the better part of the day regardless."

"It's not a matter of money," Max said at last.

"Well, what is it, then?"

"Pride in what I do." His steely gaze eventually forced the judge to
look away.

Max picked up a small rock and carefully rolled it around in his
hands, examining it from a variety of angles. He found that this exercise
kept his eyes sharp and his fingers relaxed; both traits were required of a
man who made his living with a six-gun.

"You have that in spades, marshal. I know that; so do you," the judge
said at last.

"I'm a man of my word."

"You also are no quitter, yet you are quitting on me now."

"I'm no errand boy who fetches men for you to hang." Max tossed
the stone he was holding onto the ground.

"I know that you are no errand boy, marshal."

"Do you? Your actions say otherwise."

"That remark comes close to offending me, Marshal Blake."

"Then you won't like what's coming next," Max said evenly. "You
care more about filling the town with people to watch your hangings
than you do about the men you send to do the dirty work. It's good
business to you; it's life and death to me."

"I see."

"Do you?"

"I'm not sure I like the implication or the..."

"I don't care what you like at this point," Max said, cutting him off.
"I have other concerns at the moment."

"I'd like to settle this, Marshal Blake. I really would. I like you. I
respect your work, for the most part – and you know that full well. But

you are making it difficult for me to bring about an amicable solution to our – what shall I call it? – situation."

"If you want to settle this, you have to bend. I'm happy enough to ride away now, and for good."

"I could have you arrested, sir. I could send Marshal Lord ..."

"Not likely," Max said. "I'd never look back. You know that, too."

The judge paused. "I understand that, Marshal Blake ..."

"... then fix it," Max said sharply, cutting him off.

"Enough of this. Come now and take your badge. Let's both get back to work, right here and now and with no more discussion. What do you say?"

"It depends entirely on you," Max said.

"In what way, sir?"

"On whether you ever tell me again that a hanging is more important than my life."

Judge Radford straightened a bit and cleared his throat. The color in his face had started to rise from a normal pink blush to a deep-seated red; but he settled back against a box stall and waited for a spell, concentrating hard on regulating his breathing, visibly making an effort to control himself. He looked up again, started to say something, paused, and finally spoke.

"Fair enough," he managed. "Anything else?"

"Let's talk about my next assignment."

"You have something in mind, I take it?"

Max nodded.

"Some unfinished business, perhaps?"

Max nodded again. "Aguante. Reno Walker. It's time."

Judge Radford looked hard at Max, his eyes wide with anticipation. The slight trace of a smile etched its way across his lips for a mere instant before it disappeared, and he pretended to swat at an imaginary fly.

"This would be a trail of revenge that you find yourself seeking, would it, Marshal Blake?"

"Revenge? I wouldn't call it revenge," Max said after a minute of reflection. He considered the question, wondering whether his pursuit of Reno Walker was motivated solely by the recent beating he had suffered in Aguante. He looked at the judge, his face empty, and shrugged his shoulders. "Does it matter?"

"Ah, it's an interesting question," the judge replied, "and one that will take some deep reflection on my part. But by all means let's talk. I believe that we have much to talk about, in fact. So let's do just that.

What say we return to my courthouse now and continue this discussion in a more – how shall I put it? – private setting, shall we?"

Jasper Perkins stopped his uneasy snoring long enough to turn on his side in his bedroll, snort a time or two, and resume his ragged breathing. In time, the snoring, rhythmic and steady, started up once more as Jasper settled deeper into sleep.

Max Blake turned his attention from the prospector to Buck; the horse's head was down, the great eyes closed. *The two of them are about alike,* Max thought. *Hard to tell which one's more dead to the world: Old Jasper or ol' Buck.*

Don't suppose it matters much, though I can rely more on Buck in a tight spot more than I can on Jasper – at this point anyway.

Max thought on that a minute. *And Buck is generally better company when's he's sleeping.*

Max was huddled in his bedroll, which warded off the chill of the night air. He put all thoughts of Jasper's noisy sleeping out of his mind and considered his conversation with Judge Radford once the two men returned to the courthouse and resumed their private discussion about the border town of Aguante and the outlaw sheriff who controlled it.

The judge and I don't agree on much these days, and we'll have to deal with that sooner rather than later, Max thought. *But at least we're clear about Aguante.*

His gun hand crept down to his side, gently wrapping around the familiar handle of his Colt Peacemaker. It was a move that Max often made unconsciously – something at once reassuring and familiar. He held the weapon in a caress and turned his thoughts to the sounds of the deepening night.

Chapter 11

Helping Hands

As Max Blake and Judge Radford walked the dusty main street of Twin Forks together, heading toward the courthouse to conclude their preparations for an assault on Aguante, neither man noticed the edgy cowboy who was subtly watching their every move from the shadows.

The man was smoking a stubby cigar that he nervously chewed as though it were a thick piece of meat; a stream of blue smoke curled from the tip and rose in a thin, wispy spiral over his head, flattening out on the corner of the porch overhang that covered the rough-hewn boardwalk.

Two regulars at a drinking establishment called The Watering Hole stumbled noisily out of the saloon at that moment and laughed aloud. One of the pair was tall – six-foot, seven-inches or more – with a sweat-stained Stetson pushed back on his head. The other man, slightly older and a half-foot shorter, carried himself ramrod straight and had a steady, confident look about him despite the copious amounts of alcohol he had just consumed.

The two allowed their eyes to adjust to the darkness for a moment and eventually headed down the boardwalk past the cowboy who was waiting and watching in the shadows, his back set flat against the side of the building, his left boot stuck firmly against the rugged wooden wall, his mouth furiously working the well-chewed cigar.

The saloon regulars nodded but paid the cowboy little attention as they passed. The taller of the two turned toward his partner and was about to continue an earlier conversation when the stranger with the cigar said softly, almost as an afterthought, "Hey, you boys mind a question?"

"What's on yer mind?" the taller man replied, holding up momentarily. His partner took a few more steps before he stopped to face the man in the shadows.

The stranger pulled the cigar from his mouth momentarily, looked at the end for a second or two, and then pointed in the direction of Max Blake and Thomas Radford, who appeared to be engaged in conversation as they made their way down the street.

"Them two fellas there, walking." He held out his arm and waited for the pair to take a good look. "Seems I ought to know 'em both but can't place the names. You fellas mind helping me? It's eating at me some."

"You must be a pilgrim in town if you don't know the names of them two," the tall man said. "Yer looking at the hangin' judge hisself" – the man jerked his thumb over his shoulder – "and that would be Judge Radford; he's the old galoot of the pair. And with him is his top dog deputy – no, make that top dog marshal – none other than the famous Max Blake."

"Max Blake, eh? And he's a deputy marshal, you say?" the stranger asked, nodding his head as though it suddenly made sense.

"There's nothing deputy about Max Blake, mister. He's a true federal marshal, the real thing. I guess you could even say he's something more'n jest a federal marshal round Twin Forks and the territory in general," the tall man said.

"Yeah? How do you figure?"

"Max Blake is no ordinary marshal. Wouldn't you say so, Milt?" The big man turned toward his partner and shrugged at the question he had asked, as though the answer were so obvious that even a stranger could follow the logic. Without waiting for a response from Milt, however, he continued to talk.

"Calling Max Blake a federal marshal is like saying, well, let me think: It's sort of like saying Tombstone is nothing more'n a sleepy little town, I guess. Max Blake, I think you can say, is something akin to a house a'fire."

"Naw, it ain't like that at all," Milt cut in, swelling his barrel chest and pointing a thick finger at his partner. "Geez, Big Boy, but that don't make no sense no how. I mean, Tombstone is a sleepy little town, you dumb git. Max Blake is a house a'fire, all right. But the other business yer serving up here ain't right."

"How would you say it then?" Big Boy asked. "You think yer so smart, tell me that, Milt."

Milt thought on it a minute. "Look, use any comparison you want. Max Blake is the best federal marshal in Twin Forks and surely the best in the territory. Any fool can figger that out jest by keeping his ears open and his mouth closed. And that's where you git left behind, Big Boy: You can't do neither, and especially the part about keeping yer mouth shut.

"All right, so you asked. That's how I'd put it."

"What the hell are you talking about, I can't keep my mouth closed? Gawd a'mighty, Milt, but I think you have finally..."

"I'm telling ya jest that, Big Boy," Milt cut in, "and I'm telling it straight. Every man in town knows it. Most every woman, too."

"Geez, but yer full of something," Big Boy said. "And the something yer full of smells a whole bunch like something I wish I'd never stumbled on, I swear."

"Ain't that something to say?" Milt replied. "Let me tell you and this stranger here a thing or two well worth knowing." He paused, letting his words hang in the air. Big Boy looked on expectantly; the stranger looked annoyed.

"Max Blake is tough, and he's fast with a gun – faster'n any man in the territory, so far as we know. And if he was right here right now, he'd surely ..."

Milt's eyes twinkled as he paused again.

"He'd surely what?" Big Boy asked expectantly.

"He'd surely buy us a drink. That's what he'd do."

Both men laughed at that – loud, raucous laughter that spilled out in the street, and they started off again down the boardwalk, dismissing the stranger in the process.

"Hey, hold up there a minute," the cigar-chewer called, tossing the remnants into the street. "So you think this fella Blake is special. What makes him so good?"

"Yer kidding me, right?" Big Boy asked. "I thought you said you might know Blake and the judge and jest couldn't place the names. Ain't that what he said, Milt?"

"I must have this Blake mixed up with someone else is all," the stranger replied before Milt could answer. "I'm not sure I got ..."

"Come on, mister. Everybody knows about Max Blake," Big Boy said, cutting off the stranger again. "Why, he's kilt more outlaws than they got drunks in this here saloon – and the place is full of drunks this very minute."

"Two less since we walked out," Milt added, but Big Boy ignored him.

"Max Blake is the quickest, surest shot you'll come across. If you was to go up against him, face to face, yer face would be lying flat in the dirt a cold second after the shooting started. And I'll tell you something else: Ain't no doubt about that, mister. None a'tall."

Big Boy stopped, looking pleased with himself. He folded his lanky arms across his chest and stared at the stranger, his face registering somewhere between cocky and smug.

"And then Max Blake would just ... walk away," Milt added. "He'd even leave it to somebody else to drag your sorry carcass out of the street."

"I'd say that covers it, mister," Big Boy said. "Truth of the matter is, Max Blake is far to the edge of dangerous. That's a sad fact for every killer and horse thief in the territory, but it's one best remembered."

The three men stared at each other for a moment, one to the next. Milt and Big Boy looked thirsty; the stranger pulled another squat cigar from his pocket and looked thoughtful.

"Anything else you need, mister?" Big Boy asked at last. "We got places to go and things to see and do. There's another saloon down the street that needs our tending."

The stranger shook his head and stepped out into the light. A large scar covered his face, but the two regular patrons of The Watering Hole were wise enough to ignore it. "I appreciate your help, boys. I'd offer to buy you a drink, but seeing as how you is –"

"No no – don't be hasty now. We kin be persuaded to have a drink with you, pardner, so long as you got the money to spend and the time to spare," Milt said. "What'd you say yer name was?"

"Didn't say. Call me Wesson."

"Wesson? What kind of a name is Wesson? Wes an' what, exactly?"

"It's Wesson – like Smith and Wesson." He turned to Big Boy and said, "At least it's easy to see where yer name comes from."

Big Boy was about to answer when Milt jumped in. "The way he takes to talkin' so much, you'd a thought they'd of settled on Big Mouth instead of Big Boy – don't you think?"

Milt chuckled. The stranger grunted but said nothing.

"Stop," Big Boy said to Milt and turned his attention to the stranger: "My name's actually ... well, it don't matter none. They call me Big Boy because of my size."

"You don't say?"

"Look," Milt cut in, poking his finger in the air in front of the stranger's chest, "I don't care if his name is the King of England or if you call yourself Sears an' Roebuck, so long as yer buying the drinks. Come on – we'll introduce you to all the boys, Mr. Wesson – and yer good to go till yer money holds out, at least.

"You can call me Milt. Him" – and he pointed at his partner – "you can call him whatever comes to mind, just like everybody else does 'round here."

Big Boy and Milt laughed at that and hustled back into the saloon with their new-found friend in tow. The stranger glanced down the street before he ducked inside, but Max Blake and Judge Radford were well out of sight.

The two leading citizens of Twin Forks, however, were not forgotten in the saloon conversation that followed late into the night.

It was a conversation that Richard Nash remembered quite well, in fact.

Chapter 12

The Dark Side of Truth

Thomas Radford's face was beet-red: It had distorted into a cruel half-smile, his large teeth pushed grotesquely against his thick lips, and his eyes were small slits that seethed pure hate and a violent, explosive anger.

"I've had enough of your incompetence, Marshal Blake," he raged, his meaty fist pounding the top of his desk. A stack of law books collapsed outward as his hand smacked the hard wooden surface; the scattered books crashed with a loud thump onto the floor, further enraging the judge. Saliva, mixed with remnants of his just-finished dinner, dribbled down the first and second layers of his ponderous chin.

He stood abruptly, pushing his chair backward with such force that it skidded off the wall.

"When I get through with you, sir, you will never again work as a federal marshal – not in this territory, certainly; not in any territory in the land," the judge raged, his anger intensifying as he stared at Max Blake.

"Do you hear what I'm saying? You are worse than a common horse thief. You are unreliable. You are neither trustworthy nor dependable. You have no business wearing a marshal's badge: not in my courtroom, not in my town, certainly not in my immediate presence."

The judge paused for a moment to collect his breath, his huge body working like a blacksmith's bellows to force air into his enormous chest. He pulled a white handkerchief from his back pocket, wiping his forehead and his various chins in short, jabbing strokes, leaning even closer to where the federal marshal stood.

"Am I fully getting through to you now? Do you understand what I'm about to do?"

Max Blake took a step closer and continued to level his steely gaze at the judge. "The bigger issue is what I'm about to do," he said calmly as he pulled his Colt – so quickly, so effortlessly, that it took the judge a moment to recognize exactly what had happened.

"See here. How dare you ..."

But the huge man's words were cut off by the booming roar of the finely tooled, precision-made revolver. The sound echoed off the walls of the courthouse office, even after the bullet from Max's gun crashed through Judge Thomas Radford's skull, killing him instantly.

Max fired again as the judge's body was driven into the chair behind him; it collapsed with a sudden finality to the floor, toppling the heavy chair in the process. Max had a third cartridge chambered and ready to fire, but he heard footsteps and turned instead toward the door to await the bailiff and other court officers who would respond to the sound of gunfire.

The door burst open and two men ran carelessly into the office, seeing Max first before turning to find the judge's body sprawled across the overturned chair; a growing pool of blood was seeping into the hardwood floor.

"What the hell?" one of the men managed to say before Max's Colt roared once more, catching the man flush in the chest and driving him back through the door he had just entered.

Matthew Grill, the bailiff, Max thought.

The second man – Max didn't recognize his face – used that precious instant to dive behind the judge's desk. In no hurry now, Max methodically cocked the revolver again and edged slowly around the corner.

"Good God, marshal. Yer ... not gonna shoot me, too. Are ... are ya?" the man whispered, his voice breaking into sobs as he cowered against the wall.

He looked directly into Max's eyes as the gun exploded once more. It was fired from no more than three feet away from the man's startled, ashen face.

Max Blake woke with a start, shaken by the vividness of the dream.

He blinked, steadied himself as he sat, wrapped in his bedroll, his back propped against a willowy aspen, and he blinked rapidly again to help his eyes adjust to the darkness.

He was not surprised to find his revolver clutched firmly in his right hand. He was relieved after a quick check to see that the gun had not been fired and that Jasper Perkins was still asleep in his bedroll nearby, oblivious to the night or to Max's stirrings around him.

Max had experienced the same dream three times in the past week, and he was still amazed at how real it seemed. The sequence of events was always the same: the enraged judge, the two rapid gun shots, the sounds of men running to help, and their own violent deaths.

Max shook his head, trying to sweep out the sleep and the ghostly images at the same time.

He felt his pulse returning to normal, gradually slowing along with the racing of his heart. He took a deep breath, then another, and he spent the next several moments taking stock of his surroundings before returning his Colt to the holster that was strapped to his side. He spotted Jasper Perkins, sleeping soundly on the other side of the dying fire. He could see Buck, unmoving and undisturbed a stone's throw away, as well as Jasper's mule, and he drew another deep breath.

Damn strange, he thought.

He couldn't understand why he would want to kill the judge. He also couldn't understand why he would shoot the men who ran to the judge's aid, even after it was apparent that they posed no threat. *Matt Grill is a good man,* he thought. *It's clearly the judge who deserves to die.*

The suddenness of that thought struck Max like a crashing fist. *The judge deserves to die: Do I really feel that way about Judge Radford?*

Max considered it for a while, struck by the vividness of the experience and the idea that the dream was occurring with regularity, unfolding almost methodically each time.

It's true that we don't always agree, and we've had our share of arguments, Max thought. The most recent took place only days earlier when Max tossed his federal marshal's badge down in disgust and walked out of the courthouse with a feeling of serenity for the first time since ...

"... since my uncle was murdered," he muttered aloud, and Max thought again of the elusive Paul Reyelts.

Max shook his head once more, trying to clear Reyelts from his thoughts, focusing again on Judge Radford. It was clear to Max, at least, that the judge was more interested in filling Twin Forks with paying customers to his hangings than he was in the well-being of the federal marshals who brought the outlaws in to hang. The judge disagreed with Max's assessment, reacting with predictable anger and a discussion of their differences that spilled across two long days.

Max's pursuit of Reno Walker, the murderous sheriff in the outlaw border town of Aguante, was the common ground that the judge and the federal marshal eventually found.

"You want this man because he tried to kill you when you were in search of Foster Johnson and the Morgan brothers. It was only through good fortune and your own resourcefulness that you managed to thwart his plans, which doubtless would have ended with the unjustified loss of your life," the judge told Max at the time.

"I understand that, and I respect revenge as a powerful agent – a weapon as great as a Colt revolver in some hands. But you must understand, Marshal Blake, that revenge is not the issue in my courtroom. Justice is the only issue I am interested in, and I expect that justice will be served when you return Reno Walker to Twin Forks to hang."

"That's my intention," Max said simply. "He may not see it that way."

"Indeed he may not, Marshal Blake. Be that as it may, your mission nonetheless is to return the man to my courthouse alive. Is that understood?"

"Perfectly. But I won't risk my life so that you get your hanging."

The judge had paused for a moment, wondering how hard to push the point.

"That's fair enough, marshal. I would expect nothing less of you," he said at last. "Even at that, I expect to see you bring Reno Walker here so that he can keep his date with my gallows. A lot of people will pay good money to witness that hanging. I don't want to disappoint them."

Max again considered the conversation, and he again arrived at the same conclusion: *The judge wants to get his way, regardless of the cost.*

From the day that Thomas Radford had hired Max as one of three federal marshals who kept peace in the territory, the judge had been nothing but a dedicated, hard-working representative of the court, despite his many quirks. *I wouldn't call him a friend,* Max thought. *But he's been honest in the dealings we've had, even if his needs are not the same as mine.*

The judge is a hard case, all right. But so am I – and so is the job.

The mournful call of a distant coyote momentarily put the judge out of his mind. And when he did remember the dream again minutes later, the vivid detail was gone, along with any reasons he might have had for questioning the loyalty of the man he worked for.

It was only a matter of minutes before Max Blake drifted off into a fitful sleep.

This time, however, he didn't dream at all.

At first light, Max and Jasper already were saddled up and moving. Max was leading Buck, his big chestnut gelding, through a stream bed that trickled out of the mountains to the north; the old prospector trailed close behind on his mule.

Getting Jasper to Twisted Junction and some rest and care was Max's immediate priority. But Jasper had been unusually quiet this morning, and Max concentrated instead on what he would do when he reached Aguante and confronted Sheriff Reno Walker. It was a confrontation that Max had thought about for days, and it never failed to turn his gray eyes into thin, narrow slits that were focused to a single purpose.

Reno Walker's time in the territory is up – one way or another, Max thought. *He just hasn't come to know it yet.*

It might be that the man would hang from the end of one of Judge Radford's short ropes in the town square in Twin Forks. It might be that he would die from the crash of a Colt revolver pointed directly at his heart. It might be that his death would come from any variety of events, gruesome or otherwise – and Max could picture many of them in his mind.

But Reno Walker's trail of terror was going to end; of that fact, Max Blake was certain. And he kept that thought in his head as he pushed Buck resolutely along the faint trail that led first to Sheriff Ned Clark's town, where he would leave the stubborn Jasper Perkins, before continuing on to the desert hell of Aguante.

"Hey, Max – I don't like being left behind on this, no sir," Jasper wheezed from behind, the first words he had spoken in more than a hour.

But the federal marshal paid no attention to Jasper's mumbled protests.

Chapter 13

A Side Bet

In the dark shadows of a pungent pine forest, a half-mile or more away from the main encampment of gold thieves, Iron Mike Truax was meticulously checking the mechanical parts of his Colt revolver.

He slowly pulled the hammer back on the single-action weapon, listening intently to the metallic clicks that notched the dull metal piece into place. He held the revolver close to his ear and returned the hammer to its original position, resting the firing pin on a new cartridge, before repeating the process again and then once more.

Satisfied that the Colt was in good working order, Truax watched Joe Howry load two hunks of jerked meat wrapped in butcher's paper into the saddlebags that were strapped to the broad back of his buckskin-colored gelding. Howry, a short, trim man with a starkly bald head, stuffed a package of rock-hard corn biscuits inside and called across to his partner.

"You think we did the right thing with that old man, Mike?" he asked.

Truax shook his head as he spun the cylinder on the Colt a final time before returning the weapon to its holster, which was strapped tight to his side. "Letting that old man loose was as good a ruse as we could manage," he said. "It's hard to tell what he'll say, or if he'll say anything a'tall. And whatever he says will be only half-believed anyway – but it might buy us some time."

"And we need the time."

Truax pulled the black Stetson from his head and ran his fingers across the ridges and around the creases, removing a thin line of dust. He examined the hat from a variety of angles before placing it carefully back on his head and adjusting it to sit forward and low above his eyes.

"What we need to be thinking about now is the damn Union Army, which ought to be chasing after us right about now – them and that bunch

91

of cut-throats we chose to partner up with fer this job," Iron Mike said. "I don't like or trust 'em, and it's getting harder to keep 'em in line."

"You might want to ease up on killing 'em off one by one then," Howry offered with a dry laugh. "A thing like that is like to upset a man, you know – and them boys is upset."

"Hell, you'd think a good killing from time to time would be enough to give 'em pause – make 'em think a bit before wondering who's trail boss and who should be trail boss around here. I tell ya, I'm inclined to head on back and shoot the rest of 'em, jest to let 'em know I'm serious."

Howry checked the cinches on his horse before looking in Truax's direction again. "You might want to think that one over a bit, partner," he said. "If the Army boys is on our tail, like you think, then we're gonna need them fellas in a fight. Last time I checked, dead fellers don't fight none too good. And we might well need us some hard fighters before this is all over."

"Yeah, well, it's the only thing holding me back."

"So what do you think?"

"Another good stall tactic, maybe," Iron Mike said. "There's a settlement south and west of here some, and I've got an idea of sorts rattling on and off in my head. If we ride on over and shoot Whiskey Bend up a bit like we did that last place – what's it called? Adobe Flats? – that might be enough to stall whatever's on our trail and buy us some time. Plus, the promise of some shooting will help settle the boys – take their minds off me and git 'em where they belong."

"It worked well enough the last time, over to Adobe Flats," Howry said. "Course, Whiskey Bend is a bigger town, with more people, and apt to pose some fight. And we still don't know that anyone is on our trail – not for certain, anyways."

"Oh, somebody's back there all right. The damn Union Army is not gonna let that much gold walk away and pay it no never-mind. You can bet your stake that someone's tracking us – and maybe a lot of someones. So let 'em deal with another mess in a place that don't matter none instead of dealin' with us."

"Won't it just make the Army boys more anxious to git us?"

"Maybe. But we need time to pull this deal off, and this will buy us some."

"All right, Mike – whatever you think. Just keep in mind that the men in Whiskey Bend will fight back, so check it hard a'fore you sweep in."

"That's sound advice, I guess."

"Yeah, well, you know I trust you regardless. I'll look fer you in town or just south of it when I'm done then."

"Good. That'll work. Now here's a reason to bet your life on trust."

Iron Mike reached into his coat pocket and pulled out a heavy sack of gold coins. He hefted it a time or two in his hand, judging the weight as he shifted it from side to side. Then he tossed the sack across to Howry, who caught it with a grunt and muttered, "A man could get hurt slinging this stuff back and forth."

"Jest be sure you do what we agreed. You know where to go, and you know the man to see. And you sure as hell know what to say when you see him.

"And remember, Joe, we need time. We can't pull this off without time." He paused for a moment and added, "No need to say more."

Howry nodded but remained silent. He opened one of the saddlebags, dropped the sack of gold inside, and hoisted himself onto his horse before turning to the north. He looked across to where Mike Truax was watching, adjusted the brim of his Stetson with his right hand, nodded slightly, and started off into the darkness.

"Do federal marshals dream, Ma?"

Rebecca Gray was seated at the small table in the corner of her dirt-floor cabin at the edge of Twin Forks; her son, Joey, sat across from her, fiddling with the plate of venison stew that she had spent hours preparing for their simple evening meal together. Joey's work at the livery stables after school each day usually made him ravenous by the time he arrived home, and his inattention to the aromatic food on the tidy table was a clear indication to his mother that something important was on his mind.

She looked across at the boy, her eyes filled with pride and sadness, and pondered the unexpected, unprompted question.

He looks so much like his father, she thought. *And he surprises me, too – much like his father used to catch me off guard.*

"What makes you ask that?" she said after a minute.

"I don't know, Ma. I've just been thinking about Max and Buck, I guess, out there alone on the trail somewhere, and I just got to wondering about … about maybe, well, I don't know – "

His voice trailed off, and he slumped his shoulders and then shrugged and glanced across at his mother with a troubled look on his face.

"You are worried about your friend Marshal Blake – is that why you aren't eating tonight?"

He nodded. "I guess so, Ma. I mean, I shouldn't be worried. Max is the best marshal there is – there's not an outlaw in the territory as fast. But I think it must be lonely out there for him all the time, riding from one place to another, with only ol' Buck to keep him company."

"I see."

"And, well, I just wondered if he dreamed at night, is all."

"I'm sure that the marshal dreams, just like everyone else, Joey."

She said this with a wistful look as Joey considered her words. Rebecca found Max Blake to be a good man, essentially – a careful, considerate man who clearly was fond of her son. But she also knew that he was serious to a fault and full of contradictions – and she couldn't abide the line of work that he was in.

God only knows that Joey worships him, she thought. *And Joey needs a man in his life – one who is reliable and dependable, and the marshal certainly is that.*

But Joey needs a man who will come home alive each night – we both need that. And a federal marshal is ...

"But that's just it, Ma," Joey said at last, interrupting her thoughts. "I know when I see something that scares me, sometimes I dream about it afterward – and it's usually a lot worse in the dream. Just think of all the scary things that Max sees all the time: the very worst outlaws, lots of really bad men, people trying to hurt him or kill him all the time – just about every day. And I worry that if Max dreams at night, his dreams must be just awful – the kind that wake you up with a start and make your heart race really fast and make you glad when you finally figure out it was just a dream and not real after all."

"I see. And this bothers you?"

"Well, yeah, Ma, it does. It bothers me a lot sometimes."

She wanted to cry. *It's a rare little boy I have – not so little any more,* she thought. *He's so concerned about others, though I wish sometimes – most times, really – that he would find himself a different role model.*

"I'm sure that Marshal Blake manages just fine, Joey," she said. "I'm sure that you worry about him needlessly."

"But you don't know, Ma. Max even has to deal with the judge when he's here in Twin Forks, and the judge is every bit as scary as the outlaws Max chases. I've seen it. So ... so I worry about Max is all, I guess."

"I see." She paused to collect her thoughts. "You know how strong and careful the marshal is, so I wouldn't worry too much if I were you. Eat your food now, Joey, before it gets cold."

"Promise me something, Ma," Joey said as he finally speared a thick chunk of venison.

She nodded.

"Promise me that when Max gets back, he can come over for dinner with us, Ma – so he won't be so lonely or scared for at least one time in his life."

She started to provide her automatic response: She didn't approve of the marshal's line of work, even though she knew full well that few people living in the territory – and certainly no woman living alone – would be safe without men like Max Blake ensuring the peace. The pleading look in her son's eyes made her stop, however, and she caught herself and nodded slowly in reluctant agreement.

"I promise, Joey."

"Do you mean it, Ma? Really?"

"If it means so much to you, of course I promise. Now go ahead and eat your food, and then we can enjoy the dusk together."

Chapter 14

Payments and Reunions

Jack Sloan methodically tied his horse to the hitching post in front of the dilapidated Silver Spur, one of two saloons in the otherwise thriving settlement of Twisted Junction, and smiled for the first time in hours.

He was tired, close to exhaustion, and a drink and some conversation had been on his mind from the moment he left Adobe Flats. He looked up at the ramshackle building, a crudely painted wooden sign featuring a large white spur and red block lettering fastened above the door, and rubbed his hands together in anticipation.

The Silver Spur, huh? Nothing dead inside, I'll bet, he thought as he pushed his way through the batwing doors.

Pausing momentarily for his eyes to adjust to the darkness, Sloan noted that the Silver Spur smelled like every other frontier saloon he had ever visited: The offensive reek of cheap whiskey and thick body odor and stale urine saturated the floor and the walls and even the tables and the chairs. But he ignored the stench and gladly made his way to the bar.

He pulled a small pouch of gold from his pocket and set it down on the counter in front of the bartender, a wooly, bearded man with dark, deeply recessed eyes and a worn-down face that otherwise betrayed no emotion as Sloan approached.

"What kind of bottle will this buy?" Sloan asked casually.

The bartender picked up the pouch, noted its heft, and gently pulled the drawstrings apart, spilling some of the contents into his hand. Holding the gold flakes close to his face, he pushed them around a bit with a gnarled, stubby finger and shrugged, although a slight smile whisked across his eyes for the briefest of instants.

"What's your poison, mister?" he asked.

"Whiskey – a full bottle with a couple of tall beers to wash it down."

"Seems like we can do that much and be fair about it," the barman said as he turned to pull a bottle off the back shelf. He took a dank-smelling bar towel and wiped the dust off the outside of the bottle, then set it down on the counter and produced a shot glass from under the bar. "You want the beer now or later?"

"I'll take it now if you don't mind," Sloan said, "over there" – he pointed to a table in the far corner that was well away from the front door – "if that's agreeable to you." Picking up the bottle and the shot glass, he made his way past mostly empty tables to the secluded corner.

Sloan had just finished his third shot, his eyes already acquiring a dull glaze, when the bartender arrived with two full glasses of watery beer.

"Yer not from around here, I see," he said, but Sloan didn't bother to reply to the obvious.

"That's all right. You want anything else, mister? A room for the night, maybe, or someone to look after yer horse? Or how 'bout a woman? They's hard to come by in these parts, but you look like the kind of man who jest might ..."

"Not interested," Sloan said with finality, keeping his eyes squarely on the whiskey bottle, which he deftly held in both hands. "But you can tell me where to find the sheriff."

The bartender's eyes flashed a glint of surprise, though he recovered quickly and shrugged. "You'll find Ned Clark a minute's walk down the street," he said, hooking a thick thumb toward the back wall. "What you need the sheriff for, anyways?"

When Sloan didn't respond, pouring another shot of whiskey instead and gulping it down in the same motion, the bartender shrugged theatrically and turned again toward the bar.

"Wait."

Sloan picked up one of the beer glasses and took a long, deep drink while the bartender halted his shuffle and slowly turned. Sloan finished the beer, set the glass on the table, and belched loudly. He looked up at the barman through tired, red-rimmed eyes and asked, "What's it worth to you to go'n fetch the sheriff?"

"Couple dollars, I reckon."

"Do it," Sloan said, pouring another shot. "I'll pay in gold if you git him here quick."

Jasper Perkins was worn out and saddle-weary when he arrived at the Twisted Junction livery stables, riding in with Max Blake. The marshal climbed down from his horse and stretched his legs; Jasper, hurt and grumbling, remained on his mule.

Tim Weller, the talkative livery owner, was shoeing a horse when he heard his name called and was surprised to see the territory's most famous federal marshal.

"Well hullo, Marshal Blake," he said. "It's nice to see you back with us, and bringing in some company to boot."

Max nodded.

"So, the sheriff's expecting you? Only reason I ask is he didn't say a thing to me, and he usually does if he's waiting on someone off the trail."

"He won't be disappointed to see me," Max said, "though Jasper here needs tending to first. He's been roughed up some."

"So I see," Weller replied, nodding at Jasper and noting the dried patch of blood that had stained the prospector's coat at the shoulder. Jasper grunted but said nothing. "He friendly to you or jest some outlaw yer haulin' in?"

"I'll show you an outlaw, you young pup," Jasper sputtered. "You should show a little respect – the both of you should, yes sir."

"You'll find Doc Peterson three – no, it's four buildings down the street, marshal," Weller said to Max, ignoring Jasper's outburst. "He keeps regular hours and should be around. Tell him I sent you and he'll double the rate – I get him at cards, you know. But he knows what he's doing, ol' Doc does – he's patched me up a time or two – and I'm sure he can help the old timer all right."

"I appreciate the help," Max said, cutting off Jasper's intended protests. "How about Ned Clark?"

"All I know fer sure is he's in town somewheres 'cause his horse is here. I reckon you can find him in his office or close by. Sometimes he makes the rounds, but most of the time he's …"

"I'm obliged," Max said abruptly. "You'll see to my horse?"

"Sure thing, marshal; glad to help as always."

"Good. I'm partial to Buck." Max nodded at Weller and turned toward Jasper. "Come on, old friend. Let's see if the doctor can iron out some of that orneriness."

"You think I'm ornery now, Max Blake, you jest wait and you'll see what real ornery is."

"Save your energy, Jasper," Max said. "Best save your strength, too, in case this Doc Peterson needs to carve a bit."

Max was walking alongside Jasper's mule now, holding onto the bridle, when Jasper tugged the animal to a halt. "Don't you git me started, Max, 'cause I sure ain't in no mood fer it. No doctor's gonna start carving on me, no sir. Why, I …"

But Max cut him off. "Let's just get this done, Jasper."

Max found Ned Clark minutes later, shuffling paperwork. The Twisted Junction sheriff looked up at the knock on his office door and hopped to his feet when he saw the federal marshal.

"Why Max Blake, it's good to see you again – still alive and in one piece," Clark said, holding out his hand. Max shook it without comment, and Clark took a hard look at Max's bruised face. "Looks like you had your hands full with Hoss Johnson and the Morgan boys, all right.

"We heard all about it, of course – everybody up and down the telegraph line. The wires fairly hummed with the news. My thanks again for settling up after what they did in my town."

"Glad to help, sheriff; nothing to it," Max said with a shrug.

"Your face says otherwise."

"It got in the way of a fist is all," Max said, cautiously looking around the room.

"Must be important business brings you back our way so quick, marshal," Clark said, trying nonchalantly to rub some circulation back into his right hand. "Or is this a social call?"

"I wish that's all it were, Sheriff Clark," Max said. He nodded toward a chair and asked, "Mind if I sit?"

"Of course – be my guest," Clark said, motioning with a broad sweep of his hand. "You don't need an invite to have a seat here."

Max pulled a chair free and positioned himself with his back to the wall; he could see the sheriff, the door that led out to the street, and the side door that allowed access to the empty cells in the space behind the sheriff's office.

"How's the judge?" Clark asked after an uncomfortable moment passed.

"Fine, last I saw him."

"You?"

Max nodded this time but remained silent.

"Would you care for a cup of coffee maybe?" Clark asked.

"Kind of you, sheriff, but don't bother on my account," Max said.

"No – it's no trouble. It's already made. Let me just get it off the stove."

Clark moved briskly across the room. He poured the lukewarm coffee into a well-beaten tin cup, refilled his own, and hustled back to his desk.

"I'd like to help you if I can, Marshal Blake, for whatever it is brings you back this way. I take it you've come for a reason," he said, letting the thought hang in the air.

"Kind of you, sheriff," Max said after taking a small sip. He grimaced noticeably at the bitter taste, then nodded amiably at the sheriff and mustered the slightest suggestion of a smile. He set the cup down on the edge of the desk with some finality, however, his eyes missing nothing as they held the sheriff's gaze.

"I'd appreciate a favor, sheriff," Max said at last.

"Certainly. What is it you had in mind, exactly?"

"I came in with Jasper Perkins," Max said. "He's been roughed up and likely needs a reminder to stay close for a few days."

"I know of Jasper. Most everyone in the territory does. What's happened?"

"He ran into a pack of varmints," Max said simply. "He won't agree, but I'd like to see him stay in town for a few days – till he gets his strength back, at least."

"I can see to that if you like, marshal. Is he all right?"

"He caught a slug in the shoulder. It may take some persuasion to keep him close," Max said. "Jasper doesn't like being told what to do."

"Well, I suspect I can handle it all right. Where is he now?"

"Your doctor's having a look at him."

"That would be Doc Peterson – a good sawbones. Tell me, Marshal Blake, what kind of varmint goes after an old man like Jasper Perkins?"

"Not varmint; varmints. There's a hard bunch riding through the territory. Near as I can tell, they're connected to a missing shipment of Army gold."

"Gold? The hell you say. I haven't heard anything about missing gold – not on the wires or on the streets. And gold's the kind of thing gets people talking."

Max nodded.

Ned Clark locked his fingers behind his head, closing his eyes in deep thought. "Gold turns even good men mean and nasty," he said after a minute. "You've seen this bunch, I take it?"

"Northeast of here a few days back – couple dozen or more in all. I ducked in for a close look; Jasper got tangled up first-hand. I found him two nights later." He shrugged. "You were close by."

"A good thing for Jasper, from the sound of it."

"You might have to lock him up till he mends," Max said. "He'll want to ride on."

"What about these varmints?"

"I'd be on the lookout. If I didn't have business elsewhere, I might see to them myself."

"So the gold didn't bring you back to my neck of the territory? That's a sorry thing to hear."

Max settled into the chair, his eyes boring bullet-sized holes through the Twisted Junction sheriff. "What do you know about Aguante?" he asked suddenly.

Clark leaned forward, his hands dropping down on the desk, and he whistled a single low note and held it. "Surely the judge didn't send you out on that fool's errand?"

"This one is mostly my call," Max said simply. "I'm asking because I respect your opinion and know I can trust your discretion."

Ned Clark drew a long breath, folding his calloused hands on the desk that separated the two lawmen while he collected his thoughts. "If you're heading back to Aguante, you'd best get yourself a wagon or two full-up with deputies – every one of 'em nail-hard. It's the worst place in the territory, and that's saying a fistful. But hell, marshal, you know all that – better than most men – and don't need to hear it from me."

"How about Reno Walker? What do you know of him?" Max asked.

"Only what I hear, which is more'n I want to know most days, though there's plenty to tell. The man is a killer, of course – no lawman at all. His deputies are all murderers. He keeps order by being tougher and harder than the rest of 'em – and that takes some doing. He shoots first and asks no questions – and I hear he hits what he aims at."

Clark paused and thought for a few seconds. "Yeah, and I guess there's one other thing I've heard about the man: He enjoys his work."

Max nodded, staring at a spot on the far wall, lost in thought.

"Seems he jest showed up one day – hell, I don't know, seven years back, maybe? – before you came to the territory, marshal. I was here, though, and remember it. I suppose if it weren't so out of the way and hard to get at, something would have been done about Aguante by now."

Max leaned forward again so that all four of the chair's legs were touching the floor. He moved his body closer to the desk and looked directly into Ned Clark's tough, weathered face. "You really think an army is the only way to draw him out?"

"Either that or one good man alone," Clark said after running the matter over in his mind again. "And you might be that man, Marshal Blake. But even at that, Aguante is one tough place, and Reno Walker is one hell of a tough nut to crack."

Max's eyes turned hard, and he nodded slowly and confidently as he stood and extended his hand. "It's good to see you again, Sheriff Clark," he said. "I appreciate your help with Jasper. Keep him around a few days before you kick him loose."

"I'll see that it happens," Clark said. "I'll keep an eye out for that varmint pack, too."

Max was starting for the door when he pulled up and turned to face the sheriff again. "What happened to that grinning deputy of yours – Tom Bolton?" he asked.

"I fired him not long after you were here last," Clark said. "Had to do it – he left me no choice. He was good at shooting the salt, all right, but wasn't up to the job and always full of excuses.

"As I recall, marshal, you took Bolton down a peg when you was through here – that why you ask?"

"A man looks both ways when the snake slips the rock," Max said. "You think he's got any snake in him?"

"Bolton? He never showed it when he was with me. Course, he never showed much of anything but talk and that damn grin. He left the day I sent him packing; wasn't happy, neither.

"So ... you heading out now, marshal?"

Max already was moving toward the door. "I hope to see you on the way back through – unless, of course, you want to join me on the trail to Aguante."

Clark blanched at the thought, and Max's eyes registered a brief smile. "Take care of Jasper and I'll be in your debt," he said. He tipped his Stetson and disappeared into the crowded street.

The sheriff waited a full minute, following Max Blake with his eyes, before he murmured, "Considering where you're heading, marshal, I'll be surprised if ..."

Clark stepped outside without finishing the thought and started briskly down the dusty street to meet with Doc Peterson and Jasper Perkins. He was brought up short by Johnny Seifert, the bartender at the Silver Spur.

"Man at the Spur says he needs to see you, sheriff," Seifert said without greeting or fanfare.

"Know him?" Clark asked.

"Never seen him before, but he walked in with a pouch of gold straight from the hills."

"All right, Johnny, thanks. I've got a stop to make and will come by after that."

"I suggest you get over to the Spur in a hurry if you want to find him sober, sheriff. He ain't been here but a minute, and he's already well down the whiskey trail. The man loves his redeye."

Chapter 15

Mistaken Identity

As night began to fall in earnest, a steady drizzle dampened the already depressing pall that hung like a dense curtain across the black sheen of the mountains.

A thick cover of pine needles, dark brown on the trail, was all that kept the horse from slipping. The man in the saddle kept his attention sharp and alert – his eyes constantly sweeping the surrounding countryside, looking for any sign of movement, any indication of trouble, any hint that anything at all was out of place.

A trailing army would do that to a man.

As the wind picked up and the rain blew hard into his face, he turned up the collar on his sheepskin coat and shivered once, then again – and then once more, feeling the chill run deep down to the bone.

Lots of miles to cover yet, he thought. *It'll be a long night.*

He had no idea that this night would be his last, however.

He neither saw nor heard the hidden assailant nor the crack of the rifle that cut him down in the rain and the darkness. He grunted once in surprise and slid noiselessly into the sodden ground, his right foot slipping from the stirrup. The buckskin gelding ambled off as if nothing had happened at all.

A full twenty minutes later, Tom Bolton – the former deputy from the sheriff's office in Twisted Junction – clambered off the side of the hill where he had positioned himself hours earlier. He was waiting to see whether the man he had bushwhacked with a well-placed round from a Winchester '73 would stay on the ground, or whether the single crack of the rifle might attract other men and other problems. But the only sound and movement came from the steady rain and the wind as it shifted through the boughs of the pines, and he warily crept up to the body that was motionless on the trail, face down in the mud, the right leg twisted at an odd angle.

"I got you at last, you bastard – yes I did," Bolton whispered, a wide smile forming on his wet, flushed face.

He poked at the body once with the Winchester, then again, looking for the slightest twitch or movement. He placed the rifle barrel at the base of the man's neck – *he might yet be playin' possum on me,* Bolton thought – and pushed his weight forward, hoping fervently for a reason to pull the trigger again.

The only thing that kept him from firing another round, in fact, was the thought that the sound might bring unwelcome attention.

Satisfied at last that the man in the mud was dead and beyond caring, he hooked the toe of his boot under the body and heaved it over so that he could see the face.

"Dammit," he cursed, dropping suddenly down to one knee and furiously pawing at the mud on the dead man's face to get a better look.

"Dammit to hell."

Bolton sprang to his feet, cradling the Winchester so that he could wipe the mud from his hands, his eyes fixed on the dead man. He shook his head and cursed loudly once more, and he took a savage kick at the body – almost losing his footing – and continued kicking again and again until his fury was spent.

He walked in circles for another moment or two, allowing his breathing to return to normal, shaking his head from side to side, trying to determine what had gone wrong with a plan that he thought had been perfect.

"I don't know who you are, mister," he muttered at last, almost as though he were writing an epitaph for the dead man's tombstone. "But I sure as hell thought you was that bastard Max Blake and wish to hell you was, and that's a simple truth.

"You'd be dead and I'd be happy, and that's another simple truth."

He cursed silently, and the smile that lit his face so broadly moments earlier was lost somewhere in the rain and the wind and the darkness.

Chapter 16

New Friends and Dark Tales

Jack Sloan had been drinking hard for hours, and he was a man who could consume great amounts of whiskey with gusto and enthusiasm for long stretches.

Generally, he could drink and remain coherent – something that he considered to be a blessing and a curse.

When Sloan left the settlement of Adobe Flats, he had a bottle of redeye in his hand and a look of distress on his face. The bottle lasted for little more than an hour before he abandoned it on the side of the trail with a casual flick of his wrist and pulled a second of equal potency from his saddlebags.

By the time he reached Twisted Junction and the Silver Spur saloon, Sloan had gone through two additional bottles – four in all. But it wasn't enough to get his mind off the surprising horrors he had witnessed in Adobe Flats short hours earlier.

By the time Ned Clark, Twisted Junction's determined sheriff, arrived at the Silver Spur, Sloan already was well on his way to a head-buster of gigantic proportions. Clark hailed Johnny Seifert, and the bartender pointed to the table where Sloan was seated, a half-empty whiskey bottle and a half-dozen empty beer glasses scattered about the filthy table top. He held a shot glass in his right hand; his eyes were focused on an empty spot on the wall across the room.

Clark headed toward the table. Seifert, carrying a dirty bar towel and another glass of beer, fell in line.

"My name's Clark. I'm the sheriff. You wanted to see me?"

"All of 'em's dead but one," Sloan said as he focused on Ned Clark, spotting the tin star that was pinned to his chest.

"Whoah; slow down there, cowboy," Clark said evenly. "All of who is dead?"

"All the people in that town north of here – whole town's shot to hell and all of 'em dead. Just the bartender's left, a fella named Corn. He sent me to tell you."

Sloan's eyes returned to the blank wall across the room. He had the look of a man who expected to solve the secrets of the universe, if only he could stare long enough at a single magic spot.

"Hold on, mister," Clark said. "Let's start at the beginning and see what we've got here. How about you tell me your name for openers?"

"Name's Sloan, Jack Sloan; but I ain't dead – not yet. Working on it, though."

"I can see that all right, Jack Sloan. But if you ain't dead, then who is?"

"That's what I've been trying to tell you."

He reluctantly pulled his eyes away from the wall and started to pour another drink. The sheriff, hoping to keep Sloan focused, leaned across the table and took the bottle from the man's hands. When Sloan shrugged and reached for the glass of beer that Seifert carried with him, the sheriff grabbed that as well.

"Let's hold up on our drinking till we get the rest of the story, Jack Sloan," Clark said. "Who exactly is dead, and where?"

"Every man in Adobe Flats, near as I can tell, sheriff," Sloan said, eyeing the whiskey bottle in Clark's hand. "All of 'em's dead save Col. Corn."

"The beer-slinger up in Adobe Flats is called Corn, sheriff," Seifert offered. "I've know him off and on for years, though I ain't seen him for a time."

Clark nodded, turning his attention back to Sloan. "So how do you know they're all dead?"

"Saw it," Sloan said. "I been prospecting, ya see, up in the hills to the north, and I came down for a drink. It helps keep my mind on what's important, and sometimes what to forget. So I ride in to get a bottle and the whole damn town is all shot to pieces: bodies everywhere, dead horses – a stinking mess.

"What's a man to do? I tend to a wounded horse like any good citizen, head to the saloon, and damn near get my ear shot off by Col. Corn. We start to talking then, getting to know one another and such, and here I am to tell you."

Sloan shrugged and longingly eyed the bottle again.

"Well, Jack Sloan, this tale of yours doesn't make much sense," Clark said after a moment's silence.

"It don't much make no sense to me, neither. Hell, I didn't even get to town – I was just riding in, minding my own business, you understand – when two galoots damn near rode me down trying to git away. They suggested I hightail out 'cause a pack of renegades was shooting up the place. So I head in regardless and start to converse ..."

"Wait – did you say renegades?" Clark interrupted.

"I didn't say it. They said it – the two galoots riding out of town. Them's the boys were talking about renegades."

Clark whistled softly, almost imperceptibly. "Max Blake mentioned a roving pack of gold thieves not more'n an hour ago," he said softly, as though talking to himself. "I wonder if his and yours are one and the same?

"All right, give me the rest of it, Jack Sloan."

"Give me that first," Sloan replied with a shudder, pointing to the whiskey bottle. "You mention Max Blake in the same breath with renegades and I draw the line."

"First the story; then you get the bottle."

"How 'bout you give me the beer then? You gotta understand what I saw was..."

"Talk," Clark commanded.

Sloan sighed aloud, taking a deep breath and another long look at the bottle. "There ain't much more to tell," he said matter-of-factly; he fingered his shot glass as he spoke now, absent-mindedly turning it again and again in his hand. "So I get to conversing with Col. Corn, he tells me something's got to be done and I'm the one likely has to do it, and we negotiate a bit on it.

"I get free drinks in Adobe Flats – for as long as the colonel is there, I guess. For that, I ride to your fine little town here to pass on this message. The colonel figures you got a telegraph wire and kin let someone know that something's gotta be done."

Clark took another moment to consider what he had just heard. He glanced at Seifert, who just shrugged, and back at Jack Sloan.

"Renegades of one sort or another killed every living soul in Adobe Flats 'cepting this barman named Corn – is that right?" Clark asked.

"Well, them two other fellas who were like to run me down got away as well," Sloan said. "Leastwise, I think they did. And maybe some others, too, got out or hid somewhere. Col. Corn was gonna poke around and try to scare up others who might still be alive. But the ones I could see was dead as dust, sheriff."

"How many like that – dead ones – did you see?"

"At least six in the saloon, I think. Another five or six on the street riding in and going out, and I weren't looking hard, mind ya. So how many is that, all told?"

"A damned sight too many," Clark said. "You're sure about this?"

"Sure as that bottle in your hand belongs to me."

"Here's your bottle then, Jack Sloan. Happy days."

Ned Clark started for the door. The bartender called after him, "You want I should do anything with him, sheriff?"

"You might keep him sober till the Army gets here, but I doubt it's in your power, Johnny. Just keep him close till you hear from me."

"No need to worry about me," Sloan said. "I've got me a bottle and some money. What more does a man need?"

But Clark didn't hear Sloan. He already was out the batwing doors of the Silver Spur, heading toward the telegraph office.

Sloan turned his eye on Seifert. "You know what life is?"

When Seifert shrugged, Sloan said with a flourish, "Life is a succession of bartenders, and you are the latest in a long line. I'll have me another beer."

"You should ease up some, friend," Seifert said. "I'm all for a man having a drink or two: It's good for the heart and helps the digestion – and it's good for my business. But a man who drinks like you drink?"

"Don't worry about me. You pour and I'll drink and we'll both be happy."

The batwing doors suddenly snapped open, and an old man limped stiffly into the dark room. He allowed his eyes to adjust to the gloom for a moment before heading toward the long bar.

"You the barkeep here?" he asked.

"Name's Seifert. How can I help you, old timer?"

"You can start by paying me a little respect and never mind the old timer stuff. The name's Jasper Perkins."

"All right, Jasper Perkins. How can I help you?"

"The sheriff just told me a man here'bouts had hisself a tangle with a renegade bunch north of here. That true?"

"Ask him yourself," Seifert said, pointing toward Jack Sloan. "You can save me a trip by hauling this beer with you. Want one for yerself?"

"I'm no drinking man, but I'll see he gets this."

Jasper collected the beer and gingerly hobbled across to Sloan's table. "Yer name Sloan?" he asked.

"I'm afraid so, yes. You'll forgive me if I don't stand – been here awhile, you see. And you would be?"

"Name's Jasper Perkins; sheriff out front said I'd find ya. This here beer is yers." He set the glass on the only clear spot on the table that he could find and wiped his hands on his trousers. "I'm told you had a run-in with the renegades north of here – that right?"

"I just told the sheriff all about it. Can I buy you a drink?" Sloan picked up the beer glass, belched loudly, and took a long, slow gulp.

"No thanks," Jasper said as he pulled up a chair and dropped down with a grunt. "I'm no drinkin' man – and a good thing after seeing you. But I'd be obliged to know what you saw out there, yes sir."

"What's yer interest" – Sloan stopped to gulp from a shot glass and automatically poured himself another – "Jasper Perkins? I'm surprised you know of 'em. Sheriff didn't."

"I know 'em, all right. Spent nigh on to two full days and nights with 'em a'fore I scooted free and Max found me."

"Good for you; most men who come in contact with that bunch won't end up so lucky. And this Max you mentioned?"

"Max Blake, of course – the federal marshal."

"Ah, I see; the man seems to be everywhere. You know Max Blake then?"

"As well as the next man," Jasper said. "I've known Max for years, and a good thing. I wouldn't be here talking now had Max not come along when he did, no sir."

"Well then, Jasper Perkins, I guess we have much to talk about after all."

Jack Sloan paused and looked back toward the bar again. "Mr. Seifert, sir? If you would be so kind."

Chapter 17

An Uneasy Night

Max Blake struck a thick match against the bottom of his boot and touched the flame to a sprinkling of dried leaves and small branches that he had snapped into kindling. The fire took hold, eating greedily into the coarse leaves and dried pine twigs, and he fanned the flames with his Stetson and added some larger sticks.

Within moments, he had a tidy cooking fire established among a handful of fist-sized rocks, and he broke out his small coffee pot and filled it with water from a canteen.

Max was camped for the night by a small grove of aspens and ironwood and scraggily pine trees, a day's ride outside of Twisted Junction in a small, secluded forest that he had used many times before.

He kept a watchful eye on Buck as the horse grazed on the oats and fresh hay that Max had secured in Twisted Junction. He knew from long years on the trail that Buck would detect any movement in the darkness surrounding the camp. But Buck was content as he cropped, and Max relaxed and poured some coffee into a battered cup. He dunked a piece of the jerky into the coffee, allowing the meat to soften a bit as it marinated.

He chewed thoughtfully, his eyes fastened on Buck, his mind wrapped around the problem of Aguante and its outlaw sheriff, Reno Walker.

It'll be a trick to get inside that hornet's nest and out again in one piece, he thought. *It'll be a bigger trick to pull out Reno Walker. Ned Clark was right about a wagon-load of deputies. Makes me wish I had them available.*

Max tossed another stick into the fire and stretched his legs to ease some of the day's saddle kinks. He finished the jerky, dunked a piece of corn biscuit into the cup, but frowned at the taste and decided that he had lost his appetite. He splashed the remainder of the coffee into the fire and used a green branch to separate the burning sticks.

The fire was almost out when he heard the loud snap of a twig in the aspens off to his left. Max shot a look at Buck: The horse was alert and staring into the woods.

Max was on his feet in an instant, his revolver in his right hand, and he darted quickly in a zigzag pattern toward the edge of the aspen grove, staying low to the ground. He took cover behind a clump of tree trunks and listened intently, concentrating on the area where he heard the snapping twig, confident that the night would give up its secrets.

Max waited patiently, counting the seconds off in his mind until a spotted fawn wandered into the clearing, its eyes staring intently at the dwindling fire. Max glanced across at Buck; the horse, tail swishing, was looking on curiously.

The fawn took a hesitant step forward but broke for the shelter of the woods with a sudden leap. Max caught sight of a doe moving quickly in the same direction, and he followed the pair with his eyes as their hooves drummed a steady tattoo across the soft forest floor. It wasn't until an owl hooted moments later that Max left his hiding spot and returned to douse what remained of the fire.

Buck was grazing again when Max joined the horse for a moment. "Just another restless night on the trail, old boy," he whispered. He was about to unpack his bedroll when the muffled sound of a distant rifle echoed through the night air.

A long way off, he thought – *three, maybe four miles north. Might be the renegade band. Then again, it might be... anything, anyone.*

I'd best be prepared for a long night.

Tom Bolton was cold and wet and tired and miserable and angry, and he cursed his circumstances as he stood over a shallow grave that he had carved and kicked and scraped into the hillside moments earlier, a dozen or more yards off the trail.

He wiped his hands on his coarse denim pants and cursed aloud when he succeeded only in grinding the dirt and mud deeper into his skin. The rain that had fallen steadily all night continued to pelt the former deputy sheriff and seep through his coat and down his back and into his well-worn leather boots. Small streams of runoff cascaded off the hillside and trickled into the newly carved grave, etching deep seams into the freshly turned dirt.

"Dammit," Bolton said aloud as he crossed his arms and tucked his hands deep into the folds of his coat. "This is jest one hell of a sorry mess."

Bolton's horse, which stood disinterestedly nearby, gave no notice.

The horse that had belonged scant hours before to the dead man in the newly dug grave was tied to a nearby tree, and the animal looked up at the sound and stared intently at the stranger who was shivering in the rain and the cold.

Bolton looked across to the buckskin gelding, which he had collected yards away from the body of its former owner, and eyed the saddlebags strapped to the horse's broad back. *Maybe there's an answer or two in there,* he thought.

He slipped in the wet, loose dirt as he turned, regained his balance by stabbing a hand into the ground, and cursed once more when he tried to shake off the fresh mud.

It's that damn Max Blake, he thought. *If it weren't for him, I'd still be a lawman with a future. But here I am in the muck, about to rummage through a dead man's things – dammit to hell and back again.*

Bolton stomped over to a clump of wild sweet grass that jutted from the steep hillside and used it to remove the muck. He worked on his hands for a minute and then scraped his boots at the base of the grass until most of the caked mud was left in thick, heavy clods on the saturated ground. Satisfied that he could do no better, he clucked a few times to get the horse's attention and gently stuck his hand out as he held the buckskin's steady, questioning gaze.

"I'm no threat to ya, fella," he said. "Wouldn't have bothered that cowboy over yonder had I known he weren't Max Blake. But I figured by yer size and color, you had to be Blake's horse and yer rider Blake hisself.

"You don't know where Blake is, do ya?"

The horse nuzzled the man's hand for a moment but lost interest when no food was forthcoming, and Bolton moved around to the animal's right side and started rummaging through the saddlebags.

"Let's see what we got here," he muttered, as much to himself as to the horse, and he picked his way through an assortment of cartridge boxes, an oil cloth, a can of light gun oil that was wrapped in a second oil cloth, a .41-caliber Remington derringer that was stuffed inside a small leather pouch, a hunting knife with a six-inch blade in a black leather sheath, a smaller knife with a serrated edge, but no clue to the man's identity.

"Nothing much here of interest, outside that little derringer," Bolton said as he patted the horse's flank. "Course, that little piece has found a new home – jest like you, fella – and that Bowie knife ain't a bad find, neither."

He moved around the front of the animal, ducked beneath the tethered reins, and opened the second large pouch.

Bolton reached inside and found two large hunks of jerked meat wrapped in butcher's paper, some hard corn biscuits also wrapped in paper, a half-empty bottle of corked whiskey, an assortment of cooking utensils, including a small tin for making trail coffee, and a sack the size of his fist. Surprised at its weight, he pulled open a rawhide drawstring and looked inside.

What he saw, even in the gloom of the steady rain and the leaden skies and the deepening night, brought Tom Bolton to a sudden stop.

"Now how in the hell do you figure that?" he said aloud, his voice tuned to a quizzical high pitch, a look of amazement on his suddenly beaming face.

Bolton poked his head directly in front of the horse and said: "That's a lot of gold yer packing, fella – a hell of a lot of gold. Now don't that jest beat all?"

He looked again toward the shallow grave and shook his head in joyful disbelief.

"Jest who in hell was you, mister? And what are you doing out here, dead as dirt and stuck in the ground by the likes of me?"

He laughed aloud at that, unable to contain his surprise and delight at this unexpected turn of fortune.

Chapter 18

New Pursuits

Army Lt. Col. Michael Corbin was puzzling over a map and its apparent contradiction to his current location, which seemed both to himself and his men to be somewhere at the distant edge of an unknown universe.

As he tried to get his bearings, he was certain of one thing, at least: He didn't like what he saw in either the terrain that sprawled out before him or the one represented on paper.

By his own reckoning, he should have been at least five miles away from the spot where he now stood. Tidy in all things, and a stickler for detail and discipline, he took the time now to ponder the situation. He did that by staring intently at the map, looking up from time to time to determine whether he could locate landmarks on the horizon, and then pondering the contents of the map once more in an effort to justify both.

The answer will come in time, he thought.

Lt. Col. Corbin was a no-nonsense military man from a no-nonsense military family.

Dark-haired, muscular, with a ramrod-straight bearing and a propensity to tolerate nothing out of the ordinary – especially criminals and fools – he was highly regarded and rising rapidly in the ranks of Army men destined for greatness. His father had graduated from West Point and was well-connected in military and political circles in Washington. The elder Corbin had long entertained aspirations for election to the highest office in the land. While that prospect was at best remote because of age and years of scrappy politics, it was a dream that he kept alive for his son.

The old man was determined, in fact, to see a Corbin of one age or another in the White House one day.

Spending time stationed in the hostile desert of the American Southwest was a mere stepping stone to bigger things, a fact recognized by father and son alike. They both understood that the vast territory afforded the opportunity for glory: occasional Indian uprisings, border assaults, roaming Mexican bandits, range wars, and a wide assortment of infamous lawbreakers and gunslingers – some of them well-known enough, in fact, to appear with regularity in the pages of Eastern newspapers – were in ample supply. Glory on the battlefield, and in these same newspapers, would only mean later success in the nation's capitol.

The result was that Lt. Col. Michael Corbin, due for promotion to lieutenant general within a matter of weeks, was forever looking for a good fight.

With the Army's blessing, after his father's intervention, he had assembled a light traveling squadron of up to sixty men, all of them proven fighters with battlefield experience in the Civil War or the Plains Indians wars. The squadron maintained a permanent base in Yuma, but Corbin kept his men constantly on the trail, roaming the vast territory, staying in touch by telegraph (and only when he deemed it absolutely necessary), picking and choosing the engagements that would give him the best political exposure.

He had experienced sufficient success to enjoy a certain freedom; and as long as the headlines were positive and justice in one form or another was dispensed, the Army generals and their political functionaries tended to leave the young lieutenant colonel alone while keeping a cautious, curious eye on his rising star.

Corbin was moving his men on an eastern path south of Casa Grande, heading toward the Picacho Mountains, when a rider caught up with the squadron at the edge of a rim that stretched for as far as a man could see – one that apparently could not be located on the various military maps the lieutenant colonel carried at all times. Corbin had been studying the map for fifteen minutes or more when the rider hailed the soldiers, although his approach had been watched for more than a mile by two sharp-eyed trackers who had quickly alerted their commanding officer.

"You Army boys is easy to find and hard to catch," the man said as he rode into the center of the squadron. "Which one is Corbin?"

"That's Lt. Col. Corbin," one of the men said. "You'd do well to show some respect."

"I'm here to pass on a message, not to enlist or commit Army titles to memory," the man said evenly. "Is your name Corbin, lieutenant colonel or otherwise?"

The soldier frowned, shook his head, and pointed over his shoulder. The rider nodded, a grin creasing his weather-beaten features, and moved his horse forward.

"You Corbin?" he asked as he approached the tall man on horseback with the map in his hand.

Corbin looked up after a moment. "It's Lt. Col. Corbin. What do you want?"

"Name's Steve Purchase. Sheriff in Casa Grande sent me when he got a wire from some Army boys looking for you."

Corbin didn't conceal his surprise. "What the devil for?" he asked.

"Cain't say; it ain't my concern, nor the sheriff's. But he told me to track you till I found you and give you this."

Purchase pulled a rumpled piece of folded paper from a pouch that was strapped to his horse and handed it to Corbin. "Consider the message delivered," he said as he turned his horse about, calling over his shoulder, "And good luck to you."

"Hold on there, mister," Corbin called. His soldiers quickly tightened in front of the man's horse, pinching him off, and Purchase brought the animal to an abrupt halt and turned it with a tug of the reins so that he could face the determined lieutenant colonel.

"Something I didn't make clear somehow?" he asked.

"What's this all about?" Corbin asked.

"Yer guess is as good as mine. All I know is the telegraph runner brought that message to the sheriff's office this morning. The sheriff read it, folded it up like you see it there, and told me to hunt you up and give you this personally.

"That's just what I done and all I know. I cain't tell you who it's from or what it says 'cause the sheriff didn't tell me and I don't read but a few words."

Corbin's back was rigid in the saddle as he held the map in one hand and the message in the other, weighing one piece of paper against the other.

"Anything else? It's a long ride back to Casa Grande," Purchase said at last.

Corbin stared long and hard at the rider, trying to determine if the man knew more than he was saying. Purchase, for his part, sat quietly in the saddle, returning the lieutenant colonel's stare, a casual smile etched on his face, offering indifference in return.

"Let him go," Corbin ordered after a moment.

"Appreciate yer hospitality. And yer welcome for the delivery just the same," Purchase said, nodding at Corbin before turning his horse around once more.

Corbin paid no attention to the departing messenger. He had unfolded the message and was reading it carefully, taking his time with each word. Capt. Jed Johnson, Corbin's second in command, pulled his horse in close. "A change of plans, sir?"

"It appears so, captain. It seems as though we've lost a shipment of gold – we being the United States Army – to some sort of renegade force that's operating somewhere south of here. We've been ordered by Gen. Willis to search out and destroy the renegades, and to recover and restore the gold."

"What exactly is a force of renegades, sir?"

"I'd say we're going to find out, captain. Leave it to Jim Willis to track us and then trust us to restore the peace."

"You have to wonder how the general even found us, sir."

"It may explain how the man obtained his rank, considering that even I don't know exactly where we are at the moment.

"Let's line them up in twos and march due south, Capt. Johnson."

"Yes, sir – right away. Where exactly are we heading, sir?"

"To a place we both know: Twisted Junction. We have a date with a sheriff named Clark, and I'd like to get there sooner rather than later."

"Understood, sir. I'll see that it happens."

Michael Corbin was at his finest when a forced march with well-drilled soldiers produced immediate results, and his arrival outside the bustling community of Twisted Junction made the man proud of his men and absolutely giddy about his future political prospects.

A trip that normally would have taken an armed contingent of fighting men a full day had been accomplished in a mere fourteen hours – testimony to fine horse stock, good training, exceptional discipline, and the steely will of the commanding officer.

The fact was not lost on Corbin, nor was it lost on his father when the telegram was sent from the wilds of the Arizona Territory to the hallowed corridors of Washington, D.C., from son to father, hours before. Both men knew this was the kind of event that Eastern newspapers wrote frequently and eloquently about; it was the kind of event, in fact, that

118

made military men notice and certain politicians nervous.

News of a renegade band rampaging through the Southwest countryside after the theft of Army gold was a blessing for the Corbin family, father and son both.

The old man recognized that this could be a life-altering event – the kind of moment in his son's military career that, when dealt with efficiently by a charismatic leader in the field and orchestrated in Washington by a man who knew how to manipulate the system, could produce a chain of events that might well take them both to the White House.

The elder Corbin already was priming the pump of the press.

His son, of course, had immediately recognized the assignment for the political windfall that it potentially was, although he had his hands filled with other, more pressing, matters at the moment. Still, a certain piece of his well-ordered mind remained on the distant, ultimate prize, which made the smile on his chiseled, handsome face that much broader.

He held his men in position near a series of crossroads that lead into and out of Twisted Junction and called for Capt. Jed Johnson with a low whistle.

"It's unwise for us to show a force of strength in the town at this point, Capt. Johnson," Corbin said. "The renegades may have spies about, and we should proceed with caution. Do you agree?"

"Absolutely, sir."

"Good. What do you suggest?"

The question made Johnson smile inwardly. He respected his commanding office and appreciated that the man requested his opinions and gave him the opportunity to actively participate in his role as second in command of the elite squadron. In his previous assignment, he had not been so fortunate – a fact that made Johnson respect his current commanding officer even more.

"We take a small contingent into the town and find the sheriff, sir – no more than five or six men, you and me included, with Sgt. Major McClinton in charge here. This gives us ample force should we run into trouble, but we won't look too intimidating to any spies the renegades may have posted."

"Excellent. Hand-select the men you want for the assignment, Capt. Johnson. Just be sure to include Lennox; I understand that he knows the town."

"Yes, sir."

"All right, we'll leave from this spot in five minutes. Make the arrangements and we'll see where this takes us."

"Right away, sir," Johnson said, snapping off a crisp salute.

Thirty minutes later, the two officers waited in Ned Clark's office while the sheriff poured coffee into tin cups from a battered black pot he had warmed on a wood stove in the corner.

"You must not think much of this renegade bunch, bringing only a handful of soldiers along with you," Clark said.

"There's plenty more outside of town, Sheriff Clark," Corbin said. "I understand you have some information for us?"

"Well sir, what I have for you is a man who saw first-hand the damage these renegades caused north of here," Clark said, sipping at his coffee; the grimace that immediately crossed his face clearly didn't bode well for the two military men, and Corbin put his own cup down when he saw the reaction.

"I got a man over to the saloon for you to talk with," Clark said. "His name's Jack Sloan. He rode in from Adobe Flats yesterday – said he saw the massacre first-hand and came here because we had a wire. That's when I sent out the first message that brought you here."

"Do you find this Sloan to be reliable?" Corbin asked.

"Well, Sgt. Corbin, this Sloan fella ..."

"It's Lt. Col. Corbin, sheriff."

"Right, Lt. Col. Corbin – sorry, but I ain't much for Army titles. Truth is, Sloan is a drunk. He mines a claim north of Adobe Flats and was heading in for some drinking when he discovered the slaughter there first-hand. Town's bartender was alive – a man named Corn – and this Corn fella sent Sloan here because of our telegraph station."

"What does Corn know?"

"Not much, to hear Sloan tell it: This Corn stayed low behind the bar the whole time and didn't see a thing. Best to start with Sloan. He's run through a bunch of liquor since he's been here, but he can still talk."

"Good. Let's see to that right away."

"I'll take you to Sloan, all right, but I'll tell you this first: Sloan's story is interesting 'cause it's so damned chilling, but understand, he didn't see 'em – jest the carnage they left behind. If you want an assessment of the renegades, there's two men can talk direct, though neither one's in town."

Corbin raised his right eyebrow. "Go ahead."

"The first is an old prospector, Jasper Perkins – quite a character, well known in the territory. He was held by this band for two days 'fore he got away, though he didn't have much to say about it to me. He was shot, banged up – had to visit with Doc Peterson for a spell. Anyway, I tried to hold Jasper here till you boys arrived, but he lit out today again – too many people."

"You mentioned two men, Sheriff Clark," Johnson said. "Who's the second?"

"The same man who brought Jasper to town and your best bet at getting some insight into the pack: Max Blake, the federal marshal from…"

"I know full well the reputation of Marshal Blake," Corbin interrupted, giving Johnson a sharp look at the same time. "He's as well-known in the territory as any man, on either side of the law."

"That's the plain truth of it. Ol' Wyatt himself is no more for reputation than Marshal Blake."

"How did the marshal come by his information, Sheriff Clark?"

"He's seen 'em," Clark said. "Max had his mind on other things when he was here, but he told me he got a good look at yer renegades – Army gold thieves, as he called 'em."

Clark motioned toward the door. "I'll take you over to the Silver Spur to see Jack Sloan right now," he said. "And if you pay some attention along the way, I'll tell you what the marshal told me about these very renegades you boys are so intent on tracking."

Chapter 19

Changing Strategies

"Watch out fer that damn beam there, else yer gonna git whacked in that thick skull of yers and end up dead."

"No need to worry about me. I see the beam all right. Jest move it a touch more … almost – that's it. Now hold up a minute. Let me see if I kin get me a nail in the corner here and firm it up some."

As Reno Walker walked from his office to the site where the Aguante saloon was being rebuilt with newly cut lumber freighted in from Flagstaff, the area was bustling with the efforts of a dozen men. All were carefully chosen, and all were working diligently in the hot sun to finish the job quickly.

When the Aguante sheriff gave an order, every living soul in the corrupt, gritty border town who valued his life took careful note and did his best to comply. The penalty for failure was too horrible to contemplate.

"It's comin' along nicely, sir, as you kin see," Stuart Hicks said when he spotted the sheriff. The man in charge of the operation took a moment to wipe his face with a filthy red bandana pulled from his back pocket. "Won't be long now and we'll have everything back in order, sir – like it never happened."

The sheriff nodded curtly, his face a stony mask. He carried a thick rawhide quirt, and he absently thumped it a time or two in his gloved hand; the sound snapped like a pistol shot, and it carried over the noise of busy hammering and the push and pull of a long saw that a crew worked nearby.

"How much longer, Hicks?" Walker asked. He stared intently at two men straddling long oak beams above his head, making careful adjustments in the length of the spans. Both of them, though seasoned outlaws, were careful not to make eye contact; they knew from experience that Walker could be set off by the slightest incident – including something as simple as a stray glance.

"Well sir, if we keep up what we're doing now, I'd say another six days at most," Hicks replied. "If I had me a few more hands, we could likely finish in half that time – four days at the outside."

Walker thumped the quirt again and nodded. The men working above him glanced down at the sharp report but quickly looked away.

"How many men?" Walker asked.

"Five, six more would help and not start to walk over each other, sir. We can manage all right, you understand, right now – I ain't saying we need more. It's jest that we could manage sooner with 'em is all."

"All right. Send somebody over and I'll have him do the round-up for you."

"Yes, sir. I'll put 'em to good use."

"I know you will, Hicks." He started to walk away, stopped abruptly, and turned to stare directly into the foreman's eyes. "Just don't surprise me none."

"No, sir – no surprises at all. Not from me, sir."

The sheriff held Hicks' gaze for a moment before he turned again and headed back to his office.

Reno Walker already had experienced a series of surprises, and the last thing he wanted was another.

Days before, in the span of a few short hours, two of his deputies were murdered, two other men were shot dead, half of the town's primary saloon was burned to the ground, and the men responsible for the mayhem escaped into the desert.

As he rolled the series of events around in his head once more, he cursed to himself and kicked open the door to his office. The deputies stationed on either side, guarding the office at all times, kept their eyes trained on the street. Walker ignored them as he went inside.

It's that other one I can't figure out, he thought. *And I don't like riddles.*

The solitary man who had constantly occupied Walker's thoughts since the killings was more than a riddle to the Aguante sheriff, however. He had become a threat when he somehow managed to escape from the certain death the sheriff had planned for him; Walker was subsequently forced to send Richard Nash, his top deputy, on a trail of revenge to find the man – *and I sure as hell trust Nash to kill that bastard slow and ugly*, he thought.

Walker had extracted a small measure of satisfaction by killing the two deputies who allowed the mysterious stranger to escape. But he had been uneasy since the incident, and he was uneasy now as he looked around his office and finally sat in the chair behind his simple wooden desk.

Every time he thought about the mess that had been created in those few hours, his head began to throb – and it was throbbing now.

In Reno Walker's ordered mind, the reason was simple. Aguante was a town that attracted the vilest of men. Outlaws of all sorts – murderers, thieves, rustlers, rapists, armed robbers, crooked gamblers, bushwhackers, phony medicine peddlers, swindlers – called it home. The legitimate law in the territory avoided it because of the sheer number of well-armed men. Aguante, in fact, attracted the worst of the worst; many were top gunmen who enjoyed violence and killing and mayhem and brutality and relished any kind of fight.

At the top of this pyramid of evil, Reno Walker ruled with a rawhide quirt, a rock-hard fist, and a fast gun. But he knew that his position was strong only so long as he maintained an iron grip of control. And the events of the past few days provided the appearance that control was slipping away, however subtly.

It was an erosion of image that he couldn't tolerate.

He had lost control once before, in a small mining community in Colorado where he had inserted himself by force into a position of corrupt leadership and made a small fortune stealing valuable ore. But a sudden turn of events that hinged on the single turn of a card prompted a quick reversal of fortune. He was lucky to escape in the middle of the night with the help of a woman of dubious repute and the extra gun of Richard Nash, his trusted deputy, at his side. And he had vowed never to let that happen to him again.

Aguante is my last stand, and I'll be damned if I ever let it go, he thought, a frown creasing his weathered face.

He reached into the desk drawer, pulled out a corked bottle of whiskey, and took a long slug. He grimaced, took another deep pull from the bottle, wiped his mouth with the back of his hand, and returned the whiskey to the drawer.

It's past time I heard from Nash, he thought. *He's been gone long enough now to take care of the stranger. It ain't like him to dawdle. It's high time he finished up and got back to Aguante.*

He looked up as Clyde Roberts knocked softly and shuffled warily inside. Roberts, a deputy with a twitchy disposition, was leery of the

124

sheriff from earlier run-ins and was nervous about the interruption, which only annoyed Walker even more.

"Something on yer mind, Roberts, that a simple load of buckshot won't answer?" he asked.

"Yes, sir. I, ah, hope yer kidding about the buckshot, sir."

Walker shook his head in disgust. "What do you want? You're wasting my time."

"Yes, sir. Hicks sent me over, sir – said you wanted me to find some boys to help with the work detail over to the saloon. I'm right happy to help, sheriff. Jest tell me what you want me to do, yes sir, and I'll see right ..."

"Shut that big bazoo of yers up, Roberts, or I will fill you with buckshot."

"Yes, sir."

The sheriff leaned back in his chair and rubbed the sides of his head; his headache had been dulled by the whiskey, but he was feeling only marginally better, and the sight of Clyde Roberts made him want to beat the man senseless. *Why in hell did it have to be Roberts today?* he wondered.

"All right, go find Doucette and Silverbird for starters. Tell 'em I want to see 'em in short order. Next, find McFadden and Sweeney. Tell 'em to double up on guard duty. If they got questions, they can see me – and they won't like it none. You got that much?"

"Yes, sir. Doucette and Silverbird, then McFadden and Sweeney. Anything else?"

"Yeah, then find the Dieker boys and send 'em on over."

"You want to see all three of 'em, sheriff?" Roberts asked.

"There's three all told, ain't there?"

"Yes, sir."

"So what wasn't clear to you, Roberts?"

"Nothing, sir. It's jest that one of 'em's out of town, as I understand it. I think Tommy and Paul are here. But I'm not sure where ..."

"Send me the two that are here, Roberts. No more talk, no more shuffling, no more twitching. Git moving."

"Yes, sir."

Roberts nodded with a forced smile, causing Walker to shake his head again. *Maybe I can salvage something of the day at the expense of this idiot,* he thought.

Roberts had started for the door when Walker cleared his throat, an ominous sound that brought the deputy up short. "Something else you wanted, sir?" he ventured.

"Once you find the Dieker boys, Roberts – however many of 'em are around – I want you to bring me a ten-gauge shotgun. Understand?"

"Did you say a ten-gauge shotgun, sir?"

"You got something stuffed in your ears today?"

"No, sir. It's jest, well …"

"Get cracking – don't keep me waiting. And make sure the shotgun's loaded."

"Yes, sir."

Roberts nodded quickly and almost sprinted out the door.

Reno Walker sat back and laughed out loud.

Maybe Roberts 'll come in handy after all, he thought, and he laughed again.

He leaned back in his chair and hoisted his feet to a corner of the desk, his mind turning once more to Richard Nash and the stranger he was tracking.

He thought about pulling the bottle out again when Jay Silverbird and David Doucette knocked on the door and walked into the office.

"You wanted to see us, sir?" Silverbird asked.

"Yeah. Hicks needs some help on the saloon job, and you boys know every man in town who might have some skill in the trade."

"Yes, sir," Doucette said simply. "That's a fact."

"Good. Go round up six men to work with Hicks for the next few days or so. Don't touch a single man on guard duty; we need eyes and ears in all directions. Beyond that, take any man you like. You get a hard time from anyone, tell 'em it comes straight from me. Understand?"

"Yes, sir. You want we should help with the job ourselves?"

"I've got something else in mind. I'll see you both when you finish with Hicks."

"Yes, sir."

Tom and Paul Dieker walked into the sheriff's office as Silverbird and Doucette turned to leave. The four men nodded at each other but said nothing.

"Getting to be like a freighter's station in here," Walker said casually, looking at the Diekers. "Where's yer brother?"

"He's working on the hunt down at the border, sir," Tom Dieker said. "He's been gone – what? – a handful of days now, I'd guess."

The brothers looked cautiously at each other for an instant before directing their attention back to Reno Walker, who was nodding his head thoughtfully, his mind elsewhere for the moment.

"The two of you up for some honest work?" he asked.

"Does it have to be honest?" Tom Dieker replied, and Walker laughed out loud again, noting the easy smiles that broke out across the faces of the two brothers as well.

Walker liked the Dieker boys; they were reliable, hard workers, nail-tough in a fight, and they enjoyed themselves. Both brothers had big, natural laughs that filled the air around them – and they both laughed often.

As cowboys who lived outside the law, they were trustworthy and loyal to the sheriff, which was the primary reason why Walker had sent for them now.

Paul, the oldest of the brothers, was a tall man with graying hair and a blacksmith's physique. His posture was always military straight, a holdover from his days as a Confederate Army officer. He had been wounded twice, survived despite the best efforts of poorly equipped and inept field doctors to kill him, and had taken up robbing Union Army banks after the war. Wanted posters throughout the West and southern states eventually forced him to the edge of the Arizona Territory and finally into Aguante.

His brother Tom was younger and had similar facial features, although his hair was longer and still retained its youthful coloring of light brown tinged dull blond by the relentless sun. He spoke with an easy, conversational tone that immediately stamped him as someone from the cultured South. He had entered the Civil War at the age of fifteen, survived because his brother insisted on keeping him away from the serious fighting, and followed Paul into the bank-robbing life when the armies went home.

The third brother, Jim, was something of a mystery in Aguante. He kept to himself, spoke little, and was suspicious of everyone around him except for his two brothers. He did not wear a Confederate uniform during the war, but he was still involved in the fight against the Union. His spy missions deep inside enemy-held territory provided valuable information that had helped turn a number of battles. Near the end, he had been caught and tortured for days before he managed to escape. The Union Army's relentless pursuit hardened him even more. He eventually drifted into Aguante after tracking his brothers for more than a year.

Rumors of a fourth Dieker brother persisted in Aguante; some said that he worked as an Indian agent. But if he existed at all, the brothers steadfastly refused to say.

The Diekers were, for the most part, easy-going until riled; when that happened, they were like a nest of snakes that had been poked with a sharp stick.

That, Walker knew, was their finest strength.

"I want you to take a ride for me," the sheriff said. "Pick up your brother or send for him – it makes no difference how you git him – and head straight north. Poke around in the towns and settlements up there and see what you can learn. Blend in. Don't look like a threat to anyone. Listen – don't talk. Clear?"

"Yes, sir," the oldest brother said, although he had a puzzled look on his face. "Anything in particular you want us to learn about or listen for, sheriff?"

"I can't say for certain," Walker replied. "Best I can tell you is you'll likely know it when you run across it. And when you do, report back here to me."

The Diekers exchanged quick glances before looking quizzically back at Reno Walker.

"I'm not quite sure what you want us to do exactly – meaning no disrespect, sir," Tom Dieker said. "Before we light out, I think the both of us'd like to be certain we're doing exactly what you'd like us to."

Walker nodded his agreement, aware of the confusion. It wasn't that the sheriff didn't know what he wanted the brothers to do; it was just that he was having difficulty explaining it.

He started to search for a response when Clyde Roberts knocked and walked cautiously into the office again, a large shotgun in his hand. "Stay outside a minute, Roberts," the sheriff called. "I'll let you know when I'm ready for you."

He smiled inwardly and waited until Roberts left before turning his attention back to the brothers.

"I've got a hunch, let's call it," he said. "The cowboy that got away from us, and them other bandits that shot up the place and got away? Well, that don't sit right with me; likely not with the two of you. I ain't even rightly sure that cowboy was what he pretended to be. So I want to be rock-certain if anything happens out there, it gets back to me before it arrives on our doorstep."

The Dieker brothers nodded.

"You think that stray cowboy or them others might try to bring trouble our way, sheriff?" Tom Dieker asked.

Walker merely shrugged. It was impossible to say for certain, and he knew it. He was operating only on a hunch, though he didn't want to admit that to the Diekers.

"I trust you boys to keep low, keep yourselves away from the jug, and keep your ears open," he said after a minute. "You hear of anything brewing anywhere that might cause us trouble or come our way, head on back and let me know about it straight away."

"Yes, sir," Tom Dieker said. "You can count on us, sheriff."

"I know that," Walker replied. "Just make sure we keep it like that. You can pick up some money on the way out; tell 'em I sent you and let 'em know what you need."

As the Diekers nodded and turned to go, Walker said, "You boys might like to watch some fun first."

He stood, adjusted his belt, and walked with the brothers out of the office and onto the street.

Clyde Roberts was holding the shotgun, nervously keeping a wary eye on the sheriff, the two Dieker brothers, and even on the two deputies who were stationed nearby.

"I see you brought me the ten-gauge," the sheriff said to Roberts. "It's loaded?"

"Yes, sir. I got it from the armory. It's the best one I ..."

"Hand it over, Roberts," Walker said, cutting him off.

"Yes, sir." Roberts took a step forward, looked warily around again, and handed the shotgun to the sheriff.

Walker cracked the breach, checked to see that the shotgun was loaded properly, and snapped it shut again. He looked at Roberts and said softly, "All right, I want you to start running down the street. When I get to ten..."

"I'm ... I'm sorry, sir. Did I hear ..."

"You'll be sorry if you don't get running," Walker said, "starting right now. One..."

Clyde Roberts began to run.

"Two..."

Roberts already was in full flight, his arms pumping hard, his legs churning, his boots kicking up dust and sand as they fought for purchase in the street.

"Three..."

The sudden boom of the shotgun echoed across the streets of Aguante and bounced off the faces of the surrounding buildings. The noise brought the hammering and sawing and all activity on the saloon across the way to an abrupt stop.

The sheriff smiled broadly and looked at the two Dieker brothers.

"Never learned to count past three," he said.

The men occupied with the rebuilding of the saloon quickly went back to work. The Dieker brothers exchanged glances but said nothing as they started down the street toward the stables. Faces that had peered through windows or out of doorways rapidly disappeared.

Reno Walker looked around and eventually spotted Doucette and Silverbird standing quietly near the armory.

"Told you I had another job," he said, and his laughter followed the Diekers out of town.

Chapter 20

A Grove of Aspens

Max Blake awoke from a brief, uneasy sleep with a sharp intake of breath. His eyes darted about in the hazy light of early morning as he shrugged off another lingering dream. He was in his bedroll, a dozen yards away from the small campfire he had built the night before. A second bedroll – this one with a blanket stuffed inside and his Stetson adorned at the front like a grave marker – was nestled immediately next to the doused fire.

It was an old trick but a good one – especially if a man wanted to stay alive in hostile country. And it seemed to Max that he was forever traveling in hostile country.

Buck, Max's chestnut gelding, was tethered contentedly nearby; the horse's great eyes were closed, and its tail gently swayed in the faint breath of the chill breeze that whispered off the distant, snow-capped mountains.

Max knew that if anything was stirring close by, Buck would be at full attention. Still, the cautious federal marshal took the time to mentally register every sight he could determine and every sound he could detect.

Satisfied at last that he was alone, Max shook himself out of the bedroll and rubbed some warmth into his hands and arms. Buck was alert now, roused by the marshal's movements, and Max moved briskly over to the horse and gently scratched behind the animal's ears.

"Morning, old boy," he whispered softly. "Hope you slept better than I did." He slipped a small dried carrot out of his pocket and offered it to the horse.

Max pulled the feedbag from the saddlebags, stuffed it full, and slipped it over the horse's massive head. He knew that his life depended on how well he cared for Buck, and Max was careful to look after the horse at every opportunity.

He had camped a few hundred yards away from a small but determined snow-fed stream. Max had learned long ago that camping too close to a stream was a clear invitation to trouble; the gurgling, rippling water disguised other noises – chief among them the sounds of disagreeable men trying to get the drop on a federal marshal.

Max eventually removed the feedbag from Buck's head, offered up a second carrot that he fished from the saddlebags, and walked the horse down to the stream. While Buck casually drank, Max splashed some cold water across his face, surprised again at how refreshing this simple act could be after a hard night in a hard bedroll on the hard and rocky ground of a hard and deadly trail.

"That'll shake the cobwebs loose, old boy – don't you think?" He didn't speak the words loudly enough for the horse to hear, but he said them aloud nonetheless. It was a ritual that the man enjoyed, even if the horse paid no attention.

Max filled his two canteens with fresh water, checked that the seals were tight, and nudged Buck out of the stream bed and back to the campsite. He poured himself a small tin of the cold, bitter coffee he had made the previous night, grimaced at the taste, and thought that as bad as his coffee had tasted of late, he would be better off to stay away from it entirely.

"We'll try to see some old friends today, Buck," he said gently to the horse as he began the methodical process of breaking down the camp. "It's out of the way but worth the time. And maybe a nice lady I know will offer me a decent cup of coffee."

The wisp of a narrow trail that threaded its way out of Twisted Junction and wandered north and west into the reaches of the foothills was one that Max Blake knew well from years in the territory.

He had traveled the same trail scant days before and was aware of every turn and bend, every washed-out area from a roaring creek, every spot where the undergrowth disguised all sense of direction, every rocky wasteland and watershed, every fallen tree that he would pass.

Mostly, however, he was aware of the potential trouble spots: a bluff or piece of high ground or sharp turn or copse of trees that might give a single-minded man with a long rifle, a good eye, and a steady hand the opportunity to bushwhack an unsuspecting pilgrim or wayfarer or casual traveler – or even a federal marshal. And Max Blake was anything but unsuspecting. He was attuned to his surroundings, enjoying the serenity of the ride and the relative peace of the gentle day while remaining alert and cautious at the same time.

Cautious is how I stay alive, he thought.

He had decided to pass through the small village of Indian Wells, even though it was a day's ride out of his way. But he wanted to visit for a few moments, at least, with Sally Nelson and her two sons, Josh and Jason. Only days before, Larry Nelson was killed in the Indian Wells saloon by the outlaw Hoss Johnson, late of the southern edge of the vast sprawl of wastelands that swept down into Mexico, and a revenger named Henry Grant, late of Jefferson County at the opposite end of the territory.

Max had tracked the outlaws to Indian Wells, but he arrived too late to save Larry Nelson. He did, however, stop Johnson from surprising Sally Nelson and her sons in the village home they were using: A slug from a Colt .45 fired directly into a man's chest from close range tended to slow even a determined outlaw. And as Grant prepared to back-shoot Max, Sally Nelson brought the killer down with a single shot from her late husband's Sharps carbine.

Max had been unable to express his thanks to her at the time, or even later when he attended Larry Nelson's simple funeral. But he had decided to try again now.

He pushed steadily forward into the higher elevations of the foothills, winding his way inevitably toward the tiny settlement of sheep ranchers and farmers who had been touched by senseless death and mayhem.

He had been on the trail for more than three hours, allowing Buck to chew up the miles with an easy gait, when a feeling of uneasiness started to settle over him. It was, in fact, a feeling he had experienced many times before – one he was seldom wrong about.

Max could sense that he was being followed.

It started with a slight twitch in Buck's left ear and a gentle, almost imperceptible, tug at the reins. Max, attuned to his horse, noticed the flick of the ear and could sense as much as feel the gentle tug as Buck tried to swing his head around. Max was careful not to make any sudden movements to alert a lurking gunman or bushwhacker that he was aware of a foreign presence; instead, he scanned the area ahead, looking for a spot where he could appear to casually stop and rest.

A grove of aspens on his right opened up against a long stretch of trail that skirted the low rise of a growing outcrop of red-colored rocks and patchy, clinging mesquite and thistle and acacia that climbed almost two hundred yards straight into the air. As the trail began to bend, Max nudged Buck into the aspens and urged the horse forward and well off the path. He quickly dismounted, pulled his Winchester from its scabbard, unhooked one of the canteens, and snaked his way back toward the trail after looping Buck's reins around a thin branch. He found a position behind a clump of trees that afforded an open view of the trail he had just passed and silently waited.

He kept watch for a solid hour, counting off the minutes in his mind.

His only movements were an occasional glance toward Buck, who was drowsing contentedly, showing no interest in his surroundings, and a single drink of water he took from the canteen after he was certain that no one posed an immediate threat.

Whatever was out there – whatever I sensed and Buck picked up – is gone now, Max thought. *It must not have been much, but it's better to be careful.*

Even so, he waited for another full hour, judging the time by the sun's filtered passage through the aspens, before he cautiously worked his way back to his horse. He pulled another small carrot from his pocket for Buck.

I don't mind the lost time, Max thought – *not where caution is involved. But it's odd that Buck sensed it back there, too.*

He thought on it awhile longer: *Might have been a cat. That would explain it.*

Even at that, Max couldn't shake the feeling that something, or someone, had been watching his every move. And Max Blake was a man who trusted his instincts.

I'll have to stay alert – keep a careful watch, he thought.

"We both will, Buck," he muttered.

The question that Max now considered as he pulled himself into the saddle was whether he should immediately press ahead to Indian Wells, or whether he should take his time and determine who – or what, if anything – might be behind him.

He scratched Buck's head for a moment. "No need to rush into anything, ol' boy," he whispered once he made his decision. "We'll take all the time we need."

Richard Nash wasn't sure what made him stop and dismount from his horse. It might have been the rustle of the leaves in the aspen trees that towered around him. It might have been a shift in the wind that blew cold off the ridges of the distant mountains. Or perhaps it was the leaping buck that lurched out from a sliver of game trail crossing his path, causing the Aguante deputy and cold-blooded killer to reach automatically for the revolver that was strapped to his side.

Maybe it was just a feeling in his gut that caused him to bring his horse to a stop and listen carefully to all of the sounds that drifted in around him.

He could detect the cluck and flutter of wrens and sparrows, the distinct chitter of a squirrel that was annoyed at his approach and passing, and the gentle swaying of the aspens in the light wind that seemed to reach and carry far overhead.

He also could detect a shift in the feel of the very earth around him – a sort of sixth sense that helped to keep gunslingers, and federal marshals, alive.

Something's out of place out there, he thought.

And so he waited, trying to feel the pulse of the land and the animals and the trees and the birds and the steady passing of wind and time.

After a full five minutes, rigid and unmoving in the saddle, he climbed down from his horse and slowly walked the animal into a nearby cluster of trees that afforded shelter. He carefully tied the reins around a small branch, removed his canteen and a leather-strapped Springfield carbine, and crept cautiously away from the trail. He gazed about, getting his bearings, and eventually headed toward the base of a large outcrop that rose dramatically from the level ground and stretched eastward for as far as the eye could see.

The trail he was following snaked its way past the outcrop through a series of turns and sharp zigzags. *If I get up on top and have a look around, I can spot any rider, or anything that might pass by,* he thought.

The trick will be to get up and down and not break my neck. If I can manage that, I just might learn a thing or two.

Nash edged along the base of the outcrop, looking for a way to safely climb up. He was scanning the walls, trying to determine how high he could get before a potential route would become too difficult to traverse, when he stumbled upon a fissure in the vast expanse of rock that stretched out before him. The crack initially had been hidden by a clump of gnarled junipers and patches of thistle and brush sprouting out of the boulders and smaller rocks that had tumbled to the ground through centuries of erosion. The fissure was twelve to fifteen yards wide in places and took a sharp turn to the west halfway up before it straightened again and ran on a diagonal line to the top of the ridge.

It's as a good as a set of stairs, he thought.

He slipped past the scrub and tumbleweed and picked his way around the clumps of rocks, spotting a narrow game trail. Judging by the tracks, it was used by a variety of animals to scamper up and down the outcrop. He strapped the carbine on his back, looped the canteen around his neck and across his shoulder, and pressed forward.

Nash reached the top after five minutes of cautious climbing. He was surprised by the panoramic view, which afforded him an unimpeded look at the surrounding countryside for miles to the north – and at a long portion of the same trail he had followed out of Twisted Junction as he tracked Federal Marshal Max Blake.

Nash made his way to the far edge of the outcrop, dropped to his belly, and slithered to a point by a group of boulders where he could watch the trail that snaked its way through the aspen grove below. He placed the carbine across the rocks in front of him, though he was careful to keep the sun from glinting off the shiny metal barrel and alerting anyone nearby to his presence. He took a swallow from his canteen to wash the trail dust out of his mouth, wiped his lips with the back of his hand, and capped off the canteen and waited.

The heat was oppressive, but Nash was adept at ignoring it. He kept his ears attuned to the sounds around him, though nothing he heard seemed to be out of the ordinary, and his eyes carefully and methodically examined every inch of exposed trail, every rock and shrub and bush, every living tree and creature around him.

He was certain that he missed nothing, from the early flight of a solitary magpie to the passing of a doe and two fawns an hour into his watch, and yet something didn't feel right.

I can't put my finger on it; wish to hell I could. But something's ... off kilter down there. It don't make much sense, but that's what I get, he thought.

And so he waited – for two hours, and then two hours more, and for another two hours after that, all the while watching everything that moved and most everything that didn't.

Richard Nash was a patient man – it was one of the key traits that made him an excellent tracker – and he was at his patient best now as he watched and waited and took in all of the land around him from the high perch that the outcrop afforded.

He concentrated. He searched. He studied. Yet he found nothing out of place and came to the cautious conclusion that he had nothing to fear and nothing to gain by continuing his watch.

Still, he didn't return to the level ground at the base of the outcrop until dusk was rapidly approaching and he reluctantly determined that he had to move before the pending darkness would put him at risk of falling into the fissure on his descent. He carefully picked his way along the same narrow game trail again, keeping his body close to the sides of the outcrop and making sure that his footing was sound and his boots were secure before he took each step forward.

Nash prided himself on being a careful man as well as a patient one.

That was primarily why he was so surprised when he silently worked his way back through the trees to the spot where he had tied his horse and discovered that the animal was nowhere to be found.

This ain't good, he thought. *How in hell did I let something like this happen?*

It was too dark to determine if tracks might explain what had happened to the horse, but he was certain that only two possibilities existed: *The damn beast either tugged free and walked away, or somebody stumbled onto him and I didn't see it from up top.*

He thought about each possibility for a long minute and didn't like the conclusion that he reached. *Either way I'm in trouble.*

Another thought suddenly crossed his mind – one that made him even more uneasy: *Maybe someone tracked me here and is lying in wait right now; maybe that's the reason I didn't like the feel of things.*

He listened carefully to the gentle night air but didn't sense that anyone or anything was nearby, his horse included – and that troubled him greatly.

I know for fact I tied the horse good and tight to the tree, he thought. *If this don't beat all, I sure as hell don't know what does.*

He kicked at the ground a time or two, weighing his options once more, not liking the conclusions he was forced to draw.

Caught by surprise by a dumb horse is a bad hand, he thought. *If that critter broke free and wandered off and left me here, I'm apt to end up kilt by Apaches or a damned mountain cat – or something worse. When I catch that critter...*

"... I'm as apt to shoot it as to ride it," he muttered. "Dammit to hell and back."

Richard Nash stood now in the dark in the aspen grove and considered what to do next.

His decision would have been easier had he been aware of the presence of the federal marshal from Twin Forks, who was silently watching from no more than a hundred yards away.

Max Blake had doubled back on the trail he was riding toward Indian Wells. He took a circuitous route through the aspens, being careful not to show himself and his movements to anyone – especially to a man with a rifle who might be shrewd enough to station himself on higher ground.

Always cautious, he eventually picked up the tracks of a solitary rider and followed those tracks to Richard Nash's waiting horse – and now to the man himself.

Might be this is nobody and no matter to me at all, Max thought, his Winchester pointed squarely at the man's chest. *I wouldn't bet on it, though – not out here on my trail.*

Max couldn't see the figure well enough in the dusk to recognize the man. All he knew for certain was that the cowboy was now looking for his horse – the same horse Max had lead away hours before – and that without the animal, the man was in trouble.

It'll be interesting to see how he reacts to all this, Max thought. *He's mad as hell now. I wonder how he'll be in the morning...*

The sudden hoot of a night owl in the distance caused Richard Nash, who was now prepared for certain trouble, to hunker down in a crouch next to a small aspen. Recognizing that the tree afforded almost no protection, he flopped on his belly and crawled on his knees and elbows for a handful of yards to the base of the outcrop and a section of boulders and smaller rocks that were scattered across the ground.

He waited silently among the debris, his Springfield in his hands, his revolver lying on a rock close to his gun hand, his eyes darting about in all directions, his ears straining to pick up even the softest of sounds.

But he heard nothing, and the sense of any lurking danger was remote at best, though it was active enough in his mind.

I can't wait it out here, he thought. *If someone's got the horse, that someone is likely waiting for me – close by. I need a better spot to see what happens.*

But this is a bad hand – a bad fix I'm in here – and I don't like it one damn bit.

Chapter 21

Unearthing the Truth

Lt. Col. Michael Corbin kept the telegraph wires between Twisted Junction and all points west and south humming for a solid day.

His first message dispatched a backup squadron of soldiers to Adobe Flats to help with the burial detail. His second, sent to every wireless station on the telegraph operator's list, one after another, was equally eloquent:

ATTENTION TOWN SHERIFF. STOP.
U.S. ARMY SEEKS NEWS OF RENEGADES. STOP.
ALSO SEEKS MARSHAL MAX BLAKE. STOP.
PLEASE ADVISE CORBIN, THIS STATION. STOP.

He decided to wait for a reply in the office of Sheriff Ned Clark, at times casually chatting with the man, at other times pacing the tidy work area while avoiding the sheriff's multitude of overtures for yet another cup of coffee. He often sat in moody silence, his back against the far wall, his eyes fastened on the only door in or out, toying with his hands, anxious to move, waiting impatiently.

Couriers carried orders and confirmations back and forth between the politically minded commanding officer in the town and his elite squadron of Army fighters in the field, and these served to momentarily distract him.

Mostly, Corbin wanted nothing more than to maintain an inconspicuous profile in Twisted Junction: He still had the feeling that renegade spies were lurking on every street corner and behind every building, and he was mindful of Ned Clark's words that the townsfolk looked askance at Army regulars and regulations.

And so he waited, thinking back to his conversations with the two men in Twisted Junction who knew something about the gold-robbing renegades he was chasing.

Corbin had talked with Jack Sloan about his knowledge of the outlaw pack for a full two hours on two consecutive days, at one point taking the man's constantly present whiskey bottle and emptying its contents onto the saloon floor so that the thirsty miner could fully appreciate the power of the U.S. Army – and of Lt. Col. Michael Corbin himself. But Sloan shrugged it off and called for a replacement.

"Not until I get some answers," Corbin had said.

"You already know everything I do. But I'll tell it one more time so's I kin drink in peace. You might want to make some notes on paper this time – it'll help you remember later on."

He smiled then and paused. Corbin merely looked annoyed.

"All right. I went to Adobe Flats, everyone was dead save old Col. Corn – so far as I know, at least; that everyone was dead, I mean – and here I am. I didn't see a thing, didn't hear a shot fired save one the colonel tossed at me, didn't fire a shot myself. All this time later, and all our time together, and I'm here still telling you the same thing."

Corbin at one point ordered Ned Clark to lock Sloan up in one of his jail cells – "at least until the man sobers up" – but the sheriff refused. "He's done nothing and told you what he knows," Clark replied. "Why not leave the man alone?"

They had argued the issue for a time, moving out onto the street and away from prying eyes and ears, and Corbin pressed his point first through an attempt at intimidation and then with logic. But he knew that he had no jurisdiction in Twisted Junction and no authority to place Sloan under Army supervision – and he recognized that Ned Clark knew it, too.

Sloan had used this opportunity to get the bartender's attention. "I'm in a bad fix," he said to Johnny Seifert.

"I'll say. You've consumed enough alcohol in the past 24 hours to choke a mule. How a living man who drinks as much as you can still stand and talk is beyond me."

"Hell, that ain't what I mean," Sloan said with a wry smile. "My drinking is of no concern. It's just that I don't want to be here – never wanted to be here, no offense meant – and I sure as hell don't need this attention and poking 'round by the Army boys or yer sheriff into my affairs."

"You sound like a man with something to hide, Jack Sloan," Seifert said as he polished a still-dirty beer glass.

"To the contrary, sir: I sound like a man in need of a drink, and I would appreciate it if you would oblige me. Understand that I am mindful of the words of Mr. Bill Hickock, who is fond of saying, 'Never run away from a gun. Bullets can travel faster than you can.' "

Seifert looked on blankly for a time before he gathered up another bottle.

When Corbin returned to the bar, Sloan was sitting at the same table, his back to the bartender, his hands clasped around a glass of whiskey, his face lit up in a wide smile.

"Are we clear yet, general?" he asked without malice. "Or shall we continue our discussion with civility until you go away?"

Sloan quietly and unexpectedly slipped out of town that night and had not been seen since. Ned Clark figured that he was on his way back to his mountain lair and passed that opinion along to Corbin.

"He's likely drank himself sober, which is a damn good thing, else he might have died trying," Clark had said. "If you really want him, you could probably find him on the trail headed back to Adobe Flats, though I doubt he'll want to get near the place anytime soon, given what he saw."

"I find it suspicious that he would leave in the middle of the night like that," Corbin said with conviction.

"Suspicious? More'n likely he figured you'd put him in chains and hold him, though for the life of me I can't understand yer interest: You know what transpired in Adobe Flats. I'll say it again, Corbin: It's Max Blake you want to see for answers."

"It's not like Max Blake is waiting in the saloon for me right now, Sheriff Clark."

"Well, sir, you do have the next-best thing tucked away, you know – someone else who spent real time with yer renegades."

"And you know well enough that we've talked with the old buzzard."

"Then I suggest that you talk with the old buzzard again," Clark had said.

Max Blake watched in the growing light of a rising dawn as Richard Nash repositioned himself behind a mound of rounded boulders and cautiously peered into the thick forest.

He's been careful so far, but he's getting antsy, Max thought. *It won't be long before he does something stupid.*

For his part, Nash was flat-out angry: angry at himself for being in this situation, angry at his missing horse, and definitely angry at the man he sensed was lurking out among the trees, lying in wait for him to make a mistake.

I can't stay here forever, he thought. *Sooner or later I've got to move or die.*

Trouble is, moving might get me killed faster than staying put, and neither one's a good idea.

As he continued to analyze his options, Nash determined that he had but two choices: wait for an assault and likely die, or wait for an assault that would never come and die slowly regardless from heat and thirst and exhaustion.

It was only then that his mind suddenly stumbled on a third option.

"Well I'll be damned," he muttered aloud. "Why in hell didn't I think of this before?"

Richard Nash holstered his revolver, raised his hands high in the air, and stood straight up. "I'm coming out," he called. "You want me, come ahead and stake your claim."

Max Blake watched this action with grudging respect.

That's a smart move under the circumstances, he thought. *Given the choices the man had, this was the best play he could make.*

Max kept his Winchester trained on Nash's chest and called out, "Toss your gun aside, left hand only, and get both hands high in the air again. Then we'll talk."

Lt. Col. Michael Corbin and Capt. Jed Johnson visited on three separate occasions with Jasper Perkins, the grumpy prospector once held captive by the renegade band that the U.S. Army had assigned Corbin to hunt down.

Perkins had slipped out of Twisted Junction and Doc Peterson's care despite Ned Clark's best efforts to hold him, but Corbin dispatched two of his best trackers to find the man and return him for questioning. Jasper was brought back kicking and complaining loudly; in retrospect, it was little wonder that the man was so frustrating to talk with and of such little help in the long run.

"I cain't tell you things I don't know nothing about, and you insist on asking me questions that fall into the don't-know category," Jasper had said at the start of their last discussion. "I don't like being here, and I don't like yer company, Army boys. You want answers that grow on trees, and I ain't got that one planted near close enough to my orchard."

That remark made Johnson scratch his head.

Corbin's one-word comment – "Colorful" – made Perkins smile in return.

"Well, I kin see we speak the same language at last," he said with a snort. "But I still ain't got nothing to tell you ain't already been told a'fore in one form or t'other, time and again, all told."

He looked Johnson in the eye and said, "You follow that one all right, sonny?"

"Yes, sir," Johnson replied. "I followed that just fine, Mr. Perkins."

"Good. I kin see now why the general here thinks so highly of you."

"I'm a lieutenant colonel."

"Good fer you. I'm jest an old man been shot up some who – "

"You were in the camp, Mr. Perkins," Corbin interrupted, trying to keep the prospector focused. "You saw them. You spoke with some of them. You got to know a handful of them, perhaps. Surely you can tell us something of use."

Jasper shook his head. "First off they surprised me, and then they up and caught me. They tied me, blindfolded me, kept me in the dark. I heard whispers – just whispers, mind you – of a gold shipment. When I got the chance to git my hands free and git out, I slipped away with the mule. But I was tussled up, shot. It's a good thing Max found me.

"Why he brought me here to meet up with that damn Doc Peterson and you two boys, though, I'll never know and won't soon forgive. Next time I see him, he'll git a piece of my mind, yes sir.

"And that's all of it. I don't know how many of 'em there was 'cause I didn't have no chance to count. I didn't talk to nobody that mattered none, seems to me, 'cause why would anybody that mattered talk to me? I don't know where they took me or why they took me – ask them. I don't know why they let me git away, neither.

"So when you look at it that way, truth is I don't know more than I do know – and there's nothing more to tell, no sir."

"All right, that's all well and good, Mr. Perkins, and I thank you for the assessment. Now, let's go back to the beginning once more then," Johnson had said, which prompted another dismissive wave of disgust from Jasper Perkins.

But the ongoing discussions elicited no additional helpful information, and Corbin reluctantly allowed Jasper Perkins to leave town a day later.

"If you see Max Blake a'fore I see him, you'd best tell him to watch out for ol' Jasper Perkins, yes sir," the prospector called out to Ned Clark as he steered his mule past the sheriff's office. "He won't like what I got to tell him. And you kin tell them Army boys to stay shut of me, too."

Lt. Col. Corbin shook his head at the bad memory and grumbled to himself as he waited for a response to his wire, finding himself annoyed that Jed Johnson was helping himself to yet another cup of bad coffee.

For his part, Ned Clark did his best to ignore the Army encampment in his office. He passed much of the time by walking the streets, trying to remain hopeful that the next incoming wire would chase the two soldiers out of Twisted Junction, out of his jurisdiction, and finally out his life.

"The day can't come soon enough," he told Johnny Seifert at the Silver Spur late one afternoon. "The two are like to drive me crazy just waiting around. I'm apt to say or do something rash if we don't come to a resolution soon."

Clark's reprieve came a full day later when the wireless operator ran breathlessly into the sheriff's office, the message he carried cradled in his hands like a wounded bird.

He nodded at the sheriff, who was seated at his desk, drinking his coffee and looking particularly glum, and turned to the lieutenant colonel, who again was perched in a chair, his back to the wall. "Cap'n Corbin, sir. Here's a message for you – just come in from Whiskey Bend."

Corbin almost leaped to his feet and crossed the room in seconds. He took the paper, unfolded it carefully, and read it thoroughly before turning toward Clark.

"Ah, back in business at last, Sheriff Clark," he said. "It's about the renegades – the gold thieves – not Marshal Blake. They've been spotted south of Whiskey Bend."

"Good. You'll be off then?" Clark asked hopefully.

"It's not much, but it's better than sitting here, though I do wish word about Max Blake's whereabouts would be forthcoming."

"At least there's something on your plate," Clark offered. "And if anything comes in about Marshal Blake, or something more about the renegades, I'll wire ahead to the station in Whiskey Bend for you."

"If I didn't know better, sheriff, I'd think you were trying to be rid of me."

"Don't know what would give you that notion. Every soul in the territory will breathe easier when this renegade bunch is brought to justice, and that's not likely to happen with you sitting here all day."

Corbin pulled a coin from his pocket for the wireless operator. "I appreciate the service," he said before turning his attention back to Ned Clark.

"You are quite right, sheriff," he said. "It's time to put some miles under foot and find these bandits. I appreciate your hospitality, sir, and the offer to forward news. And I look forward to seeing you again, Sheriff Clark."

"No need to thank me, Corbin. It'll be thanks enough when you run down that thieving pack, I'd say. We'll all sleep better."

Max Blake remained hidden in the brush, closely watching as Richard Nash pulled his revolver, using his left hand to reach across his body and grasp the wooden handles with two fingers. He dropped the gun on the ground, raised his hand in the air again, and walked forward, scanning the trees as he moved, looking in vain for his pursuer.

"That's far enough," Max called. "State your business."

"I'm jest a drifter passing through, looking for a little honest work in the next town," Nash lied. He still couldn't see his adversary, but he hoped that a good story might give him an advantage – or even save his life. "Lost my horse somehow and am stranded afoot out here in the middle of ..."

"Save it," Max interrupted. "You're no more a drifter than I'm the sheriff of, say, Aguante."

The word struck Nash like a blow to the face. He knew instantly that there was no reason to pursue his ruse; whoever was out there knew full well who he was – and likely even knew, or at least suspected, what he was up to and why he was there.

Nash also thought it likely that this was the same man he had been pursuing for days now: Federal Marshal Max Blake.

It was not a comforting feeling. Nash had learned from Milt and Big Boy, the two hard-drinking cowboys he had run into days earlier in the marshal's home base of Twin Forks, that Blake was a handful for any man – and he believed it now.

"What do you think you know, stranger?" he asked, although he could see no one ahead of him.

"I know who you are and where you come from," Max said. "I even have a good idea about who sent you, and why."

The words were especially chilling because they came from directly behind Nash, and he would have sworn that only seconds before he was talking with a man who was immediately in front of him.

He started to turn when he felt the cold barrel of a long rifle pinch into his back between his shoulder blades.

"No need to move," Max said. "Keep your hands high and tell me why I shouldn't shoot you right now."

"Well, Max Blake, yer a lawman, for one thing," Nash said.

"So I see that we know each other."

"I wouldn't go that far. But I'll ask you to remember that you work for the law."

"That's funny coming from you," Max said. "You're supposed to be a lawman. But that doesn't stop you – or the rest of Walker's tin star killers – from shooting a man in the back, or taking him out for a buggy ride in the desert."

Nash said nothing. There was nothing, in fact, that he could say.

"What's your name?" Max asked after a minute.

"Nash. The name's Nash," he said, knowing full well that there was no reason to pursue further lies. He paused for a moment and added, "How did you know?"

"I felt you on the trail two days back."

"How did you know where I'm from, I mean?"

"I saw you, in the jail with Walker and one or two others, days back," Max said simply. "That scar is hard to forget, though I never forget a face."

"So what do we do now?"

"This can go any number of ways," Max said. "I could shoot you now, and no one would question it. I'm a lawman, as you point out, but I could accept it in time."

Nash started to turn and protest, but Max shoved the Winchester's barrel harder into his back.

"Then again, I could get you running and shoot. I'd tell the judge that you tried to escape. Judge Radford wouldn't be happy – he'd rather see you hang – but he'd likely understand."

"Then there's the third way," Max said.

"Yeah, and what's that?"

"You get on your horse and I take you to the nearest town with a decent jail and an honest sheriff. That's the best I can do. I've got more pressing business than you."

"And how do you figure to do that, Blake? You think I'm gonna just let you tie my hands? You think I'm gonna volunteer to climb up on my horse and let you lead me to certain death?"

"Something like that," Max agreed. With a quick flick of his powerful wrists, he turned the Winchester about and caught Nash in the back of the neck with the heavy wooden stock. The killer crashed to the ground with a grunt and a dull thud and was motionless at Max's feet.

Max was reaching into his pocket for rawhide straps to secure the man's hands when the distinctive whine of a high-caliber Sharps repeating rifle cracked the air. He could hear the bullet power past his ear and strike with a deadly thump into a nearby tree.

Max was in a crouch in an instant and moving in a broken pattern into the trees to his right. Another shot, then a third and a fourth, cracked the still air around him.

He found shelter behind a mid-sized pinion pine and peered out, trying to determine the shooter's position. A fifth shot a moment later revealed it: A man was stationed behind a scattering of large rocks close to where Nash had been hiding moments before. Max could see the glint of the sun on the rifle barrel; he also saw that the shooter was looking in the wrong direction.

Maybe I can work my way behind and get the drop on him, Max thought.

He looked down and spotted a rock as large as his hand. Picking it up, he tossed it far away to his left and ran in the opposite direction when the rock clattered to the ground and more rifle fire erupted.

Max was eighty yards or more away from the gunman now, and he wanted to move closer before risking a shot and exposing himself to additional fire. Staying low, he silently slithered along the ground for ten yards, then twenty, then thirty, using the trees as cover, moving slowly and carefully, making almost no sound whatsoever.

Max was no more than thirty yards away when the man with the Sharps suddenly thought better about his position. With a quick move, he swung himself up on his waiting horse and raced the animal down the trail, staying low in the saddle, his rifle held in one hand. He was out of range in an instant, gone entirely in another.

Max caught only a brief glimpse of the man's face, but it was enough.

"Tom Bolton," he muttered. He shook his head at the thought.

Max again considered his brief contact with Bolton, Ned Clark's former deputy from Twisted Junction. Bolton was hardly old enough to be a man, and his most redeeming feature was a smile that was both broad and stupid – as stupid as the attack he had just mounted on a federal marshal.

Ned Clark won't be happy about this turn, Max thought.

A single shot from a small revolver shattered the air, and Max could hear the solitary whine of a bullet pass close to his head once more.

"Nash," he muttered, finding immediate cover behind a tree. "What next?"

Chapter 22

The Trail to Whiskey Bend

Lt. Col. Michael Corbin pushed his men through the desolate Arizona landscape that rolled across miles of sand and sagebrush and low-slung, barren mesas on the way to the freighting colony of Whiskey Bend.

Only hours earlier, a wire from the town's sheriff found Corbin as he waited impatiently in Twisted Junction, an outpost of determined settlers a two-day ride to the east. The message was simple:

RENEGADES SIGHTED NEAR HERE. STOP.
BRING LOTS OF GUNS. STOP.
SIGNED, JOHN HAWKINS, SHERIFF. STOP.

Corbin was unhappy, however: He found himself short on facts and long on speculation, and he didn't like the hand that he had just been dealt.

Based on conversations with Jack Sloan and Jasper Perkins in Twisted Junction, Corbin determined that the renegades had carved a wide swath of terror and murder after stealing a shipment of U.S. Army gold. Rumors aside, no living man in a position to tell could explain exactly how much gold was involved, how many men were riding with the pack, what the intentions of the renegades were or might become, or where they were heading and why.

Even Corbin's superiors in the U.S. Army hierarchy refused to stamp out the rumors or speculate aloud about the possibilities, likely because of embarrassment.

All Corbin knew for certain was that his squadron had been dispatched to find and stop the renegades and recover the gold. He also recognized that his mind should be devoted solely to that task, calibrating the necessary maneuvers to ensure a thorough victory. Instead, he continued to think about Max Blake, the federal marshal from Twin Forks in the heart of the territory.

The reason was simple: Blake had seen the renegade encampment first-hand and attained at least a passing assessment of its strength, which was something that Corbin desperately wanted. *Max Blake is the key to how we proceed,* he thought as he pushed his men aggressively forward on a relentless march toward Whiskey Bend. *I'd bet Blake even knows this Hawkins and could lend a hand there.*

Because he had never been in contact with the Whiskey Bend sheriff, Corbin was uncertain about the sheriff's assessment that ample firepower was required to deal with the renegades. *It might be the man's prone to exaggeration,* Corbin thought. *Or maybe he tends to be overly cautious. Given what we suspect about these renegades, that might even be a good thing.*

His thoughts returned to Max Blake again and how he might locate the marshal and obtain a first-hand report about the strength of the renegades and the character of the Whiskey Bend sheriff. But Corbin knew that he couldn't make it happen by wishing. Even though he had sent messages up and down the line to every settlement in the territory with a telegraph operator, no sightings of Max Blake were reported.

The lieutenant colonel pondered the ramifications.

Capt. Jed Johnson, Corbin's second in command, noticed the distant look on his commanding officer's face, gradually edged his horse through the traffic of the moving column, and eventually pulled alongside.

"You look bothered, sir," Johnson yelled, interrupting Corbin's thoughts. "Can I help?"

"Tell me that Max Blake is waiting up ahead with some news we'll want to hear, captain," he called over the clatter of horses' hooves.

"Wish I could, sir," Johnson replied. He paused for a moment. "Might be we'll hear something in Whiskey Bend, sir. Sheriff Clark said he'd pass along any word. Most likely someone's spotted this Blake by now."

"I hope you're right, captain," Corbin called. "It would make our job easier. But we'll deal with it."

"Yes, sir."

"Keep them moving, Jed. The sooner we can meet with Hawkins, the sooner we'll know what we face."

The former Confederate soldiers who had banded together to steal a shipment of U.S. Army gold were camped a handful of miles from the tiny settlement of Whiskey Bend. A dozen men were huddled away from the main encampment and out of earshot of Iron Mike Truax, the ruthless leader who had pulled the renegades together.

The men had been riding together for two solid weeks. Chief among their dubious accomplishments was successfully securing a gold shipment in a surprise raid on an Army caravan making its way across the desert. They next raided nearby Adobe Flats, killing most of the town's occupants, in a ruse to delay their pursuers. But a general sense of distrust and unease had settled in.

Days before, Truax and one of his trusted lieutenants took the wagon carrying the gold into the night. Truax returned with the wagon a day later, and at least some of the men suspected that it was noticeably lighter. Instead of confiding in his men, however, Truax insisted on leading them in a round-about pattern of random attacks on tiny outposts, with no sense of purpose or direction.

Only Iron Mike's iron-fisted control, his quickness with a six-gun and willingness to use it, and the backing of at least six other fast gunmen who blindly followed his every command had prevented a bloody confrontation. But the mood of at least a handful of the renegades was changing daily, and it was not changing for the better.

Slim Berning chewed a piece of jerky methodically. He was a man ill-suited to the outlaw life – there were even rumors that he had once been a law enforcement official of one sort or another before the war – coming, as he did, from a wealthy Southern family. He had fought with distinction as an officer in the Confederate Army during the latter days of the conflict, although a quick tongue and an impulsive brush with authority cost him his rank near the end. He came to the attention of Iron Mike Truax because of the incident, however, and each man recognized a strength in the other.

Truax saw Slim as a man who had the respect of his men – the same men, in fact, who had followed Slim in helping to fill out Iron Mike's renegade force. Slim saw in Truax a way to regain some of the family wealth that was lost during the war. But Slim secretly despised Truax, recognizing him for the bully and tyrant that he was; and Iron Mike was slowly coming to realize that Slim Berning's lack of respect for authority was a problem and not a strength at all, regardless of how many men he had brought to the deal.

It was becoming readily apparent, in fact, that the two men would clash before long.

Slim glanced across to the campfire, where a dozen men were gathered fifty yards or more away, and pointed with a bony finger in the general direction of the big man who sat steely-eyed, away from the others and well out of earshot.

"Iron Mike's gonna be the death of us all, sure as hell," Slim said. "I ain't afraid to say it tonight, nor tomorrow, nor the day after."

"You sure as hell don't say it direct to Iron Mike, though – do you, Slim?" a gnarled former soldier who was missing most of his left arm said with a wink to the others who were gathered about. The man had a graying beard that was full and bushy and long hair that poked at odd angles outside the tattered edges of his dusty Johnny Reb cap, a staple that provided him with his nickname.

"A man would be a damn fool fer that," Slim replied. "You know Iron Mike'd shoot any man of us as soon as look at us, and that's a true fact. I mean to say – what I meant to say – is I ain't afraid to say it to you boys, and that's what matters.

"Besides, you know how cranky I git when I ain't had nothing to eat save this here jerky. I could eat something right now."

"This ain't about food, you old fool," Thom Adams said. "And it sure as hell ain't about telling us we need be on the lookout fer Iron Mike. We know that already.

"The trouble with this here deal is Iron Mike's calling all the shots, and he's got hisself backup. There ain't a lot to talk about less'n we all make a move against him – and that means all of us. And I don't likely see that happening anytime soon.

"I ain't sayin' I'm right, mind ya. It's jest the way I see it."

Slim poked another bony finger toward the spot where Mike Truax was seated when a grizzled man with long sideburns hissed, "Git yer finger down else he sees you, Slim. What in hell are you thinking? It's risky enough we sit here away from the main pack, you ask me."

"Relax, Harvey, and don't worry none 'bout – "

"But I cain't relax, and I sure as hell is worried; you should be, too," Harvey Bones said. "We're on a fool's errand to start with. Why hell, we got half the Union Army on our tails, and that ain't the worst of it."

Johnny Reb sniffed at that as he scratched at his stump. "What's worse than half the Union Army on our tails, I wonder?"

"You could start with the name of Iron Mike Truax," Harvey replied. "And there's a couple of others I kin think of right off the top of..."

"Enough, Harvey," Slim cut in sharply, glaring at the man for a moment. "You, too, Thom – enough already. Let's git our business settled here and inch on back to the fire a'fore Mike takes notice and ambles this way. I ain't got the words to discourage him or settle his mind tonight, though I expect I'll give it some thought."

"So what are we gonna do?" Harvey asked.

Slim waited a moment to see if anyone had an opinion. When no one did, he nodded slightly and assumed the role of leader once more.

"We got a handful of options open. First off, we stay quiet and go along and hope fer the best. It don't seem likely this whole business will end good, or if we'll be alive and kicking when it's done, but it's one to consider."

"The payday at the end is something else to consider," Johnny Reb volunteered. "That needs to be put on the table, too."

"All right, fair enough," Slim said. "So that's fer starters. Next, we kin cut and run right now, or as soon to now as we kin manage. We won't be the first to do it. Ol' Mike sent that ugly basket of snakes – what the hell was his name? – out to ..."

"Fuller," Thom Adams said.

"... check on one thing or t'other – yeah, it was Fuller, all right – and we ain't seen him since. I figger that he cut and got out when he could."

"Naw, Fuller not being here don't mean nothing," Johnny Reb said.

"Well it don't mean nothing good, I'll give you that," Slim replied, looking annoyed. "Seems plenty plain enough to me that Iron Mike kilt off Fuller, jest like he kilt off Dirk and the rest of ..."

"We don't know that Fuller's dead, Slim," Toad Wright said. "Might be he is. Might be he is and ol' Mike didn't do him in. Then again, might be he's run off. Might even be he's guarding the gold right now. Might be he's ..."

"... as dead as old Coley's mule," Slim finished the thought. "Fuller ain't smart enough to do the right thing – never was. The thing of it is, we jest don't know – and that's the problem when you git yer arms 'round it. So I'll say it again: We've got to figure out what we kin do as a group."

"There's something else we might think about," Johnny Reb said.

"Yeah? What's that?"

"We kill off Mike Truax and them that's loyal to him and take all the gold."

"Jest one problem with that," Thom Adams said.

"You mean other than the one where we all git kilt off first?" Harvey Bones asked with a mirthless chuckle. "That's all I see happening if we take that path – every man of us ends up dead."

"Naw, hell, that ain't the problem I see," Adams answered.

"Well, jest what is it then, Thom?" Slim asked.

"The problem is the damn gold, you old fool," he said. "Iron Mike knows where the gold is, and we don't, less'n you think it's still on that wagon – and I fer one ain't buying that pig in a poke fer a minute. No sir. So long as Mike has the knowing of the gold and keeps it from us, then he's safe as a newborn in his mother's arms."

The men were silent for a moment, their thoughts running in myriad directions.

"We kin still cut and run and save our skins," Jack Conway said at last. "We won't get rich, but we won't git dead, neither. And I'd rather be broke and alive than the other way I see this going."

He looked around, and a handful of the men nodded. Others, however, were noncommittal, and Conway threw a stick on the ground and looked across at Slim with a shrug.

"So we got ourselves a problem, and we is gonna have to figger a way to solve it a'fore long," Slim said at last. "Much as I'd like, we cain't do it now 'cause there's too much thinking at stake here. Besides, we been here long enough – ain't no sense in pushing our luck and risking Mike's taking notice."

"So what do we do?" Toad asked.

"Let's give it twenty-four hours," Slim said after a moment of consideration. "We kin sit down to vittles – if'n there's any to be had – a day from now and take a quiet vote if we git the chance. That will give us all some time to think about which way we might want to go. That sound right?"

"Yeah, that's good by me," Johnny Reb said.

"I kin wait, I guess," Toad said.

"Me, too," Harvey offered. He looked hard at the two men who sat nearest to him and added: "You boys right with that? Jack? Bob?" They glanced at each other and then back at Harvey and nodded, although they said nothing aloud.

"What about you, Thom?" Slim asked.

"We kin use the time to try and draw a bead on the gold," Adams said. "The whole thing might change a day from now. Hell, anything kin happen. But another day is fine, so long as we take action right after. If we wait too long, we're jest inviting trouble – and you know trouble's comin' our way regardless. The sooner we pick a trail to follow, the better."

"It's settled then. We find a spot tomorrow and decide it – if we kin manage it without being seen.

"All right," Slim said with some finality, "I say we break it up and amble over to the rest of 'em – maybe a couple at a time. You right with that?"

"Sure," Johnny Reb said. "Who wants to git up with me and warm up some by that fire off yonder?" He stood and looked around at the men. When no one moved, he shrugged, turned, and started walking toward the campfire where Mike Truax, Rand Townsend, and the rest of the renegade pack had settled.

"Suit yerselves," he called over his shoulder.

"Hey, wait up; I'll head on over with you," Bob Strickland said. He picked himself up from a mid-sized rock he had used for a seat and lumbered after Johnny Reb. "Hold up a minute, else I pull out my hog-leg and slow you some."

"That ain't likely."

Slim chuckled and elbowed Thom Adams. "Come on," he said, nodding his head toward the fire. "What say we settle in at the camp there?"

"I'd sooner go and – "

"Save it, you ol' buzzard," Slim cut in. "You've had enough to say fer one night."

An hour later, as Slim was sitting by himself near the fire, his mind deep in thought, Iron Mike Truax casually ambled by. The big man kicked at Slim's outstretched feet and stared intently into his eyes.

"Interesting congregation you had going on some time back, Berning," Mike said. "What the hell was that about? You thinking of setting up a church – doing a little preaching, maybe?"

"Naw, Mike – nothing like that," Slim replied as casually as he could muster; he had rehearsed his answer a dozen times, just in case he was challenged. "Sort of a coincidence we ended up there. I thought the fire'd be pitched there, and the next thing you know, well, it weren't – and we had already started talking about a card game, and one thing you don't want to do is interrupt discussions when it comes to a game of ..."

"That's a pile of horse dung, Slim," Mike cut in. "I got my eye on you – and it's gonna stay there till you give me reason to turn it elsewhere. You got me?"

Iron Mike Truax didn't wait for an answer; he turned and stomped off into the darkness.

Slim shuddered but didn't say a word. He looked across to where Thom Adams was stretched out yards away, but Adams appeared as though he had missed the exchange entirely; his eyes were shut, and his Stetson was pulled low across his brow.

It's no good; I'm runnin' outta time, Slim thought. *Mike's got my number, the bluelegs is chargin' behind us – and maybe something else is comin', too. I kin feel it.*

He kept his back against a tree that night, and he was still wide awake and watching when the sun began its slow rise in the eastern sky of early morning.

Chapter 23

A Fork in the Road

Max Blake crouched, Winchester in hand, and scurried behind a solitary Ponderosa pine as the bullet from Richard Nash's revolver whined over his head.

Dammit. How did I miss a gun? Max wondered as he dove for cover.

Blending his muscular body against the honeycombed bark of the tree, the federal marshal kept his face hidden and listened carefully to the forest sounds around him as the revolver's echo faded into a deathly stillness. Even the chatter of birds had ceased; the only noise that he could immediately detect came from the steady winds that whipped off the distant snow-capped mountains, rustling the upper branches of the elegant Ponderosas and the roundly swaying smaller aspens.

Max scanned the ground and spotted a branch, a foot in length and about an inch thick, that had snapped off and withered in the turn of seasons. Careful not to expose his position, he tossed it with a hard flick twenty or more yards to his left. The stick clattered into the bark of a Ponderosa, and Max broke to his right as a single gunshot was snapped off in the opposite direction.

He stayed low and ducked behind another pine, then peered around the edge and scanned the area. He remained motionless, his eyes darting back and forth, looking for the slightest sign of movement among the trees.

His diligence was rewarded moments later when he caught sight of a tan Stetson jutting out from the far edge of a thick pine. He focused intently on the area and watched closely as more and more of the hat emerged until he could make out the face of Richard Nash, intently peering at the spot where the tree branch clattered minutes earlier. Nash apparently was searching for either movement or sound and was puzzled to find neither.

Found you, Max thought. *Now it's just a matter of surprising you.*

Max was prepared to wait all day if necessary – unmoving, unbending, oblivious to the elements and external forces – to find the right angle of attack to exploit Nash's position.

He didn't have to wait long, however: The corrupt deputy, apparently anxious to dispatch the federal marshal and make his way back to Aguante, decided to force the issue instead. Nash crept slowly away from the pine that had provided him with effective cover and headed in a low crouch toward the general direction where he figured Max Blake was hiding. The killer was soon down on his hands and knees, inching his way cautiously forward, his body moving in rhythmic shifts as he crawled deliberately ahead.

Max spotted a small revolver of polished steel extended in Nash's right hand and silently inched his Winchester into position and took aim at the distant gun. *If I can disarm him and take him in to hang, justice is best served,* he thought. *But if I miss this shot, it's anybody's guess as to how this will turn out.*

Max drew a short, silent breath, held it, and squeezed off a single shot.

A shout of surprise and anguish echoed through the forest an instant later as the revolver skidded out of Nash's grasp and the Aguante deputy rolled on his back, holding his wounded right hand tightly to his chest, writhing on the ground.

"Gawd a'mighty," he yelled. "What'd ya have to do that fer? You damn sight could've kilt me."

Max chambered another round into the Winchester and directed the weapon at the injured man as he made his way through the trees. Nash was groaning loudly, rocking back and forth on a bed of pine needles. Max could see that the man's hand was bleeding freely. *The bullet must have passed directly through,* he thought.

Max spotted a .31 caliber Beals Pocket Model revolver lying on the forest floor and picked it up with his left hand while he kept the Winchester trained on the wounded man; he examined the gun for a moment before tucking it away in his belt.

"What's wrong with you?" Nash gasped, looking up. "You damn near shot my hand off."

"Where'd the gun come from?" Max asked, annoyed at himself for missing it during his initial contact.

"Let me have it a minute and I'll show you," Nash said through gritted teeth.

Max guessed by the size of the Beals that Nash had tucked it into his boot for insurance, just as Max himself carried a Reid's Knuckleduster behind his belt buckle for similar emergencies. An extra weapon close at hand often was a necessity in the lawless lands of the territory – the difference between life and death – and he knew at once that he had been fortunate.

"You might want to get a piece of cloth on that hand before you bleed to death," Max said after a minute. "Can you move your fingers?"

"How the hell should I know?" Nash complained. "What's it to you, anyways?"

"There's not much call for a man with one hand," Max said. "Besides, you'll look better swinging from the judge's gallows with both hands behind your back."

Nash snorted angrily and glared for an instant before wiggling his fingers, one at a time, staring intently now at his hand. A steady flow of blood oozed from both sides of the wound. He moved his thumb and fingers back and forth a few times and looked up. "Satisfied?"

"It's nothing to me," Max said. "It's your hand."

"Well, it still works and no thanks to you." Nash grimaced in pain again, clutching tighter at the wound. "Listen, Blake, I don't have a piece of cloth of any size. My kerchief must be in my saddlebags, which you stole when you took my damn horse. I'm gonna need something to tie this off with."

"Use the sleeve of your shirt," Max said. "No need for you to bleed on mine."

"That's a hell of a card to deal a man you just bushwhacked," Nash whined. "I figure the least you can do ..."

"... is get you moving," Max finished. "I'll help – and don't even think about trying to bolt. That would be a bad mistake."

He placed the barrel of the Winchester directly on Nash's chest – "twitch and you die right here," he said softly so that the words carried some menace – and then reached down and gave the man's left shirtsleeve a hard yank, but the material held firm.

Max pulled his Bowie knife, eyed Nash carefully for an instant, and used the blade to rip a three-inch gash in the seam. He continued to press the barrel of the Winchester into Nash's chest as he returned the knife to his boot, his eyes never leaving the Aguante deputy's, his finger resting gingerly on the rifle's trigger.

"This won't hurt much – unless you do something stupid," he said and again jerked at the shirtsleeve. The flannel tore in a loud rip at the seam, and Max gave it one more tug, pulling it loose.

"Wiggle out of that and use it to bind your hand," he said as he backed a few feet away. "The tighter you tie it now, the less likely some quack'll cut it off later. If we were in Twin Forks, I'd send you to Doc Strand. He can patch a man today and watch him hang tomorrow."

Nash scowled at the thought.

"This Doc Strand sounds like he's no better'n you and that damn judge you answer to."

"Doc Strand is a better man than you'll ever know or appreciate, and the judge has his moments, not that it matters here," Max said. "You'd best tug that tight if you want to do it any good. The nearest town is Whiskey Bend, which is out of my way but best for you. I know the sheriff well enough; not sure about a doctor, though."

Nash cursed loudly as he pulled the severed sleeve down his arm and began to wrap his hand, wincing in pain with every movement. "I'll tell you plain, Blake, if our situations were different and reversed somehow, I'd have me a ..."

"I know exactly what you'd do," Max said, cutting him off. "Let's go – on your feet now. We've got some traveling to do if you want that hand tended by someone other than yourself."

Nash struggled to his feet, clutching his hand, his shirtsleeve wrapped tightly around the wound. Even at that, Max could see the blood seep through the dirty fabric.

"You mean to say you won't give a man a ..."

"... a hand?" Max finished. "Let's get moving. We've got a three-hour ride, and I'll be surprised if you make it past the first hour."

Richard Nash looked down at his hand and then directly into Max Blake's steel-gray eyes.

He wasn't sure what sight scared him more.

Lt. Col. Michael Corbin had pushed his squadron hard for four solid hours when he caught the eye of Capt. Jed Johnson, his second in command, and signaled a halt. They were nearing Whiskey Bend, and Corbin wanted to use both surprise and discretion to his advantage.

He had previously sent riders to approach the town from two directions. Their orders were to assess the situation in the settlement, determine if the band of renegades that Corbin's squadron was chasing could be located, and report by nightfall at the foot of the mesa overlooking the settlement. They were to contact no one, including the town's sheriff, John Hawkins; that was a task Corbin saved for himself.

The remaining soldiers now circled their horses around Corbin and Johnson, waiting for instructions.

"All right, men," Corbin said softly, "let's tend to our mounts and disappear into the rocks: No talking, no campfire, no unnecessary movements – nothing until we get a better idea of what's out there. Are we clear?"

He looked carefully about, assessing each man's eyes, and nodded. "All right, see to it, Mickey."

"Yes, sir," Sgt. Major Michael McClinton said as he looked about. "All right, lads, you heard the man. Let's be quick about it."

As the men climbed off their horses, Corbin turned to Johnson. "Post the usual lookouts, captain, and be sure to cover all exposed perimeters. Remind each man that we are expecting two of our own – no surprises then."

"Yes, sir," Johnson replied. "I'll see to it right away."

"Good, Jed. We've done good work today. Let's be sure the men know it."

Corbin pulled a map from his saddlebags and took advantage of the fading light to study the surrounding territory carefully, comparing one to the other.

The map is a flat piece of paper, he thought. *It doesn't give you a feel for the contours of the land and the hidden spots that can hide a gunman – or a pack of gold thieves.*

He found the mesa on the tattered parchment, noted its location in reference to the point where the town should be, and gazed out into the increasing gloom. He spotted two tiny points of faint light, perhaps from lanterns, off in the distance and nodded as he glanced from the map to the land and back again until the natural light was gone. Corbin carefully refolded the map, dismounted, and handed the reins of his horse to McClinton, who was patiently waiting nearby.

"You'll see to my horse, sergeant major?" he asked.

"Of course, sir. And would the lieutenant colonel need anything else?"

"Thanks, Mickey, but I'm right. Carry on."

"Yes, sir," he said, the Irish lilt in his voice as distinct as it was on the day that he left County Cork as a boy.

McClinton was a career soldier who had served with distinction under Gen. Ulysses S. Grant during the American Civil War. He was a tall man with a barrel chest and hands as large as thick steaks. His hair, tinged gray as it peeked out the sides of his Army-issue hat, was gone on top except for a few wisps that he jealously guarded and fussed over when no one was about.

He had stunning blue eyes that commanded attention and a kindly face with a florid complexion that his mother had called pure Irish strawberries. He was a match for any man in a fist fight and was equally handy with a Springfield rifle.

McClinton had been assigned to Corbin's squadron three years previously, and he took an immediately liking to his commanding officer. He had noted more than once that Corbin was destined for greatness – far beyond the scope of an ordinary Army life; greatness that only wealth and privilege could provide, in fact – and he determined that he would faithfully serve the rising star.

The acknowledged bond between the two was apparent to every man in the squadron, enhancing McClinton's role among the enlisted men significantly.

For his part, Corbin relied on his sergeant major, even more than he did on young Capt. Jedediah Johnson. He knew that McClinton would stand by him in any situation and support him in any circumstance – from a simple saloon fight to an encounter with a hostile renegade band of gold thieves. He fondly called him Mickey, just as McClinton's mother had done so long ago in Ireland.

Best of all, he could picture McClinton as a faithful bodyguard and trusted adviser when Corbin made it to the White House one day.

"See to your own needs, too, sergeant major," Corbin added.

McClinton snapped off a salute, took the reins of his commanding officer's horse, and led the animal to an area where the other Army mounts were being secured and fed.

"All right, you two, clear out of the way while I take care of himself's horse," McClinton said. "Look sharp, or I'll have a go at ya meself."

Max Blake pulled on the reins of his horse and whispered softly into the big gelding's ear: "Hold up a minute, Buck. Something's out there."

He looked across at Richard Nash, who was riding alongside, and tugged on the rope he had fastened around the neck of Nash's horse; Max had secured a second line around the Aguante deputy's left ankle and tied it to the stirrup, and the man's left hand was tied to the pommel of his saddle with a rawhide strip that left him little room for movement.

His wounded right hand, still strapped with the flannel sleeve pulled from his shirt, remained free.

Buck pulled to a halt, and the movement roused Nash, who had drifted off in the saddle.

The deputy's hand had stopped bleeding, but it was still throbbing with a dull ache that served as a constant reminder of what had happened to him only hours before. Nash, in fact, was beginning to appreciate the formidable skills of the federal marshal from Twin Forks, and he cursed as the reality of the moment set in again.

"Dammit, Blake, now what?"

"Quiet."

The single-word command, and the forceful way it was uttered, forced Nash to look quickly about. He listened carefully, detecting no sounds on the night air. He tried to get his bearings but couldn't determine where he was, exactly. He only knew that he was being led to Whiskey Bend, and he hoped that he would arrive soon: The constant pain in his hand made him increasingly fearful that the wound would start to fester, which could lead to amputation or even a slow death.

"Something's out there," Max whispered after a minute.

He looked at Nash in the fading light. "A move to run is your last."

Nash nodded. He knew the best he could hope for was that Max Blake might be surprised, even killed, on the trail – *and given the man's skill, that ain't likely to happen.* Beyond that, a quick arrival in Whiskey Bend so that his hand could be properly tended was a good alternative in Nash's mind.

And after that – well, there'll be time enough after that to get the drop on him somehow, he thought.

Nash touched his wounded hand to the brim of his hat and whispered through clenched teeth, "Whatever you say."

Max quickly dismounted and secured Buck to a clump of trees. He took the rope tied to Nash's horse and the second rope that was fastened to the man's ankle and tied both securely to a nearby tree before edging up to the Aguante deputy.

"I'm going to look around," he whispered. "Sing out, you die. Try to get free, you die. Doubt what I say, you die. Whatever is out there is likely to kill you before I do; but make no mistake that I'll see to it regardless if you try to run. Understand?"

Nash nodded again, keeping his thoughts to himself, and Max Blake disappeared into the night.

Chapter 24

A Starry Night

"Look at all them stars." Slim Berning poked Thom Adams on the arm as the two men, flat on their backs in their bedrolls, looked up at the heavens.

They had settled yards away from the guarded campfire that the renegade band of gold thieves had pitched two miles south of Whiskey Bend. Slim could make out Iron Mike Truax in the distance, and he knew from long experience that the farther he stayed away from the man, the longer he was likely to stay alive.

"What of 'em?" Adams replied after a minute.

"Lots of 'em up there is all. That's a nice slice of moon, too," Slim said. He turned his head slightly to look at Adams and added, "I'll tell ya straight up, Thom: If every one of them stars was a single gold coin, we'd both be flush and no need to run with this pack of wolves."

Adams sniffed at the thought. "If wishes was horses, then beggars would ride. If frogs had wings, they'd fly instead of hop. If every shot I fired flew straight, I'd ..."

"All right – I hear ya plain," Slim said, cutting him off. "You need a rosier disposition, if you ask me. What you need is a ..."

"... a cowboy beside me who will shut up and leave me in peace," Adams finished, rolling on his side away from Slim.

"Just an observation is all," Slim said after a minute. "Just thinkin' out loud's all I was doing."

"Think to yerself then," Adams grumbled. "I'm getting old and crotchety, and this ground is rock-hard and don't do my disposition, as you call it, much good. It don't do much for my sleep, neither – any more'n yer jabbering."

The two were silent for a moment. Adams closed his eyes once more, content that he had gotten in the last word. Slim watched the spectacular light show overhead, imagining for a moment that he had wings and could rise and fall at will among the stars, swooping up and down like a soaring eagle.

His reverie was interrupted by the disagreeable face of Iron Mike Truax, which suddenly loomed overhead, blocking a large patch of the night sky from his view.

"What's all the damn noise about?"

"Noise? I didn't hear no noise, Mike," Slim said cautiously. "Did *you* hear anything, Thom?" Slim glanced across at Adams and saw that the man was feigning sleep convincingly.

Slim looked back at Truax and shrugged. "Didn't hear a thing, Mike."

Truax stared down for a full minute, his face twisted into a perpetual scowl, his eyes alive with malice. "I told ya before, Slim Berning, I had an eye on you," he said at last. "Now I got both of 'em on ya. You hear me?"

"No need for harsh words, Mike," Slim said with a nod. "You know I'm on board with you – me 'n Thom both. Yer the big bug, Mike, and make no mistake by me."

Truax was silent. He glared at Slim for a long moment and glanced once across at Adams, who was breathing loudly now, his eyes tightly shut, before he disappeared into the night.

Slim tried to listen for the man's footsteps, but he heard nothing. He kept his eyes open, blankly watching the parade of stars overhead. He turned after a moment and looked across at Thom Adams, shifting his weight slightly off his bedroll. "We've got to do something about ol' Mike," he whispered. "We are running outta time, I tell ya."

But Adams gave no indication that he was awake, and Slim eventually looked up at the stunning expanse of sky and stared long into the night, his mind racing, his right hand closed around the well-worn wooden grips of his Confederate LeMat revolver.

He was still awake when he heard the clatter of a rock falling from the edge of a mesa off in the distance. But he paid no attention and soon drifted into a light, fitful sleep.

The light of a quarter-moon and a billion stars brought Max Blake to the edge of a mesa that he knew from memory overlooked the freighting settlement of Whiskey Bend.

He crouched behind a wide clumping of good-sized rocks and scattered boulders and sensed as much as saw the surrounding expanse of earth and sky.

Looking to the north, he could see shimmers of moon-tinged light reflected from the fast-moving stream that wound its way out of the snow-capped peaks of the central territory and curled like a lazy serpent across the broad band of the high desert. He recalled hearing stories about the legendary Carter Thomas, founder of the crossroads town, who had lost a wagon filled with cases of high-powered rotgut in the sluicing currents of the stream after a flash flood – an incident that gave Whiskey Bend its name.

In the far distance, off to the west, he could make out twin pinpoints of light that he quickly determined were beacons to the town itself – *likely the back end of the stables*, Max thought. *Every drunken cowboy needs a light to saddle up his horse.*

Directly below him, however, he could sense the presence of men.

Max picked up a rock the size of his fist and tossed it over the edge of the mesa, keeping the arc short so that it would clatter and carom along the sides of the vertical walls until it skidded to a stop at the bottom.

Max waited, listening intently.

When the only sound he heard in return was the faint trailing echo of the discarded rock, he selected another chunk of rounded limestone, this one larger and heavier, and nudged it over the rim.

The rock fell thirty feet or more before it caught the jagged edge of the cliff, clattered off, skidded and ricocheted, and eventually crashed into the rock-strewn base of the mesa far below.

"Now what do you suppose, sweet Jaysus, is causing all that racket above us? Goats, d'ya think?"

"Goats, is it? Unless you want a visit from me boot, you'd best shut yer gob and keep it shut, Patrick O'Flynn. And I mean right now."

As the words carried to the top of the mesa where Max had positioned himself, he smiled inwardly and turned away from the rim.

Army boys, straight from Ireland, Max thought.

He knew that entire regiments of the U.S. Cavalry were filled with broad-shouldered Irishmen who had escaped the poverty and the forbidding bleakness and despair of their native island and found themselves welcomed into the soldier's life in America. The Irishmen he knew from the months he had spent on his uncle's Wyoming cattle ranch were hard workers and reliable fighters who followed orders and generally were appreciative of the opportunities they received in the wilds of their newly adopted land.

Max hurried back to the spot where he had secured Buck and Richard Nash, the captured Aguante deputy. Max could see that the man was again slumped in the saddle. His right hand remained wrapped in his torn flannel shirtsleeve, which Max had pulled free to help staunch the bleeding of a bullet wound; his left hand was tied to the pommel with a rawhide strap.

He's asleep or passed out, he thought. *Then again, maybe it's a ruse – an act.*

There's no easy way to tell, but it's best to be cautious.

Max pulled his finely tooled revolver and cautiously approached from the right, placed his Colt firmly against Nash's ribs, and gave the barrel a sharp nudge. Nash's eyes jerked open, and he looked wildly about for an instant, trying to find an enemy to fight.

"Quiet," Max whispered. "Just checking."

Nash turned to his right and looked at his captor with angry eyes. "I was sleeping, for gawd's sake," he hissed loudly. "It's the only relief I kin get from the throb in this hand you tried to shoot off."

"I'll make it permanent if you don't keep quiet," Max whispered calmly. "The Army's below us. We're going in."

"Like hell we are," Nash said loudly. "I ain't riding into no Army – "

"They likely have a field surgeon," Max said as he untied the rope that was fastened to Nash's horse and then swung up on Buck. "If you want to save that hand, you'll do as you're told. You can start by staying quiet – might be others lurking about."

Max turned and looked directly at Richard Nash. "Understand?"

Nash nodded. "Yeah, I hear you all right, Blake," he said softly this time. "But you gotta know, my hand's getting worse every minute. It hurts, I tell ya. I think it's starting to fester some."

"The Army will see to it," Max said. "Meantime, keep your mind off it."

"Yeah, and how am I gonna do that? You won't even let me light a cigar."

Max shrugged. "Anything that works. You can count to a hundred, or think of a thousand ways to escape; of course, that'll just get you shot again."

"Brilliant."

"Take a look overhead," Max said as he nudged Buck forward again. "There's a lot of sky up there to count, one star at a time."

Jack Sloan dismounted from his tired horse and, weary himself, climbed the steps of the Adobe Flats saloon. Night was falling fast, and the dim lantern beams that peeked through the dingy windows were the only man-made lights that Sloan could detect: Every other building in the once-thriving settlement was deserted, as dead as the town's former occupants.

He paused for a moment, looking back to the street and then overhead at a million shining stars. He turned his head both right and left and saw millions more lighting the sky in either direction.

His glance took in the Big Dipper, and he followed the handle automatically across to the North Star, just as he had been taught as a child. He sighed deeply, thinking of all the bad decisions through all the hard years, before he finally turned again to face the saloon.

Sloan approached the batwing doors and called out, "Hey, Col. Corn – you in there?"

"Who wants to know?" the cranky bartender yelled in reply.

"I'm coming in. Keep yer finger off the trigger of that scatter gun you keep back of the bar and pour me a drink instead."

"Jack Sloan? Is that you?" Corn hollered when he recognized the voice, and Sloan pushed his way inside and looked around the dimly lit interior, taking in every corner in every direction, before turning his full attention to the man behind the bar.

"Place looks a might better'n last I was here," Sloan said as he edged forward, a smile working its way across his weathered face. "You look about the same, though, colonel – not much of an improvement at all."

"That right? Well, it's dandy to see you, too, you ol' buzzard. You look fit enough for a man tries to drink hisself to death every opportunity he gets. Speaking of which …"

Corn pulled the cork on a bottle of his best whiskey, which he selected from a long row on the shelf behind the restored bar, and poured a generous shot. Sloan eyed the bottle, picked up the glass, saw but ignored the chip in the rim, and held it aloft for an instant in the bartender's direction.

"Here's to ya, despite yer ugly face," he said before taking a long drink. He swallowed, smacked his lips a single time, and looked across to Corn, smiling broadly. "So the Army came to help you out?"

"They showed up two days back," Corn said, refilling Sloan's glass. "Thanks for getting out the word. It's appreciated."

"Least I could do for a man in need," Sloan said before emptying the glass in a single gulp. His eyes watered momentarily, and he nodded at Corn and managed another weak smile. "It's at least as good as I remember it, and maybe a whole bunch better – so I'll have me another, if that's agreeable."

"It's on the house, just like I promised," Corn said.

"It's the very thing that brought me straight back here," Sloan replied, sliding his glass across the bar. "You've a fine, steady hand. I'd be most pleased if you joined me."

Corn filled the tumbler and looked carefully at Jack Sloan. The man's eyes were bloodshot, and he looked as if he hadn't had a decent night's sleep in days. "You all right, Sloan?" he asked. "You look like hell."

"I don't look any worse'n you do, colonel."

"I've got reason," Corn said in turn, shaking his head slowly. "There was five of us left alive all told. That's all. Three of 'em's already talking of moving on.

"The bastards kilt nigh on to fifty people here; some I buried myself. The Army boys – young kids mostly – took care of the rest and lit out this morning. They was holed up over to the other side of the street in the mercantile shop" – he pointed with a thick finger out the batwing doors – "and gawd only knows what they thought. Some of the pups got sick at the sight and the smell; saw it myself. No wonder they was in such an all-fired hurry to git."

Sloan listened thoughtfully before taking another careful inventory around the room. The dead bodies that had littered the floor short days earlier were gone; the tables, chairs, broken bottles and beer glasses, scattered playing cards and poker chips, and assorted coins had long since been replaced or pocketed or simply discarded.

"Place looks empty," he said at last.

"Place *is* empty," Corn said sadly, and he poured himself a drink after refilling Sloan's glass. "The Army boys refused to set foot in here; orders, they told me. And now they're gone, and, well, nobody's left. It's tough to regrow a town, you know. No one wants to come back; everybody wants to forget.

"That's the pity. The place is empty and likely will stay so – and not a thing I kin do. You think that fool of a judge or the undertaker that got themselves shut of here 'fore the shooting started will ever come back and start again? Not likely."

Corn swatted at a fly, his eyes empty, his face blank.

"Still, a man's got to drink to something," Sloan said after a long silence. He looked at Corn and raised his glass. "Here's to death and rebirth – and to an amazing night full of stars. Have you taken a look outside?"

"I have not," Corn said.

"Then bring that bottle and we'll have a long look together."

Corn stared at Jack Sloan and laughed, for the first time in a long time. "I guess I'll drink to that."

Jasper Perkins had been on the trail from Twisted Junction for hours, working his way into the higher elevations of the Picacho Mountains, his thoughts darting in as many directions as there were brilliant stars in the night sky.

He did his best to ignore the pain in his shoulder from the bullet wound he had sustained days earlier while escaping from the renegade camp, where he was held hostage for two days. The easy escape still bothered him.

It's almost like they wanted me to git away, he thought. *That flying bullet was as much a mistake as it was anything else* – and he considered that possibility for some time.

He came to a fork in the path he had been following and urged the mule toward the northeast, taking a narrow game trail he knew well from searching for traces of gold in the unforgiving rocks. The mule, a bulky, stubborn beast with an uneasy disposition, snorted in protest, prompting Jasper to talk aloud to the animal in a scolding, biting tone.

"Listen up, you, and listen good, yes sir," he said. "You'd best behave yerself or I'll trade you in for a big horse. Or maybe I'll have you spend the day with that damn Doc Peterson and see how you like that, yes sir. That'd put an end to your crankiness."

Jasper snorted, mimicking the mule; the mule, unimpressed, brayed loudly as the grade in the trail began to increase, tugging incessantly toward the right side of the path, which forced Jasper to correct his animal's rambling route.

"Come on, mule," Jasper grumped. "Another hour or so and we'll be far enough shut of them Army boys so's not to give 'em anymore thought."

Jasper glanced up at the array of stars that cast a clear light on the twisty trail he was following into the high country, his mind suddenly shifting to Max Blake.

I know Max meant well when he dumped me back in Twisted Junction, he thought. *I know he was jest trying to make sure I was gonna be fit to fight again. But ...*

He looked ahead as the mule drifted off the trail again, and he cursed silently and tugged on the reins. "Come on, mule," he muttered. "No sense getting mad at me, no sir.

"But the next time I see Max Blake, I kin tell ya, he's gonna hear from me about what I kin handle and what I can't anymore. And he jest might be surprised."

First off, though, I gotta get this shoulder feelin' some better, he thought. *'Cause it don't feel too good right now.*

Jasper sighed deeply and forged ahead into the night, grumbling at the mule, certain in the conviction that he would run into his friend the federal marshal again – and he hoped that it would be soon.

"I tell ya, mule," he muttered. "Max Blake ain't seen nor heard the last of ol' Jasper Perkins, yes sir."

"You ever sit out in the desert at night and watch the shooting stars?"

Jay Silverbird looked across the buckboard at David Doucette as the two Aguante deputies rattled and bounced along on the front seat of a nondescript wagon built of plain oak boards that were stained dark crimson in spots. William Barber, late of the Oregon territories and a one-time reputed bank robber and medicine peddler who had made his way to Aguante months earlier, rattled and bounced along in the back.

William Barber was beyond noticing the condition of the trail or the wagon, however.

William Barber was beyond noticing anything at all.

"Now why in hell would you ask me a fool question like that?" Doucette replied at last. He eyed Silverbird curiously for a second or two and then stuck a stubby cigar back into his mouth and chewed at the end.

"I mean, jest what the hell kind of question is that to ask, Bird?" he said when no immediate answer was forthcoming. "Think about what we are doing right now, and you stop to ask me about shooting stars?"

Silverbird shrugged, a contented cat's smile crossing his face.

"Take a look at that sky," he said at last. "You ever see anything as pretty as that? I mean, fer as far as you kin see in any direction, the sky is just filled up with stars. Hell, it's a wonderful thing to behold, my friend. All we need is some shootin' stars up there, and we can run the deck on this night."

He looked over at his partner and added, "That's all I'm saying."

"That's what you think about when we cart a dead man out to the desert?"

"And jest what kin I do about that, Davey? The sheriff filled this man up with lead, and it's somehow our job to clean up. You want me to say I'm sorry about this Barber character? Hell, I didn't care much for Mr. Barber to begin with. He was slow in life, and he's slowing us down now in death."

"That all true enough, but it don't make it right to shoot the man in the back," Doucette said. "The whole thing is getting outta hand. You know I'm right, too."

"I ain't sayin' yer wrong. Hell, I agree with you: The whole thing is outta control and we both know it. But we been through this: What kin we do?"

"Besides clean up the mess, you mean?"

"Exactly."

"Well, hell, I don't know. That's the truth of it: Not one man among us knows what to do – less it's to sit and wait to see who the hammer falls on next."

"And hope to hell it ain't us."

"Right."

Silverbird brought the wagon to a halt, and he looked overhead again. The light from the moon lit a thin trail that snaked its way through clumps of Russian thistle and scrub brush. He stared in peaceful serenity at the night sky, enjoying the sight as though he were seeing it for the first time.

"There, look – did you see it, Davey?" Silverbird said suddenly, stabbing his finger up into the air and holding it there, pointing in the direction of the Big Dipper.

"See what?" Doucette grumped, looking about.

"The shooting star, you fool. Hell, it was right in front of yer face, were you only looking fer it."

"Didn't see a thing; don't want to see it, neither. Let's get this buggy moving – kin we jest agree to that?"

"No need," Silverbird said after a minute. "We've gone far enough, and it don't matter much to our dead friend in back whether we drop him here or somewheres else. Last time I checked, Mr. Barber weren't bent on talking much. Let's jest dump him here and take in the sky for a bit."

"You take it in all you want," Doucette said, climbing down from the buckboard. "I'm pulling that body out the back right now. You gonna help me?"

"Sure," Silverbird said. He, too, hopped down from the rickety seat and started around to the back of the wagon. "Ain't no use our making more outta this than's necessary."

They each grabbed a boot and pulled at the same time. Barber's body, which was leaking fluids from four bullet holes, skidded across the hard timbers; a second tug and a mighty toss from the two deputies brought it to a sudden thump on the sandy desert floor.

Silverbird looked down. "Amen to that."

"No need to say more," Doucette added, and they returned to their seat on the wagon.

They were silent for a moment. Silverbird continued to look up at the countless stars overhead; Doucette stared at nothing, chewing on the stub of his cigar, his mind running in circles at a problem that had no easy solutions.

Silverbird made no effort to move the wagon forward. Doucette didn't notice.

"I'll tell you what, Bird," he said after a long minute passed. "All we seem to do is clean up after the sheriff these days. He makes a mess; we clean it up. He can't control his temper; we clean it up. He loses his head at some dumb puncher like this one; we clean it up. He can't keep his hands off his gun; we clean it up."

He pulled the cigar stub out his mouth, tossed it hard into the desert, and looked intently at his partner. "I'm damn sick of cleaning up after the man, Bird. I don't want to do it no more."

Silverbird continued to stare up into the vast reaches of the heavens. He nodded after a moment, however, and said softly, as though talking to himself, "I think we ought to ride north, Davey Boy – right now. We know the Dieker brothers are up there somewheres, poking about. And who knows fer sure where Nash is off to? Other'n that, we kin move slowly and pick our way across to Denver, maybe, where we ain't much known and no one cares."

"Or we kin go to California," Doucette suggested. "I'd like to see some of that country again 'fore I pack it in."

"It don't matter none to me," Silverbird said.

"Just so long as we go," Doucette added.

The two men looked at each other and laughed.

"Yeah, it's time to git out," Silverbird said. "Live free or die."

Chapter 25

Connections and Reconnections

"Look sharp now, you two. I've a feelin' in me bones tonight."

Sgt. Maj. Michael McClinton spoke the words softly, the way a man would whisper into his lover's ear.

"Absolutely, sir: Whatever you say, sergeant major."

"Don't push it, Phelan; you either, O'Rourke, or I'll have ya both on horse detail for a month. It'll pay you two eejits to respect me hunches."

"But we already do, sir…"

"Just stay sharp and steady, the both of ya, till we hear what himself has to say."

"Yes, sir."

"If you don't mind me asking, sir, what sort of feeling do you have tonight?" Army Pvt. Matthew O'Rourke asked.

"It's the banging of them rocks down that wall behind us has me a bit on the touchy side," the sergeant major said. "Can't ya feel it, lads?"

"Yes, sir."

"Of course, sir. Absolutely."

O'Rourke and Army Pvt. Sean Phelan glanced quickly at each other with amused smiles but turned immediately serious again when they saw the stern look of disapproval.

"There's no time to play the fool, me boyos," McClinton snapped. "We're in a war of it, ya know – and a deadly serious one, it is."

McClinton studied the two enlisted men carefully – "I've got me eye on you half-wits," he muttered – before moving off into the shadows.

McClinton, working with Capt. Jed Johnson, had stationed guards to the left, center, and right of the squadron, and he was checking his men now. He knew that with the squadron close to Whiskey Bend, and a reported area sighting of the murdering gold thieves they were chasing, no lapses in security could be tolerated.

The mesa's vertical wall of solid rock immediately at his back provided both a comfort and a concern to McClinton. It was unlikely that an attack could be mounted from behind: It would take skilled climbers with ropes to manage that kind of assault. But a determined group of men stationed on top of the mesa could wait until daylight and fire down on the squadron with no possibility of retaliation.

Hell, they could pelt us with bloody rocks from above, he thought, *and drive us into the open. It would be a massacre in minutes.*

McClinton stopped to consider the predicament. It was unlikely that his commanding officer, Lt. Col. Michael Corbin, would alter his plans for the evening: reconnoiter the town, try to ascertain the location of the renegades – if, in fact, there were renegades nearby – and determine the logical next steps to take. McClinton wouldn't consider raising the issue with either Corbin or the squadron's second in command, Capt. Jed Johnson, in any event. He understood and accepted his role.

So it's left to me to see that we don't get surprised from above after all that clatterin' up there, he thought.

McClinton edged his away around the perimeter of defenses he had established to the east and considered the distance he would have to cover to skirt the vertical wall and find a trail to the top.

It'll take two hours or more on foot; less than half that time with a horse, he thought. He tried to make out the outline of the mesa's rim in the light cast by a crescent moon and a collection of brilliant stars. *Makes me wish I'd committed the lieutenant colonel's map to memory, or at least had one in me own back pocket for a quick peek.*

McClinton made his way back to the area where the horses were quartered among a nest of boulders and two long lengths of rope. "O'Flynn," he whispered.

"Right here, sir," Pvt. 1st Class Patrick O'Flynn said in muted reply.

"Saddle me horse: Make it quick now, Patrick, like a good lad."

"Yes, sir. Might I ask what the ..."

"No you may not. Just get it done, me bucko. I've a little errand to run is all."

McClinton quietly hailed 1st Sgt. Seamus Lennox, who had pulled himself to attention nearby when the sergeant major approached, and said: "Get the word passed to the sentries up and down the line. I'm going out fer a look up top. I'll be gone two hours or so, and no surprises on me return. Are you right there, Seamus?"

"Aye, sir."

175

Lennox snapped off a salute and disappeared into the darkness. McClinton could follow his progress by the clattering noises that his boots made against the rocky ground.

"Sure an' yer all set here, sir," O'Flynn said as he approached again and handed off the reins of McClinton's horse with a flourish. "Mind yer step in the dark, sir."

"You take care yerself; I don't want to be shot on me return," McClinton said. "I'll be comin' in from this direction, you understand" – he pointed with a gloved finger toward the east – "so watch for it. Am I right?"

"Yes, sir."

"No itchy fingers now, O'Flynn – "

"No sir."

McClinton shook his head in mild disgust and pulled himself into the saddle, ignoring the creaking of leather that carried far away on the night air. "You watch yourself, lad – and everything else around you."

"Yes, sir."

"All right. I'm off then and a fine thing it is."

Max Blake was adept at picking out unexpected sounds in the night, and he brought Buck to a halt and gave the rope attached to Richard Nash's horse a hard tug.

When Nash looked up, Max gestured for the wounded Aguante deputy to keep his mouth shut and his eyes open. Nash nodded in understanding and deliberately cocked his head to one side and then the other, trying to pick up stray sounds that might have attracted the marshal's attention seconds before.

He looked back at Max and saw that his captor was alert, his eyes moving rapidly about, sensing as much as hearing the various noises that carried across the darkness.

A moment went by, then another, and Max suddenly heard the sound again: the distinct clop of a horse's hooves against solid rock.

He glanced at Nash and pointed, but the outlaw already had picked it up and nodded, pointing in the same direction, his teeth gritted tightly against the stabbing pain in his wounded hand.

Max made another series of gestures – *stay still and stay silent* were close approximations – and Nash nodded as Max climbed down from Buck, quickly tied the rope that was attached to Nash's horse around a young sapling, and vanished.

Richard Nash sighed deeply. He was in a hard place, and he knew it. An attempt at escape would likely mean a sudden death; and even if he did manage to get away, he was convinced that without immediate medical aid, the gunshot wound to his hand would quickly kill him regardless.

There's no use making a run for it, he thought after a minute – *not with my hand shot to pieces. Blake would kill me in no time, and I'd be beyond caring. Best I can do is stay low here, find the Army doctor, and take my chances on down the trail.*

Then I kin get the drop on Max Blake.

Sgt. Major Michael McClinton had been on the trail for forty minutes or more, carefully picking his way across a landscape strewn with large rocks, shale, sheets of scree and talus that covered vast acres, and enormous boulders – all interspersed with sweet grass and Russian thistle and an occasional twisted and stocky scrub pine – when he felt the cold steel barrel of a revolver pressed into his side.

"A sudden move'll be yer last," a voice hissed.

McClinton nodded but said nothing. He was careful to keep his eyes ahead and his hands cupped over the pommel of his saddle, gently holding the reins.

"Yer one of them soldier boys, I take it."

"Was it the uniform that gave me away then?" McClinton asked calmly.

"Don't git smart with me, old man. There's two ways you come outta this, and only one of 'em's any good. Me? I don't care one way or t'other. What's it gonna be?"

"What do you want?" McClinton asked.

"I'm hunting a man."

"Would that be me then?"

"Course it ain't. Why would I hunt an old Army jackal like you?"

"If yer not hunting me, laddie, why are ya standing there with a gun stuck in me very ribs?"

"Thought you might've seen the man I'm after. He's a federal marshal named Blake. He's in the area – close by, I think – and he'd likely find the lot of you. Leastwise, that's what I'd do if I was in his boots."

McClinton paused for a moment to collect his thoughts. "I've heard of yer man Blake all right," he said at last. "Most folks have, and well you know it. But I've never seen the man and wouldn't be after knowing him." He looked to his right at the man who was pushing the revolver into his ribs and added, "I'm sorry to disappoint you, lad."

"So what are you doin' out here, away from yer – "

McClinton was startled by a sudden flash, a glint of cold steel, and the thump of a revolver crashing down on the head of the man who had been holding him hostage, and he stared wide-eyed as the gunman slumped to the ground.

"Easy now; no sudden moves," a second voice said.

McClinton nodded but said nothing, unsure whether he should rejoice or curse this new turn.

"You're a bit far afield from the rest of the squadron," Max Blake said, a statement rather than a question.

McClinton nodded but again offered no reply.

"You were heading up top because you heard the rocks on the mesa walls awhile back," Max said quietly. "You wanted to make sure the perimeter was controlled."

McClinton's surprise showed in his face, and he cocked his head to one side but remained silent.

"How long since you left Ireland?" Max asked after a moment.

McClinton looked sharply toward his new captor. "Yer a gypsy, is it, and can read the future and the past and a man's mind as well? What's this all about then? And who are you now to save me from that blighter in one instant and torment me in the next?"

"It's all right, sergeant major," Max said. "I'm a federal marshal; my name's Blake. I sent out a call for you, or someone like you, by pushing those rocks off the mesa wall."

"Yer the same Max Blake this pup you just thumped is after, I take it?" McClinton asked.

"One and the same," Max said.

"Well then, Max Blake, I'm a happy man to meet ya, and me commanding officer'll be a happy man as well. He's been looking fer you the better part of four days or more – ever since we heard yer name in Twisted Junction."

Max thought about the connections for a few seconds and said, "You've talked with the sheriff there and are after the stolen Army gold."

"Ah, you've a right bright head on yer shoulders, Max Blake. Me name's McClinton; you know me rank, I gather, from the stripes on me shirt. And to answer yer question, it's a long time indeed since I left me mother's home in Ireland.

"So let me ask then: Who in the name of sweet Jaysus is this lad lyin' here on the ground?"

Max lowered his Colt as McClinton climbed down off his horse and stretched.

"His name's Bolton. He's a former deputy who worked for Sheriff Clark in Twisted Junction. Clark sacked him some days back, and he's been tracking me since."

"And why would he be after trackin' you?"

"That's a question I'll have to ask him when he comes around."

Max prodded Bolton's rigid body with the toe of his boot. Satisfied that he was still unconscious, he turned to McClinton and asked, "Who's your commanding officer?"

"That would be Lt. Col. Michael Corbin," McClinton said.

"Of course," Max said, almost to himself. "Send the best to catch the worst."

"You know the man then, I take it?"

"Only by reputation," Max said. "You boys are the Army's troubleshooters for the territory – you've made quite a name for yourselves."

"The same can be said about Max Blake," McClinton said.

Max shrugged. "I've got a prisoner stashed out there. Keep an eye on this one while I bring the man in. Then we can talk with your Lt. Col. Corbin," Max said.

"Do you need a hand, Max Blake?" McClinton asked.

"Funny you should mention hand," Max said. "Just give me a minute and see for yourself."

Chapter 26

The Start of a Plan

Max Blake climbed down from his chestnut gelding and gave Buck a quick check as a half-dozen soldiers, following Sgt. Major Michael McClinton's orders, secured the two prisoners.

Tom Bolton was groggy from the rap he took to the back of his head; it was doubtful that he knew what had transpired since he stuck his revolver into McClinton's ribs an hour earlier, thinking that he had the advantage, and awoke instead strapped across the saddle of his horse.

Richard Nash's wounded hand continued to throb and ache; he had momentarily removed the shirtsleeve covering the wound and was startled to see that the area around the gunshot already had turned an ugly blackish purple and crimson. He was now convinced that only immediate attention could save it.

"I demand to see a doctor," he sputtered as he was pulled off his horse by Pvt. 1st Class Brendan McMullen.

Handling a man of Nash's stature was an easy chore for McMullen. He was as strong as he was tall and solid, with rippling muscles that his uniform could barely contain and little tolerance for annoying or offensive civilians – traits he immediately attached to the Aguante deputy.

"You'll make no demands of me, ya snipe," McMullen said. "You'll do as yer told and no more – and make no mistake, the sergeant major will do the tellin' and not you. Do you understand me, bucko?"

"I'm telling you, I need a doctor," Nash complained bitterly. "That man over there" – he pointed at Max Blake, who was still looking carefully at Buck – "damn near shot my hand off."

"You'll bugger off till I tell you different," McMullen said. "Fer all I care, that hand of yers…"

"...could use some lookin' after," McClinton finished as he approached the two men, now standing inches apart.

"I appreciate yer concern, Brendan darlin', but what kind of hosts would we be if we didn't offer our guest some Army hospitality?"

McMullen sniffed as McClinton poked Nash's arm with a giant fist and added, "Am I right, sir?"

"Look, have all the fun you want, but I demand to see a doctor," Nash said. "And I mean right now."

McClinton looked the man over and shook his head, as though he were dealing with a recalcitrant child. "See here, me little man," he said at last, "I'd be only after too happy to accommodate yer needs. But what makes you think we freight a doctor around to look after the likes of you – and you just wandering by?"

Nash looked confused. "I was lead to believe that – that ..."

"You shouldn't believe everything you are told," Max Blake said as he approached the group. He stared hard at Nash, whose expression was rapidly turning from puzzled to angry, and then at Tom Bolton, who was standing silently nearby, a wide smile on his face but a vacant look in his eyes.

"Even so," Max added, directing his gaze again toward McClinton, "your field surgeon might have a look at these two just the same."

"Yer right, Marshal Blake," McClinton said. "Yer after catching me havin' a bit of gaff with the lads is all."

Max nodded. "I'd appreciate seeing Lt. Col. Corbin as well."

"The word's been sent that yer here, Marshal Blake. I expect he'll be with you shortly."

Max nodded. He looked across at Bolton again and gave some thought to a series of questions when the soldiers around him snapped to attention.

"Ah, the famous Max Blake," Corbin said as he approached, providing a quick salute to his men and then holding out his hand. "It's long passed the time when we met."

Max took the man's hand, noticed the powerful grip, and answered with one of his own. "A pleasure. Your reputation precedes you."

"Ah, reputations. We both have much to talk about then. Is it true that you've been feuding with your judge, Marshal Blake?"

Max's eyes registered a tight smile. "And you'd rather be called President Corbin than Gen. Corbin," he replied.

Corbin's face broke into a wide grin. "I see that we know each other well. Very good, indeed."

The two men held each other's hard gaze for a moment, like prize fighters assessing an opponent's strengths. Corbin turned at last toward the two prisoners and scowled. "Which one of you is from Aguante?"

Nash stepped forward. "I'd offer a salute, but this man you seem so anxious to know damn near shot my hand off," he said. "I demand to see a doctor and …"

"Quiet," Corbin snapped. The simple command stopped Nash immediately. "You are a common criminal and will get no quarter here. You'll fare best if you keep your mouth shut; do I make myself clear?"

Nash started to protest, thought better of it when he caught the look on Corbin's face, and nodded but said nothing.

Corbin then looked toward Tom Bolton, who grinned back disarmingly. "Is this man all right?" Corbin asked. "He looks, well, off in the head somehow."

"I col'-cocked him when he held a gun on your sergeant major," Max offered.

Corbin turned to McClinton and waved his hand toward the two prisoners. "Have the doctor look after these two, sergeant major. Then secure them and post extra guards. The patrols are starting to come in, and I expect to be on the move inside an hour. Get 'em cracking, Mickey.

"Marshal Blake?" he said, turning toward Max again. "Let's move across the way and see if we can learn something from each other."

Sheriff John Hawkins walked the back alleys of Whiskey Bend, listening intently to the various sounds that drifted in on the chilly early morning air.

He had been patrolling the streets for hours, cautiously watching for any sign of suspicious activity, silently blending into the darkness that surrounded him. The saloon had closed an hour earlier, and the only lights he had spotted since were the two at the livery stables behind him and the small glow of a lantern from his office window.

The town was boarded shut, with no one about, and yet he still could sense pending trouble – *something evil,* he thought.

He looked toward the east and could almost percieve a gathering force near the mesa.

He turned toward the south and closed his eyes, and a chill ran through him. *They're still out there – close by, too. Waiting.* He instinctively put his right hand on his revolver and found some comfort in the familiar feel of the holstered Remington.

Hawkins edged away from the corner of the shed he had used for momentary cover and made his way through the alley past the back ends of a series of ramshackle buildings. His night vision, aided by the startling light of a sliver of moon and a sky full of brilliant stars, was exceptional. Yet he saw nothing out of the ordinary: pieces of his shadow as he walked, the silent passing of a mongrel behind the steakhouse, an occasional sailing cloud that momentarily obscured the moon.

I can't spot it, but it's out there all right, he thought – *somewhere in the night.*

Hawkins cautiously made his way back to his office and silently closed the door when he entered. His deputy, Bob Stebner, a fixture for years in Whiskey Bend, was asleep in a chair in the corner, and Hawkins went over and gently shook him awake.

Stebner's eyes popped open with a start, and he looked wildly about the room for an instant before finding Hawkins' face. "Whoah. You startled me, sheriff. Gawd a'mighty – is everything all right?"

"You'd best get up and stay sharp, Bob," Hawkins said. "I've got a feeling that something's about to break out there. We should get outside and keep an eye on it – whatever it is."

"Your feelings are as good as a preacher's word for me," Stebner said as he roused himself from the chair and stretched. "You think that renegade bunch is comin' in at last, maybe?"

Hawkins shrugged. "Might be the renegades are tired of waiting to move on us; might be something else entirely. I can't get my hands around it yet."

"It could be the Army boys you sent fer, sheriff," Stebner said hopefully. "We could do with a break."

Hawkins thought about it for a minute, running his hands through his hair. "Let's just say I wouldn't count on it. But whatever it is – whatever's coming – we'd best get ready and get the men on alert."

"I jest wish the trouble'd wait till I git me a good night's sleep; that ain't asking too much," Stebner said as he followed the sheriff out the door and into the street.

"You'll have plenty of time for sleep when this is over."

"You make it sound like it'd be fer good, sheriff," Stebner snapped. "I ain't interested in that kind of sleep. I'm jest thinking forty winks is all."

Federal Marshal Max Blake and Lt. Col. Michael Corbin had talked for an hour.

The conversation started out casually, with each man recounting people and places the other would know and could connect to. Corbin talked in long sentences; he was surprised that Max Blake was a man of few words.

The discussion soon turned to the band of gold thieves terrorizing the area, Max's assessment of the strengths of the outlaw group, his surprise at hearing what had taken place in Adobe Flats, and ideas about what might be done to bring the renegades to justice. And as the two men sipped coffee from battered tin cups, surrounded by armed sentries, the hint of a plan began to form in the agile mind of the federal marshal.

"I might have something," Max said after a moment of thoughtful silence passed. "But understand that this pack and the gold are your concern; my business is elsewhere – in Aguante."

Corbin nodded. "We've been aware of the mess there for some time," he offered. "But with Apache raids and border assaults and that series of range wars, and now one bunch after another of renegades and roving thieves – well, it just hasn't been high on the Army's list of concerns."

"Maybe we can help each other."

"How so, marshal?"

Max set his coffee tin down and leaned closer, looking directly into Corbin's dark eyes. "You've heard of putting all the rotten eggs in a single basket?"

Corbin looked puzzled. "Certainly," he said. "It's a time-honored adage; and in many cases, I suppose, it makes sense. How does it apply here?"

Max shrugged, as though the answer were apparent. "Why not drive the renegades into Aguante?" he asked simply.

Corbin stared blankly for a second. "Say that again."

"All I'm suggesting is that ..."

"... is that we put all of our rotten eggs in a single basket," Corbin finished.

"Exactly," Max said. "Aguante's the right basket."

Corbin sat back and let out a low whistle.

"It's a bold step, I'll give you that," he said at last. "But I'm not sure how it benefits us, marshal. Won't it make our job twice as difficult? By your own assessment, there are thirty or forty of the renegades in all. There must be three times that many able men in Aguante – perhaps more."

Max nodded. "Based on what I saw, five or six are top guns and the rest likely know their way around a fight. You'd have your hands full, all right."

"So what do we gain?" Corbin asked. "It seems to me that we would just make the job that much harder."

"How many men do you command?" Max asked.

"There's thirty with me now," Corbin replied, "Every one's a top fighter, of course: well-trained, field-tested, tough. You said it yourself: We're the best of the best."

"How many more men are at your disposal with a single wire sent by telegraph out of Whiskey Bend?" Max asked.

"As many as I want or need, I'd guess – the rest of my squadron, certainly … a regiment if I wanted one," Corbin said, and the pieces that Max Blake laid out on the table suddenly fell into place.

"I see. Yes, this could be momentous. Running down these renegades would make the Eastern newspapers. But cleaning up the most corrupt town in the territory at the same time?" His face lit up in a wide grin. "That's more than a newspaper headline, Marshal Blake. That's a stepping stone – and perhaps a big one."

Max picked up his coffee tin again. "Well, there's that," he said. "From my view, we clean up one mess by cleaning up another. If you buy in, all I want is to handle the Aguante sheriff."

"I don't have any problem with that. For all I care, you can string him up or shoot him full of holes – or both, or worse. But understand that this will be an Army operation, Marshal Blake."

"It's all yours, including the glory," Max said. "My concern is Reno Walker. As for the rest of it – well, the rest is up to you."

Lt. Col. Michael Corbin started to laugh. He clapped his hands together and laughed even harder. "The more I think about this, the better I like it," he said at last.

"I'd suggest we find Sheriff Hawkins in Whiskey Bend and get an assessment from him about the renegades," Max offered. "After that…"

"… after that it's textbook Army," Corbin said. "With credit, of course, Marshal Blake – with much credit due."

Max shrugged. "All I want is to shut down Aguante."

"Then let's do exactly that."

Corbin picked up his coffee tin and extended it toward Max.

"Here's to success," he said. "Success and glory."

Chapter 27

An Alignment of Resources

As the muted colors of a reticent morning sun began to slowly rise against the back of the mesa, casting long shadows across the high desert, Lt. Col. Michael Corbin's fighters struck out in a double column toward Whiskey Bend.

Max Blake, the federal marshal from Twin Forks, rode next to Corbin near the head of the column. Capt. Jed Johnson rode immediately behind the two men.

Close to the rear, between four well-armed Army regulars, were Richard Nash, the Aguante deputy sent to kill Max Blake, and Tom Bolton, the former Twisted Junction deputy who had tried to settle a score with the federal marshal that only he understood. Both men were disappointed with their efforts. In addition to becoming Army prisoners, Nash's right hand was festering from a gunshot wound, and Bolton was slow to recover, hours later, from a crashing blow to the head that left him uncomprehending and mute.

The squadron's surgeon was a commissioned officer affectionately called Doc Sawbones.

Capt. Lewis Sayre was a career Army officer and surgeon with deep-set blue eyes that commanded attention and a face that might have been copied from the likeness on an ancient coin. He was more than six feet in height and was as interested in maneuvers and precision drills as he was in healing soldiers wounded in action. He made quick decisions in the field, and he knew when to let nature take its course – a trait that set him apart from other physicians who had learned their craft on the battlefields of Antietam and Gettysburg and similar places of slaughter during the Civil War.

Sayre met with Corbin before the squadron assembled for the march into Whiskey Bend. He expressed general optimism about saving Nash's hand after a bullet from Max Blake's Winchester had passed through it and the wound quickly became infected. He confessed, however, to being less certain about Bolton's condition.

"Some details then, Sawbones, on both," Corbin said.

"I've cleaned Nash's wound and provided him with a decent field dressing, sir," Sayre said. "The next few days will tell, but with luck and a constant eye, he should recover."

"So he'll have two hands when he hangs," Corbin said. "Fine. How about the other one – Bolton? What's his condition?"

"It's hard to put a finger on the problem, sir," Sayre replied. "He's fit enough to travel, but I'm not certain that he knows where he is or why he's here. Then again, I can't be certain that he isn't faking a medical condition."

"An interesting proposition," Corbin mused. He watched the flight of a distant bird for a moment, weighing myriad possibilities, trying to determine in his own mind whether Bolton was clever enough to outsmart his field surgeon. "Let's assume that he isn't faking, as you put it, captain: Have you seen this sort of thing before?"

"Once or twice, sir, and generally they come around in a day or two," the doctor said. "But Bolton looks as though he might have been problematic before this, which complicates the issue. I'll keep him under observation, of course; but there's not a lot I can do for him in field conditions, and your guess is as good as mine as to how it'll end."

"Fair enough, Sawbones; do your best," Corbin said. He considered the situation for a moment, his eyes hooded in thought, and added: "Perhaps you can find some help in Whiskey Bend. I don't want it said that the Army didn't do all it could in this matter. Newspaper people are apt to ask questions about this sort of thing."

"Yes, sir."

Corbin turned to Max Blake, who had been listening to the conversation. "What's your take on this man, marshal?" he asked. "Do you think Bolton can outsmart us?"

Max thought about Tom Bolton for a moment: his first encounter with the deputy in Twisted Junction weeks back, his later discussion with Ned Clark about the man, and the attack that Bolton had mounted on Max short days ago. *What I don't know about Tom Bolton could fill a good-sized book,* he thought.

"I didn't hit him hard enough to cause serious damage, or at least I didn't think so," he said at last. "But Ned Clark indicated that Bolton had been thumped weeks earlier by a back-shooter named Grant."

Max stopped for a second and shrugged his shoulders, looking toward Sayre. "It just might be …"

"… that the combination of the two blows caused serious damage," the doctor said, finishing Max's observation. "That information will give me something else to think about, Marshal Blake."

"You can treat an injury of this type?" Corbin asked.

"Not like you can set a broken bone, no sir," he said. "The best I can do is watch him carefully and see if he responds beyond that smirk he likes to show. Time, and rest, will do the work for us – if, in fact, it needs to be done at all."

"You'll keep me appraised," Corbin said, a command rather than a question.

"Absolutely, sir."

Corbin nodded and refocused his energies as the doctor moved away. "I've been giving some attention to your proposed plan, Marshal Blake," he said. "I've considered a number of options and have planned for several changes …"

"It seems likely that any course you take will depend on what Sheriff Hawkins tells us," Max replied.

"I'm afraid I don't follow."

"Hawkins has seen this bunch – and recently. For all we know, the renegades moved into his town after your scouts passed by last night and are waiting there now."

"I hardly think that would be the case. Not after what our …"

"I'm sure the sheriff in Adobe Flats would have told you the same thing, but he's not talking."

"Yes, I see your point." Corbin looked thoughtful for a moment, his eyes intently focused on a distant point on the horizon. "So what do you propose, Marshal Blake?"

Max looked puzzled. "I'm surprised you'd ask."

"I'm not above asking for help from expert sources – and I consider you to be an expert source."

"Fair enough. Send out four scouts for a final look," Max said after some thought. "Two ride into town; the other two watch. If things appear normal, move ahead. If things change after the scouts leave, the two in the field raise the alarm. That way, you lose two men – four at worst – and not your squadron."

"You'd make a fine commanding officer, Marshal Blake," Corbin said after a minute of reflection. "You might want to consider a military career. The Army would covet a skilled fighter like yourself – a man who knows the territory and the hostiles who invade it."

Max arched his eyebrows and looked hard at Corbin. "I've found it easier to deal with the Indians in the territory – the hostiles, as you call them – than with the killers I've tracked for the judge." Max shifted his weight and added, "You might want to consider that if you ever make it to the White House."

Corbin gave Max another appraising gaze as the marshal slowly climbed into the saddle. Max scratched at Buck's ears and patted the chestnut gelding's neck reassuringly, holding his eyes on the lieutenant colonel.

"I'd love to continue the conversation, marshal," Corbin said as he pulled himself up and nudged his horse forward.

"That's the politician in you. My only interest is bringing outlaws to justice."

Corbin found Capt. Jed Johnson with his eyes and waved his hand forward, and the squadron quickly began to assemble in marching formation before moving ahead.

"We'll see what this Hawkins has to offer," he said.

"Providing he's still alive."

The morning sun had lifted over the top of the mesa, chasing the shadows and searing the air with a wind-fueled heat that baked the earth. Max looked off to the south and thought for an instant that he detected the glint of metal in the distance. But he saw nothing more, even though he continued to watch for signs as the squadron pushed ahead, kicking up a ribbon of dust into the high desert air.

Sheriff John Hawkins followed a train of trail dust off in the distance with deep-set blood-shot eyes as he stared intently from a second-floor window of the Whiskey Bend Hotel.

Hawkins was looking east, toward the distant mesa that framed the town, watching for half an hour or more. He had been awake for three straight days, but his concentration remained sharp.

The hotel afforded him a perfect view of the rolling landscape to the east and south of Whiskey Bend. Hawkins knew that the trails leading to the more prosperous settlements in the territory – places like Twisted Junction and Twin Forks – lead directly east. The renegade band that had terrorized the area for days had been spotted and scouted south of the settlement.

Hawkins determined that trouble would most likely come from the south and that help in any form, if it came at all, would arrive from the east, where he had sent an answering telegraph to a lieutenant colonel named Corbin.

He looked back to the south again, willing himself to spot something – anything at all – that he could identify as a threat. But the land looked empty and desolate for as far as he could see, and he shrugged and turned to follow the dust trail again.

Someone's coming, he thought. *A lot of someones, likely. It might be this Corbin. Then again, it might be the renegades, circling to set a trap.*

Above the mesa, large white cumulus clouds were stacked like cords of firewood set aside for winter. *There's like to be a thunder storm later today,* Hawkins thought. *That might be of some help, if it's bad news that's out there.*

Hawkins turned and walked quickly from the hotel room, taking the wooden stairs two at a time to ground level. Dennis Whitlock looked up from behind the hotel's counter as Hawkins walked past, and he nodded at the sheriff, straightening the starched collar of his white shirt at the same time.

"See anything of interest, sheriff?" he asked.

"Someone's coming our way – from the east," Hawkins replied. "Can't tell yet if it's good news or bad, but we'll find out soon enough."

A look of concern crossed Whitlock's face. "Should I … I mean, should we …"

"No need to get worked up till there's something to get worked up about. I'll let you know, Dennis, but things are on the move, so don't wander too far. And you'd best keep a rifle handy – just in case. There's a chance we'll need it."

"All right, sheriff; that seems like good advice."

"Thanks for the use of the lookout."

"Any time, sheriff. No need to ask," Whitlock said as he reached under the counter in search of his shotgun.

Hawkins moved out of the hotel and found his deputy, Bob Stebner, on the opposite side of the dusty street, engaged in conversation with three men near the steps of the general store. Hawkins nodded to the others and said softly to Stebner, "Time to move, Bob. We're about to get company."

"What is it, sheriff?" Frosty Bell asked, stepping forward. He was a gentle man with brooding eyes and a wild beard who took his name after riding into town during a late-season blizzard with so much ice and snow frozen to his face that hot towels provided by the town's barber were needed to thaw him out.

"Riders are coming in from the east," Hawkins said. "From the dust trail, it might be thirty men or more."

"It's likely the Army boys you sent for," Bell said. "High time, I say, what with the renegade pack so close and all."

"I'd like to think you're right, Frosty," Hawkins replied. "But I'm not one to take chances."

Stebner, anxious to act, asked, "You want me to fetch up the reinforcements, sheriff?"

"Let's line up every able man we can find, starting with these three" – and he pointed toward Bell, Leon Austinson, and Neil McGill, all longtime freighters who had been in Whiskey Bend since its founding. "How 'bout it, boys: You up for a little show of force?"

"It's past time you asked, sheriff," Austinson said. "Just say where and when and I'll be there. My hands shake some, but I kin use a door jamb to steady up my aim all right."

"I stand with you, sheriff," McGill said.

"And that goes for me," Bell added.

"Good. Knock on every door you see and raise every gun you can. If we station men in every door and window along Main Street, we at least won't be surprised at whatever comes our way."

"Sounds good to me, sheriff," Stebner said. "I'll get right on it."

"You mean we'll git right on it," Bell said.

"Get going then," Hawkins added. "We've got thirty minutes or less before our visitors ride right through the front door. I want to be ready for 'em."

"Let's jest hope it's the Army and not that other bunch."

"Let's hope," Hawkins said. "But let's be ready in case it goes the other way."

Twenty minutes later, Army Scouts Brendan McMullen and Seamus Lennox approached Whiskey Bend from the east, cautiously eyeing every building they could see from the far edge of town.

"What do you think, Brendan?"

"Hard to say, me boyo," he replied. "If we ride through, we are like to get our arse's shot off – pardon me Irish – and fer no good reason."

"And if we don't, we are just as like to get 'em shot off by yer man Lt. Col. Corbin."

"Aye, it's a hard place we've been put in, Seamus."

"That's the truth of it."

As the two sat on their horses, debating whether to make a wild dash through the dusty main street, a lone man stepped out from a door in the middle of the cluster of ramshackle buildings that marked the town's immediate center and began walking slowly toward them.

"It looks like we've got company then, Brendan."

"Indeed," Brendan replied. "Who do you suppose we're lookin' at, then?"

"Yer guess is as good as me own."

"I was thinkin' the same."

"Given and taken it's the town sheriff."

"Given."

"Taken."

John Hawkins could hear some of the banter as he approached, and he called out loudly: "We've got twenty rifles trained on the two of you – more on the way. State your intentions."

"We're with Lt. Col. Michael Corbin's squadron. I believe you sent for us, sir," McMullen called. "The lieutenant colonel wants us to assess the town – to make sure yer not overrun with renegades, as he puts it."

"Well, that makes sense enough. My name is Hawkins. I'm the town sheriff."

"That's the way yer man described it, all right," McMullen called back.

"My man? What man? Who are you talking about?"

"Why, yer man Max Blake, the federal marshal," McMullen replied and turned to Lennox. "What's the name of the place this fella Blake hails from, is it, so I kin tell the man?"

"How the devil should I know? It's yer job to ..."

"You are riding with Marshal Blake?" Hawkins interrupted impatiently.

"Right you are. He's back with the rest of the lads as we speak, sir."

"Come along then," Hawkins replied. "But just so you know, we'll keep the rifles trained on the lot of you, or at least until I see Max Blake."

The pair nodded before galloping back toward the squadron, picking up the two additional scouts along the way.

"Can you imagine the look on himself's face when I tell the man a show of force is all we git for our efforts to help?" McMullen called.

"Imagine the insolence."

"Some people have no sense."

"True enough," Seamus added.

"And it's this fella Blake that impresses the man. I'm tellin' ya, Seamus, Army life is far harder than I ever thought possible."

Chapter 28

The Ticking Clock

John Hawkins was a fastidious man who appreciated punctuality, good grooming, manners, civility, and a positive attitude.

His attire was always immaculate – from the cut of his trim black Stetson, which he wore straight ahead and low above his eyes, to the polished shine on his two-toned leather boots. He favored dark, laundered trousers and white shirts tied at the neck with an inch-wide black ribbon that he fashioned into a bow tie each morning, always taking the time to ensure that the loops he produced were perfect in size and shape.

He liked to think that his conduct, and the way he treated the good people around him, reflected both on himself and his town.

At the same time, Hawkins loathed laziness, sloppiness, avarice, those with a disdain for women, and the ill-treatment of animals large and small. He didn't care much for drinkers or gamblers, though he tolerated them as a means of financial security, and he was especially unbending on drifters with no apparent means of livelihood or support.

He took an immediate dislike to Richard Nash, the Aguante deputy who was quickly deposited into the Whiskey Bend jail.

"That's no lawman," he told the Army regulars who accompanied Nash once the squadron arrived in Whiskey Bend, dusty but well-rested after a night spent at the base of the towering mesa east of the settlement. "It's clear that this man is little more than a hard-shell criminal."

"Easy what you say," Nash said in turn. "You can talk direct at me, you know, and not jest at these Army slobs. I can even answer questions on my own. And I got me a badge – just like the one you carry."

"You'll do well to keep your mouth closed until you are spoken to,

194

sir," Hawkins replied. "And that's going to be a long time coming." He looked intently at Nash for a moment and added, "I trust that we understand each other now."

Hawkins was less sure about what to make of Tom Bolton, who was safely deposited in a jail cell next to Richard Nash and retained a wide, grinning smile on his simple face. But the man had a vacant look in his eyes, and Hawkins had the feeling that if he knocked on Bolton's door, no one would be there to answer.

"How did you get mixed up in all of this, son?" Hawkins asked of Bolton after the soldiers left and only Bob Stebner, the Whiskey Bend deputy, remained behind. But Bolton's reply was a gap-toothed grin that was both disturbing to witness and as constant as the rising of the sun in the east.

"I'd say that boy is off in the head somehow," Stebner offered after a moment of reflection. "He sure don't look or act right to me anyhow, sheriff."

"If you want my opinion …"

"I warned you once, Mr. Nash. I won't abide having to speak with you again, sir," Hawkins said sternly. He looked intently at the man, gauging his eyes the way a mountain cat judges a potential meal, before he turned toward Stebner again.

"It might be you're right, Bob," Hawkins replied. "Then again, it might be an act – a way for this fella to try and cheat the gallows. But we'll get it straight in time."

"Time is something that we don't have a lot of," Max Blake said as he walked into the sheriff's office after tending to his horse at the town livery. He stepped into the small room in the back where four cells were lined against a wall of heavy oak timbers, his eyes taking in the strength of the bars and the locks on the narrow entry doors.

"Marshal Blake: It's a genuine pleasure to see you again, and so soon at that," Hawkins said, extending his hand. "You remember my deputy?"

Max nodded toward Stebner. "It's good to see you both again."

Stebner smiled broadly, and the three men left Nash and Bolton behind and moved into the main office.

"It was a relief to see you riding in with the Army, Marshal Blake," Hawkins said. "Considering what's nearby, it's a pleasure, in fact – though something of a surprise.

"What's your assessment of this Army outfit, marshal?"

"You did the right thing by calling them in," Max said. "The commanding officer, a man named Corbin, will be along in a minute and you can judge for yourself."

"From the way they paraded through as they rolled in, you'd think the man was running for some sort of elected office," Hawkins said.

"You'd be closer to the truth than you know," Max said. "But he's a good soldier – a good man, too, I suspect – and his outfit is filled with fighting men."

Hawkins nodded, grateful for Max's assessment. "That's reassuring, marshal. I'm mighty glad to hear it."

He paused and picked up a sheet of paper from his desk, using it as a fan to chase some of the heat away from his face.

"Our livery man is taking care of your horse then?" he asked after a minute.

"The place is packed with your people and a handful of soldiers. Buck seems to be in good hands," Max said.

"Good. That's fine, Marshal Blake."

"You want some coffee, marshal – or something stronger maybe?" Stebner asked. "I kin fix you up with just about anything you like."

"No thanks."

"Listen, marshal," Stebner said, "I know you want to get into this business about the renegades and all, and the sheriff and me is anxious to tell you what we know ..."

"Let's just wait till the cavalry shows up," Max said. "Then we can go over it together."

The three sat in silence for a moment.

"The Army boys are taking their own sweet time of it," Hawkins said at last. "Is the man waiting for drums to beat or a horn to blow?"

"Just like 'em, you ask me," Stebner added. "Why, I remember the last time ..."

The front door swung open at that moment, and Lt. Col. Michael Corbin and Capt. Jed Johnson walked purposefully into the office. Stebner let his remark hang in the air, waiting and watching carefully.

"I believe you sent for these gentlemen, sheriff," Max said by way of casual introduction.

"I did, indeed, and am glad to see you both," Hawkins said, standing and shaking hands briefly with both men. "My name's Hawkins; I'm the town sheriff."

"I'm Lt. Col. Corbin. This is Capt. Johnson. We received your telegraph in Twisted Junction, sir, and are here to help."

"This man here" – Hawkins pointed with a gloved thumb – "is my deputy, Bob Stebner."

After another round of handshakes, Hawkins looked again at Max and said, "I still don't understand how you got mixed up with the Army, marshal."

Max shrugged. "Not a lot to it, really."

"Let's just say we were heading in the same direction," Corbin said, anxious to take control of the conversation.

"Sheriff, your telegraph sounded urgent, and I brought my squadron in as fast as we could get here. I'm anxious to hear what you saw and what you know – and why you called for a lot of guns. The renegades are heavily armed, I take it?"

Hawkins sat again behind the wooden desk and indicated that the others should pull up chairs as well. Stebner went to the door, looked out on the street in both directions, and stood watch as the two soldiers and Max Blake pulled up simple wooden chairs and sat patiently while Hawkins fiddled with a coffee cup.

"Well, we wanted the wire to get your attention – and it did, which is a good thing," Hawkins said.

"Then the message was a fabrication?" Johnson asked.

"A fabrication? No, hardly that. The wire was fact, all right, Capt. Johnson – do I have that right?" Johnson nodded, and Hawkins grunted. "I've seen this gang first-hand, gentlemen. I wish I had not; there's no fabrication in that."

Corbin immediately warmed up to the man. "In you own words, then – if you please, Sheriff Hawkins," he said, his arms extended as though waiting for an orchestra to follow his lead.

"Three days ago, maybe four, a freighter by name of … aw, what's the man's name again, Bob? I don't see him often enough to recall …"

"You mean ol' Kevin Lee?" Stebner called over his shoulder.

"Yeah, exactly, Kevin Lee. I only see him three, maybe four, times a year, and a man tends to forget names and such.

"Anyways," Hawkins continued, "Lee comes running in here like he had a fright. He starts jabbering at me, and I tell him, 'Hey, slow down, ol' boy, and tell me what's got you so excited.' He sits down, right where you are now, and tells me about bringing in a load of lumber from north of here when he spots this column of dust off in the distance.

"Well sir, he slows down and finally gets out his spotting glass. He takes a look and figures he's watching thirty men, maybe more – his words again, you understand – with two wagons loaded up. The men are armed to the teeth, apparently guarding whatever's in the wagons, and

Lee tells me everyone one of 'em looks to be nothing less than a crack shot."

Hawkins took a sip of coffee then and noticed for the first time that his guests had not been invited to join in.

"I'm sorry; you boys surely want some of Bob's coffee here. Bob makes a decent pot, you understand. Hey, Bob" – he called loudly, and Stebner turned from watching the door and glanced back at Hawkins – "would you get our guests some of your brew?"

"Please continue, sheriff," Corbin said. "Time might be a factor that we need to consider here."

"Right. So I think hard on all this and figure this band is likely the renegades you're chasing. From the description on the wire, they've got this missing gold with 'em on the wagons, and I figure they are close by – not too far away, south as the crow flies, judging from Lee's recollections.

"But I can't just take Lee's words for all this; he's a freighter, you understand, and untrained in these matters. So I leave Bob in charge and head out south that night. I'm still a mile away, mind you, and I already can tell these boys mean business. There's a lot of 'em around, they are all well-armed, and they appear to be waiting on something or someone. So I come back in and send you the wire to answer your own."

Hawkins stopped as Stebner set down three tins and began pouring hot coffee from a battered pot. "Looks like a change in the weather," Stebner said. "The clouds are building up over the mesa in big black stacks – happens this time of year in the afternoons, you know."

Corbin nodded his thanks to Stebner but ignored his weather forecast. Instead, he turned intently toward Hawkins again. "Anything else of use, sir?" he asked.

"Just that they're still out there in the same spot," Hawkins said. "I've sent scouts out twice a day and again at night since we spotted 'em, mind you. These are good men, too – men I trust. They know how to stay low and out of a bullet's path. Course, I went back out once or twice myself, just to keep my hand in. And I don't like what I see out there – especially being so close to town."

Hawkins sat back in his chair, and Corbin and Johnson exchanged brief glances. "Sheriff, how many men do you figure are out there?" Johnson asked.

"Let's split Kevin Lee's number and call it thirty-five," he said. "It was tough to keep track of all the comings and goings, but that's safe. All the scouts agreed to that, too, give or take."

"And their exact location?"

"I'll sketch you a map, of course – but I'll take you out and show you directly, at your convenience. We've been able to come and go without notice so far."

"It might be that they know you are looking and don't care," Max said.

"Well, that's not a comforting thought, Marshal Blake," Hawkins replied after a moment's consideration.

"And the gold?" Corbin asked with a nod, leaning forward in his chair, his eyes intently holding the sheriff's. "What do you know of the gold, sir?"

"I can't say for sure, not even if there is any gold," Hawkins replied without hesitation. "We haven't been able to get close enough to see what's in the wagons – none of us could manage it, you understand – so it's only a guess. But I figure they've got something stashed, and it might well be gold. They have some big draft horses ready to hitch up to the wagons when the time comes."

"So why are they still here? What are they waiting for?"

"Well sir, I can't answer that for sure, either," Hawkins said. "We've all thought about it – talked about it, you understand – all of the scouts I sent out there and me. The best I can figure is the renegades are waiting for something or someone – or maybe both at once. Other than that, well, your guess is as good as the next fella's."

"Have you noticed anyone hanging around town – someone you don't know?" Max asked.

"Yeah, now that you mention it. But it was two, maybe three, days before the renegades – if these boys are your renegades – showed up."

"Tell me about the strangers," Max said.

"Well, there was three of 'em," Hawkins said after closing his eyes, as if picturing the events he had witnessed days earlier would make them come alive in his mind again.

"My guess is they were related somehow – brothers, or cousins maybe. They did their best to stay low. But you could tell if you watched them closely – and I did just that; watched 'em close, I mean – that they knew each other. I mean, I always keep a close eye on strangers when they come to town, and I kept a close eye on these three.

"They were here, I think, two days before drifting on. They left alone, one after another, but within an hour of each other pulling out, and they all headed east, toward Twisted Junction when they left. That's another reason I think they were connected somehow. I suspect they met up outside of town and headed down the trail together."

"Did you get any names?"

"They never said, and I never asked; didn't think it was necessary."

Hawkins called across the room to his deputy: "Hey, Bob, did you get the names of them galoots we spotted hanging around town a few days back?"

"Never did," he said, looking over his shoulder again before turning his attention back to the street.

"Do you think they were connected to the renegades?" Max asked.

"Well, I hadn't until you mentioned it just now," Hawkins said, running his hand through his thick gray hair, which was neatly trimmed and parted in the middle. "I'm still not sure of it, comes to that, though I wouldn't bet against it. They played some poker over to the saloon – strictly small stakes, you understand – at different times with different regulars. Judging by conversations I overheard, they were curious about what goes on in Whiskey Bend, but not overly so. And they didn't say a thing that made me suspect much. Had that been the case, I would have run 'em in" – and he pointed now to the jail cells behind him.

"Which reminds me, marshal, what's your pleasure on these two you've got behind my bars?" Hawkins asked.

"I'd be obliged if you could keep them a spell," Max said. "I'll wire Judge Radford for his preference. It might be he'll want me to bring them in. He might send another man across: Dave Lord, perhaps." Max thought about it for a few seconds and shrugged. "Maybe he'll have another idea entirely; he often does."

"Whatever he wants is fine with me," Hawkins said. "I'm happy to help, Marshal Blake. But I've got to say I'm surprised you don't want to take them back with you."

Max shrugged. "I've got another priority at the moment. These two just happened along. They'll have to wait."

"I see."

Hawkins clearly was expecting more, but Max added nothing else; his eyes had taken on a distant look, as if he could see something that the rest of the men in the room could not.

"You've done a fine job to date, sheriff," Corbin offered at last, breaking the silence. "You kept an eye on the renegades without losing anyone – which is something of a surprise – and you posted sentries and sent for reinforcements. There's not a lot more a man could do."

"I'm obliged, and more so if you'd scrape that mess out there" – he pointed through the window of his office – "off my boot and clean away from my town.

"You boys are equipped to handle this sort of thing," Hawkins continued. "It's well beyond me and the resources we have here. I've been worried these renegade boys would run roughshod into town, killing everything that moves, the same way they did in Adobe Flats. We've been ready for 'em, mind you, with rifles stationed and eyes to the south, as good as we can manage it, but it's been of some concern to me and most everyone here, even so."

Corbin, as though acting on an internal directive that only he could sense, suddenly stood. Johnson took his cue and got up an instant later.

"Sheriff, I thank you for the assessment," Corbin said. "We'll send scouts to gauge the situation in its present state – with your help, of course. And I'll keep you informed as best I can about our intentions."

Hawkins got to his feet and extended his hand. "I appreciate that, Col. Corbin," he said. "I'll say it again: I'm happy to have you and your men here. I'll run you out personally at your convenience, though I hope it's sooner rather than later."

Corbin shook the man's hand and turned to Max Blake, who had remained seated, his thoughts elsewhere.

"Marshal Blake? I'd appreciate an additional word with you, sir. Outside, if that's all right."

Max looked up, focused on Corbin's words, and nodded. He stood and tipped the brim of his Stetson to John Hawkins. "I'm obliged for the good work, sheriff," he said. "You run a good town – a clean town. It's a pleasure."

"That means a great deal coming from you, marshal," Hawkins said.

Bob Stebner, who was keeping watch at the window, suddenly turned around. "Hey, we've got something brewing out here, boys – besides the weather, I mean. You'd better come and take a look."

Iron Mike Truax was in a foul mood, which helped keep fools out of his path.

He stood on a high piece of ground that overlooked a narrow gulch and gazed off to the east, where the rim of a distant mesa ran in a straight line until it was lost behind a grouping of low-slung scrub and cacti and large clumps of thistle off to his right. He was looking for any sign – a wisp of trail dust, a hint of moving color, the glint of metal against the sun – that might indicate the presence of a rider. But he saw nothing, and he was becoming concerned, his frustration spilling over into a growing knot of anger that welled inside him like an infected wound.

He kicked at the ground, stepped around a cactus to gain a different sight advantage, and stared off into the distance for a full five minutes, his eyes shifting back and forth, methodically searching every inch of the distant landscape. But all he saw was the furrowed, rolling earth and spots of stubborn vegetation that clung to its sides.

It ain't like Joe Howry to be late like this, he thought. *He's been held up somehow, or something's wrong. And I don't like it when things go wrong – not by a long shot.*

Truax turned his focus toward the distant edge of Whiskey Bend, two miles north from the site where he was camped with the renegades. He was waiting for the return of his longtime partner and a solution for converting the Army gold his men had stolen into currency that they could dispense without suspicion.

Maybe the answer's in Whiskey Bend, he thought. *What if I took a ride in and had me a look around and a little fun to boot instead of jest waitin' here?*

He considered the thought for a moment before rejecting it again as too risky – *though I'd sure like to get in there and crack a few heads and get me a bottle or two; maybe even find a woman.*

He turned at the sound of footsteps and was surprised to see Rand Townsend approaching from the south. Behind him, five-hundred or more yards away, the main encampment of renegades had spent an uneasy two days of waiting and grumbling, and Truax had the feeling that Townsend's arrival would only signal trouble.

"I told you to leave me alone," he said, the challenge in his words ringing as clear as the bellow of a trumpet.

"You told me to let you know if I spotted anything in the air, Mike, and I'm doing that now," Townsend said. He was a tall, solid man with long black hair that ran in cascading waves over his muscular shoulders. He maintained a full beard that he meticulously trimmed each morning with a carefully stropped straight razor. He favored colorful shirts and often wore a bright feather in his Stetson. He liked to keep his boots and his holster and even his saddle polished, and he liked to talk.

Townsend also had a penchant for confrontation: He was confident of his abilities with a gun and his fists – and he was afraid of no man, Iron Mike Truax included.

It was a trait that Truax did not admire, however; instead, it made him nervous, and he looked at Townsend through eyes that were as cold and as hard as tempered steel.

"There's a bunch of 'em yammering back there about it being time to go," Townsend said casually. "Normally I wouldn't pay it much mind, but the long wait in the same place with no action – for whatever good reason – has made some of the boys anxious. I been hearing the same talk for the past two nights, and it seems to be growing louder, so I'm passing it along."

He held Truax's gaze for a minute and then shrugged when the man said nothing. "Thought you'd want to know," he added and turned to head back to the encampment.

"Bring me good news next time or no news. You understand?"

"Sure, Mike – anything you say," Townsend said as he turned to face Truax once more, his eyes hard, his hands at his sides. "You told me to speak up when I heard something that weren't right. Well, things ain't right back there, so I'm passing it on – like you told me. You may not like what I say, Mike, but you can't have it both ways."

Truax snarled, his lips twisted in a strange caricature of annoyance. "Here's something you can't have no two ways then: I don't like you, Rand Townsend," he said. "And I intend to do something about that one of these days."

Townsend smiled affably. "You keep shootin' the men you hire, and there's gonna be no one left to do the heavy lifting, Mike – 'cept maybe me and you. When the horse falls to his knees, the big guns come out, you know.

"But here's something for you: I ain't gonna go down easy, and you know that full well. Might be you take me down. Then again" – and Townsend paused and looked hard at Mike Truax, the geniality gone from his face, his eyes as thin as flat gold pieces – "then again, you just might be the one that don't walk away."

The two men stared at each other, one minute stretching into two.

Iron Mike Truax made no movement.

Rand Townsend remained in place, his right hand close to his holstered revolver.

The sudden crack of thunder overhead surprised them both and broke the tension.

"Looks like a change in the weather," Townsend said, a smile gradually creasing his face. "That might be a good thing."

Chapter 29

A Change in the Weather

"Jest what do ya suppose that damn fool's doing?"

Bob Stebner turned from the door of the sheriff's office and called across to John Hawkins, who was concluding conversations with Michael Corbin and Jed Johnson of the U.S. Army and Federal Marshal Max Blake of Twin Forks.

"You'd better take a gander at this, sheriff," he added, shifting his gaze between Hawkins and the street. "Right now."

Hawkins turned with a curious look, his eyes wary and focused into narrow slits. He knew his deputy well enough to recognize that something was wrong on the streets of his town. He also knew that the last thing he needed was an unwanted distraction while important guests were in his office.

Hawkins started for the door when Stebner looked out again and called over his shoulder, "You might want to see this, too, Marshal Blake. He's calling out your name, after all."

Max already was moving toward Stebner. Without conscious thought, he pulled his Colt .45 and held the revolver in the same way that you would shake the hand of an old friend. He looked down briefly, snapped the cylinder open to determine that all of the chambers were properly loaded, and expertly flicked the weapon back into the black leather holster that was strapped to his leg.

The movement was graceful – a ballet of precision and timing – and the Army officers picked it up and glanced at each other for an instant, their eyes communicating the fluid beauty of the maneuver, their minds recognizing instantly that words were unnecessary.

Stebner stepped into the middle of the open door and called out, "What the hell do you think yer doing, Lenny?"

"You let me call him out proper," Len Wilcox yelled. "Jest git outta the way, Steb, 'fore I drill you to git at him."

Stebner shrugged and called back, "Have it yer way, you damn fool. You *do* know who yer calling out, right?"

He turned back inside the office, stepped away from the door, and held up his hands in a what-can-you-do motion as Max Blake and John Hawkins approached.

"That damn fool Lenny Wilcox is out there, sheriff, and he's calling out Marshal Blake. Don't know what fer – cain't imagine what would possess him to do something that fool stupid."

Hawkins looked outside, shook his head in disbelief, and turned his attention to the federal marshal. "Wilcox has been in town a year or so, Marshal Blake, and never a problem. I am surely at a loss to explain this," he said.

"Hey, Blake: Git on out here, you no-good bastard, and let's see who's got a fast gun," Wilcox called loudly from the middle of the street.

Thunder suddenly rolled in the background – a deep, throaty rumble that grew increasingly louder as the light streaming from the windows turned from bright afternoon sunshine to the muted shadows that precede a mountain storm.

Max shrugged. "I don't recognize the face or the name," he said.

"Like most everyone else in town, he's a freighter. He hauls whiskey, mostly, but he'll carry all sorts of goods: lumber, barrels of flour and sugar and such for the general store – hell, whatever pays well at the moment," Stebner said.

"Never knew him to be crazy, though, Marshal Blake. I cain't imagine what's eating at him. Why hell, the Len Wilcox I know is a quiet, gentle man."

Max looked out from the edge of the window at a thin cowboy of medium height standing alone in the street, his right hand held close to the holstered revolver at his side. The man wore a dusty, wide-brimmed Stetson, a dark flannel shirt that was speckled with the gray of trail dust, and leggings that appeared to be tattered dark denim. A pair of spurs was attached to his boots, which were stained with sweat and spotted with dried mud.

A burst of rain splattered on the street as another peel of thunder shattered the silence. The rain increased in intensity, as though someone had opened the flood-gates of a dammed stream, and pools thick with black mud began to form on the street.

Wilcox stood resolutely, his left hand clenched in a tight fist.

"I don't know him," Max said after a minute. "And we've got no time for this."

Hawkins pushed his way past Stebner and stood in the door frame, just out of the lashing rain.

"Len Wilcox, it's Sheriff Hawkins," he called out. "I don't know what's got into you, boy, but you'd best put it away right now. You hear me?"

"Git out of the way, sheriff. It ain't you I'm interested in." He dismissed Hawkins with a withering look and called out loudly again, "Hey, Blake, stop hiding behind the law and face me like a man, you yella stinkin' coward."

Max took hold of Hawkins' right arm and gave it a slight tug. Hawkins turned, saw the look in the marshal's eyes, and stepped back into the office. "I'm sorry, Marshal Blake, but I don't know what to tell you."

Max nodded as he pushed past Hawkins and stepped out to the front of the sheriff's office, planting his boots solidly on the boardwalk that fronted the wooden buildings along the street. "It's all right," he said softly. "I'm used to this."

Len Wilcox smiled grimly when he saw Max Blake. He fought the urge to pull his holstered revolver on the spot but held himself back: *He's got to know first. He's got to understand why he's gonna die.*

Wilcox waited, but Max said nothing; he only stared grimly, his hat pulled low over his eyes to shield the torrents of rain, his hands steady and close to his sides.

The marshal's silence was unnerving, and Wilcox shivered involuntarily.

The rain now hammered the town and the freighter in the street, striking his clothing and his exposed skin like stinging needles, but Wilcox was more attentive to the eerie silence that seemed to envelop him.

"You recognize me, Blake?" he said at last.

Max stood silently on the boardwalk, his right hand flexing near his revolver, his eyes narrowed against the rain.

"Didn't think you would," Wilcox called. "You don't even remember it, most likely. But I do – like it was yesterday. I kin see you standing there, that damn gun of yers blastin' away.

"You kilt my cousin dead in the street in Pueblo Springs. Two years ago, and you shot him to pieces and left him in the dirt, then rode outta town like you could come and go as you please."

Wilcox ignored the rain, which was coming down in torrential sheets. He stood anchored in place, the water sluicing past him as it coursed its

206

way through the wheel ruts left by the freighters' wagons that moved in long strings in and out of the town. Another crack of thunder shattered the air with a sound like cannon fire.

"I ain't forgot all this time," he called. "I heard you was here some weeks back, Blake – brought it all back again. You was lucky then 'cause I was up in Flagstaff. But here you are now."

A shaft of lightning brightened the sky in the distance, and the deep rumble of thunder quickly followed, rattling the windows of the sheriff's office. Wilcox was startled by the proximity of the blast, but he held his ground.

"Len, you get your sorry carcass out of that street and stop this," Hawkins called out from the door. "No good will come from this – no need for you to die today."

"The only man among us gonna die today is him," Wilcox called back, though his eyes never left Max Blake's. "I been patient all this time. I been following my own trail of revenge, and here it comes walkin' right up in front of me. It's a sign.

"So ... are you ready to die, Blake? You gonna make amends with the Lord a'fore I kill you dead?"

He spit out the words like a curse, frustrated that the federal marshal had not acknowledged him in any way.

"You even remember my cousin, Blake?" he called, filling the silence again. Another crack of thunder peeled loudly overhead, and he had to yell to be heard above the incessant pounding of the rain. "They said he was a horse thief and kilt a man, but that ain't true – none of it – and you don't even recollect it. You cain't even bring to mind his name, can ya? Do you have any idea ..."

The sudden bellow of a Colt .45 barked twice in the storm, its distinct whine whistling across the street and bouncing off the oak timbers of the general store and the bank. Wilcox had his eyes focused on Max Blake, and yet he looked hard now and saw that the marshal had his revolver in his hand; a wisp of gunsmoke trailed away in the rain and the wind.

Wilcox lurched forward as though he had been shot, but he felt no pain and was surprised that he found himself still standing. His mind, reacting slowly, instructed his hand to reach for his own revolver, and he did this now, trying desperately to hold his balance in the slippery street. But his hand dropped to an empty holster as another peel of thunder rumbled in the distance. His fingers caught the shattered top of the leather instead, and he looked down as though time had stopped and wondered dully why he was unable to come up firing.

As rain water rolled off the brim of his hat and through his outstretched hand, he saw that his holster had been ripped apart. He caught sight of his shattered revolver an instant later, lying behind him in the muddy water that coursed around his boots. And he stared again in disbelief at Max Blake, who stood unmoving and unwavering in the rain.

"Damn you to hell, Blake," Wilcox called, raising his right hand in a fist and shaking it at the federal marshal. "This ain't finished."

Bob Stebner brushed past Max and moved rapidly into the street, his revolver pulled and pointed at Wilcox. He picked his way across the slippery muck and grabbed the freighter by the arm. "Yer a sight lucky to be alive and don't even have the sense to know it. What were you thinking, trying to draw on the likes of Max Blake? A man would have to be thick as a post to try a fool thing like that."

"Lemme go," Wilcox hissed, pulling his arm away. He tried to reach down in the mud for his revolver, but Stebner deftly kicked it away and stuck his Remington into the freighter's side, getting his attention.

"That gun of yers ain't no good, you dumb fool. He shot it clean out of yer holster and then again to pieces right out of the air. He could've done the same to you. So you listen and listen good: Yer gonna walk into that jail, and yer gonna do it without another word. Understand?"

"But he killed my cousin, Steb. Bobby was kin to me, and it falls to me to make Blake pay for what he done."

Hawkins had moved onto the boardwalk next to Max, and he turned to stare at the federal marshal. "You mind telling me …" He let the words trail off when he saw the look that lingered in Max's eyes, which were still fixed on the squirming Len Wilcox.

Hawkins glanced down at Max's Colt, shook his head in amazement, and walked gingerly into the street to help his deputy subdue the still-angry freighter. He took the man's left arm and pulled it hard as Stebner pushed his revolver deep into Wilcox's ribs. The rain was easing, and the thunder that moved with it rolled off to the east.

"Enough of this nonsense," Hawkins said. "If you don't stop right now, I'll be the one shoots you full of holes."

Wilcox continued to struggle, but the fight was out of him. As Stebner and Hawkins pushed him past Max through the door leading into the sheriff's office, Wilcox called over his shoulder, "You satisfied now, Blake? You feel better now?"

Max could smell the odor of cheap whiskey and fear and sweat that even a hard thunderstorm couldn't mask.

Max turned and followed the men inside. He deftly flicked his Colt back into the finely tooled holster at his side and glanced at Lt. Col. Michael Corbin, who had witnessed the episode from the relative warmth and comfort of the sheriff's office.

"We've got no time for this nonsense," Max repeated.

Corbin stared back at the federal marshal, not fully comprehending Max's words.

"You wanted to talk," Max offered this time. "Now might be a good time."

Corbin shook his head, as if to clear it, and he looked at Max Blake the way a man might examine an entirely new species of animal.

Capt. Jed Johnson snapped to rigid attention and offered up a firm salute. "That was excellent shooting, sir," he said. "I'm honored."

"It was that," Corbin said, finding his voice at last. "Unexpected, certainly, but a perfect solution, Marshal Blake."

Max shrugged and looked through the door to the rack of jail cells at the far corner of the sheriff's office. Richard Nash, the Aguante deputy, was in one. Tom Bolton, the former Twisted Junction deputy, was in the middle cell. Len Wilcox, his clothing soaked, his boots mud-stained, made no protest as Hawkins and Stebner searched him and forced him inside a third cell.

Bolton grinned widely. "Welcome," he said. "Gettin' a might crowded."

Nash looked at the newcomer and called out, "Good thing he didn't come between me and you, Blake – and I don't care what happened out there just now."

"It's over for you," Hawkins said softly, although an undercurrent of menace crept into his words. "I've told you before not to speak until you are spoken to. I expect that you will pay for your remarks before it's all said and done, Mr. Nash."

Nash's hand crept unconsciously to the long scar that ran across his face, but he said nothing.

Wilcox sat sadly down on the floor of the cell, his eyes empty, his face wet and flushed, his arms clutched and folded under his chest with a pressure that made his knuckles turn white. Water dripped from his clothing onto the floor of the cell, and the mud from his boots slowly dropped off the leather and fell in dark clumps that stained the wooden planks beneath him.

Stebner turned away from the cell. "Quite a storm out there for a minute," he said casually, winking at the sheriff.

Max directed his attention to Corbin once more.

"What's on your mind?"

"The rain's about let up," Corbin said, nodding toward the door. "Let's head to the stables – something of interest there."

Max followed Corbin and Johnson as they headed outside. He stopped and turned when Hawkins called out, "Marshal Blake?" He caught and held the man's gaze, and Hawkins added, "I want to thank you for doing what you did just now. The ending could have been … far uglier."

Max glanced at Wilcox for an instant, but the man remained on the cell floor, his eyes fixed on a spot that only he could determine. Max looked back at Hawkins, touched his hand to the brim of his Stetson, and followed the two Army officers into the street.

"If that don't beat all," Stebner said when the three men walked out the door.

"That was the finest display of six-gun mastery I've ever seen," Hawkins said, his eyes flickering. "And I've seen some skilled craftsmen in my day."

"Hey, sheriff, could I say a word?" Richard Nash called.

Hawkins looked hard at the man, who was standing with his hands on the bars of the cell. "Not a single word – now or later."

When Max entered the Whiskey Bend stables with Corbin and Johnson, he spotted a dozen soldiers lounging in various corners of the building. Four were playing a game of cards; two others were tending Army horses. The rest were engaged in scattered conversations.

All of them snapped to attention when the two officers walked in, their hands automatically generating a perfect military salute, although their eyes drifted toward the federal marshal. Buck, content in a middle stall, nickered when he saw Max.

"Sergeant major," Corbin said, his eyes immediately spotting Michael McClinton, "a word, if you please."

McClinton stepped out of the shadows and again saluted his commanding officer. "Yes, sir," he said.

"At ease, sergeant major. I'd like you to show Marshal Blake what you found in Bolton's saddlebags."

McClinton nodded. "With pleasure, sir." He turned toward Max. "If you'd follow me, Marshal Blake," extending a long arm before him and pointing a finger toward the far bank of stables. "You might find this interesting, sir."

McClinton walked briskly through the stables, scattering three enlisted men who lingered nearby. "Out of the way, you mutts. There's real work to be done here."

He turned back toward Max and said, "If you don't keep at 'em constantly, they're like little boys who steal the sweets from the pantry, the lot of 'em." He raised his eyebrows then and added, "That was some piece of shooting, marshal, if you don't mind me saying. I was tending to the guards and saw it all."

Before Max could reply, they reached the far wall and McClinton opened the right-side pouch of the saddlebags that he had pulled from Tom Bolton's horse.

"After you surprised Bolton and saved me own sorry carcass, I back-tracked his trail a bit and found two horses tied nearby. One of the animals was his, all right; the second was recently acquired, shall we say – though how, exactly, who can say?

"Yer man Bolton might have come by it honestly, though I doubt it. He might have stolen it, saddlebags and all, from a livery or the back end of a saloon, perhaps – again, a difficult thing to assess. Or he might well have surprised some poor rider and bushwhacked him, taking the blighter's horse and belongings.

"Anyways, we opened this not more'n five minutes after we arrived in Whiskey Bend and this very spot. And this, sir, is what we found inside."

McClinton reached into the saddlebags and pulled out a sack of gold coins, splaying a handful out across his massive fingers. "It's fine gold, as you can see – a fortune, truth be told," he said.

"The marshal knows what gold looks like, sergeant major," Johnson said.

"Ah, but does the marshal recognize *Army* gold?" McClinton asked.

Max took a coin and studied it carefully, judging both the weight and the markings. "A twenty-dollar gold piece, fresh from the mint," he said. He looked from McClinton to Johnson to Corbin and added, "How do you suppose Tom Bolton got his hands on Army gold?"

"We were hoping you might explain it," Corbin said.

Max looked at the coin again, holding it up to a shaft of afternoon sunlight that streamed through a fly-speckled window and cast a distorted rectangle on the dirt floor at his feet. He turned it over, examining both sides as though the answer could be found on the shiny metal surface. Then he flipped it, end over end, high into the air, deftly caught it in his left hand, and handed it back to McClinton.

"It's unlikely that Bolton is connected with the renegades," Max said after a minute. "They wouldn't have him. He found it – stumbled on it somehow – or stole it. Either way, he's lucky to be alive."

Max shrugged his shoulders and looked hard at Corbin. "I'm only guessing. You can always ask him."

"We intend to do just that," Corbin said. "It's just that with his head the way it is, the answers he provides, if any, will be suspect at best and likely not helpful." He shrugged and stared through the window, wondering whether he had somehow missed a vital piece of the puzzle connecting the unlikely Tom Bolton with the gold.

"My hunch is that Bolton encountered the renegades and somehow survived it, taking this bit of gold at the same time. I don't know how that happened, but I don't know how else to explain it."

"I'm sure you'll solve it in time," Max said. "As for me, I've got other concerns – south of here, past the renegades."

"Fair enough, Marshal Blake. I know you are anxious to get moving – likely with good reason," Corbin said. "But we still have some work ahead of us."

"How so?"

"Your plan is for us to drive the renegades into Aguante, where we take out the entire snake's nest – am I correct?"

Max nodded.

"What if the renegades don't cooperate? What if they move in any of a hundred other directions? My men are good, but we may not be able to control those killers once we start driving them."

Max smiled at Corbin, as though he already had solved the puzzle and was waiting for the right moment to offer the solution.

"Richard Nash might help," Max said. "All he needs is a little play-acting from us – and the chance to walk away from the jail."

"An interesting suggestion," Corbin said as he ran his hand through his hair, the idea playing in his mind. "With the right prompting …"

Max picked up the thought: "… we get Nash to steer the herd straight into Aguante."

Chapter 30

A Parting of Trails

Max Blake sat on the edge of a desk in the sheriff's office in Whiskey Bend, his mind already in a distant place. He was absently gazing through the window, watching traces of thin morning clouds race above the second-floor cupola of the general store across the street.

He had oiled his revolver moments earlier and was wiping the weapon down from memory with a brown-stained cloth. The pungent smell of light machine oil and solvent meshed with the aroma of strong black coffee and the sour stench of perspiration from men who had not bathed for days and the fine trail dust that drifted in from the wagon traffic on the street and hung in the air like the peel of a church bell.

Army officers Michael Corbin and Jed Johnson were discussing the success of the ruse they had used the night before which allowed Richard Nash to walk out of the jail and escape into the night. A number of maps of the territory, some of them hand-made and sketched out on sheets of butcher's paper, were spread out on the floor around them.

Corbin was convinced that Nash already was in the renegade camp, alerting the gold thieves to a pending attack from two U.S. Army units.

Johnson agreed with the assessment.

John Hawkins, the Whiskey Bend sheriff, was less convinced and said so. "It ain't likely the man just walked out of town and is now a part of that pack. I don't care how many seeds we planted.

"Truth is, Nash has lots of choices. He can head direct to Aguante, which is what I'd do, and lay low, hoping interested parties forget him. He could head direct to Mexico – knowing he's wanted by the Army and Marshal Blake here. He could even hang around and try to get back at the marshal or the rest of us when we ride out."

Hawkins paused for a few seconds and glanced around the room. "The man has plenty of choices – despite the line of malarkey we fed him through the jail bars. The only way you can tell for sure what he's up to is see how it plays out once you get there. When you see Nash with the renegades, then I'll believe it."

Hawkins shrugged and leaned back in his chair, as though he had made the final statement on the matter.

Corbin turned toward Max Blake. "You've been mighty quiet, marshal," he said.

Max turned away from the window. His eyes found Corbin's and held them for an instant, and then he looked at Hawkins for a long time, as though he had discovered something about the sheriff that he hadn't known before. Max appreciated the way that Hawkins spoke his mind and dealt with adversity and took care of his town – solid traits that he too seldom found in the men who pinned a tin star to their shirt.

"It doesn't matter what I think," he said at last, "though I expect Sheriff Hawkins is correct – about a lot of things. We won't know till we hear from your men."

"Your opinion matters, Marshal Blake," Johnson said. "It's just that, well, I think we did a good job last night laying it out so Nash could act once we left his cell unlocked. I figure he's only got one move, and that's direct to the renegades."

"We'll see it when we see it and not a minute before," Hawkins said matter-of-factly. He looked across at Corbin, who was seated with his feet propped on a corner of the desk, his black boots shined to a deep rich luster, a map in his hand. "This wire you sent last night: You got the reply you expected, I take it?"

Corbin nodded and pulled a gold watch from his pocket. He opened the cover and studied it for a few seconds. "An entire regiment should be gathering west of here within the next two hours. We are talking about a lot of men, a lot of noise, a lot of commotion, a lot of trail dust. A blind man will be able to see it coming."

He looked across the desk from Hawkins and back to Johnson and Max Blake and then back to Hawkins again: "When the renegades see that, sheriff, they are going to run. And if this Nash has done his job, as we expect, they will run straight to Aguante. I don't see how it can be any simpler."

"They might just shoot Nash when he gets close," Hawkins said. "Why you think this is going to end well – for us or for Nash – is beyond me."

214

"It won't be long now and we'll all find out," Corbin said, stretching out in the chair, his hands absently fiddling with the edges of the tattered map.

Max flicked the Colt back into the holster at his side. He carefully folded the gun cloth and set it down on the desk with a nod to Hawkins. "I'm going on ahead then – into Aguante," he said. "By the time I bend around the renegades, the regiment will attract attention, so now's the time to move."

"What are your plans then, marshal?"

"I'll poke around Aguante – learn what I can, see if I can smoke out Reno Walker somehow. I'll try to get word to you, but I wouldn't count on it."

"What if I send a man with you, Marshal Blake?" Corbin asked.

"I work alone," Max said flatly.

"I could force the issue."

"Not likely."

"I could wire the judge – what's his name? Radford? I could wire your Judge Radford right now and insist."

Max raised a single eyebrow in Corbin's direction. "You do what you have to, but it won't change the situation," he said.

Corbin began to speak and then thought better of it. He looked toward Jed Johnson instead. "Captain, notify the sergeant major to organize the men. I want to be ready when Lt. Gen. Mitchell's men arrive; see that it happens quickly."

Johnson jumped from his chair. "Yes, sir," he said. "Right away." He turned toward Max Blake then and added, "It's been a pleasure, marshal. I hope to see you again soon, sir." He saluted and moved briskly toward the door.

Richard Nash couldn't believe his good fortune.

He had been sitting on a cot in his jail cell, listening to the scattered discussions among the two Army officers, the Whiskey Bend sheriff and his deputy, the federal marshal from Twin Forks, and one or two others whose voices he did not recognize – likely additional Army personnel, he figured.

The snippets of conversation he had picked up were enlightening: a contingent of renegades camped to the south of town, a regiment of Army regulars arriving from the nearby fort to help kill or capture the renegades and return a stolen shipment of Army gold, a rivalry between the fighters commanded by Lt. Col. Corbin and the head of the incoming squadron – the highly touted Lt. Gen. Gary Mitchell – and a roundabout discussion of Aguante and the law's aversion to the town that housed the territory's worst criminals.

A man could play this information to his advantage, he had thought at the time.

But a man would have to be someplace else – anyplace else – besides the inside of a jail cell in Whiskey Bend to make use of the information he now possessed.

And then the unexpected happened: The deputy serving the nighttime meal was distracted by a disturbance in the office and failed to relock the cell bars once he had placed the food inside.

Nash had said nothing, of course, and set his plate and cup under the bars and pushed both toward the outer door once he had finished so that there would be no good reason for a man to recheck the locks.

Within an hour, an incident on the street pulled the men out of the building. Richard Nash used this moment to slip out of his cell, duck unnoticed out the main door of the sheriff's office, creep silently around the back of the building, and race past the edge of town and into the blackness of the night beyond.

Len Wilcox, in the adjoining cell, was asleep. Tom Bolton was wide awake but said nothing, his eyes vacant, his face contorted into a broad smile – as though he knew something that no one else did.

Nash had run the events around in his head for some time but could determine no other angle than good fortune and the stupidity of an overworked deputy to account for his escape.

The thought of a ruse on the part of his jailers had not crossed his mind.

He understood that a contingent of deputies, and perhaps even some soldiers, would look for him once his disappearance was noticed. But regaining his horse was out of the question: It was quartered in the town's livery stables with the livestock from the Army and well-guarded as a result.

And so he made his way on foot, moving quickly and silently, toward the only place in the territory where he might have a chance to escape: the renegade encampment.

If I act fast and catch some luck, I might get out of this mess entirely, he thought. *The Army won't chase the renegades till that second bunch of soldiers arrives. If I can get to 'em first – warn 'em about what's coming – I just might save my neck.*

And if I can manage to do that, I'll get another shot at Max Blake.

He headed due south, his eyes alert, his legs churning up yards with determined, forceful steps, his mind roaring with information and ideas and potential plans and strategies.

Nash's hand was throbbing again. The ointment that the Army doctor had used on it had helped; but that was hours ago, and he was again concerned that infection would set in. He was concentrating on the shooting pain that ran up his arm in short but excruciating bursts, in fact, when he felt the sudden thrust of cold steel into his back.

"Get 'em high where I kin see 'em."

He did as he was told, making no effort to respond or turn.

"Yer as good as dead, cowboy," a man's voice said. "You must be one of them Whiskey Bend galoots comin' out fer another look. Well, you got too close this time, so it's gonna be yer last look."

"Don't make a mistake here," Nash said as casually as he could manage.

"What's that supposed to mean?"

"I just escaped from the jail in that town back there," he said. "I've got information that's valuable – about what they are planning to do to you boys."

"Who are you talking about? What kind of information?"

"Not here – and not now," Nash said. "I want to see the big bug. You take me to him, and you'll live a whole lot longer."

"What makes you think Mike Truax'll talk at the likes of you?" the man asked.

"If this Truax fella won't talk to me, he's gonna die – along with the rest of you, and right soon enough. Stop wasting time here and get a move on."

"I don't know. My orders are to ..."

"This is your chance to move up a notch," Nash said. "If Truax don't like what I have to say, he can kill me and be done with it. But if he learns some things that save the whole bunch of you – well, think how good you'll look then."

"You kin do that, mister?"

"I can do that."

The big man behind him, his breath smelling like rotted meat, his body odor foul and overpowering, thought it over. "What'd you say yer name was?"

"Didn't say, and it don't matter. All you need to know is I can save your neck and the neck of every man here."

217

"I'll take a chance with you," the renegade sentry said, making up his mind. "Meantime, empty yer pockets nice and slow, and let's have a look at what's inside. And mister, if you move even an inch in the wrong direction, it'll be the last inch you ever moved in. You understand me?"

Nash nodded and slowly turned out the pockets of his denim pants, one at a time, cringing at the shooting pain in his hand.

Tom and Paul Dieker looked out across the great expanse of desert that stretched before them like a never-ending painting. For as far as they could see in any direction, the earth was a barren landscape of reddish sand and hard rock, exposing the dust-tinged green of occasional clumps of Russian thistle and creosote bush and cacti, the faded brown of wispy sweet grass and dead tumbleweed, and an assortment of cracks and crevices and small gulches that appeared like long black snakes in the distance and ran off into the earth, remnants of the work of eons.

Off to the south, a tall mesa rose against the blue sheet of sky, its red rocks gleaming against the muted light of the setting sun.

Dave Dieker, the third Aguante outlaw brother, was a hundred yards or more ahead, and he turned his horse around now and looked back.

"What the hell are you two looking at?" he called loudly.

Tom glanced at Paul, and the two of them smiled – big, wide grins with eyes shining and their mouths curled up on the corners.

"Ain't you seen it yet?" Tom called back.

"Seen what?"

"The elephant. You take a good look across the way, brother" – he pointed with his right arm, stretching it out toward the east, his index finger aimed like the sight on a gun barrel – "and I don't see how you can miss it."

Dave Dieker looked in the direction that his brother indicated, staring hard at the earth and the sky and the landscape between the points where the two met. He moved his eyes back and forth, trying to find something of interest – anything at all that would justify the attention that his brothers showed. But he spotted nothing but the barren landscape, and he turned and shrugged. "I'm missing it and beyond caring. Let's jest move on. We've got a distance to travel yet."

He pulled at the reins and turned his horse back toward the east, carefully choosing a trail that avoided the distinct rifts and rents and fractures in the land.

"I'm afraid our brother doesn't appreciate the finer things in this world," Paul Dieker said. "I don't think he'll ever find that elephant of yours."

"I'd agree, brother," Tom replied. "But if a man looks hard enough, why, you can see it off in the distance."

"It's as plain to me as the horse you sit on – and a whole bunch bigger."

"It's as big as a house."

"It's at least as big as an outhouse."

The two men laughed and nudged their horses forward and moved along at a slow pace, in no hurry of catching up with their brother, who was three-hundred yards ahead now and gaining.

"You know what I'm thinking?" Tom said after a minute.

"I can't imagine but know you'll tell me at some point," Paul replied.

"All right, you talked me into it."

"I did? What did I say?

"You said you wanted me to tell you at some point. I guess now's as good a time as any," Tom said.

"Hell, it don't matter what I say. Just go on ahead and say whatever's on your mind, brother. You will anyway."

"I'm thinking we ought to keep on riding east."

"Well, we are riding east – right toward Twisted Junction."

"I know that," Tom said. "That was the plan. We check out Whiskey Bend, which we just did, then we check out Twisted Junction and whatever else we can find. But I'm thinking now that we keep on moving – past Twisted Junction and Twin Forks and keep on riding clear into New Mexico, maybe. Or maybe we should head on to Colorado; it's been awhile since we been there. Might be we should go on up to Wyoming – or even into Montana; I hear tell the mountains in Montana are pretty as a song."

"What brought all this on a'sudden?" Paul asked.

"It ain't so sudden," Tom said. "I been thinking on this hard for some time now – since we left Aguante. You know Reno Walker's aching for a bullet. Trouble is, when the bullets come flying – and they will – I don't want a stray one to find me, let alone a well-aimed one."

He looked hard at his brother and added, "And I sure as hell don't want one to find you – or David."

"You think it's that bad then?"

"Yeah, I do. It's been bad a long time, and it got worse when that puncher showed up and got the sheriff all worked up. What – five or six good men dead since?"

"We've got ties to Aguante, you know," Paul said. "And we all got our faces hanging on sheriff's walls across the West."

"If we go back to Aguante and stay, we're gonna die there," Tom said after running his brother's words around in his head for a minute. "I ain't anxious to die in Aguante like that fool Clyde Roberts. I ain't anxious to die anywhere no time soon, mind you, but I sure as hell don't want to git it in Aguante. I got a bad feeling."

Paul Dieker pulled his horse to a stop and shook his head, looking at his brother as though he had spotted him for the first time in a long time. "Truth is, I've had the same feeling fer a spell myself. I don't know what David thinks – ain't said nothing to him nor him to me – but I think we need to talk about it some."

"Might be the time for talking's past," Tom said. "If we ever want to see that elephant out there, Paul, roaming the West and getting harder to find every minute, we need to move – away from Aguante and away from Reno Walker." He looked at his brother, his eyes like reflecting pools, and added, "I don't know what else to tell ya."

"I'll think on it," Paul said. "I'll talk to David. But I got no hankering for Montana or Colorado; we been there, and we left it fer good reason. Oregon's always interested me, though, and might be worth a look. Even at that, I got to think on it some."

"You think on it, so long as you come to the same conclusion in the end. But don't take too long, brother. We are about out of time. Tell me you can feel it, too."

"What makes you think you got something to say worth my time?" Mike Truax asked.

Richard Nash stood a mere five feet from the renegade leader, holding his wounded right hand gingerly, his eyes steady, his face neutral. He knew that the next few minutes would mean the difference between life and death, and he steeled himself for a difficult encounter.

"I know things I ain't supposed to know," he said.

"Hell, I do, too. That ain't much."

"I know things about you."

"All right, talk yer way out of a bullet," Truax said, his six-gun in his hand, cocked and pointed at the man's chest.

"My name's Nash. I'm from Aguante." He saw the look on the faces of the men around him at the mere mention of the border town; it was a look of appreciation and perhaps even a little fear. He also saw that Iron Mike Truax registered no recognition at all; he simply stared holes straight through the man before him – as though he could care less what Nash had to say.

"I got shot a day back by a federal marshal named Blake. Blake is hooked up with a squadron of Army boys lead by a man named Corbin. You fellas have been shooting yer way around the territory, and you took something the Army wants back – like a lot of gold. That's why this Corbin is on yer trail."

Nash paused for a breath, and Mike Truax grunted at the delay. "Keep talking," he said, prodding with the end of his revolver. "You ain't said nothing of interest yet."

Nash shrugged, though the man's words chilled him. "I heard them talking in the jail. Corbin wired for a regiment of Army regulars to deal with you. The plan is to kill every last one of you – 'no prisoners' were his exact words – and take back the gold."

Truax grunted again. "You heard all this – back in a jail cell in Whiskey Bend?"

"That's right."

"How'd you get out of the jail and out of the town with a federal marshal and a sheriff and a squadron of soldiers hanging about?"

"I got out because I'm good."

"And the reason yer telling me all this now?"

"Look, I got no great hopes here. I stay in Whiskey Bend, they hang me – either there or back in Twin Forks. But if I can get back to Aguante, there ain't no man alive can touch me."

"What makes you think no one can get at you in Aguante?"

"I heard 'em all say it: the Army boys, the sheriff, even the damn federal marshal. All they could talk about was how dangerous Aguante was and how they all stayed shut of the place because of it."

Mike Truax took his meaty left hand and scratched at the whiskers on the side of his face, his mouth half open, his eyes half closed in thought. He tilted his head to the side, as though considering a new hand of cards, and eventually turned back toward Nash.

"When's this regiment expected?"

"Tomorrow morning," Nash said. "They plan to slaughter you right here – every last man. They talked about shooting you full of holes and leaving you for the buzzards – a warning, as they put it, to discourage others from stealing Army gold."

"Well, they can't slaughter us if we ain't here," Truax said after a minute. "And I got me an idea of where we might want to go and buy us some time."

"If you are thinking about Aguante, I'm here to offer my services," Nash said. "I can …"

The sudden explosion from Mike Truax's revolver cracked in the night; the bullet caught Richard Nash directly in the belly. His eyes gaped in surprise as his hands closed around the wound; he looked down, saw the blood seep through his fingers and into the stained dressing that the Army surgeon had used to protect his wounded hand, and he looked back into the vacant eyes of the renegade leader.

He saw only cold indifference in return.

"I know the way to Aguante," Truax said. "Hell, most every man here knows it." He slowly, deliberately, cocked his revolver and fired a second time. The bullet slammed into Nash's chest with a heavy thump and drove him off balance, his legs buckling behind him as he hit the ground with a muted thud.

Truax turned to the big man responsible for bringing Richard Nash into the camp and looked coldly at him, his eyes dark and menacing.

"You ever ignore a direct order from me again, Jim Dutoit, and you'll git something worse than this man," he said, his revolver pointed at the lifeless body on the ground in front of him. "You understand?"

"Sure thing, Mike. The only reason I …"

Truax's face contorted in anger, and Dutoit stopped talking and turned away, moving back to his post as quickly as he could manage, afraid that a gunshot would hit him in the back at any second.

But Iron Mike Truax already had forgotten about the sentry. He turned toward the men who stood around a small cooking fire and said, "All right, we break camp right now. Spread the word. We travel light, and we move fast – due south. Joe Howry will have to catch up with us."

Chapter 31

A Roundabout Return

Max Blake considered a thousand possibilities in his quest to end Reno Walker's outlaw empire in Aguante, and his thinking always returned him to the same word: Trouble.

Behind him, the settlement of Whiskey Bend, perched near the edge of a broad mesa, a swift stream flowing through its northern flank, was occupied by a U.S. Army cavalry squadron that was itching for a fight – and for glory.

To his immediate right, three miles or more to the west, the renegade pack lead by the murderous Mike Truax was cloaked in secrecy, waiting for the arrival of something, or someone, that only the vicious Truax understood.

Somewhere behind him, a regiment of U.S. Army regulars was moving into position to help drive the renegades into a box to the south.

And directly ahead or him, thirty miles or more on a straight line to the border, was the outlaw town of Aguante, a settlement that sparked fear into the hearts of even the bravest occupants of a harsh and unforgiving land.

"We must be fools to head back to Aguante, Buck," Max said softly, patting the horse's broad neck as the animal picked a careful path through the sage and scrub on a night lit by a crescent moon and an ovation of stars overhead. "But that's the hand we've been dealt."

Buck gave his head a slight shake and pressed forward.

The ol' boy has a nose for trouble, too, Max thought.

The idea of facing Reno Walker again gave Max little satisfaction. He knew that revenge for the beating he had suffered at the hands of Walker and his men weeks earlier was a concept that meant little in the long run.

He had sought revenge for his uncle's murder years before and succeeded in killing two of the ranch hands who robbed and then fatally shot Edward Blake while Max was asleep in an upstairs bedroom. But a third man, the elusive Paul Reyelts, managed to escape and remained free all these years later, his trail as cold as a mountain grave. And while Max still looked for news of Reyelts, the burning hatred of his youth had given way to a dull nagging in his heart.

Maybe justice is all I'm after with Walker – just a part of the job, he thought. *A trail of revenge is a certain path to disappointment and trouble – sometimes even death.*

Max considered that possibility for a long time as Buck continued to navigate a route away from the renegade encampment and the approaching Army regiment that was moving into position west of the gold thieves. The sure-footed horse didn't vary in speed or direction, his pace as steady as the striker of a tightly wound clock.

In the long run, Max figured that Reno Walker meant no more to him than Hoss Johnson meant – or the two Morgan brothers, Freeman and Weasel, or even Tom Culpepper and Johnny Dole and Len Wilcox's forgotten cousin and other hard-baked outlaws he had faced with a loaded six-gun and a deadly stare: desperate men about to die on the wrong side of an unforgiving law and a sure-handed federal marshal.

But his thoughts continued to return to the dangerous Reno Walker and the trouble that awaited him in Aguante. The town was filled with the worst men in the territory: desperate, deadly killers who found a measure of comfort in the presence of each other and the protection offered by the corrupt sheriff and his deputies.

Walker will be a handful. But he's no more to me than Reyelts is now, he thought.

And he let that idea drift in and out of his consciousness as Buck moved steadily forward and the moon shifted positions again and a faint light began to show itself across the ridge of earth in the east.

The vegetation that was so plentiful in the higher elevations near Whiskey Bend began to give way to the sparse, sun-baked sand and rock and red dirt and dust of the rolling desert that stretched in an endless succession of miles on a direct line into Mexico. A series of broken, wind-blown tumbleweeds moved in the faint breeze like soldiers engaged in tireless parades across the landscape until they snagged on gnarled scrub and clumps of sagebrush and creosote bush and thistle and cholla cactus, marking the land with a dried-up, used-up look.

Occasional breaks in the landscape – arroyos and short-end canyons and dark rents in the earth caused by volcanic uplift and the steady erosion of wind and sudden storm – gave way at last to the sprawling, monotonous desert floor.

Even in the hour before the sun began its relentless march across the forbidding landscape, driving shadows like cattle, the heat of centuries simmered on the surface of the earth.

Max tugged Buck to a halt, climbed from the saddle, and broke out the two canteens. He took a sip of fresh water for himself and savored the sweet taste for a moment before taking a small drink. He looped the strap around his shoulder and opened the second canteen, cupped both of his hands together, and filled them with water that he offered to Buck. The chestnut gelding tasted the water eagerly, and Max repeated the process four more times before he capped the canteen and returned it to the saddle horn. He took a final taste from his own canteen before strapping it to the horse's flank, and he took Buck's reins and began to walk.

"We've got a long way to go, Buck," he whispered. "Let's take our time; save our strength."

Max began to assess his situation once more, trying to find an approach to Aguante that would minimize the danger to himself and to Buck. But he knew that outside of the element of surprise, he held few if any cards. *In fact, too much is simply out of my control,* he thought.

After all, there was no way to gauge how Walker and his deputies would react when the renegades showed up in Aguante – *if they even show up.* And the prospect of both a squadron and an entire regiment of U.S. Army regulars arriving on Walker's doorstep at the same time was simply too unpredictable to plan around.

Too much can go wrong, Max thought, shaking his head. *The whole thing spells trouble. I can either stay out of the way and let the Army settle it, or control what I can and leave the rest to chance.*

But leaving things to chance was a dicey concept: Max knew from long experience that men who left things to chance often ended up dead, their fate sealed by those who were more fortunate, or more careful, or who had planned more meticulously.

"I've got to get in early and get Walker alone," Max said suddenly, and he climbed back into the saddle and scratched at Buck's ears before urging the animal forward again.

"That's all there is to it, Buck. We've got to get there first."

Buck lifted his head, his nostrils flaring, his wide eyes searching the landscape, and he surged ahead, moving inexorably toward Aguante.

The steady thump of hooves echoed across the miles like a monotonous, muffled drumbeat.

"That's either a brave man or a crazy one – maybe a little of both," Capt. Jed Johnson said.

He was talking with Lt. Col. Michael Corbin as the two men walked from the Whiskey Bend stables toward the sheriff's office. The street was alive with activity: People milled about, talking, some pointing at the two Army officers, while freighters moved wagons loaded with a variety of goods in and out, the first time in three days that the inhabitants of the small settlement felt at ease.

"What did you say, Jed?" Corbin asked as though he had been tapped suddenly on the shoulder and was surprised to find someone standing beside him.

"You look like you're a hundred miles away, sir," Johnson replied. "I was talking about Max Blake. You seem to be concentrating on something else entirely."

Corbin nodded in the direction of a handful of men who talked animatedly in front of the barber shop and bath house. "It's good to see the town wake up again," he said.

"Yes, sir," Johnson replied. "From what the sheriff says, our presence is appreciated."

Corbin nodded thoughtfully. "What was it you said a minute ago – something about Max Blake?"

"I said he was either an awfully brave man or a crazy one – I can't tell which. Perhaps he's a bit of both, sir."

Corbin took a deep breath and allowed a smile to cross his face. "Max Blake is a man with no patience for lawbreakers and fools. He's smart, calculating – definite officer material. It's a shame he's working for that judge in Twin Forks and not for the Army."

He paused momentarily, removing his hat to smooth his hair, and he looked at Johnson as though he had just discovered a universal truth. "And he is without question the best hand with a six-gun I've ever seen."

The two men walked up the steps leading into the sheriff's office, and Corbin added: "I wouldn't worry too much about Marshal Blake. It's the men in his way who require our pity."

John Hawkins looked up from his desk as the two officers approached. He set a fistful of paperwork aside and stood, motioning for the pair to take a seat.

"No thanks, sheriff. We've only come to pay our respects, sir," Johnson said.

"So you're all set to move out?" Hawkins asked.

"We'll start steering the renegades toward Aguante within the hour," Corbin replied. "Still, you'd best be prepared to keep a sharp eye for trouble. You never can tell about a pack like this; they've been unpredictable so far and may be again."

"I understand," Hawkins said. "There's a lot of ways they can go."

"They might try to loop straight north and find some protection right back here," Johnson said. "We'll try to keep them moving south, of course, but it's something they might consider. You might want to prepare for the possibility, sir."

Hawkins nodded. "Hard telling what they'll do when pressed," he said, "but that does present a concern. I'll set up a wall of men with a good eye and station them looking south. If trouble comes, we'll be ready."

"Just make sure you shoot at renegades and not at my soldiers," Corbin said.

Hawkins laughed. "We can still tell the difference between blue and gray outfits."

Corbin nodded his approval and hooked a thumb toward Johnson. "Gather them up then, captain, while I have a final word with Sheriff Hawkins here."

"Yes, sir." Johnson turned toward Hawkins and added, "Good luck to you, sir."

As Johnson moved briskly into the street, Corbin extended his hand. "It's been a pleasure, Sheriff Hawkins," he said. "But a last word of caution, if I may: Don't trust Bolton. I certainly don't – and I don't think that Marshal Blake did, either.

"How Bolton did it is mystery. But he got his hands on gold the renegades stole, and he had resources to do it – resources not apparent to me. It wouldn't surprise me if he's playing possum, waiting for help to spring him from that cell you've caged him in."

Hawkins nodded thoughtfully after a moment. "You might be on to something," he said at last. "He's playing awful dumb for a simple whack on the head – especially after this much time. But how can you tell for sure?"

"Just be careful with him. Don't give him the chance to whack you on the head in return," Corbin said as he started making his way toward the door.

"Listen, Lt. Corbin – one other thing."

Corbin turned and held Hawkins' gaze as the sheriff shifted from one foot to the other. "Not everyone does, I reckon, but I consider myself to be a friend of Marshal Blake's. You've got a rough trail out there, and I know the marshal is going to be somehow right in the middle of it. Still, some of us in the territory would feel a sight better if he made it through this scrape in one piece."

Corbin laughed hard for the first time that day. "I'll tell you what I told my captain a few minutes ago, sheriff: It's the man in Blake's way needs to watch out. I don't suspect a little thing like a renegade pack is any match for your marshal friend."

Corbin offered a casual salute, turned smartly, and walked through the door.

"It's not the renegades that worry me," Hawkins said softly. "It's that damn mess in Aguante."

Max Blake could feel the midday heat bake through his clothing and settle deep into his skin as he approached a wash that dropped suddenly ahead of him, stretched forward a hundred yards or more, and tumbled downward into a long, narrow rent in the earth. He climbed off Buck and, taking the horse by the reins, walked into the wash and approached the small chasm.

"This will do fine, Buck," Max whispered.

He led the horse down a thin game trail into the fissure, which dropped gradually for thirty feet or more; already he could feel the heat lessen as the chasm's sides eclipsed the direct beating of the relentless sun overhead.

Max pulled the saddle and blanket off Buck's back, broke out the canteens, and took the time to thoroughly wash the trail dust out the horse's mouth and nostrils. He took a small drink himself, then pulled a brush from the saddlebags and stroked Buck's flanks, murmuring into the animal's ears as he patiently worked.

He eventually returned the brush to the saddlebags and next checked Buck's shoes for lodged stones, loose nails, or other damage. Satisfied that the horse was in good condition despite the heat, Max took off his Stetson and turned it over, pouring an inch of water inside, and offered it to Buck. When the horse finished, he put the Stetson back on his head, appreciating the momentary coolness that it provided as the remaining water trickled into his shirt, and he returned to the top of the rim to survey the surrounding landscape.

Nothing moved for as far as he could see in any direction. A light breeze caught his face, and he took the time to savor it before returning to the inside of the chasm, suddenly aware of how tired he was.

"Make yourself comfortable, ol' boy," Max said softly, stroking the horse's neck. "We'll be here till dark. Then we'll move on to Aguante and have a look around."

Max stretched out on the ground, using the saddle to rest his head. He was asleep within minutes, his arms folded over his chest, his left boot crossed atop the right.

The men who approached the chasm wore dark clothing and moved silently.

Two were carrying rifles – old Springfields that looked like U.S. Army issue from the Civil War; three others had cocked revolvers in their hands.

They were hard men with years of trail experience, used to killing with a gun or a knife or their fists, confident in their abilities to walk away from any fight with any man.

The fact that there were five of them in all increased both their boldness and their confidence.

The leader raised his arm, bringing the group to a halt. He signaled for two men to skirt the edge of the chasm and travel halfway down the rim on the left side; he made a similar signal, and a third man moved to the right edge and peered over from that point.

Satisfied that he had the man below caught in a cross-fire from which there could be no escape, he motioned with his head for the fourth man to follow him into the wash and then down again, along the narrow game trail, to the bottom of the chasm itself.

They moved silently, carefully lifting their boots and setting them down again so that no stone would be dislodged and no sound, however faint, would echo off the rocky walls beside them.

The leader could see the outline of a horse in front of him and then began to make out the form of a solitary figure sleeping nearby, his head propped against a saddle, his Stetson pulled low over his eyes. A grim glint of hate entered the leader's eyes for an instant, and he thought of himself as a big cat approaching a slumbering fawn.

He recognized a slaughter when he saw one, after all, and the thought made him smile.

The leader held his left arm high in the air so that those above him, as well as the man at his side, could see the signal. He extended his revolver and took a careful, calculating bead on the sleeping man's chest, and then dropped his hand and fired.

Max Blake's eyes popped open with a start, his hand already clutching his Colt revolver.

He saw that Buck was drowsing near his feet, the horse's head unmoving, eyes closed and ears indifferent, the tail softly swaying in the currents of air that found their way into the chasm. Max took a deep breath then, recognizing that the lurking killers he had pictured in his mind were the products of a nightmare.

Damn, another dream: There's no one here but Buck, he thought.

Max shook his head, trying the clear the vividness of the scene from his mind. Buck stirred and opened his big eyes and looked back at Max, then moved over and nudged the marshal's head with a cold, wet muzzle. Max got to his feet and quickly scrambled up the game trail to a sheltered spot on the rim. He looked out across the landscape, using the fading light of day to try and identify any human shape, any foreign presence – anything that would indicate trouble.

But the land was barren, and the only movement he could detect was the faint rustle of sage and thistle in the soft hum of the evening breeze.

He spent a full five minutes at the rim, looking carefully in every direction, taking the time to ensure that he was alone, sweeping the images from the dream farther back into the dark corners of his mind until they disappeared entirely.

Satisfied at last, he hurried back to where Buck was waiting.

"Time to move, old boy," he whispered as he grabbed the heavy saddle and effortlessly swung it up onto the horse's broad back. "We've got a date with the Devil, and he won't wait forever."

Chapter 32

Final Debates

Lt. Col. Michael Corbin studied a hand-drawn map he had sketched from memory on a piece of butcher's paper the night before, memorizing the various lines and circles to ensure that every possible plan of attack was considered and reconsidered.

He looked again at the notations he had made in the margins, reading and reading again his thoughts and observations after discussions the previous evening. He considered a comment that Sheriff Hawkins had offered and another that came from Max Blake, each noted in his tiny but exacting script. A suggestion from Sgt. Major Michael McClinton held his attention for another moment, and he looked up now and spotted the big Irishman in the center of the line.

The Army is held together by men like the sergeant major, he thought.

He formed a tight-lipped smile at that and concentrated on the map again, nodding as one course of action and then another played through his mind. His men waited silently, confident that Corbin's careful, meticulous preparations before a battle provided them with advantages that could mean the difference between life and death.

Capt. Jed Johnson sat astride his horse a few yards away, watching his commanding officer carefully, knowing that there was nothing he could add at this point that would make a difference in the course of the next few hours. He had seen Corbin work strategic wonders with a map before; he recognized that a map in the lieutenant colonel's hands was at least as effective as a Springfield carbine or a Colt revolver.

Another full minute passed before Corbin looked up from the piece of paper, as though he had detected a change in the weather or the passing of a predatory animal. His eyes moved cautiously about, taking in the forbidding earth that stretched before him one more time, his face grim with determination.

He pulled the pocket watch from his vest, opened the casing, and checked the time in the faint light of the early dawn. He secured the watch again and looked across to Johnson, nodding once, his eyes muted, giving away nothing.

"At your convenience, Jed," he said casually. "At your convenience." Johnson snapped to attention and flashed a quick salute. "Yes, sir."

Three miles to the west, Lt. Gen. Gary Mitchell studied the landscape ahead of him, fidgeting on his horse, shifting his weight from one side of the saddle to the other. He considered and reconsidered options that he already had been over a dozen or more times, trying to ensure for a final time that he had done everything possible and considered every risk and option and opportunity available to him.

Mitchell was a career military officer who wanted no other life. He was born into a family of money and privilege and had enrolled at West Point and received his first commission before his twenty-first birthday. Thirty years later and a veteran of the American Civil War and numerous Plains Indians encounters, he was considered to be both reliable and unpredictable – valuable attributes in a fighting man. Although diminutive and almost totally bald, he was a commanding figure because he was decisive and gave no quarter; his men respected him and were proud to serve in his regiment.

Mitchell looked far down the line of soldiers to his left and right, each man mounted and ready for action, backs straight, eyes directed ahead. He nodded his approval at the mirror image of military efficiency.

"How are we on time?" he asked Sgt. Major James Cox, who was mounted on a tan quarter horse close to Mitchell's right side.

Cox, a veteran of countless confrontations in two wars, patiently checked the time again on his pocket watch, squinting in the soft light to ensure that he was reading the dials correctly. "Another minute, sir," he said.

"Very good, sergeant major," Mitchell said. "Let's prepare to move them out."

Cox urged his horse forward and broke hard to the right, sweeping past the line of cavalry regulars. He circled about at the end of the long row, returned to his original spot, nodded to his commanding officer, and made the same pass along the line of men to his left. He halted at the end of the column, examining the eyes of the young soldiers before him, sensing anticipation and a trace of fear. He nodded at a young private, holding his eye momentarily, then turned his horse again and made his way back to the center of the column. "The men are ready, sir. Shall we proceed?"

Lt. Gen. Mitchell relaxed for the first time in a long while, the relief visibly stretching across his gaunt face. He savored the moment – it was little moments like this, after all, that added up to a career – and replied in a firm voice: "Very good, sergeant major. At your leisure."

Iron Mike Truax had been on the trail for two hours, pushing his men forward at a brutal pace, ignoring the oppressive heat as the sun climbed higher and the air grew thick with trail dust.

Rand Townsend pulled his horse alongside Truax and called, loud enough to be heard above the thrumming of forty or more horses in close proximity, "We'd best rest the teams, Mike, or we'll be hauling those wagons by hand."

Truax threw Townsend an ugly glance, then spit off to his left and wiped his mouth with the back of his free hand. "You think I don't know that?" he called back.

"Knowing it and doing it ain't the same."

"Listen, Townsend, and you'd best listen good …"

"There's no use getting worked up at me," Townsend shot back.

"I'm not done talking …"

But Townsend cut him off once more: "I'm giving you my advice – nothing more and nothing less." He started to peel his horse back and called out, "And it's damn good advice. Take heed fer once."

Truax grunted. *When this is all over, I'm gonna have a short talk with that bastard,* he thought. *And he won't like what I got to say.*

Truax pushed on for another twenty minutes before he spotted a jumble of rocks and boulders, scattered across a chunk of desert no larger than the footprint of a small building. He brought a halt to the procession of mercenaries by riding to the front of the pack and circling his horse.

"All right," he called out as the trail dust blew past in a heavy blanket. "You know what to do. Do it."

One by one, the men climbed off their horses and dusted themselves off. They broke out canteens, took cautious sips, and sponged out the mouths and nostrils of their animals.

Slim Berning, Johnny Reb, Thom Adams, Toad Wright, and Harvey Bones gathered near the back of the contingent, their faces streaked with sweat and dust, their mouths chalky dry. Slim kept his eyes on Iron Mike, who was talking with one of the teamsters near the wagons, fifty yards ahead.

"I thought he was gonna run the horses to ground and kill us all that time," Toad said as he pulled the blanket off his mount and laid it and his intricately carved, hand-tooled saddle across the top of a small boulder.

"The man has put us in a hard spot again," Adams said. "We are gonna have to get us a handle on this, and soon, or we'll end up bones in the desert."

Slim faced the men, his eyes flicking from one face to the next, his hands nervously pulling at a piece of thin rope. "We all know the cards we hold," he said softly. "And we're past the point of decidin' which side of the table to stand on."

Slim tossed the rope into the sand at his feet, turned his head in Iron Mike's direction again, and grunted softly when he saw that the big man was still engaged in a lengthy discussion near the wagons.

"All right, here's the way I see it – not that any of you is asking," he said. "If we ride away now and Iron Mike or Townsend or one of the other guns sees us, we die in the desert – plain and simple. If we ride away now and get shut of Mike and Townsend and the rest, we save our skins but get no gold fer our efforts. And if we ride into Aguante like ol' Mike wants, the chances are better'n fifty-fifty that we die, with no gold to boot."

Slim shrugged and turned again to catch sight of Truax's whereabouts, concerned that Iron Mike could somehow overhear his words. "The man makes me nervous," he said at last. "If you ain't a'feared of him, you likely ain't alive.

"So, you boys got any bright ideas? I'd say we're about to run out of time."

Johnny Reb shuffled his feet. He started to talk, thought better of it, and adjusted the dirty Confederate cap on his head, his eyes boring holes into the toes of his boots. He looked at Harvey Bones, who shrugged his shoulders and maintained his silence.

Adams stepped forward. "We're gonna run out of breath if we ain't careful here," he said. "A fistful of gold ain't worth a spit in the sand if a man ain't alive to spend it. So I think we need to git away – maybe slip out of Aguante once we get there."

"I don't know," Johnny Reb said. "I'd like to get me a taste of that gold first."

"I'd like some of that myself," Bones added.

"We cain't have it both ways," Adams said. "I agree with Slim: We either get out with our skins and no gold, or we stay and die. Either way it's no gold – but at least we live to try again."

Johnny Reb scratched at his beard, wrestling with the greed in his heart and the voice of reason in his head.

Slim nodded slowly, his eyes darting back and forth between the two men. He bent down and picked up the rope he'd tossed to the ground minutes earlier and started working the twisted strands around his fingers, an exercise of rote and reflex.

"We can git out first chance in Aguante," he said, keeping his voice muted. "We stay low and slip away when Iron Mike is occupied elsewhere. There's like to be a show of force on both sides when we pull in. We can use that to slip free."

Adams didn't hesitate. "It may well be we can't wait that long, but I'm in."

"Good. What do you think Toad? Reb? Harvey?" Slim asked.

"I'm in," Toad Wright said, turning away from the group without another word.

"Hell, I know yer right, Slim," Johnny Reb said. "But we is sure walkin' away from a lot of easy living."

"That's one way to put it," Adams said. "It's also cheating a certain death. You look at it that way, Reb, and it don't seem bad."

"We're running outta time, Reb," Slim said. "You do what you want, like always. But if you don't tag along, you won't be around next time, plain and simple."

Sheriff John Hawkins and his deputy, Bob Stebner, were doing their best to organize the men of Whiskey Bend into a fighting force that could fend off a possible attack by the renegades to their south, and they were running into surprising resistance.

Hawkins was frustrated; Stebner was disappointed and took every opportunity he could to express his mounting anger.

A growing number of Whiskey Bend residents seemed oblivious.

"I tell ya, it ain't our job no more," the owner of the general store, Milo McMillan, said as Hawkins and Stebner met with a gathering of men in the street. "You did right by sending for the Army. Now it's their turn to earn their pay. Why should we risk our necks again?"

"It's a precaution and nothing more," Hawkins replied evenly amid murmurs and rumbles from the more vocal men in the group. "If the renegades double back …"

" … then it's the Army's job to double back after them," McMillan interrupted. "I'm telling you, sheriff, it don't fall on us now to do the Army's work."

"I cain't believe what I'm hearin' here today," Stebner said.

"That's easy for you to say, Steb; you're getting paid to keep the peace," Bob Beattie said. "I'm a banker; I'm no hired gun. That's why we pay you and the sheriff here to take care of this kind of thing for us. Milo's right – it ain't our job."

Stebner started to answer, his face turning a deeper shade of red as the veins knotted in his neck, when Hawkins grabbed him firmly by the arm and gave it a hard tug.

"There's a misunderstanding here," Hawkins said, giving Stebner a determined look as he tightened his grip on the deputy's arm. "We're not going after the renegades. We just need to protect our interests in this town one more time.

"The Army's gonna roust the renegades and drive them south, toward the border. But there's no telling what that gang will do in turn. All I'm asking is if they head toward us, we drive them back to the Army with some well-placed rifle fire.

"What could be easier than that?"

"Why don't the Army leave some men here to make sure this don't happen?" Beattie asked.

"Why don't they just send up some reinforcements now?" McMillan called.

Frosty Bell pushed his way through the crowd, tugging at his full beard, his face contorted in anger.

"You should be ashamed of yerselves – every last one of you," he said as he neared the spot where Hawkins and Stebner stood. "We're being asked to protect the investment in our town one more time. It seems those with the most to protect" – his eyes locked onto Beattie's for a moment and then found McMillan's – "are the ones least likely to help and most vocal about it. That's a sad thing."

He turned toward Hawkins and said, "Sheriff, I stood with you before, and I'll do it again now. I'm an old man, but the fight ain't left me yet."

Bell squinted hard at McMillan, who turned and walked back to his store, a look of disgust on his face.

"Truth be told," Bell added, "I hope the bastards show up. I been itchy for a scrap all day – one with some meaning, anyway."

Hawkins nodded his thanks at Bell. "We need a dozen rifles on the lookout till we know for sure the renegades are on the trail south," he called out, looking around at the gathered faces once more. "We've got five – no, make that six – right now. How about the rest of you? Mr. Beattie?"

"I'll speak for him," Stebner said, stepping forward and grabbing Beattie's arm. "He can stand watch next to me."

Beattie started to protest, but the look on Stebner's face made him reconsider.

"That's a brave thing yer doin' today," Stebner said as he nudged Beattie out of the crowd. "Everyone using the bank will think better of you now."

Beattie glared at Stebner for an instant but recognized that he had been outmaneuvered. "I guess I can spare some time," he said with a shrug, his voice little more than a whisper.

"Well now," Stebner said, a smile curling around his mouth, "that's a generous offer, Mr. Beattie. Guess I won't have to make that emergency withdrawal after all."

Hawkins took advantage of the shift of opinion among the men to recruit a handful of others, issuing rifles from his office.

"I suspect we won't have to use these. And as soon as it's over, we can all can get back to something approaching normal," he said as Stebner assigned the men to strategic positions along the back edge of town.

Hawkins edged away from the group and gazed at the monotonous desert landscape that stretched south toward the border, a distant look in his eyes.

"But that won't be the case for everybody," he muttered. "Not by a long shot."

Chapter 33

A Question of Timing

Max Blake warily approached the outcrop overlooking the border settlement of Aguante in the murky darkness of early night. He had walked the final two miles to reduce the hoof noise and trail dust that would point to his arrival, leading Buck with the horse's reins in his left hand, his gun hand close to his holstered Colt.

But all was silent as he arrived at the base of the rocky outcrop that towered over the town, providing an unobstructed view of the dusty main street and the central saloon that attracted much of Aguante's attention and support.

Max slipped Buck's reins over a weathered pinion pine and stealthily scampered halfway up the overlook. He paused, listening carefully for signs of life. When he heard nothing except the distant jangle of a tinny piano and faraway voices that carried softly in the light breeze, he cautiously made his way up to the top.

Even in the filtered light of the crescent moon through passing strands of wispy clouds, Max quickly determined that this spot had been used recently – *by a sentry, from the looks of it, and a messy one at that.* He considered several possibilities but thought it most likely that the site was being used by Aguante deputies watching for strangers who made their way out of the desert to the infamous border town.

Empty whiskey bottles littered the ground, along with scattered pieces of cigarette paper. A chunk of wood and thin shavings beside it indicated that the watcher was bored with his assignment: The wood was simply being whittled down to nothing, its sharpened point now stuck in the ground, the shavings pushed into an uneven pile. Boot prints, likely from a lone man, were scattered to all corners of the outcrop.

If he did his job well, Max thought, *I'd be in Reno Walker's jail cell*

238

right now – or on the back of a buckboard heading out to the desert. It makes me wonder where he's gone – and he gave that thought some hard consideration.

Max worked his way to the bottom of the outcrop and spotted a narrow trail leading into Aguante. *Now I know,* he thought and returned to where Buck was tied, stripped off the saddle and blanket, sponged out the horse's mouth, and scattered some oats from his saddlebags onto the ground. "We'll find you some water directly," Max whispered and then scrambled to the top again for a more careful assessment of the town.

He could detect activity on the main street, even from this distance and the little available light: Groups of men, often as many as four or five, were entering or leaving the saloon, engaged in animated discussions. Their voices carried into the night, but the words and conversations were indistinct. Max could hear the piano and a woman's voice, singing a song better suited to a church than to a public house in the vilest spot in the territory.

Within minutes, he picked up the figure of a solitary man, his hand tightly gripping a small package, making his way out of town instead of turning south down Aguante's main street.

That's odd, Max thought. *The man has nowhere to go except –*

"– except right here," he muttered aloud. "He's making his way back here."

I was lucky pulling in when I did. A few minutes either way ...

Max checked his Colt, ensuring that the revolver was fully loaded and in perfect working condition. He pulled the Knuckleduster that was tucked behind his belt buckle and checked it as well, mentally calculating whether the seven-shot derringer might be a better weapon for what he was about to do. *I'll have to see when the time comes,* he thought.

Max watched as the returning sentry picked his way clear of town and found the trail to the outcrop. Max eventually could hear the clatter of boots on the rocks that lined the path below, and he crouched behind a group of boulders that clung to the north edge and waited. The moonlight at his back, momentarily free of passing clouds, cast a long shadow across the jumble of rocks.

When the sentry crested the rise and came into full view, Max could clearly see his face and the whiskey bottle that he tenderly held.

The sentry was short and stocky with a wide mouth and a full beard flecked with gray hairs and loose dirt and dust from his climb. He was breathing loudly, clearly trying to catch his breath, his chest and heavy stomach pumping in and out like a blacksmith's bellows. The man's clothes were filthy: His denim trousers and boots were covered with splotches of thick mud, and his flannel shirt was tattered and ripped at the elbows. Even his Stetson had a ratty, tattered look to it.

The sentry carried a single-action revolver – *maybe a Merwyn and Bray; it's hard to judge in this light* – strapped to his right side. Max could see a chip knocked out of the end of the wooden grips and wondered whether its owner might have used the weapon as a hammer at one time.

The man leaned against a smooth-shouldered, waist-high rock on the side of the outcrop closest to the town. He sighed loudly, pulled the cork on the bottle, and took a long, deep drink, his lips greedily wrapped fully around the end.

"Perfect," he muttered when he finished with an audible gulp, shaking his head from side to side and using the back of his hand to wipe his mouth. "Nothing like it."

He took another pull and smacked his lips when he finished, looking at the bottle with appreciation before placing the stopper into the neck and setting it down at his feet.

He turned and eased his frame slowly to the ground, his back pressed against the rock, a look of sleepy satisfaction on his face. He pulled his dirty Stetson off his head, placed it next to the bottle at his side, and closed his eyes. His breathing was calm and slower now, steady and easy, and within minutes he was fast asleep, oblivious to the dangers lurking around him.

Max slipped from behind the boulders and was at the man's side in an instant, sticking the Colt deep into the sentry's amply padded ribs while removing the man's battered handgun from its holster.

"No sounds; no sudden moves," Max whispered as the man's eyes popped open in dull surprise. The sentry nodded once, his eyes wide and unblinking, and Max used his boot to kick the bottle out of the way and eliminate a potential weapon.

"What's your name?" Max asked as he held the man's frightened gaze.

"Folks call me Rufus. Don't kill me mister; please."

"Nobody will die if you do as I say and answer questions quickly and truthfully," Max said. "Understand?"

Rufus Baxter nodded.

"Good. Where's Reno Walker?"

"I cain't say for certain," Rufus said without hesitation. "It ain't that I don't want to tell you, mister. It's jest that I ain't seen him 'round tonight."

"He's close by?" Max asked.

"Oh, I'm certain enough of that. He don't leave Aguante much these days. And when he does go somewheres – like down into Mexico, maybe – well, let's just say everybody breathes a little easier when the sheriff's gone."

"He sleeps in his office then?" Max asked.

"No, though he spends most of his time there. He's got a room at the hotel; second floor, Two-Oh-One is the number. And he don't sleep alone. He's got a woman friend, Fanny Franks, though her real name is Stephanie; she owns the big saloon."

"Keep talking," Max urged, nudging the Colt into the man's side.

"No need to stick me with that thing, mister. I'm talkin' all right. The hotel rooms up and down the hall are filled with deputies. It ain't easy to get up there unseen, and it ain't easy going unnoticed once yer there. I know 'cause I been there a time or two."

Max nodded. *It's clear the man is willing enough to talk,* he thought. *The trick is to figure out whether he's telling the truth.* "Does the sheriff's room face the front or the back of the street?" he asked after a moment.

"The back end; it faces the back side."

"How many rooms do you pass before you get to Two-Oh-One?"

"It's the first one when you get to the top of the stairs – on your right. The sheriff likes to come and go as he pleases, I guess, so that arrangement works."

"You're singing pretty good, Rufus," Max said. "If the sheriff heard that you were talking so much ..." He let the thought hang in the air.

"Well, that considerable sidearm stuck in my ribs is reason enough fer me to talk," Rufus said with a grunt. "But it ain't no secret the sheriff don't have many friends left. He's kilt off a half-dozen or more men in the last couple weeks alone – good men, mind you – jest out of meanness and to keep the rest of us in line. He's got me up here, watching day and night, like I weren't worth nothing else, all 'cause of something that went wrong some weeks back. And he's been worse since he sent out his top hand and ain't heard a word since, as I hear tell."

"This top hand have a name?" Max asked, instantly making the connection.

"He goes by the name of Nash now, and he's a mean cuss. His being gone so long don't bode well, neither. The sheriff seems to think, near as I hear it talked about on the street, that Nash was either kilt or he run out on him, which makes the rest of us easy targets. Personally, I don't think Nash would up and run. He and the sheriff go way back, as I hear it. But who kin say fer sure?"

Rufus paused to catch his breath, and he looked hard at Max. "The thought has occurred to some of us to hightail it out fer good; a good-sized bunch already done such. Trouble is, most of us are wanted. And me? Well, I ain't much good no how. My eyes ain't reliable, my back gives me grief at night, my shoulder ain't much good since I took that fall – and hell, mister, that ain't the half of it.

"You want to know, I'm wore out and like the bottle too much, and I ain't anxious to start over."

"Are you interested in staying alive?" Max asked.

Rufus nodded, sighing deeply. "Yes sir, I surely am anxious fer that."

"Let's see if we can make that happen then," Max said. "But it's going to require some work on your part."

Rufus nodded. "As long as you are carrying that gun of yers, mister, you've got my attention." He held Max's eyes for a few seconds and then asked, "Don't I know who you are? I mean, you look right familiar to me somehows."

"I wouldn't worry about it," Max said. "The less you know, the better your chances of waking up in the morning."

"Hey there, Rufus."

Rufus Baxter nodded to the man on the dusty back street and kept walking.

Immediately on his left, a Reid's Knuckleduster in hand, Max Blake walked along with Buck, his chestnut gelding, trailing behind. The two men, trying to appear casual, made their way toward the Aguante stables at the end of the street. It was a path that Max remembered well: The last time he was here, he had been knocked cold from behind, beaten nearly senseless by the town's outlaw sheriff, and tossed onto a buckboard for a one-way trip to a bullet in the desert.

The Knuckleduster had saved Max then, and he was counting on the small derringer to keep Rufus Baxter in line long enough to make it to the stables, where he could secure the captured deputy, tend to his horse, and prepare for an assault on the stronghold of Reno Walker.

"You did fine there," Max whispered as they continued down the street and away from the moving cowboy.

"Course I did. You ain't got to prod me much to keep me moving, mister. I can read a stacked deck."

"We'll see," Max said simply.

They were within fifty yards of the stables when a man wearing a tin star walked out from the shadows. He was tall and angular in appearance, with a rawboned face and lean, hard muscles, and his eyes were like a lizard's in the dark shadows of the street.

"That you, Rufus?"

"You know it is, Jerry Berger; you got eyes same as any man. And you was expecting someone different maybe?"

"I was expecting you to be at yer post, keeping watch," Berger said, stepping closer and eying Max and Buck with a look as sharp as barbed wire. "Who's yer friend?"

"Spotted him not more'n twenty minutes back," Rufus said, ignoring the sharp end of the Knuckleduster in his ribs. "Jest showing him to the stables is all."

"What's yer name, cowboy?" Berger asked, looking directly now at Max, his gun hand lingering near his holster.

"What's your interest?" Max replied evenly; he had positioned himself so that Berger couldn't see the derringer, but the angle left Max at something of a disadvantage if both Aguante men decided to turn on him.

"Don't get smart with me, pilgrim. I represent the law here, and that's all you got to know. What's yer name?"

Max held the man's gaze, but he could tell that Berger had shifted his right hand even closer to his holstered revolver. "Names don't mean much," Max said with a shrug. "I've had more than my share. Today you can call me Pepper."

"Pepper, is it? Well, if that's yer name today, what the hell was it yesterday?"

"Salt," Max said.

Berger scowled, the lines running across his forehead like railroad tracks, his eyes narrowing. "I don't like yer looks or yer smart mouth," he snapped. "What's yer business in Aguante?"

"I thought the business of Aguante was nobody's business," Max said.

"You thought wrong."

Rufus Baxter, who had stood silently by, shifted his weight to his left leg – he winced slightly as Max followed the movement with another nudge of the Knuckleduster – and looked hard at Berger.

"You two boys is gonna get into a spat a'fore you know it, and there ain't no need," he said. "Fer gawd's sake, Berger, ease up. This man is all right; I already grilled him some. And last time I looked, this is exactly the kind of man comes through Aguante every day. Ease off, I tell ya."

"Don't you tell me what to do, Rufus Baxter, you dumb old fool. I ought to shoot you full of holes fer that."

"It's high time someone told you what fer, Jerry Berger," Rufus countered. "And I'll tell you another thing, dammit ..."

"Enough."

In a single smooth motion, Max switched the Knuckleduster to his left hand and pulled his Colt .45; the derringer was now pointed no more than a foot from Berger's face, while the Colt was covering Baxter.

"Unbuckle the gun belt, then get your hands high," Max said to Berger. Watching carefully, he added: "Slowly now – no sudden moves."

"I knew there was something off 'bout you," Berger said, as though this sort of surprise was an everyday occurrence, and he dropped his revolver and holster to the ground using his left hand, his gun hand held in the air. He looked at Max for a moment and finally let his eyes travel across to Rufus Baxter, and he added with a hiss, "And I'll send you to hell for this, Rufus."

"You truly are dumber'n a post, Berger," Rufus said. "You think I'm supposed to give you warning when this man has got a gun stuck hard in my ribs? I used to give you credit fer some smarts, but this shows how wrong I was all along."

"Quiet," Max said with enough ice in his voice to instantly silence both men. "Rufus, pick up the reins and lead my horse into the stables. Watch how you move." Max stepped back to give Baxter room, his eyes now locked onto Jerry Berger, his Colt cocked and aimed directly at the man's chest.

"Let's go," Max said once Rufus moved off to his right, staying well clear of the Aguante deputy and whistling softly as he made his way toward the stables.

"Nice and easy now – no surprises," he added.

"I'll give you a surprise you won't forget," Berger said, moving slowly forward and falling in line behind Rufus. "Then I'll take care of that bonehead in front of me."

"Bold talk," Max said as he picked up Berger's holstered revolver and gun belt, his eyes never leaving the deputy's back. "An empty chamber makes the loudest noise."

Berger stiffened, but Max closed the short gap between them instantly and pushed the barrel of his Colt hard into the deputy's back. "Don't try it," Max said, "unless you want to die on the street."

"One shot will bring out half the town," Berger said.

"It won't matter to you; you'll be dead."

Berger thought that over for a moment; he grunted softly as he continued to move grudgingly forward, his hands still held high in the air.

They entered the wide livery doors with Rufus Baxter quietly leading Buck and Max's Colt still pressed firmly into Jerry Berger's back.

"You want I should water yer horse down, mister?" Rufus asked.

"You want I should water yer horse down, mister," Berger mimicked, his voice tuned to a high nasal, seemingly oblivious to the revolver barrel pressed hard into his flannel shirt. "I thought you said you was took by surprise, Rufus; looks to me the two of you is working together, thick as thieves. You wait till the sheriff hears."

"You jest don't get it – do you, you dumb ox?" Rufus replied. "What the hell am I supposed to do here?"

"You might try something like this," Berger said and quickly spun around, throwing a wild punch at the same time, hoping that the sudden move would catch Max by surprise. But the marshal simply stepped forward, pulling the man so that the momentum from the punch caused him to lose his balance and fall face down onto the dirt floor. Max placed his right boot on Berger's neck and pushed down hard, keeping the surprised deputy on the ground.

"I'm gonna break yer ..."

"You are going to stay quiet," Max cut him off, pushing even harder into the man's back and leaving him suddenly short of breath. "Rufus, leave the horse for a minute and find some rope. I've got an idea that might just save your life."

Max looked at Jerry Berger, who had twisted his head sideways so that he could breathe easier, and added: "It might even save yours."

Berger grunted loudly again and churned his legs in an effort to get free. Max shoved him hard to the ground again with his boot, but the man continued to struggle.

"I'm gonna get up and kill you dead, mister," Berger wheezed. "I'm gonna ..."

Jerry Berger didn't finish the sentence. Rufus Baxter, a broken axe handle in his hand, swept in from Max's right side and whacked Berger hard in the back of the head. Baxter stepped back when he saw Max's Colt aimed squarely at his heart, and he quickly dropped the piece of wood to the dirt floor.

"Always did talk too much," he said simply, a nervous smile creasing his face.

"You almost caught a bullet there, Rufus," Max said evenly.

"Truth of it is, I figure I got me a better chance with you than I got with him," Baxter said with a shrug. "I hit you and he gets back up and shoots me full of holes for payment. And no offense meant, mister, but you don't look up to the job."

"You might be surprised," Max said. "When will he be missed?"

"Berger? Tomorrow morning, soonest, less things have changed."

"What about you?"

"Me? Hell, it could be days, if a'tall, though only the sheriff kin say fer certain."

Max considered the situation and made a quick decision. "Then we'd best get busy," he said. "We've got some work ahead of us."

Chapter 34

An Unlikely Alliance

"Rufus, saddle your horse."

"You mind tellin' me why?"

"When you're done, throw a saddle on this fella's horse," Max Blake said, ignoring the question while he hog-tied Aguante deputy Jerry Berger. "You get the chance to ride out and maybe save your life."

Max glanced at Rufus Baxter, who reached down to the dirt floor of the Aguante stables, picked up a chunk of rock-hard mud, and tossed it back and forth from one hand to another, nervously assessing the predicament he found himself in.

Hours earlier, his only concern was staying out of the way of Reno Walker, the murderous Aguante sheriff, while he kept watch from the top of the outcrop overlooking the outlaw haven near the Mexican border. Now he found himself working with a stranger who, rather than killing him, seemed to be willing to help him.

Baxter was confused and afraid, and each emotion showed itself clearly on his rugged, weather-beaten face, which was streaked with sweat in the dim lantern light.

"Listen, mister, my life ain't gonna be worth a spit in the corner once the sheriff gets wind of this, even if it's mostly my own choosing. I don't know what you got in mind exactly, or why, but I kin tell you it'll lead to no good – not fer you and sure as hell not fer me. You ain't half the hard case the sheriff is, no offense meant."

When Max didn't answer, Rufus added, "I guess I ain't nearly afraid of you as I am of the sheriff – even if yer the one with the gun."

Max stopped binding Berger's feet with rawhide strips that had been secured from the tack room and looked across at Rufus Baxter, who stood near the end of series of stalls. He watched intently as the man fiddled

247

with the clump of mud, catching it first with his right hand and then with his left, his fingers a whirlwind of motion and energy as his mind tried to grasp the dilemma that he found himself in.

Max decided to chance an explanation of what was about to happen in Aguante. *He'll accept the hand I deal him, or he'll find himself in more trouble*, he thought. *Let's see how it plays out.*

"What are you wanted for, Rufus?" Max asked.

"Cattle rustling."

"Did you do it?"

"Yes, sir, I did."

"How long ago?"

"Hell, I don't rightly remember. It's been five years or more, I'd guess, since I been on the owlhoot."

"You made your way to Aguante because of that?"

"Yes, sir. I didn't like the thought of some bounty hunter or sheriff catching me and stringing me up on account of a few head of cattle. I ain't a bad man, as such. I jest got mixed in with the wrong band of thieves is all. I followed 'em down the line and into Aguante and been here since. Most of them I rode in with drifted on, though one or two ran afoul of the sheriff and ain't with us now."

"That seems to happen often in Aguante," Max said.

"It don't make none of us happy, neither, but what's a man to do? You don't live long if you go up against the sheriff and his men. Better to join 'em than try and beat 'em, I guess, but we still ain't happy. I ain't happy, at least."

Max expertly finished the knots that bound Jerry Berger's hands and feet before he looked up at Baxter once more.

"By this time tomorrow, nothing will be left of Aguante," he said. "Anyone still alive will likely hang at the end of an Army rope."

Baxter looked puzzled. "How in hell you gonna manage that, mister?" he blurted.

"The Army's heading in from two directions," Max said. "They should be here by dawn. They'll be armed, and they won't ask questions."

"Hard to imagine," Rufus said, his eyes wide with disbelief.

"The man heading the Army attack is interested in two things: justice and glory," Max continued. "He won't stop until he gets both."

Rufus slumped to the floor at that bit of news, numb and discouraged. "So who in hell are you, mister? You don't look like no bluecoat to me."

"I'm a federal marshal," Max said. "My name's Blake. I've been here before – not all that long ago, in fact."

"I knew it – knew you looked familiar," Rufus said, tossing the clump of dirt onto the floor, his face lit in a tight, grim smile. "You was here when all hell broke loose and the saloon was burnt near to the ground. Am I right?"

Max nodded. "I didn't torch the saloon, but I was here."

"Sure you was," Rufus said, his excitement apparent. "You was beat up bad and somehow got out – got the jump on ol' Jim and Pete. The sheriff weren't none too happy 'bout that. He kilt the both of 'em, you know."

"The sheriff is the reason the Army's coming in," Max said.

"He's a damn sight crazy, you ask me," Rufus said, though he looked from side to side, as if checking for someone lurking and listening in the shadows. "This is a town run on fear as much as bullets. That's why when I'm told to git up top the hill and stand watch, I do it and stay quiet. Only time I leave is when the bottle runs out."

Max nodded. He had come to appreciate the man's candid nature and honest assessment of the brutal laws that controlled those who lived in fear in Aguante.

It also was clear to Max that Rufus Baxter wasn't much of an outlaw.

"I'm taking a chance with you," Max said after a minute. "You can ride out and take this man with you."

"He'll kill me the first chance he gets," Baxter said, pointing at the prone body of Jerry Berger. A large lump the size of a hen's egg had appeared on the back of the deputy's head, and a trickle of blood ran through his hair and onto the back of his neck.

"Give him no chance for that," Max said. "Head due north to Whiskey Bend with Berger strapped over the horse."

"They'll shoot me up in Whiskey Bend – if I even make it that far."

Max finished with Berger, and he stood, helped Rufus to his feet, and directed him to toss a saddle on Berger's horse.

"When you get to Whiskey Bend," Max continued, ignoring Baxter's concerns, "tell the sheriff – his name is Hawkins – that I asked you to bring this man in. Tell him Berger is wanted for murder and should be held till he hears from me. That'll be good enough."

"What if Berger runs his mouth?"

"He likely will. Just tell Hawkins that I'll explain it all later."

"Well, I guess I kin do that. It beats waiting to git kilt right here – and sooner rather'n later, to hear you tell it."

"Good choice," Max said. "If you run into the Army on the way, and you might, give them the same story. They won't question you much.

They've got other business."

"Then what? What's to become of me?"

"It's up to you. Head in any direction you like; take a chance. Five years is too long to keep much paper on you, if your crime was rustling. If I find out otherwise, and I'll check, I'll track you down myself."

"You won't have to. You'll never see me again – no need."

"There's one other thing you should know," Max said as an afterthought. "It's about the renegades."

"Renegades? What renegades?"

Max shrugged. "I'll tell you what I know while I see to my horse."

Reno Walker was staring at the ceiling in his office, his boots propped on the scarred wooden desk at the end of the wall farthest from the door. The front two legs of his chair were well off the ground so that he could lean back, maintaining his balance with his feet, and think.

Things were falling apart around him; he could sense it, but he wasn't sure what to do about it. He grew angry each time he considered the situation, which only added to his confusion.

His deputies were restless and uneasy.

The outlaws who relied on his protection were equally nervous. A number of them actually had slipped away in the night, *heading down into Mexico, no doubt, trying to steer clear of my six-gun.*

Even Fanny Franks, the pretty saloon owner he kept company with, had been distant and aloof of late.

The thought left him momentarily discouraged.

Normally, he would share his suspicions and frustrations with Richard Nash. But Nash was long gone from Aguante. He had been on the trail for days now, tracking a man responsible in Walker's mind, at least, for creating much of the unease in his town.

His top deputy might be gone for weeks or months, in fact: Nash's orders had been to track and kill a silent stranger who even now haunted the sheriff's dreams.

Walker had no doubt that Nash would succeed in time. But excessive time was something that he despised. Time gave people the opportunity to think. And thinking gave people the chance to question, to doubt, to nibble at the edges of his authority.

It's like a sore that festers and won't heal, he thought as he balanced his weight on the chair, his eyes closed, his mind lingering on the point. *I can feel it eatin' away...*

The same thing had happened to him once before, in a mining town in the Rockies of Colorado, and he had been lucky that time. He had escaped with Nash's help, and the two men eventually drifted to the desert and set up the Aguante operation.

But a change was creeping into the town and the minds of the men and women who drank and gambled and lived and died there; to Reno Walker, at least, it was as real as a bullet, and it had to be stopped.

I'm the man to fear, the one to reckon with here; every one of 'em knows it, he thought. *But something ain't right out there. I kin almost see it and smell it, but I can't get my hands wrapped around it. And that worries me.*

Walker understood that fear was a great motivator, and he pulled it like a fifth ace in a stacked deck at every opportunity.

They all know that crossing me is a fatal mistake, he thought, his gaze directed at the ceiling, his mind wandering through a litany of failures and missed opportunities and perceived slights and corner-of-the-eye looks and shadow dealings that he couldn't quite put his finger on but recognized as troublesome, as truly worrisome, regardless.

He stood suddenly, the chair striking the wooden floor with a solid knock, and paced back and forth in front of his desk. He crossed to a rack of Winchesters on the wall and lifted one into his hands, automatically cycling the lever action to pump a fresh shell into the chamber. His finger tightened on the trigger, sensing the tension, gauging the feel of the mechanism. He slowly released the hammer with his right thumb, allowing the firing pin to nestle on the back of the cartridge.

This all started with that drifter and the big fella and his partner, and then the fire at the saloon. And I won't rest easy till every last one of 'em responsible is shot to pieces.

Walker pulled a whiskey bottle from a drawer in his desk and took a long, deep gulp; the liquid burned his throat as it coursed through his system, providing a sense of satisfaction and comfort. He sighed inwardly, took another drink, and returned the bottle to the drawer again. Tucking the Winchester under his arm, he strolled out of his office and onto the street, his confidence improving with each step.

One look around town, he thought. *Maybe I'll find me a head or two to bust up some; that should get me to feelin' better.*

Max Blake ducked out of a small door at the rear of the Aguante stables, his Winchester in his left hand, and crouched low to the ground, allowing his eyes to adjust to the darkness.

He noted after a few seconds that he was within yards of the spot where one of Reno Walker's outlaw deputies had crashed the butt of a pistol into the back of his head weeks before. Max patted his belt buckle, feeling the outline of the Reid's Knuckleduster that was safely tucked behind it. The derringer had helped save his life on that occasion. This time around, Max was counting on larger weapons – his Winchester and Colt Peacemaker among them – and smarter decisions.

And the Army – can't forget about the Army, he thought.

Off in the distance, he could hear the chatter of a lone jay. Beyond that, and the soft sigh of the night breeze, all was still on Aguante's dusty streets.

Max tried to detect any sounds from Rufus Baxter, who had left the stables minutes before, walking his own horse and leading Jerry Berger's, with Berger hog-tied and strapped on, down the arroyo to the south and out into the dark cover of the night. But Baxter had slipped silently by and passed unnoticed; his plan was to move west for an hour and then due north, picking up the trail toward Whiskey Bend.

With luck – and it would take some luck with the renegade pack driving to the south – Baxter would arrive by noon the next day in the stronghold of Sheriff John Hawkins.

He'll need a break, and I hope he finds it, Max thought. Then he darted into the street, staying low, making his way toward the two-story structure that housed Aguante's lone hotel and boarding house.

I'll need a break of my own to chase Walker out of there without some sort of dust-up, Max thought. *If I can just ...*

His thoughts were interrupted by the sudden crunch of boots walking on the plank steps of the building immediately ahead of him. The boards were unsupported, which made the wood creak loudly, the sound unmistakable in the night air. Max halted in mid-stride, crouched lower, and pressed his body against the side of the building; he pulled the Winchester into his chest so that the barrel pointed skyward.

He kept his head still, turning his eyes toward the sound of the boots, which were now on solid ground again and approaching along the edge of the street in Max's direction. He could detect the lone silhouette of a man, a rifle held with one hand, walking quickly and looking directly ahead, moving toward the stables.

Must be another deputy, Max thought. *There's too many of them and not enough of me. And I don't want him stumbling on Buck.*

Max moved his eyes steadily along, following the man's progress down the street, holding his breath until the deputy was well past.

Max waited until the man was out of sight before slipping silently around the edge of the building. He quickly doubled back on the opposite side, moving stealthily through the shadows, the Winchester cradled so that his gun hand was free. He reached the far end of the stables, ducked his head around the corner, saw nothing, and moved forward once more, listening for tell-tale sounds.

He heard a boot scrape against solid wood and the creak of a door opening. Max waited a moment and then another before he made his way down the side of the stables building to the midway point, where a small window afforded a look inside. Pushing the Stetson back on his head so that the brim wouldn't get in the way, he edged his face slowly forward until his left eye was level with the bottom portion of the window. The two lanterns provided enough residual light to reveal any movement, even through the dirty glass, but he saw and heard nothing.

He was so intent on concentrating on the interior of the building that he didn't hear the footsteps creeping up from behind until the last instant. *The man's good,* Max thought quickly. *He's double-backed on me. I'll have to be smart here and get lucky.*

Without turning around, Max held up his right arm as a warning signal to the man approaching behind him. "Watch it," he whispered, just loudly enough to be heard, his face still pressed up to the window. "Got a stranger skulkin' in here."

"That you, Berger?"

"Quiet," Max said, disguising his voice as best he could with a low hiss. He again thrust his right arm skyward and moved it quickly back and forth, as though he were throwing an apple. "I can see him. Look over here."

Max could sense as well as hear that the man was almost directly in back of him now, and he knew that his ruse wouldn't last much longer. He kept his face pressed against the glass and hissed again, "Get on the other side here ..."

As the man started to move alongside, Max swung the butt end of the Winchester in a single violent upward motion, catching his quarry full in the stomach with the hard wooden stock. The surprised man clutched his belly and doubled over, trying to catch a ragged breath, and Max raised the Winchester again and brought it down with a firm thump on the back of the man's head. The stranger went down in a heap with a sudden intake of breath and was still in the dirt.

One less skunk to deal with, Max thought. *I'll just get him inside and tie him in a stall, out of sight.*

He grabbed the man by his collar, gave a hard tug, and noticed for the first time that the material was made of fringed buckskin. Startled, Max bent down and rolled the prone body over, looking into the man's face for the first time.

"Well I'll be damned," he muttered.

Chapter 35

Final Preparations

Max Blake was seldom taken by surprise, but the dirt-smudged face of Reno Walker, eyes closed and muscles slack, unmoving and unaware on the dusty ground outside the Aguante stables, gave him a decided start.

"I'll be damned," he repeated softly.

A thousand thoughts ran through his mind, and another thousand scattered impulses raged through his veins. Primary among them was immediately ending the Aguante sheriff's senseless reign of lawless terror.

But he drew a deep breath. *I'm a federal marshal, not a killer with a badge,* he thought with conviction.

Max quickly looked around, trying to determine whether the brief scuffle attracted attention. But he saw and heard nothing out of the ordinary, and he looked carefully at the fallen outlaw, checking for signs that the sheriff might be faking.

Max removed the sheriff's revolver and rifle and set them on the ground along the edge of the livery's rough-hewn walls; he placed his own Winchester against the timbers of the stable's exterior. He took Walker's hat, pulled the inch-thick strap from the band, and used it to bind the man's hands, looping the rawhide through the sheriff's thick leather belt before cinching it tightly.

Max next used both of his hands to grab Walker's jacket and shirt collars. Struggling with the dead weight, he pulled the prone body – the boots dragging on the ground, heels down – through the small door at the back of the stables.

Max stopped for a moment to catch his breath before again hauling the man into one of the empty horse stalls, where he dropped the body unceremoniously into the filthy straw. Seeing that Walker still had not stirred, Max scrambled to the spot where he had worked earlier to secure Jerry Berger, the deputy Rufus Baxter had carted away. He returned to Walker's side with additional rawhide strips to further bind the sheriff's hands and feet and a kerchief that smelled of sweat and horse, which he knotted in the center and used as a gag.

As a final piece of security, Max took a thin piece of rope, tied one end around the sheriff's feet, and secured the other end to an iron O-ring that was fastened to a post at the front of the stall.

Momentarily satisfied, he ran outside the livery, collected the weapons he had left moments earlier, brushed the sheriff's heel prints out of the dirt, and circled the entire building to ensure that he was alone. He waited patiently at all four corners of the building, listening and watching, trying to sense as well as spot or hear potential danger.

But he turned up nothing suspicious and eventually went back inside, where he checked on the sheriff again. He prodded at the man's ribs with his right boot and, getting no response, began a systematic search of the occupied horse stalls. *One of these horses belongs to that murderer,* Max thought. *The beast deserves a better fate.*

As he worked his way through the stables, trying to determine which horse the sheriff owned, Max heard approaching voices and ducked into one of the empty stalls.

He peered across to the side door, where a long shadow suddenly chased itself across the dirt floor in the dim lantern light. Max could smell cigarette smoke and, removing his Stetson, snuck a glance around the corner of the stall where two men stood at the entrance. It was too dark to make out their features, but their voices carried well on the night air and he wondered whether that alone might be enough to rouse the sheriff.

They'll hear him stir if he's awake, Max thought, *and that'll mean trouble.* He silently pulled his Colt from the black leather holster and listened to the conversation.

"Hell, I don't know what to think anymore," one of the pair said. The man sounded weary and worn out to Max, his voice thick with cigarette smoke

"It's almost as if he just ain't interested," the same man continued. "He's been that way since the fire. But what do I know? Maybe he's gone loco in all this heat."

"You reckon all you want 'bout the sheriff. I'll stay away from that thinking."

"So, you see him in here?"

"I don't see nothing in here," the second man, who was younger and had more vitality, replied with a shrug. He turned toward the center of the stables and called out in a voice that made Max wince, "Hey, Berger, you in here?" He paused a moment as if waiting for a reply and finally said, "Hell, he ain't here. I don't know where he got to, but he sure ain't in here."

"He's supposed to be in here, ain't he – either right here or somewheres close on by? So what do you think?"

"Maybe he's off to the saloon fer a drink or two. How the hell should I know?"

"The saloon's closed, you blankethead."

"Then maybe he's chasin' after a gal somewhere hereabouts – might even have one up in the hay back there. Who kin say?"

"And maybe the sheriff'll bust him upside the head if he finds out he ain't at his post, you reckon? The sheriff catches him playing the fool, and I'd say Berger is headed to the bone orchard fer sure. Silverbird and Doucette will see to that right quick enough, though I ain't seen much of them lately, comes to that."

"It don't matter. If the sheriff keeps bustin' heads, there won't be none of us left to haul the bodies or defend the place. And that includes you and me."

The older man pulled a last long draw from his cigarette – Max could see the coal-red end light up a weathered face with a wild gray beard – and he tossed the burning stump onto the dirt floor and ground it in with the toe of his boot. He laughed and said, "Now who in hell is gonna attack Aguante? You'd have to be crazy to even think it."

"The law don't know we got ourselves fewer guns by the day 'round here, what with the sheriff acting the way he is and half the cowboys in town slipping out in the dead of night."

"You reckon maybe that's where Berger's gone?"

"Berger is none to bright to figger that out. Nah, he's around somewheres. Come on, let's get out and find him."

The two men turned toward the darkness outside. Their voices carried on the night air, and Max could still hear them as they moved away.

"I'll tell you this, partner: It's always amazed me the Apaches don't come sweeping in here and clean the place out. I don't figger we'd stand a chance. But you think I could ever git the sheriff to listen? Not a chance."

"Maybe the Apaches have carted off Berger – you think?"

"As if they'd want him."

The men laughed at that, and their voices trailed off at last into the night air.

That was lucky, Max thought when he could no longer follow the conversation. *The last thing I need right now is a shootout, which is exactly where that was heading.*

Max moved away from the corner of the stables and looked carefully up and down the rows of stalls. The perspective was immediately useful: In the far corner, away from the other horses, a muscled, well-brushed black gelding was tethered to a stall that was cleaner and decidedly larger than anything else in the building. A hand-tooled black leather saddle and finely crafted bit and reins were stored nearby on a sawhorse made of crossed lodgepole pine with a thick oak beam in between.

That's the one, Max thought. *It's the best-looking horse here, though it doesn't hold a candle to ol' Buck.*

He approached the horse carefully from the left side and whispered softly, soothingly, as he brushed at the animal's neck from the outside of the stall. The horse stirred and turned toward Max, swishing its tail leisurely before dropping its head contentedly again.

This is a fine piece of horse flesh, Max thought. *Let's see if I can get a saddle in place and get out of here in one piece before the Army shows up.*

As Max placed a blanket across the gelding's back and followed it with the saddle, a sudden thrashing from the other side of the stables caught his attention.

Awake at last, Max thought. *He won't be happy when he sees me.*

I wonder how long it'll take before he figures it out.

Max finished cinching the saddle and fastened the bit and reins in place before he raced back through the shadows to the stall where the sheriff was snorting muffled curses through the gag in his mouth, his tethered limbs straining to break free.

Max knelt down and grasped Walker by the hair, turning the man's head to the left so that he could look directly into the outlaw's face. The sheriff's eyes were thin slits, but they widened in surprise at the sight of the federal marshal. Max had seen the look before: It generally registered on the face of a gunfighter who wasn't fast enough, or skilled enough, or quick enough, or resourceful enough, to stay alive.

"My name's Blake. I'm a federal marshal," Max said simply. "I'm taking you in for trial before Judge Radford in Twin Forks." He looked hard at the man and added, "You won't like the result."

Walker pulled his head loose from Max's grip, leaving a chunk of hair behind, and bellowed a cry of rage through the kerchief that was stuffed into his mouth.

"We can't have that now," Max said, and he drew his fist back and crashed it into Reno Walker's jaw, sending the man reeling into blackness again.

Max studied the prone body carefully for a moment and then whispered, "Just one more thing to do before we go."

He returned to the door at the back of the building, checked for any signs of lurking deputies along the outside walls of the livery, and disappeared into the night.

Rufus Baxter could hear the thunder of hoof beats long before he could see the massive dust cloud that stretched across the wide expanse of desert like a low-slung brown cloud against the horizon.

He slowed his horse to a walk and continued forward. Jerry Berger's horse, a roan-colored mare, trailed behind. Berger was awake and alert again, his body strapped and tied across the saddle. The red kerchief that was knotted at the center and tied around his head was an effective gag that muffled the curses he yelled continuously at Rufus.

"The Army boys are coming for ya, Berger," Rufus said loudly so that his voice could be heard above the steady drumming of incoming horses. "You kin hear 'em plain enough up ahead. You'd best keep yer mouth right shut if you want to live another day."

He pulled his horse to a halt as the columns of soldiers came into full view in the early light of dawn and called to the trailing outlaw, "Course, it don't matter much to me if they hang you now or later."

Berger's muffled protests were drowned out as the lead column approached and drew to a halt twenty yards or so directly ahead of the patiently waiting Rufus Baxter.

A thick cloud of dust drifted into his face, and he turned the horses around, loosened the kerchief around his neck, and pulled it across his mouth and nose to filter out the stifling dirt. It took more than a full minute for the dust to clear, and Rufus finally turned the horses to the north again to see thirty Army Springfield carbines pointed directly at him.

Time to be bold, he thought, and then called out, "One of you fellas named Corbin?"

"That's Lt. Col. Corbin," a voice answered. "Who's asking?"

"Anything you say," Rufus muttered and yelled back: "My name's

Baxter. Max Blake sent me on an errand – said I might run into you boys. I've got a message or two to deliver and a prisoner to take north, and I'd appreciate yer putting them rifles down."

Rand Townsend edged his horse around a cluster of men huddled at the fringe of a small encampment on the rim of a dry gulch miles north of the border.

The renegade band of gold thieves had halted its hard ride for the second time in an hour, resting the pack horses hauling two heavy wagons, and Townsend was trying to assess the condition of the animals and the sentiments of the men to share with the murderous Mike Truax.

He didn't trust Truax – few men running with the renegade pack did – and he knew full well that somewhere along the line, and likely sooner rather than later, the two of them would settle their mutual dislike with six-guns and flying lead.

"Hey, Rand – hold up there."

Townsend pulled up his horse and turned as Slim Berning and Thom Adams approached. He tipped his Stetson and nodded. "What's on yer minds, boys?"

"It's true we're headed to Aguante then?" Adams asked.

Townsend shrugged his big shoulders and chased a persistent black fly away from his face. "That trouble you some?" he asked.

"Just curious is all, though it does give a man pause," Adams replied.

Slim snorted loudly. "It troubles me a wagonload."

Townsend shifted in the saddle and waited.

"Aguante is a town of last resorts, Rand. Ain't a man here don't know that. Ain't a man here don't understand what heading there means," Adams said, edging past Slim and positioning himself directly in front of Townsend's horse. But he could sense immediately that the big man wasn't buying it.

"Near as I can tell, it means we get out of the line of fire from the hounds on our tails. The chances of them tracking us to Aguante are as skinny as Slim here," Townsend said, grinning.

"You kin laugh all you want, Rand, but it's deadly business fer every man-jack of us here," Slim said. "And I'll tell you something else you likely ain't thought about yet."

"Keep yer voice down, Slim," Adams hissed, looking nervously about, but Slim ignored the advice and moved in closer.

"I'll take a chance and say this 'cause I think yer a reasonable man," Slim said. He paused, organizing his thoughts, and looked across at Adams as though seeking approval before he plunged in again.

"We've been on a hell-ride fer days now after shootin' up that town to the north, and it won't git no better in Aguante," Slim said at last. "We may well git shut of the Army there, but we'll be up against a gang of cut-throats every bit as bad as them that's been chasin' us – and maybe a whole bunch worse."

Townsend was intrigued. "What makes you say that?"

"You know Aguante's reputation. You really think we kin jest ride in and hole up fer who knows how long and have no trouble? Hell, Rand, only a man with a death wish would come up with a plan like that."

Townsend almost laughed. "It's Iron Mike's plan, Slim. Take it up with him," he said at last, shrugging his shoulders.

"Take it up with Iron Mike," Slim repeated with a snort. "You say that like it's possible to make a point with the man."

Townsend turned his horse about and started to move off.

"You know I'm right," Slim called. But Townsend merely raised his hand, his fingers pointing skyward, and nudged his horse ahead.

"You think we did the right thing?" Slim asked after a minute passed.

"I think we need to pull out – and soon," Adams replied. "Townsend don't like ol' Mike any better'n the rest of us, I suspect, but he can't act. We're out of time. We got the Army at our backs and the Devil as a partner and hell itself ahead of us."

"You thinkin' tonight?"

"I'm thinkin' right now."

"Good," Slim said. "What about Reb? How 'bout Harvey, Jack, Toad, and the rest of 'em who feel the same?"

"It's their call," Adams said. "When we mount up again, I say we hang back, keep our pace slow, and cut due west after a time."

Slim Berning nodded. "Come on then. Let's git."

As the pair moved through the shadows toward their horses, Rand Townsend drifted through knots of men who we tending to their animals or talking in groups of two and three. A handful of men acknowledged him with a nod, but they were careful what they said when he was nearby: It was common knowledge that Townsend talked regularly with Iron Mike Truax – and that fact alone made everyone nervous.

Townsend was aware of the role he played now that Joe Howry's return to the renegade band was suspiciously overdue. He also knew there was precious little he could do about the distrust directed his way.

None of that matters. All I want is my share of the gold, he thought – *that and a clear shot at Mike Truax before it's all over.* He weighed one wish against the other for a moment and couldn't decide which he wanted more.

He was still wrestling with the thought when he saw Iron Mike talking with the teamsters in charge of the wagons. The three men were arguing again, and Townsend took the opportunity to nudge his palomino directly behind the renegade leader.

"Five more minutes and then we move," Truax said with finality.

"If we don't rest these teams awhile, Mike, we're gonna be packing that gold on our backs," a freighter called Will said nervously.

"It'll be on your back, not mine. Jest get them animals moving when it's time."

He spun around quickly and glared at Townsend, who sat patiently on his horse, listening to the conversation with a smile lighting his face.

"What the hell do you want?" Truax snapped. "You look to be enjoying this."

"This'll just take a minute, Mike," he said, and he motioned with his head for Truax to put some distance between himself and the teamsters. Iron Mike turned toward the pair and said, "Git movin' – and five minutes is all you get." He looked back at Townsend and hissed, "Now what?"

"Aguante's a mistake, Mike," Townsend said, his voice neutral, his face empty.

"Yeah? Who says that?" Truax shot back, his eyes raging with anger.

"The men, for starters. They don't like it. Aguante presents problems."

"Of course Aguante's a problem. You think I don't know that? A man would have to be half-baked to head into Aguante with two wagons loaded up, no matter how many men and rifles he had. Hell, Townsend, even you could figure that out – and you wouldn't need to take no vote, neither."

"Ain't nobody out taking votes, Mike. But the men do talk."

"I know that, too," Truax fired back, continuing to glare at the man. "You jest don't give me enough credit. Never have. That'll change, though."

"It ain't that, Mike, and you know it. Nobody cares who gets the credit for what and who don't. All anybody cares about is the gold. And the men think Aguante …"

"Enough," Truax growled, cutting him off with a brutish snarl. "We ain't going to Aguante. We was never going to Aguante. We're headed straight to the border. The last thing I'd do is turn the gold over to that

262

pack of weasels in Aguante, and that's jest what'll happen if we ride in there."

Townsend thought that over for a moment and shook his head in agreement. "Good," he said at last. "Will and Ryan there are right about the stock, though. Them freight horses need rest. Hell, we all do."

"You jest be ready to move when I tell ya, dammit, and not another word 'less you want to eat a bullet. You follow?"

Townsend started to reply in kind but reconsidered. *Not here – not now,* he thought. *The gold is all that matters now.*

"Anything you say, Mike," he said and touched the brim of his Stetson.

"It's coming, ya know," Truax said, his eyes drilling holes into Townsend.

"You bet," Rand replied, confidently returning the man's unflinching stare. "And you ain't gonna like it when it does."

Chapter 36

A Sign in the Dark

"Watch for the signal now. Be patient and wait for it, sergeant major."

"Yes, sir. How exactly will we know when we see it – the signal, I mean, sir?"

Lt. Col. Michael Corbin chuckled at the question. He was standing on the outcrop overlooking Aguante in the exact spot where Max Blake and Rufus Baxter first scuffled and then formed an unlikely alliance scant hours before. It was the exact spot, in fact, that Baxter had recommended to Corbin and his squadron – "but only if you want the bird's view of the place and what the marshal's gonna do," he had said a short time earlier when their paths crossed on the trail.

"I suspect we'll know Marshal Blake's signal when we see it, Mickey," Corbin replied after a minute had passed. "There's nothing subtle about the man that I can tell."

"Yes sir, and a rare thing, that."

Sgt. Major McClinton glanced across at Corbin for an instant, a smile creeping across his ruddy face, and he stared intently down from the outcrop into Aguante's main street. Even in the dim light from a crescent moon that found only sporadic holes in the passing high clouds, he could clearly see the front entrance to the town's main saloon off to the right and the two-story hotel, which was immediately across the dusty street.

"Hold on a minute. Isn't that something, maybe a man down there – over on the right side of the street near the hotel?"

"It looks like two men, to be exact. Let's keep an eye on them, sergeant major," Corbin said after staring intently at the street below.

"Yes, sir. You think one of 'em might be the marshal, sir?"

"Highly unlikely, unless he's picked up some additional support. He's not going to find a lot of friends in Aguante."

"I guess not, sir," McClinton said. "So what do you suppose those two are up to at this time of night?"

"Technically, it's morning, sergeant major. And my guess is those two are likely on patrol." Corbin looked across at McClinton quizzically. "You seem a bit yappy tonight, Mickey. Is something troubling you?"

"Me, sir? Not a'tall. It's the marshal that's been on me mind."

McClinton shrugged then, pausing momentarily. "You don't think they're looking for the marshal, do you, sir – those men down there, I mean."

Corbin chuckled again. "If the sheriff down there had any inkling that Max Blake was in his town right now, he would ring every bell and beat every drum personally – and every man in Aguante would be on alert.

"No, sergeant major, the marshal is down there somewhere, all right. But nobody else who's alive or awake knows it. I suspect they will, however – and soon."

The men on the street below stopped momentarily in front of the saloon while one of the pair lit a cigarette; it appeared to McClinton and Corbin that the two shared a laugh before they continued past the saloon and slipped out of sight again.

"A thought just occurred to me, sir," McClinton suddenly said. "You don't think Marshal Blake is dead, do you?"

The words made Corbin stop and look hard at McClinton. "Dead? I'm astonished that would come to mind. What makes you ask that, of all things?"

"Well sir, it's another possibility is all. If no one is after beatin' drums or ringin' bells down there, and they aren't, maybe the celebrating's over, sir."

Corbin turned as Capt. Jed Johnson, his second in command, scrambled to the top of the outcrop, before he found McClinton's eyes once more. "If Max Blake were dead, sergeant major, they would still be ringing bells and beating drums. Just be patient and watch for his signal. It should be any time now.

"You have a report for me, Capt. Johnson?"

"Yes, sir," Johnson replied, stopping for an instant to salute. "Lt. Gen. Mitchell sends his regards, sir. He has the town surrounded, sir, and is waiting for your signal. He told me to report that the only activity going into and coming out of Aguante all night long was that Baxter fellow we ran into, trailing that outlaw behind."

"And the renegades?" Corbin asked.

"Just as you suspected, sir: They avoided Aguante and are heading toward the border. Lt. Gen. Mitchell has some of his best trackers on them, sir. He said they were slowed down by the stock pulling two trailing wagons."

"The gold, then."

"It would seem so, sir."

Corbin nodded thoughtfully, his eyes still on the street below. Johnson and McClinton stood patiently by.

"He didn't mention seeing Max Blake going into the town?" Corbin asked after a minute.

"No sir. I specifically asked him about the marshal, in fact. It might well be that Marshal Blake already was in Aguante when the regiment arrived."

"And it might be that he's already slipped past everyone."

"That's unlikely, sir. We are talking about an entire regiment, after all."

"A man as resourceful as Max Blake could slip past Gen. Mitchell and his men easily enough, Capt. Johnson."

"I guess that's true, sir. We know he's out there somewhere; that Baxter fellow told us that much."

"Hold on," McClinton interrupted, and Corbin and Johnson both looked toward the sergeant major and then followed his line of sight to the street below, where a dull orange and red glow was sparking the night sky near the saloon.

"Unless I miss my guess, gentlemen, we have just heard from the elusive Max Blake," Corbin said. "Sergeant major, you have three minutes to prepare the men. Capt. Johnson, alert Lt. Gen. Mitchell that we strike in exactly five minutes from your arrival; he'll know when it's time because all hell will break loose down there.

"Questions, gentlemen?"

When Johnson and McClinton remained silent and unmoving, Corbin nodded with satisfaction. "Excellent. We go in hard, and we show no mercy."

"What about Marshal Blake, sir?"

But Corbin already was moving down the trail that lead from the outcrop to his waiting horse below.

"You think we're shut of 'em yet, Slim?"

"Hard to say."

Confederate raider Thom Adams grumped at that, listening to the drumming of horses' hooves around him, waiting impatiently. He tracked the rise of the sun to the east for a time, watching as the rocks turned from a shadowy gray to glowing orange and burning red and the last of the stars winked out overhead. He caught sight of a hawk, circling high above the distant horizon, and followed the raptor until it moved beyond his vision. He finally called across to Slim Berning again. "So, you think we're shut of 'em now?"

"Gawd a'mighty, Thom, who's to say? I sure as hell ain't no expert."

Slim and Thom Adams, along with Harvey Bones and Johnny Reb, were riding at a steady pace west of the trail leading toward Aguante and the border. The men had slipped away from Iron Mike Traux and his renegade band thirty minutes before, lagging at the end of the column of riders, waiting for the pack to pull ahead before gradually turning their horses away from the rising sun.

But the uncertainty ahead of them was nothing to the lingering fear that caused them to look back over their shoulders, time and again, hoping that no one – and especially not Mike Truax – was tailing them now.

"I think we're clear," Johnny Reb called out as he pulled his horse alongside Slim's. "They cain't be following now."

"They can if Iron Mike knows we lit out," Slim called back. "It's too soon to ease up, Reb – too soon to relax."

"Ain't gonna relax. Jest saying what I think is all."

"Where we heading, Slim?" Thom Adams called.

"To the big cactus and then on to Yuma," Slim called. "We git to Yuma, then I say we kin rest a spell, but not before."

"We ain't likely to git that far," Harvey called across now in alarm. "Take a look behind."

Slim threw a glance over his shoulder and caught a wisp of trail dust. He pulled his horse to a slow halt and turned to take a closer look. He used his hand to shield the rising sun from his sightline and watched with unblinking eyes. The others had pulled up and were gathering around him now, also looking back to the east, trying to assess their fate in the column of dust that chased after them.

"What do ya think?"

"Too soon to tell."

"That ain't good; maybe we should ride hard."

"If they're coming, Harvey, they're coming and no use us runnin'.

We won't git far and won't git shut of 'em."

"I think it's one man alone," Reb said. "Not enough dust back there fer more."

"You think?"

"Yeah, one man alone," he added after a minute went by.

"So who is it?"

Reb continued to stare, absently scratching at his stump, but he didn't answer.

"Let's not give him an easy target," Slim said, getting down from his horse. "Split up some – don't all bunch up in one place." He pulled his Spencer carbine from the scabbard attached to his horse and moved away from the animal, getting down on one knee and sighting along the barrel toward the approaching target. Harvey Bones and Thom Adams did the same, moving sideways in a line twenty yards or more apart.

Reb remained in the saddle, unaware of the activity around him, watching carefully. He could make out the outline of a man now, riding almost casually along on a dun-colored mare with an easy gait.

It was the horse that gave it away.

"It's Toad," he called. "Hold yer fire."

"You sure?"

"Course I'm sure. You can see it plain as I can, you look hard enough."

"My eyes ain't what they used to be," Slim said with a shrug, standing again and tucking the Spencer under his arm.

It was another full minute before Toad Wright, a big smile crossing his narrow face, pulled up and nodded to each man in turn. "Slim. Reb. Harvey. You, too, Thom."

"Took you long enough," Slim said.

"Leave it to you to complain."

"What about Jack Conway?" Reb asked.

Toad merely shook his head.

"You see anything behind you, Toad?"

"Nothing, and I been watching. I saw you pull back and was too close to Townsend and Dave Berns to follow right off," he said. "Had to wait some is all. Here now, though. What's the plan?"

"Plan?" Slim snorted. "What plan?" He looked at the men around him and laughed for the first time in months.

Chapter 37

The Muster of Cavalry

Max Blake cautiously picked his way down the back streets of Aguante toward the town's primary saloon, his Colt revolver in hand. He stayed low to the ground, moving from building to building, his eyes darting toward every dark corner and potential hiding place where an on-duty deputy or hired gun might lurk.

He had rummaged through the livery and collected several rags, which he doused in kerosene emptied from lanterns hanging on the back wall, and a handful of wooden matches that he had found in a metal box nearby and stuffed into his pockets.

He knew his route well: He had been in Aguante short weeks before and could vividly remember making his way through these same back streets in his relentless search for Hoss Johnson and the Morgan boys. He briefly recalled surprising an Aguante deputy and the satisfaction of knocking the man senseless. He also recalled with distaste his capture and subsequent beating moments later; he had been fortunate to escape.

No sense looking back. I'm close to the saloon, Max thought. *The hotel is just around this corner –* he peered from the edge of an outbuilding and could see the two-story hotel clearly in the filtered light – *there it is; and the saloon is across the street.*

All I need to do now is ...

Max was brought up short by two men – *deputies, judging by the hour* – engaged in conversation in the middle of the street. They were arguing about the disappearance of the man assigned to the stables and whether they should wait or report at once to the sheriff.

One of the pair, a tall, slender man with a narrow face and unruly hair that sprouted from his coal-black Stetson like obnoxious weeds, was lighting a cigarette. Max could hear him pause and offer the makings to the second deputy. When the man declined – "You know I only smoke cigars," he muttered indignantly – they resumed their discussion about the missing stables guard.

"It's unnatural," the man with the cigarette said. "It ain't like Berger to skip away from his post like that. You know how the sheriff'll react, and so does Berger. I tell ya, Charlie Boy, something ain't right about it."

"He's either sawing logs somewheres, which is what we should be doing right now, or he's over to the Red House and bedded down fer the night, which is something else we should be doing," Charlie Boy Albus replied. "Ain't he some sweet on that little gal with all them black curls? Eva Mae?"

"She's worth the thought. So let's check the house and see fer ourselves," Stevie Bauer said in return.

"Hell, if we try to go banging in there, Erin Lynn'll have us hog-tied and never let us back inside again, no matter how much money we'd bring along. No sir. Let's jest relax some and Berger kin tend fer hisself."

"And if the sheriff finds out?"

"Finds out what?"

"That Berger ain't at his post – what do you think?"

"It's still on Berger."

"It may end up on Berger all right, but the sheriff might not see it that way," Bauer said with a shrug. "And if the sheriff don't see it that way …"

"… then the sheriff might put it on us, and I don't like that," Albus finished. He paused and made a snorting sound, mumbling something that Max couldn't make out.

The two men started to drift down the street again, talking softly, their voice carrying even as they moved away into the blackness of the night.

If they only knew about Berger, Max thought, and he moved around the edge of the hotel, listening intently to the muted conversation before slipping silently across the street and making his way to the back of the saloon.

Max spotted an abandoned pile of charred lumber that had been pulled from the walls of the saloon and discarded haphazardly after the fire set by Freeman Morgan and Hoss Johnson weeks before during their escape from Aguante.

Thinking quickly, he holstered his Colt, set the rags down at the edge of the building, and began leaning some of the long timbers against the newly constructed building, his energy focused on a single task.

"Git yer hands up, mister. Now."

Max cursed to himself as he felt the cold steel of a revolver grind into his back, and he quickly raised his hands. A man behind him pulled Max's Colt from its holster and tossed it on the ground a few yards away.

"Who are ya? What are ya doin' here?"

"Name's Radford," Max improvised. "I'm working with Berger."

"I didn't know Berger had him a partner, and I don't recognize you no how." The man circled around so that he could look directly at Max. He wore a badge and was of medium height, though thick in the middle with dirty clothing. He also had a mean, vacant look in his eyes, which were coal-black in the early morning darkness.

Max shrugged. "Sheriff just paired us. I'm new to town."

"I don't know nothing 'bout you."

"I could say the same. Take it up with the sheriff," Max said casually.

"Don't you tell me what to do, mister. Where's Berger?"

"He's working over there," Max said, pointing behind the saloon. The deputy turned his head automatically, and Max used the instant to slip in tight and wrench the revolver from the deputy's hand. He pulled the Knuckleduster from his belt in a swift, fluid motion, his fingers naturally fitting into the brass handle of the frame, and brought it down on the back of the man's head with a vicious thump. The deputy crumpled to the ground, and Max wasted no time dragging his unconscious body behind the lumber pile.

Didn't hear him, he thought as he checked to see that the man posed no additional threat. *Too many of these jackals about – time to get this done and get out of here.*

He scrambled back to retrieve his Colt before tossing the deputy's weapon aside. He knocked the Colt against his hand a couple of times to shake any loose sand or grit from the barrel; he opened the cylinder with a snap and spun it, checking the action, listening carefully to the mechanism's workings, and he shook it again before returning the weapon to his holster and resuming his task.

He worked silently and efficiently now, moving without sound, stacking the charred wood into a makeshift lean-to. He inserted the fuel-soaked rags halfway up the sides, close to the new timbers, and pulled a kitchen match from his pocket. He ignited it with the nail of his right thumb, held it downward to grow a larger flame, and touched it to the rags, which immediately caught and flared.

The fire quickly chewed into the fuel of the charred timbers and worked its way up toward the fresh lumber of the exterior walls. Max pulled another piece of wood from the pile and used it to prod the now-blazing fire, which already was crawling high up the sides of the saloon. Then he tossed it onto the stack, and the pile collapsed to the ground and hungrily started working its way along the base of the building.

There's something about the desert air that makes a fire catch quick and burn hot, Max thought. *Corbin should see this for miles.*

He looked around again, ensuring that he was still alone, formulating his route back to the stables and Reno Walker.

Max raced across the still-deserted street and stopped at the corner of the hotel. He grabbed a rock as round as his fist and tossed it through the hotel window, bringing the large sheet of carefully hand-lettered glass crashing to the floor.

That ought to get some attention, he thought, and then he was gone.

Lt. Col. Michael Corbin scampered down the side of the outcrop that overlooked Aguante, his mind devouring a hundred ideas as he approached the base of the rocky hill and surveyed his waiting men.

Corbin called for his horse and then swung his big frame into the saddle and waited silently while Sgt. Major Mickey McClinton secured his mount and moved alongside. Corbin cleared his throat and addressed his squadron.

"Gentlemen, this is a moment of opportunity for us all," he said softly but firmly, his words carrying clearly in the crisp air of early dawn. "We've been given a great responsibility this day: to reduce to rubble a blight on this territory – and we will do exactly that."

He paused and glanced up and down the line at the soldiers he commanded. "Show them no mercy, gentlemen, for they will show you none. Do your duty. I expect no more of you and can ask no more. Are we clear?"

He waited theatrically for a full minute as Capt. Jed Johnson approached the column from the west. "All right," Corbin said at last, his eyes determined, his face resolute. "Good luck to you all."

He turned to McClinton. "Take them out, sergeant major. Do us proud."

"With pleasure, sir."

"Capt. Johnson?"

"Yes, sir," Johnson replied, leaning forward in the saddle.

"If you would be so kind ..."

The two officers peeled their horses to the end of the column and waited as McClinton directed the squadron forward toward the south side of the outcrop, holding the men in place as they waited for the signal to begin the attack.

Corbin consulted his pocket watch, squinting in the dim light to read the hands before he snapped the cover closed and returned it to his vest.

"Lt. Gen. Mitchell sends his compliments, sir," Johnson said. "He's anxious to get started, sir."

"I would hope so, Jed," Corbin replied with a chuckle. "On both counts."

"Do you think Marshal Blake's had enough time to get out, sir?" Johnson asked after a moment of silence.

"I expect so," Corbin replied. "He knows what's coming – what's at stake. He doesn't want to get caught in a fight between the rabble in that pathetic town and the U.S. Army."

Corbin shook his head slightly and shifted his weight. "I'd say Max Blake already is two steps ahead of us and three steps out of Aguante."

"Very good, sir. It's been my experience that your instincts are always right."

A broad smile lit up Corbin's face at that, and he beamed back at Jed Johnson. "I knew it all along, of course," he said. "You are a perceptive young man destined for greatness, Capt. Johnson," and both men laughed.

Corbin looked straight ahead again, and he started counting silently, ticking off the seconds of an imaginary clock that was approaching high noon in his mind. He casually pulled the Springfield from the scabbard strapped to his horse, taking his time as he unhooked the leather binding that secured the carbine in place, and he shucked a cartridge into the trap and pointed it skyward. The seconds were ticking down, and he glanced at Johnson once more and nodded; then he whispered softly, "At your pleasure, Mickey," and fired the Springfield into the air as the morning sun began its steady rise to mark a new day.

Lt. Gen. Gary Mitchell heard the high-pitched single shot distinctly in the crisp morning air. He nodded to his regimental bugler, 1ˢᵗ Sgt. Charles Hayes, and said, "If you would, Mr. Hayes," and the soldiers of Mitchell's regiment spurred their horses forward at the sound of the incessant charge.

Mitchell and Sgt. Major James Cox, who was assigned to stick close to his commanding officer, remained in place as two-thirds of the regiment raced forward. Mitchell could follow the movements of the galloping soldiers from the trail of dust kicked high in the air, and he looked on with satisfaction as a broad brown cloud filled the sky and stretched from the north end of Aguante to the south end in a solid, unbroken wall.

This'll be over quickly unless we've missed something, he thought. *And we didn't.*

He turned to Cox. "What's your assessment of the resistance we can expect, sergeant major?"

"Light, sir. They'll be preoccupied with the fire," he said, pointing in the general direction of Aguante with a thick finger. "My guess? They won't know what hit 'em – from either side."

Mitchell smiled. "Corbin's men will get there first and claim the glory. But I suspect we'll have plenty to do – here and out there," and he swept his hand toward the unceasing, merciless desert that stretched forever in front of him, backlit to a dull red by the rising sun. He paused for a moment and added, "Let's just hope we don't shoot each other in the cross fire."

The sound of a galloping horse drew the pair's attention, and Mitchell spotted one of his scouts approaching from the west. The man was charging quickly, and he pulled his palomino to a halt at the last instant, facing his commanding officer directly, and snapped a short salute.

"Beg to report, sir," he said at the same time.

Mitchell returned the salute casually and nodded. "Go ahead, mister," he said to his most reliable tracker, 1st Sgt. Bernard Vogel, a career soldier with years of experience in Indian campaigns throughout the Western United States.

"Thank you, sir. The renegades are moving south and four miles behind," Vogel said, pointing back to the west. "We count twenty-seven men in all. They've been slowed some by the wagons, but it's clear they want no part of Aguante."

Mitchell nodded. "They have no idea of what's in store for them, then?"

"No, sir. We've stayed well clear – we tracked their dust as much as anything else – so they've had no chance of spotting us, sir."

"Good. That's fine, Mr. Vogel."

"Thank you, sir. And your pleasure, sir?"

"Patience, first sergeant: Patience, if you please. We have plenty of time before they reach the border – am I correct?"

"Yes, sir."

"Good. Sgt. Major Cox, would you please give Capt. Stuart the word to take the remaining men and follow Mr. Vogel here?"

"Does the general care to add a personal message, sir?"

Mitchell laughed softly. "The return of the Army's gold shipment, of course, sergeant major."

"Very good, sir," Cox said. "And a little glory of our own, I might add, sir. There's no sense in giving Mr. Corbin all the credit."

"No doubt," Mitchell said with a smile. "All right, Mr. Vogel, straight to 'em now and no mistake. A lot of gold and a lot of lives are at risk – and a barrel full of Army revenge."

"Yes, sir. No mistakes at all, sir."

Vogel saluted his commanding officer and turned his horse again, edging slowly forward so that Cox could move in beside him.

"Capt. Stuart and his men are waiting across the way," Cox said.

"Good, sir. We collect them and ride hard – a nice little trail of revenge, I'd say."

Max Blake heard the single shot from a Springfield carbine, followed a brief moment later by a distant Army bugle, and he knew at once that he needed to make up time if he wanted to survive.

The rock he had thrown through the window of the Aguante hotel created an immediate stir which quickly turned into panic on the dusty streets. Within minutes – far sooner than Max had anticipated, in fact – Aguante was filled with men who were surprised and then angry to see the town's main saloon ablaze once more. And while the fire was drawing everyone toward the saloon, Max had to be careful to avoid pockets of men, all of them well-armed, who had heard the stirrings and were stumbling out of buildings and small huts throughout the settlement.

He could hear the steady ringing of a bell behind him – a signal that would bring every living soul in Aguante out into the streets – and he figured that the Army fighters who surrounded the town already were charging hard.

I need to get Walker on his horse and out of here before the shooting starts, Max thought. *And it won't be easy.*

He ducked behind an outbuilding, avoiding a group of puzzled men hurrying toward the saloon, and ran quickly to the end of the side street, which in turn lead directly to the back end of the stables. Max crouched low again, moving across the exposed corner in a quick run, his Colt held firmly in his right hand. He slipped alongside the now-familiar walls of the livery and began to work his way toward the back entrance when he detected muted voices inside the cavernous building.

Max stopped at the window, which was situated midway along the wall, and cautiously raised his head for a look inside.

Damn it, he cursed.

He could see the same two deputies he had followed outside the saloon minutes before as they searched for the missing Jerry Berger. The pair was now occupied in the corner where Max had left the trussed and unconscious Reno Walker minutes earlier.

It was instantly clear, however, that Walker was awake and talking and about to be freed from the ropes and rawhide straps that Max had used to secure him.

I've got no time for this, he thought, and he raced to the door at the back of the livery.

Chapter 38

Sweeping Out The Old

Max Blake burst through the back door to the Aguante livery and called out in a commanding voice, "Don't move; you're all under arrest."

The two deputies he had seen on the streets moments before, searching for the missing Jerry Berger, were crouched over the highly animated form of Reno Walker, trying to untie the knots that bound the sheriff's trussed feet.

Charlie Boy Albus and Stevie Bauer looked up in surprise at the sight of a federal marshal, a steely resolve in his piercing gray eyes, pointing a Colt .45 revolver in their direction.

"I'll be damned," Albus said, raising his hands in the air. Bauer took a step back but said nothing.

"Shoot him or we'll all be damned," Walker hissed, struggling to get free.

"Bad idea," Max said calmly, his revolver pointed directly at Charlie Boy's chest.

"Get down on your face – both of you. No sudden moves."

"Shoot him, Charlie. Bauer, shoot him. Dammit, somebody shoot him," Walker screamed; he was sitting up now, pulling at the rawhide strips that still bound his feet. His face was beet-red and contorted with rage, and his eyes burned holes in the two stationary deputies who were looking directly at Max – and clearly not liking what they saw.

"You shoot him, you think it's such a good idea," Albus said matter-of-factly, though his eyes didn't leave Max Blake's. "He ain't got no hog-leg pointed at you."

Charlie Boy dropped slowly down on his knees, his hands still high in the air, and calmly spread his lanky frame out on the dirt floor. Walker was infuriated. "He'll kill us all, you damn fools," he yelled, and Stevie Bauer apparently believed it. He snuck a quick look at Charlie Boy, who was now sprawled face down, his arms outstretched, and bolted behind the sheriff, trying to find cover by the oak-framed wall of the horse stall as he reached for his holstered revolver.

Max snapped off a single shot from his Colt Peacemaker, and the diving deputy yelped as he crashed into the wall.

Walker jerked his head around to the spot where Bauer landed with a thud, trying to determine exactly what had happened; the shot had startled him, and he snapped his head back again and tugged at his bindings and tried to locate Max. But the federal marshal had slipped away after the gunshot and was out of Walker's sightline.

"He's moving, Bauer," Walker shouted to his deputy, his hands furiously trying to tear the rawhide loose from his tightly bound feet.

"I'm hit. He damn near shot my foot off," Bauer screamed back, ignoring his six-gun, which had clattered against the wall and skidded to a stop in the dirt.

"He's gonna finish us all off if you don't ..."

The sudden eruption of gunfire outside the livery brought Reno Walker up short. He cocked his head momentarily, trying to determine what had gone wrong on the streets of his town, and the sounds that he heard were chilling: volley after volley of rifle and revolver fire, mingled with the incessant ringing of a bell of alarm and the muted cries of men under attack. He knew at once that Aguante was being threatened by a well-armed, hostile force, and he was helpless to do anything about it.

"He hit me in the damn foot," Bauer whimpered, but Walker ignored him, trying to count individual shots outside the livery but quickly giving up, recognizing that the bad situation he found himself in was growing far worse with each passing moment.

"Yer a damn fool, you ask me," Charlie Boy, still face down in the dirt, called across to his partner, though he didn't move an inch.

"Shut yer bazoo, ya coward; he's out there somewheres," Walker yelled at Albus. He again pulled on the rawhide strips that were fastened like leeches around his boots, trying to work the knots free, and he cursed in frustration and looked up again to see Max Blake staring directly into his eyes.

"Bad idea," Max said, his Colt inches away from Walker's face.

"This all started with you – all of it," Walker snarled. "What'd ya do with Nash?"

Max shrugged. "Don't count on him to help."

Bauer grunted loudly from the corner, his eyes clouded in pain. "You shot me in the damn foot, you bastard," he wheezed before slumping down again. "What'd ya have to go and do that for?"

"I'm gonna kill you, mister," Walker said an instant later, his eyes seething with hate. "Should've seen it through myself last time. You'll pay for coming back."

"That's big talk for a man in trouble," Max said, his eyes never leaving Walker's.

"Come on," Walker called out suddenly, glancing around the stables once more. "There's three of us and one of him."

"He tried to shoot my foot off," Bauer complained again. He was clutching both hands around his left boot as he sat curled in a corner of the horse stall, his mind fastened on the growing stain below his ankle. "I ain't got none to spare, ya know."

Walker ignored Bauer and tried to kick at Charlie Albus, who was silent and unmoving on the ground. "Git movin', ya coffee boiler. Do something," the sheriff yelled, his voice now high-pitched and hysterical. But once again it was Stevie Bauer who reacted to the sheriff's taunts.

"I ought to shut you up, Walker, ya damn weasel," he called across to the sheriff. "Should've done it long before; all of us should've got a hand in it. Yer the one with the big mouth 'round here."

"Stove it, you," Walker hissed. "I'll git you when I'm done with this bastard."

"I'm tired of yer talk," Bauer mumbled. He reached for his revolver and picked it up slowly, as though he controlled all manner of time.

"Drop it," Max ordered.

But Stevie Bauer ignored the federal marshal and aimed his revolver at the struggling Aguante sheriff. "Should've never let it git this far," he said softly, as though he were talking to himself.

Max tried again. "Put it down now," he called.

"I don't know which one of you to shoot first," Bauer said through clenched teeth, fighting the pain in his foot.

"Kill him," Walker urged, snatching a glance at Bauer.

"No. You first."

As Bauer deliberately cocked the hammer on his Rigdon-Ansley revolver, his hand wavering, Max fired his Colt. Charlie Boy Albus moved his head for the first time, turning to see what had happened to his friend. He glanced back for a moment, then dropped his face into the dirt again and remained silent and motionless.

"I'm gonna enjoy killing you, mister," Walker said, but it was difficult to hear his voice above the constant thunder of gunfire on the streets as it drew ever closer to the stables.

Max had his revolver trained directly at Walker again. But he said nothing, choosing instead to concentrate on the erupting gun battle outside the livery.

Sgt. Major Michael McClinton heard the high-pitched whine of his commanding officer's Springfield and raised his right arm high in the air. He turned slowly in the saddle to face a line of eager fighters, and he bellowed in his clear tenor the simple battle call he had used a hundred times – one that never failed to rouse his charges and spur them eagerly forward:

"Let us go amongst them."

With loud, raucous whoops and yells, the squadron swept forward – guns drawn, eyes wide, faces grim and determined – into the fire-lit streets of Aguante.

McClinton smiled grimly as he lead the charge, his reliable Smith & Wesson revolver held high in his right hand, his eyes darting back and forth in search of targets, his horse held steady on a straight line to the burning saloon.

He could see the activity directly ahead now – men running about, some with buckets or shovels, while others were standing silently by, watching as the saloon burned – and he called over his shoulder, "Mr. Lennox, on me left if you please."

A column of men followed the lead of 1st Sgt. Seamus Lennox and broke toward the hotel side of the street and began firing. Startled men who had concentrated on the roaring fire at the saloon seconds earlier turned in amazement as a column of Army regulars swept in, their revolvers cracking with deadly precision.

McClinton peeled his column directly toward the saloon and fired his revolver accurately and assuredly as he thundered past pockets of men who were so surprised at the sudden appearance of the Army force that they stood and gaped – their mouths open, their eyes wide with shock – even as they were targeted by the charging soldiers.

The column moved past the saloon now, and McClinton brought the men up with a loud bellow, raising his right arm momentarily. He casually reloaded the Smith & Wesson, watching the mayhem before him with a knowing smile etched across his face, and he caught sight of Lennox's force on the opposite side of the street.

McClinton nodded toward Lennox, their eyes locking in a wordless and unnecessary exchange, and he called out again: "Gentlemen – once more, if you please."

Aguante deputy Spanky Parker selected that moment to rush into the street with a Spencer rifle. He took careful aim from no more than fifty yards away, finding McClinton in his gun sights, when Pvt. Matthew O'Rourke spotted the man and fired his revolver three times in rapid succession. His first two shots missed the mark, the bullets kicking up dust in the street, but the third shot sent the surprised deputy crashing into the dirt, his rifle clattering harmlessly away.

"Good, lad," McClinton said calmly with a nod toward O'Rourke. "If you'd be so good as to reload, me bucko, we'll try this again."

Lennox urged his men forward at that instant, and the Aguante deputies and hired guns and outlaws who moments earlier had been occupied with saving the saloon now were scattering in all directions, trying to find shelter from the advancing soldiers. Many had their handguns drawn and were wildly returning fire in the confusion.

The echo of a bugle's charge bellowed from the west of Aguante, growing in intensity as it drew nearer, and McClinton smiled at the sound. "I think the cavalry has arrived," he shouted above the incessant din of gunfire.

"Are you quite ready, Mr. O'Rourke?"

"Ready, sir."

"Let us go amongst them," McClinton yelled, and his men whooped loudly and charged down the main Aguante street once more.

Stuart Hicks was trying his best to organize a bucket brigade on the streets of Aguante: barking orders, directing traffic, working hard to save the saloon that he had only recently put back together after a disastrous fire weeks before.

"Where in hell is the sheriff?" he called at one point, but there was no response – only confusion and angry shouting and imaginative cursing and general disorder and chaos and confusion.

"For gawd's sake, get those buckets moving," Hicks shouted, pointing at a cluster of men standing nearby who wanted to help but were unsure of what to do. "Kline, take charge there and get them organized.

"King, get over here – now, dammit. You – Pence? Kelly? – haul that damn thing out of the way. Move it, man."

But the barked orders of Stuart Hicks were largely ignored in the bedlam that ensued when the entire back of the building began to crumble in the blistering heat and solid wall of flame that rose high into the morning sky, the sparks and embers catching in a gentle breeze and drifting into the desert. As the building collapsed in on itself, large chunks of the side walls ripped away and crashed down as well; the flat roof fell with a tremendous roar that sent towering clouds of orange and coal-red embers shuttering into the sky.

Hicks threw his hands up in disgust. He could see that the building was lost – all of his hard work from the past weeks gone in an immense spiral of flame and heat and crumbling timbers and shattering glass – and he looked around again at the grim faces of the men who were milling about on the street.

Where in hell is the sheriff? he wondered again.

"Hey, watch that," he called, pointing toward an outbuilding that was used for storage behind the saloon. Embers caught in the cedar shakes on the roof, and the wood was starting to spark to life. "Don't get yerselves caught between the shed and the saloon …"

"That building is full of whiskey," a deputy named Ernst shouted, and a dozen men scrambled with buckets and tried to douse the flames.

Hicks was about to help when he heard a sound that stopped him cold, and he cocked his head to the east and concentrated. *That's gunfire – lots of gunfire,* he thought.

He turned slowly around, puzzled, and gaped at a squadron of U.S. Army soldiers sweeping down the street, pushing their horses expertly forward, their guns blazing.

"What the hell is this?" he muttered aloud and then repeated the phrase, his eyes glancing about in disbelief, his body frozen in place as the acrid smell of black powder and sulfur and burned timbers wafted through the air.

This isn't possible, he thought, though his mind registered a bugle's call off in the distance.

He turned to run toward the hotel across the street when a bullet ripped through his shoulder, knocking him to the ground with the force of a well-landed punch. He groaned, looked up to see a dozen or more men on horses charging past, all of them dressed in U.S. Army uniforms, firing randomly at every moving man on the street.

"Where in hell's the sheriff?" he mumbled. He tried to crawl out of the street and then gave in to the darkness.

Max Blake focused on the man who called himself Charlie Boy. The lanky Aguante deputy was lying on his belly in the stables, his arms outstretched, his head held high enough to keep an eye on the federal marshal who had a Colt revolver trained on him from no more than a dozen feet away.

"You want to live?" Max asked.

Charlie Boy nodded but said nothing.

"Don't listen to him, Charlie," Walker called. "He's the law and can't be trusted."

"The way you can be trusted, you mean?" Charlie Boy spat back at the Aguante sheriff, though his eyes never left Max Blake. "I'm listening, mister."

"Good," Max said. He took three brisk steps and pulled the man's revolver out of its leather holster. Max tucked the gun, a nicely made Allen & Wheelock .36 caliber side-hammer revolver, into his belt and said, "All right, on your feet, nice and easy," as he stepped away.

Charlie Boy slowly picked himself off the ground, his eyes locked on the federal marshal, his face registering confusion and fear.

"He's gonna kill us both," the sheriff snarled. "You play along with him, you die – cause if he don't kill you, I sure as hell will."

Max glanced at Reno Walker, who was still tugging at the rawhide that bound his feet, and issued a one-word command: "Quiet." The menace in Max's voice brought the sheriff up short.

"Tie him up again," Max said to Charlie Boy, pointing in the sheriff's general direction with the end of his revolver. "Gag him first. Make it quick; then you get your chance."

Charlie Boy nodded and scrambled next to the sheriff, who was seething but motionless now as Max moved his Colt into position. The deputy picked up the dirty horse kerchief and stuffed the knot in the middle into Walker's mouth before pulling it tight behind his head and tying it off at the ends. "High time yer mouth got shut," he muttered before looping the same ropes Max had used earlier around the sheriff's wrists, pulling them tight and tying them off in a series of half-hitches.

The sheriff began to struggle again, but his curses were muffled by the kerchief in his mouth, and Charlie Boy ignored the outburst.

"Get his legs again," Max ordered, and Albus picked up a second piece of rope and bound the sheriff's ankles tightly together.

He stood when he was finished and looked at Max. "Lots of shootin' out there, mister. You mind telling me what in hell …" He let the words drift away, waiting for the federal marshal to respond.

"Get his horse ready," Max said instead, pointing across to the largest stall in the building. "Do it fast; do it right. I'm right behind you."

Charlie Boy nodded again and moved quickly across the floor of the stables. "I'm on it," he said. "You don't have to prod me none."

"I worry about everybody," Max muttered. The gunfire from outside the stables was growing closer, and Max recognized that he was rapidly running out of time.

"All right," he said when Charlie Boy finished with the cinches, "hoist him up, then tie him tight – feet and hands looped underneath. Take an extra blanket."

"He's pretty good size," Albus said with a shrug. "I might need a hand."

"You'll figure it out," Max said. "Be quick about it."

Charlie Boy hitched Walker's horse to the stall and studied the struggling sheriff, trying to determine how to best strap the man across the saddle. He bent down and got his arms around the sheriff's chest from behind in a bear hug, but Walker immediately began to thrash about wildly, his words muffled and indistinguishable but still conveying his rage as his eyes flamed.

Charlie Boy rapped the man's head with an open hand. "Hold still, dammit, or I'll kill you myself and make this a sight easier," he grunted, hoisting the sheriff onto his feet. When Walker resisted again, trying at once to sit back down, Max stepped closer and pointed his Colt directly in the sheriff's face.

"Enough," Max said.

The man's eyes went wide again, but he stopped struggling.

Charlie Boy pushed the sheriff forward and hefted him up and across the saddle, gasping with the effort. He caught his breath momentarily, and Walker used the moment to try and wriggle back down. But Max caught him by the back of his shirt with his left hand and held him in place.

"Hurry now," he said to Albus. "Strap him on. When you finish, you can take your chances outside."

"What's out there, mister?" Charlie Boy asked as he started to work the ropes. "I got to know what's waiting fer me."

"Nothing you can't handle," Max said. "There's an Army regiment on one side and a squadron on the other, working their way through town. I'd steer clear of them."

Charlie Boy Albus shook his head in amazement, but he didn't stop his work. He bound the sheriff's hands and feet again with a rope that he cinched beneath the horse after placing the spare blanket under the animal's belly. He looped a second rope around the body three times and tied it off at last on the pommel of the saddle. "Good enough?"

Max nodded his approval. "It'll do," he said. "Take off your trousers and go."

"Take off my pants? What fer?" Charlie Boy huffed.

"Who would shoot a man with no pants?"

Chapter 39

Payment in Full

Although the hostility had been growing for weeks, the spark that started a raging fire in Iron Mike Truax resulted from a tiny moment on the trail.

Rand Townsend pulled his horse alongside Truax's as the renegade pack of outlaws raced toward the border with two heavy wagons in tow. Townsend edged in close so that the unpredictable Truax's gun hand was restricted, and he smiled thinly and called out so that he could be heard above the steady drumming of horses' hooves. "The freight horses are worn down, Mike."

Truax looked across at Townsend in disgust and yelled in return, "So what?"

Townsend expected the hostility in the reply, and he didn't miss the opportunity: "So it's time to do something right fer a change."

Townsend's words were a challenge that Iron Mike could no longer ignore, and he cursed and pulled abruptly on the reins of his horse, slowing the animal enough so that he could free his gun hand. In a fluid, easy motion, he pulled his revolver from the leather holster and cocked the single-action Colt, aligning the barrel directly at Townsend's suddenly exposed back.

Townsend, however, was quick for a big man. Sensing as well as eyeing Truax's rapid movements, Rand pulled his own horse sharply to the right and swung his body low and off to the side of the saddle.

The move likely saved his life. But he was still in danger, and he knew that, too.

Townsend, his tall frame tough and rock-hard, slipped out of the saddle and rolled off his horse on his right side. He kept the startled animal between himself and Mike Truax, holding onto the reins as firmly as he could to help stop the horse's forward momentum. He heard a

286

gunshot – he could sense the bullet as it whined past his head – and he rolled as he hit the ground in a stirring of dust and sand, tossing aside the reins of his horse and reaching for his holstered revolver. Another bullet cracked at his feet, striking close enough to kick small chunks of rock across his boots, and he pulled his revolver and snapped off a shot at the still-saddled Mike Truax.

The bullet caught Truax in the left shoulder, knocking him backward and off his horse. He hit the ground hard, breaking his fall with his wounded shoulder, turning at the last instant so that he wouldn't land on his head. His revolver clattered out of his hand and skidded across the sand, and he groaned and cursed loudly and tried to recover but recognized that he was in trouble.

Rand Townsend slowly picked himself up from the desert floor, his revolver trained at Iron Mike's chest, his eyes laughing.

"You ain't got the guts or the sense," Truax challenged, clutching at his shoulder, his eyes holding Townsend's.

"Yer wrong on both counts," Townsend said as he pulled himself up to his full height and moved forward, towering over Truax as the renegade leader sat motionless in the dirt. "You been wrong all along."

The remaining outlaws slowed their horses as they charged past the two men, uncertain what to do. The freighters handling the reins of the draft horses spotted the commotion as they trailed the pack and drew the teams to a welcome halt.

Townsend ignored the activity around him and calmly pulled the hammer back on his Colt revolver. "Yer move, Mike," he said softly, though every man in the pack heard the words clearly.

"Shoot me and you never see the gold," Truax replied, taking a moment to wipe the sand out of his greasy hair and off the side of his sun-baked face. He was looking for his revolver, trying to gauge whether he could make a lunge and come up shooting. But the weapon was out of his reach and half-buried in the sand, and he wasn't sure that it would fire properly even if he could reach it in time.

"That so? Seems to me all we need to do is open up them boxes," Townsend said casually, as though he were talking to a child. "Then we kin all get a piece of yer share."

"And yer as dumb as yer horse," Truax said with a menacing hiss. "You go ahead. Open them boxes right now and see what yer share is – see if you kin yet kill me off."

"What are you telling us, Mike?" a teamster named Tribbett called out as the renegades edged closer, waiting to see how Townsend's move would play out.

"I'm saying the gold ain't in the wagons – what do you think I'm saying? Yer all of you thick as boards – every last man here."

"So if it ain't in the wagons, jest where in hell is it?" Tribbett asked.

A sudden gaping hole in his chest toppled the teamster off the buckboard before Truax could reply, however, and the renegades – one after another – looked up in surprise to a hail of bullets and a line of charging U.S. Army regulars.

Lt. Gen. Gary Mitchell watched the destruction of Aguante with a look of calm satisfaction on his face.

"It's righteous work we are doing here today, sir," Sgt. Major James Cox said, waving his arm in a sweeping motion toward the burning outlaw town.

Mitchell nodded. "We'll see when it's all over," he replied softly.

He was looking through a small, telescoping lens so that he could better follow the ebb and flow of the fighting, which was moving from building to building on the dusty Aguante streets.

From his vantage point on a small rise, he counted eight bodies in the two streets he could monitor with an unimpeded view through his lens. It was difficult to tell from a quarter-mile away, the distance Mitchell estimated he was clear of the fighting, but he figured with some certainty that all of the dead were Aguante outlaws.

Scouts galloped to his position every few minutes, calling reports from the fighting, relaying observations and questions from his field commanders. Mitchell listened intently to what the scouts had to say, nodding – sometimes smiling, cursing a time or two – and providing directives when necessary.

To each scout he would ask the same question: "Dead or wounded?"

Each time the reports came back the same: "No casualties at this time, sir."

From all reports, the Aguante resistance was weak and ineffective – sporadic at best, which was a surprise. It was apparent that fewer men were defending the outlaw border town than initially had been anticipated. Or perhaps, Mitchell considered, the deputies and hired guns and outlaws who had sought refuge there refused to fight and were either holed up in the buildings or trying to sneak away to the desert.

"Sir, we've got a lone man on horseback leaving from the south," Cox said, pointing off in the distance.

"I see him, sergeant major." Mitchell turned his telescope toward the departing man and following his progress for a moment. "He's trailing a horse; looks like something's strapped on the back."

"It could be a man on that second horse, sir – looks about right. And he's heading toward us, not skulking off to Mexico."

Mitchell continued to peer through the lens. "Unless I miss my guess, that's the federal marshal from Twin Forks." He watched awhile longer, following the man on horseback for a moment. "Send two men out to bring him in; I'll want a word with him, sergeant major. Tell the men you select to proceed with caution."

"Right away, sir."

Lt. Col. Michael Corbin was back atop the outcrop that overlooked Aguante, his right foot planted firmly on a large rock, his arms resting on his raised knee, his eyes locked on the streets below.

Everywhere he looked, soldiers from his own squadron or from Lt. Gen. Gary Mitchell's regiment controlled the streets. The pockets of resistance that had initially sprung up were soon swept away in the chaos of charging horses and determined men wearing the blue uniforms of the U.S. Army.

He had spotted two separate incidents where soldiers apparently were wounded by gunfire, but he had detected no fatalities except for the Aguante outlaws. Corbin counted nine bodies directly in front of the town's main saloon, and he could see three more near the hotel.

The saloon continued to belch fire and thick columns of smoke, and the flames had spread to three other buildings, aided by the morning winds and Corbin's orders to his most trusted men moments earlier: "Nothing stands when we are done," he had said. "We leave no buildings, no reminders. We flatten it all – it blows away in the wind."

In time, no one will know that Aguante ever existed – unless, of course, they read about the accounts of its destruction in the finest newspapers in the land. He chuckled at the thought.

Corbin heard a disturbance at the base of the outcrop and spotted a handful of women, their ornate dresses billowing in the rising breeze, gathered in a group near three of his fighters. One of the men called up, "We've salvaged Aguante's treasures, Mr. Corbin. Have a look for yerself, sir."

"You'll act the gentleman, Mr. Feeney, now and always," Corbin called back as he surveyed the scene below.

"On me honor, sir, and have no fear of me manners," Feeney replied with a laugh, and the men with him joined in as well.

"Hey, you up there," one of the women called. Corbin could tell that she was diminutive, with a full head of long blonde curls that fell from her shoulders like a cascading waterfall. Her dress was deep red, and it clung tightly to her full figure. "I demand to know who is in charge of this ... this wanton destruction. You are burning my business to the ground, and I have rights. Who do I see about that?"

"I'm the man to see," Corbin called down, tipping the brim of his hat. "The name Corbin, ma'am. To whom do I have the pleasure of addressing?"

"You must be new to Aguante, soldier boy," she replied. "I'm Fanny Franks, and that's my business on fire."

"Well, I'm sorry, Miss Franks, for your inconvenience," Corbin called back, and he smiled tightly as he spoke. "But you've been dancing with the Devil, ma'am, and it's time to pay the bill."

"What about my rights?"

"Consider yourself lucky," Corbin said dismissively as he looked out again toward the burning town. "Mr. Feeney," he called down after a minute, "be sure these ladies are afforded every courtesy."

"You can count on me, sir."

"I'll be down directly; I want to get a closer look at the action. See to my horse," Corbin called, and he turned away from the ledge and scrambled down the game trail.

Max Blake took a full minute to check the rear of the Aguante stables before he ventured cautiously out of the building. He was leading Reno Walker's horse, with the captured sheriff strapped across the saddle and firmly secured with ropes and rawhide, and he knew that his best chance to escape the mayhem with the sheriff in tow was to slip away quietly and unnoticed.

It was a daunting task: Max heard round after round of gunfire, the shots echoing off the walls of the buildings. He figured that most of the action was centered near the saloon, which was two streets back toward the east, but it was steadily creeping his way.

They'll shoot first and ask no questions – on both sides, Max thought. Still, he kept his federal marshal's badge in his left hand, thinking that it might be useful if he were spotted by an Army patrol.

He made his way across a clearing and eased down a razor-thin game trail on a steep slope leading to an arroyo at the back edge of Aguante. He whistled softly, and Buck, his chestnut gelding, looked up and nickered. Max had left the horse earlier, loosely tied, with a bucket of water and fresh hay and oats that he had carried from the livery.

"It's good to see to you too, boy," Max whispered as he approached. "Lots of commotion out there to get your interest."

He scratched at the horse's ears for a moment and then swung up into the saddle. "Nice and easy, fella," he whispered. "We head north, back to Whiskey Bend, with some company," and he urged Buck forward.

Although he heard constant gunfire from behind, Max saw no sign of escaping Aguante outlaws or Army regulars in pursuit, and he allowed Buck to pick a path away from the arroyo and around the scrub and thistle of the desert floor.

He was on the trail for five minutes, moving at a brisk pace, when he saw Buck's ears twitch in a manner that generally suggested trouble. Max pulled his Colt from the finely tooled holster strapped to his side and scanned the immediate area. The land rose and fell in a series of faults and breaks – interspersed with stumpy scrub, clumps of prickly pear cactus, and Russian thistle – and he could picture a man hiding in any number of potential lairs, sighting a rifle, waiting for the right angle or correct yardage or a shift in the wind before pulling the trigger.

He deftly slipped off Buck, listening to the desert around him, trying to block out the gunfire that rolled across the sand like tumbling ocean waves, his eyes scanning the horizon in every direction. When Reno Walker started to struggle against the ropes that lashed him to his horse, Max whispered, "You'd best stop if you want to see tomorrow."

Buck was now staring off toward the northwest, his ears forward and alert. "Someone's out there all right," Max whispered. "I can feel it, too."

He waited patiently, ignoring Walker's muffled curses behind him and the constant gunfire from the town. Max's Colt .45 was cradled in his right hand, and he pulled his Stetson low to keep the glare of the rising sun from his eyes.

Buck's ears twitched again, and Max heard the sound of horses' hooves before he caught a glimpse of two approaching riders.

"Marshal Blake? Are you out there, sir?"

The voice carried clearly, drifting on the currents of the morning air despite the incessant bellow of repeated gunfire, and it caught the federal marshal by surprise. Max remained silent as a result, waiting until he got a closer look. When he clearly spotted two U.S. Army regulars approaching cautiously, looking about in his general direction, he called out firmly: "State your intentions."

"Marshal Blake? Is that you, sir?"

"Keep talking," Max said.

"We've been sent by Lt. Gen. Mitchell, sir," one of the men called. "You were spotted by the general, sir."

Max stood, his finger on the Colt's trigger, and he nodded as the soldiers drew closer.

"My name's Blake," he said. "I'm a federal marshal." He pointed back toward the trailing horse and added, "I'm taking this man to Twin Forks." Walker started thrashing about on his horse again, his voice muffled by the kerchief stuffed in his mouth. But it was apparent that he was both ignored and ineffective in his protests, and he stopped fighting his bindings and eventually was still again.

"Seems like you've got a handful there, marshal. I'm 1st Sgt. Timothy LaLonde; this is Pvt. Don Black with me, sir," the man said, pointing toward his partner, though his eyes never left the federal marshal's. "We're here to escort you safely away from the fighting. If you'll follow us, Marshal Blake, we'll take you and your, ah, baggage directly to Lt. Gen. Mitchell, sir."

For reasons that Max could not understand – and he contemplated the significance of the moment for days afterward – his mind abruptly focused on Rebecca Gray and her son, Joey, the young stable boy in Twin Forks. It was a fleeting thought, gone from his head almost as quickly as it appeared, but it somehow provided a measure of comfort amid all of the chaos and mayhem that surrounded him.

He determined much later that the image of the two – mother and son together – jumped into his thoughts because of their inherent goodness and the way they stood apart from his world, which was populated with outlaws and murderers and brutality and the worst kinds of men and the dregs of a society bound by no laws, no honor, no humanity.

Max tipped his Stetson to the soldiers and nodded again. He could smell sulfur and gunpowder and burning timbers and the stench of certain death in the distance, and he looked out again toward Aguante and stared for a moment, his mind empty, concentrating on nothing.

"I'm right behind you," he said after a minute.

Chapter 40

And Then There Were None

No one was certain how it happened, though fingers were pointed in a variety of directions afterward.

By then, of course, it was too late.

Deputy Bob Stebner had finished his early morning rounds through the dusty streets of Whiskey Bend and returned to the sheriff's office an hour after sun-up. He busied himself with paperwork and what he referred to as tidying – keeping his corner of the office neat and orderly.

He ultimately secured two thick hunks of stale bread, an apple that he split in two with his long knife, and two cups of lukewarm coffee from the storage area in the corner; he arranged the breakfast on serving trays and entered the back room containing the jail cells by pushing open the unlocked door with his boot.

It didn't occur to him until later, after he had discussed the events with Sheriff John Hawkins a number of times, that the door should have been shut and locked tight.

Stebner stopped first at the cell holding Len Wilcox, the young freighter who had tried to pick a gunfight with Max Blake, and slid the tray under the bars.

"Come and git it, Lenny," he said with a grunt as he stooped down, pushing the tray beneath the bars and into the cell. "You'd get better fixins if you weren't stuck here, ya know. Sheriff says yer out tomorrow anyways – no law against being stupid."

Wilcox was asleep on the cot in the corner and didn't budge, his rhythmic breathing softly carrying across the room, and Stebner pulled himself upright again and shrugged indifferently before moving down to the next cell.

He expected to find Tom Bolton, the half-witted former deputy who was being held on attempted murder and robbery charges and a half-dozen other crimes that Hawkins was still working out.

"All right, Bolton, here's something fer you," Stebner said, talking to a lump in the cot. "It ain't much, but it's better'n you deserve."

Stebner stooped to slide the tray under the bars, but he was surprised when he leaned his hand against the iron door and it swung inward with a loud creak, unlocked and suddenly wide open. Stebner let the tray clatter noisily to the floor. He pulled his revolver and ran to the cot, where he poked at the blankets with the barrel.

"Nothing," he muttered as the gun met with no resistance, and he cursed softly and tossed the blankets on the floor. "Now what in the hell's happened here?"

He glanced wildly about, shook his head when he assured himself that the cell was empty by staring intently in every corner, beneath the cot, and even at the ceiling, and he added aloud in a mumbled sigh, "The sheriff sure ain't gonna like this." Stebner stalked out of the building and onto the street, his revolver clutched in his hand with a death grip, a look of stunned disbelief on his face.

He located Hawkins within minutes, and the two men rechecked the jail cell once more, prodding Wilcox for information, before making a quick scan of the town's streets and the livery stables.

Bolton's horse and saddle were gone – that much, at least, was certain. Frantic questioning by the two lawmen turned up a single fact: No one in Whiskey Bend remembered hearing or seeing anything unusual throughout the long night.

"It's like that boy just got up and walked out of that cell, and there was nothing there to stop him from doing exactly that," Hawkins said as the two men examined the area behind the jail, trying to determine how Bolton managed to slip away.

"He had help, sheriff, though fer the life of me I can't say where it came from," Stebner replied. "No other way to it. He ain't got the brains to manage on his own."

"He was smart enough to ride out of town," Hawkins replied evenly. "He was smart enough for that."

"Then he had to have help; ain't no other way around it."

"Unlikely, though I can't think of another explanation, Bob," Hawkins replied after running through the possibilities. "Are you absolutely certain that –"

"I'm telling you, sheriff, it happened jest like I told ya," Stebner interrupted. "I went in, and he weren't there. Wilcox claimed he didn't hear a thing; I prodded him a time or two, same as you.

"I didn't hear a thing – not all night – and I was around and weren't sleeping, neither."

Stebner paused and kicked his boot in the dirt, digging a small trench with the toe. "Maybe it was all that grinning he did that somehow sprung him – opened the doors up somehow like magic. Ya think?"

"We'll eventually find the truth, provided we get him back," Hawkins said after a minute's hesitation, thinking the event through again – and again coming up empty. He started to say something, paused, shook his head as though he were in pain, and finally added: "All right, Bob, let's see if we can mount a posse and find him; he can't have gotten far. I see the two Ditchen boys are back, so deal them in. Get Frosty Bell, Leon Austinson, Gary Haugen, the two Fladwood brothers, Stan Kenyon, Neil McGill for sure – the toughest men you can find."

"Yes, sir – I'll git right on it. That boy can't be far off yet. But the rest is downright spooky – unless he had some help."

"The best way to find out is to find him," Hawkins said with finality, and he stalked off toward the stables.

Morning broke gray and overcast in the eastern sky as the looming mountains snagged passing clouds and stacked them in the air, one after another, like stuffed sacks of flour.

Max Blake was heading north again, toward Whiskey Bend. Buck, his big chestnut gelding, chewed up the miles with a steady gait. The sun that burned off the early morning clouds had shifted halfway to noon, Max figured, and the heat of another oppressive desert day already was beginning to take its unrelenting toll on every living thing it touched.

No more desert work, Max thought, wiping his forehead with the back of his hand. *It's too hard on Buck, and it's not doing me any good, either.*

Reno Walker, Aguante's outlaw sheriff, was strapped upright in the saddle of his black gelding, his hands tied and fastened around the pommel, his feet bound and strapped to each other by a rope that hung loosely beneath the horse's belly. A knotted gag was stuffed into his mouth and securely fastened at the back of his head.

Max glanced backward as Walker started a run through another long string of muffled curses and complaints, the rage in his face apparent as the veins in his neck grew as thick as binding twine. But Max shrugged indifferently and looked ahead again. He had listened to the man's uninterrupted tirade when three of the soldiers in Lt. Gen. Gary Mitchell's regiment helped him secure Walker upright on his horse for travel north, away from the Aguante battlefield; it was all that he wanted to hear from the outlaw for a long time to come.

"You'll get a chance to yell at Judge Radford," Max had said as the gag was inserted into Walker's mouth. "You might as well save it till then."

It was readily apparent that Walker was uncomfortable, but Max figured that it was better than the man deserved and preferable to the way that Max had forced him out of Aguante: strapped and tied across the saddle, lying on his belly and unable to absorb the steady beating from the horse's natural gait.

Walker continued to rant, his muffled voice carrying clearly through the high desert air even though the words were indistinct, and Max eventually slowed Buck until he was riding side by side with the sheriff.

"You'll do well to hobble that lip," he suggested firmly.

Walker glared for an instant and then threw curse after curse into the gag again, his mouth working hard against the wet, dirty cloth.

"If you force that rag out of your mouth, I'll have to shoot you," Max said matter-of-factly.

When Walker launched into another tirade, his eyes wide, Max added: "I'll start with the bottom lip and work my way up to the top one – one tooth at a time."

He held Walker's stare, ensuring that the outlaw recognized the seriousness of the threat. Max brought Buck to a halt then and pulled Walker's horse up abruptly as well. He thought for a moment that the outlaw might rant again. But the rage went out of Walker's eyes, and he stared straight ahead to hide the sense of hopelessness that he suddenly felt, and Max eventually nodded and nudged Buck forward.

Max shifted his weight and thought again about his conversations with Lt. Gen. Gary Mitchell and later with Lt. Col. Michael Corbin as the assault on Aguante raged on short hours earlier.

Mitchell's regiment handled the bulk of the Aguante fighting, it had seemed to Max, although Corbin's squadron of Irish fighters was instrumental in making the first sweep through the town and securing its most potentially volatile hotspots: the primary street, the area immediately around the main saloon and hotel, and the sheriff's office.

In all, sixty-three outlaws were dead and another thirteen – Charlie

Boy Albus among them – were captured during the Army's dual-force onslaught. In addition, twelve women currently were secured and in the custody of Army troops. Two patrols also had been dispatched to determine if any outlaws had tried to sneak out of the town on foot.

Mitchell's regiment sustained the loss of three soldiers; five more were wounded. Two of Corbin's men were wounded during the fighting, neither seriously.

Corbin's field surgeon, Capt. Lewis Sayre, was still tending to the injured when Corbin left the fighting and finally met with Max and Mitchell. The Army commanders discussed strategy for a few moments while Mitchell's men helped Max secure Reno Walker on his horse.

The dead outlaws and town deputies were stacked in rows like cordwood on the northern edge of the town, and two dozen or more of Mitchell's men were busy with small trenching shovels, digging a long, shallow grave. Max could hear the shovels slicing into the sand as he viewed the action from afar with the Army commanders.

When Walker was secured to his horse and got his first look at the bodies, he barked loudly through the gag, doing his best to work it out of his mouth. Corbin eased his gaze across to the sheriff and said, without a trace of sympathy: "You got off easy, mister. But your time is coming – sooner than you think."

The hate reflected in Walker's stare was as real as the searing sun and the reek of sage and the stark blue cast of the open sky, but Corbin held the man's eyes until the outlaw finally turned his face back toward the slaughter.

Once the town was secured and the livery emptied, every building on every street was systematically torched. Within minutes, the sky was dark with thick clouds of billowing, roiling smoke that drifted eastward in the prevailing winds, blocking out the sun. The air smelled of charred wood and kerosene and soiled rags and clothing and bedding and accumulated debris, and the sounds of exploding whiskey and rye and bourbon bottles and shattering glass could be heard for miles across the desert floor.

A band of Apache warriors silently appeared from the south and watched the fire from a distance, but they disappeared quickly toward the border after assessing the strength of the gathered infantry nearby. Corbin and Mitchell surveyed their movements with interest as the town burned and the smoke and stench drifted with the winds, and Max nodded and said, "Naiche and his men."

"You know him, Marshal Blake?" Mitchell asked. "I'm surprised."

"The surprise is that you don't," Max replied.

When Max finally left the two Army officers – shaking hands with both, heading north toward Whiskey Bend – no word had come in from Mitchell's scouts about the renegade band of gold thieves. Corbin was itching for a piece of that fight as well, already making plans to move his squadron south.

It seems like weeks ago, not hours, Max thought as he wiped the sweat from his face, snapping his mind back to the present.

Max glanced toward the eastern sky and figured that he was still three hours from the relief that Sheriff John Hawkins' hospitality provided. *That'll tire Buck some in this heat, but we'll rest in Whiskey Bend for a spell,* he thought.

"We'll both catch a good meal, boy," he whispered to Buck, leaning forward in the saddle and scratching at the back of the horse's head. "I'll get a shave and a hot bath, and for you, old fella, a nice rest – what do you think?"

Buck pushed steadily forward, and Max was soon lost in his thoughts – of Judge Radford, of the gallows that stood outside the courthouse in Twin Forks, of the now-silent outlaw who trailed behind him, trussed and defeated.

Tom Bolton was quick, all right.

And he wasn't nearly as dim-witted as he pretended to be.

He chuckled inwardly at that. *They might think I'm dumb, but it ain't so – less it's dumb like a fox,* and that thought made him laugh out loud.

Escaping from the jail cell in Whiskey Bend was easy. All he had to do was distract for a moment and then pick the pocket of Bob Stebner, the friendly deputy sheriff, to secure the key to his jail cell.

Bolton had waited until the middle of the night, certain that the man in the cell next to him – a freighter named Wilcox – was asleep, certain that Stebner was walking his rounds on the streets, before he spit on the key and the hinges to provide some lubrication and silently opened the bars.

He crept noiselessly past the sleeping Len Wilcox, returned the key to the top drawer in the battered corner desk that Stebner used – *they'll wonder fer a long time how in hell this happened,* he thought, grinning broadly – and then simply slipped out the front door after securing a Winchester lever-action rifle and a box of cartridges from the rack on the wall behind the sheriff's desk.

Bolton crept around the corner of the building, used a narrow alley to position himself behind the row of buildings that fronted the main street, and made his way cautiously toward the livery stable. He found his horse and saddle, unguarded and untended. He was disappointed that his saddlebags had been rifled and the newly acquired gold coins were missing, but he was not surprised: *Hell, I would've stole that gold myself. In fact, I did steal it* – and he couldn't help but chuckle at the thought.

He saw nothing of Stebner. Everywhere that he looked, in fact, the streets were deserted.

Within minutes, Bolton boldly walked his horse away from the western edge of town, the newly acquired Winchester cocked and ready for trouble in the crook of his arm. But the expected trouble never came, and he mounted his horse and trotted the animal a mile toward the west. He eventually looped to the south and started to pick his way through the rocky terrain of the high desert that stretched for miles toward the border, using the light of the moon and the multitude of stars overhead to navigate.

He had heard plenty of talk about the renegade pack while he was secured in the jail cell, and he was heading in that direction now – hopeful that he might track the gold thieves and somehow throw in with them. Bolton now figured that the gold he took from the man he had killed on the trail days before – a man he had mistaken for Make Blake – was somehow connected to the renegades, and he might be able to use this knowledge to work his way inside.

It could give me leverage if I play my cards right, he thought, his face still formed into a broad grin. *And if that don't work out – well hell, I can still shoot Max Blake.*

The thought of killing the federal marshal made Tom Bolton laugh out loud again, and his voice carried across the desert for a long time.

The grudge he carried against the federal marshal was as real to him as the horse he rode, the stolen Winchester he carried, the very land he now traveled.

Bolton had always considered himself to be a lawman worthy of respect; it was simply a matter of waiting in the wings before taking over Ned Clark's sheriff's duties in the bustling town of Twisted Junction and then moving on – perhaps even one day becoming a federal marshal and working for Judge Radford in Twin Forks.

But all of that changed in his mind, the dream suddenly dead and empty, on the night weeks before when Max Blake rode into Twisted Junction in pursuit of Hoss Johnson and the Morgan brothers.

In Bolton's simple mind, in fact, Blake had shamed him in front of his friends by knocking his feet off the top of the sheriff's desk, by telling him to wipe the silly grin off his face – *by treating me without the respect that one lawman always gives to another lawman.* Blake's reputation as a tracker and fast gunman, famous throughout the territories, may have been well-deserved; but to Bolton's way of thinking, his disregard for a fellow lawman was something that he could not abide, and he began to brood on the matter.

As Bolton considered it, Ned Clark seemed to become more critical of his performance and far less tolerant of the work that he did within days of Blake's arrival in town. Clark blamed it on Bolton's preoccupation with Blake; Bolton blamed it on Clark's jealousy and inability to appreciate his deputy's obvious talents as a lawman of considerable skill.

Truth is, he can see I'm destined to become sheriff, and he's afraid for his job and nothing more and is listening to that bastard Blake, Bolton thought.

Within a matter of days, Clark told him to pack up and leave Twisted Junction for good – confirmation in Bolton's twisted thought process that his dismissal was orchestrated entirely from Twin Forks.

It's all Blake's fault – it all goes back to him, Bolton thought now as he made his way south toward the border.

Max Blake is gonna pay for what he done to me. Jest you wait and see.

He threw his head back and laughed aloud again as he shifted the Winchester from one arm to the other, and he laughed for a good long time.

Chapter 41

A Trail of Revenge

Tom Bolton, late of Twisted Junction and years short of common sense, positioned himself at the far corner of a dry gulch carved in the desert floor halfway between Whiskey Bend and the Mexican border, waiting patiently.

He had tied his horse to a clump of mesquite at the far end of the arroyo before finding cover behind a scattered pile of boulders left behind when the earth shuddered and rolled eons before, leaving behind an ugly gash on the desert floor.

In the distance, he watched a pair of hawks circle aimlessly above the miles of rock and sand, riding the air currents and thermal troughs with breathtaking precision and dexterity. He imagined what it must be like to fly, keeping an eye on all moving things, untouchable from great heights, magnificent and imperious.

Sure wish I could fly like a bird, he thought, *'cause it sure would make this job a whole bunch easier.*

Bolton couldn't fly, of course, but he could afford to be patient on this day, and he knew well the benefits of caution. These were traits he had learned from his former boss Ned Clark, Twisted Junction's sheriff, and they served him well now as he kept his eyes directed to the south, a stolen Winchester cradled across his lap, loaded and ready.

He had missed the renegades by hours, he figured, though he could tell easily enough where they had camped in the desert south of town. And so he concentrated again on finding and killing Max Blake, certain that he could eventually join the gold bandits in Mexico.

A few hours, a few days – it didn't matter. Bolton knew that if Max

Blake survived his venture into Aguante – *and that in itself is a long reach,* he thought – the marshal eventually would return to Twin Forks. He also knew that the trail home passed directly through Whiskey Bend, where Bolton had escaped from a jail cell hours before.

Sooner or later, if he's still alive, Blake is gonna show up. And when he does, me and this brand new Winchester I'm holding will be ready – jest as surely as the turning of the earth.

A stack of enormous black thunderheads rolled across the sky, and Bolton listened with appreciation to the low, throaty rumble of threatening storms coughing in the distance. The passing clouds provided a welcome if momentary break in the sun-fueled heat, and he sipped at the water in his canteen and enjoyed the brief respite. But the thunderheads passed to the northeast and the rumblings grew more distant with each fleeing minute, and the sun again broke loose from the thick swarm of clouds and continued its relentless attack on the parched earth.

The hawks drifted away on the desert currents and were soon gone from sight, and Bolton concentrated on the trail that stretched before him, running north and south, waiting for any appearance – any sign – that would indicate the presence of a man on horseback.

At one point, he thought that he heard the drumming of distant hoof beats, and he scanned the horizon to the north for what seemed like an hour or more. *That might be a posse out of Whiskey Bend working my tail,* he thought, *though there ain't no man tough enough to get me.* But he gave up when the threat, more imagined than real as he saw it, passed from his mind, and he again turned his attention to the trail that he hoped would eventually produce Max Blake.

"Sooner rather than later," he muttered aloud, taking a small rock and tossing it out into the desert. *I plug Blake and let him look in my eyes a'fore he dies, jest so he knows it was me. Then I kin catch up with them bandits and git me a share of that gold.*

"Yes, sir," he said aloud, reaching for another rock, "a cut of the gold and no Max Blake, and I'll be ace high till can't see."

Max Blake was watching for the glint of a rifle barrel reflecting in the sun, and he reacted with the instincts and quickness of a mountain cat when he saw it.

He was heading north, drawing ever closer to Whiskey Bend, when Buck, his chestnut gelding, twitched his ears and snapped his head quickly off toward the left side of the trail. The flash of the rifle barrel in the overhead sun sparked off the top of a boulder at the edge of a dry gulch, and Max pulled Buck up and cut the horse sharply to his left and behind the trailing Reno Walker and his black gelding.

The single shot from a Winchester lever-action rifle rolled across the desert floor in a dull wave of murmuring echoes; the bullet struck solid flesh with a sickening thud.

Walker's cry of pain and surprise was muffled by the gag that covered his mouth, and he slumped in the saddle and rolled to the side of his horse, held upright only by the ropes that bound his hands and feet.

Max was off Buck instantly, pulling the big animal to the ground in a sudden, efficient maneuver that man and horse had practiced many times. He glanced across the desert floor at Walker's horse, which had bolted before coming to an awkward halt, and Max quickly estimated the distance and the time it would take him to reach the wounded outlaw sheriff. He tried to spot the position of the shooter, pulling the Bowie knife from his boot as he scanned the immediate area ahead of him, and he patted Buck's neck and sprinted, crouching low, on a hard zigzag course toward Reno Walker.

Two shots barked out, kicking up sand behind him, and Max positioned the black gelding between himself and the shooter and quickly sliced the ropes that held the outlaw upright in the saddle. He pulled the wounded man down into the sand, returning his knife to his boot, and slid his Colt out of its holster. Two more shots from the distant rifle sprayed sand and pieces of rock across his chest, and he cursed softly and slithered away from Walker as the gelding bolted again. He waited for a brief instant before jumping to his feet and, staying low to the ground, ran hard until he hurled himself behind a thick clump of mesquite at the side of the trail.

Max knew that Walker and his gelding were vulnerable; and he was painfully aware that Buck was in jeopardy as well, although the horse would not move until Max whistled or called. He looked across to where Buck waited on his side, and he silently cursed again.

Max had found no time to pull his rifle from the scabbard attached to his saddle when the shooting began, and it was too dangerous now to return for the weapon: Gunfire in that direction almost certainly would strike Buck.

Max drew a deep breath before scrambling north and west, drawing fire away from Reno Walker and Buck, his movements erratic and unpredictable. He dove for a solitary paloverde tree, which stood like a lone sentinel on the desert floor, as three consecutive shots struck the ground around him, and he caught his breath for a moment before chancing a look to the north. Another shot from the Winchester peeled into the bark of the paloverde directly above his head, and Max tucked himself low to the ground again and rested on his back as he considered his next move.

His Colt was cradled in his hand, but Max knew that the bushwhacker was too far away to use the revolver effectively. The best he could do was continue to work his way forward until he discovered the shooter's position. It was a dangerous plan, and he knew it; one movement that was too slow, or one lucky shot, and he would be in the same position as Reno Walker – wounded and defenseless in the dirt.

Or I might end up dead, he thought.

"Not good," he muttered. "Not good at all."

He drew another deep breath before sprinting across the desert floor, and he turned his head toward a spot a dozen yards away that he felt he could reach in safety. He stumbled, caught his balance, sensed before he heard the bullet as it whined past his ear, and dove to the ground in a shallow depression that offered precious little protection.

Max looked about frantically, trying to locate a better position, when he heard the staccato beating of horses' hooves, coming in hard from the north. A quick glance showed a ragged line of men on horseback, their clothing dulled by trail dust, their rifles and carbines glinting in the noonday sun. A thin smile crossed Max's face as he counted ten riders sweeping toward him in a line that stretched across the horizon in a bobbing, shimmering wave of color and sound and motion, heading directly toward the shooter.

A whoop and a yell carried clearly across the great expanse of desert, and Max spotted a tall man in a black Stetson in the center of the column, his arm raised, edging forward in the saddle and urging the riders on either side to follow his lead. The big man yelled again, and the crack of high-caliber ammunition bellowed in savage bursts.

Max followed the line of fire and spotted for a brief instant the solitary gunman running hard away from the charging riders before disappearing from sight, as though he had been swept off the earth by an unseen hand. Max shook his head and refocused his eyes, studying the spot where the racing figure had been mere seconds before, but he saw nothing more of the dry-gulcher.

Another round of rifle fire barked out, and Max holstered his Colt and stood slowly as two of the charging riders swept past the spot where the bushwhacker disappeared and drew closer to his position. He kept his hands at his sides and waited until he saw John Hawkins, the Whiskey Bend sheriff, swinging his horse directly toward him, a broad smile sweeping across his face.

Hawkins hailed his deputy, Bob Stebner, and the two lawmen pulled their horses up immediately in front of the federal marshal from Twin Forks. A rolling cloud of dust swept past Max, and Hawkins waited until it cleared before he spoke.

"It seems I've come to your rescue this time, Marshal Blake," he said.

Max nodded at Hawkins for an instant, wordlessly acknowledging his thanks with a simple smile, and then whistled loudly. Buck scrambled to his feet at the sound, shook the dust and dirt from his big body, and loped across the sand to Max's side. The horse nudged at Max's right shoulder until he pulled a carrot from the saddlebags. "What an old beggar you are," he whispered, patting Buck's head.

Max then pulled himself into the saddle and urged Buck toward the spot where he had left Reno Walker in the dirt minutes before. "Who's the shooter?" he called over his shoulder.

"It's Tom Bolton," Hawkins said, pulling alongside. "He snuck out of the cell sometime last night – not sure how. Looks like we happened along at the right time."

"We heard the shots from over yonder and came in thinking it was Bolton all right," Stebner called. "He's pinned in an arroyo across the way" – he gestured with his arm in the general direction of the shooting. "I expect we'll flush him out directly."

Max nodded. "I've got a surprise of my own here," he said and nudged Buck along until he was looking down on the still form of Reno Walker. The outlaw's eyes were closed, and a look of anguish stretched across his face. The man's buckskin trousers and jacket were soiled with dirt and dust; his face was streaked with grime and sweat and the oil that seeped from his hair. His Stetson was lying nearby, partially crushed and covered with sand, exposing the ugly rent in the sheriff's shattered ear.

A growing stain pooled at his side, turning the earth a muddy deep-hued red.

"It's Reno Walker," Max said simply.

Stebner whistled, and Walker's eyes flickered open at the sound. He tried to focus in the glare of the noonday sun until another stab of pain stitched itself across his face.

"Water," he muttered, too faintly to be heard.

Max swung out of the saddle and knelt at the outlaw's side, ignoring the occasional gunshots that echoed across the desert floor from the nearby gulch.

"Water," Walker repeated, and Max turned to Hawkins. "Sling me down one of those canteens," he called, catching the deerskin-covered tin when Hawkins complied. Max pulled the stop and offered Walker a drink, carefully pouring small amounts into the man's half-open mouth as he tilted his head forward. Walker sputtered and coughed before closing his eyes again.

"I'm done in," he whispered. "At least you don't get" – the words caught in his throat, and a violent cough wracked his body and a trickle of blood leaked from the side of his mouth – "at least you ... don't get to hang me."

Max nodded. He offered the canteen again, but Walker shook his head slightly.

"Tell Nash I tried ..." But the words caught again, and he choked and couldn't finish the thought. The outlaw's eyes closed, and Max thought that he was gone and started to stand again when the dying sheriff stirred once more.

"Blake, I want ... message ... my wife," he muttered, each word coming with a painful effort. "My name's ... Rentfro. Her name's ... Mary. She's in –"

The sheriff's body visibly slumped, as though all of the air inside had suddenly gushed out, and his hard, doll's-like eyes stared up at nothing.

Max stood, cursed softly under his breath, turned, and tossed the canteen back to Hawkins.

"What'd he say at the end, marshal?" Hawkins asked.

Max started to reply, then shook his head and climbed back into the saddle. He shifted his weight, glanced at Hawkins and then Stebner before turning his head toward the sporadic gunfire in the distance, and muttered, "Nothing – of any use, at least," but his words were indistinct.

He swung Buck toward the gulch where Bolton was pinned by the Whiskey Bend posse, pulled the Colt again, and nudged Buck forward. Hawkins fell in line on Max's left, with Stebner trailing behind after latching onto the reins of Walker's horse. Max kept his eyes focused directly ahead. "Let' put an end to this," he said.

"Yes; you are quite right, Marshal Blake," Hawkins replied.

Tom Bolton was tucked beneath a protruding rock that provided cover from directly above and the far side of the narrow canyon's walls. John Hawkins leaned forward in the saddle, looking intently over the rim. A barrel-chested man with a wild beard pointed out Bolton's position.

"What do you think, Frosty?" Hawkins asked at last.

"He's like a tick plugged into a hound down there," Frosty Bell said. "He's gonna be tough to roust outta that spot, and it's too risky to send a man over the side – he's like to get shot quick and no reward fer the effort."

Hawkins called out loudly: "Tom Bolton, it's Sheriff Hawkins. Give it up, son; there's no place to go and no way to get there."

Hawkins' words echoed off the walls of the gulch but were met with silence.

The Whiskey Bend sheriff tried again: "Bolton, listen to me and you'll see the sun again." He paused, waiting for a reply, and added after another moment of eerie silence: "The only way out is through us, and that's not gonna come easy. Come on out of there now and stop this."

But there was still no reply, and Hawkins shrugged and turned toward Bob Stebner. "Any suggestions?" he asked.

Stebner cocked his head and considered the dilemma. "Some," he said after a minute. "We could starve him out. And he can't have much water, if any. But fer something quick – well, yer guess is likely better'n mine."

"I'll get him out," Max said.

Both men turned in surprise. "How do you propose to accomplish that, marshal?" Hawkins asked.

"I'll call him out. He's been trying to kill me. I'll give him the chance."

"Sorry, marshal, but I can't allow it. It would be the same as executing Bolton, and I won't abide that – even if he deserves it."

"I'm only suggesting that we draw him out," Max said. "Once he's up, you take him and I ride away. Work out the details with Ned Clark; he can have him."

Hawkins rubbed his fingers on the bridge of his nose, tired of the chase, and finally nodded in agreement. "All right – be my guest, Marshal Blake," he said. "It's better'n waiting him out. If you lure him up, we'll surprise him – and no gunplay."

"Good," Max said, and he turned his attention to the rim of the gulch as Hawkins whispered instructions to Frosty Bell and Bob Stebner.

"Bolton," Max called out after collecting his thoughts. "It's Max Blake." He paused momentarily, letting his words echo off the rocks. "It's just you and me. Hawkins and his men ride; the two of us settle it."

The silence that followed was tangible. Hawkins edged his horse closer to the rim, and Stebner climbed down from his mount and peered over the side as Bell huddled with Neil McGill and Gary Haugen from the posse. Max was about to try again when a thin voice carried upward on the hot currents of air.

"I'll come on up, Blake. I'll kill you when I do."

Max caught John Hawkins' eye before calling down: "First things first. I'll get rid of the posse. Then you come up and we end this." He nodded again toward Hawkins, and the sheriff motioned for McGill and Haugen to hide behind boulders at the top of the rim. When Hawkins was satisfied, he called down, "All right, Bolton, it's Sheriff Hawkins again. We're pulling out. You sure you don't want to – "

"Let it go," Bolton called back. "It's between me and Blake. Clear out now.

"Blake, you tell me when it's jest you and me. Then we finish it. And no tricks – understand? I want the chance to kill you fair and square."

Hawkins waved his remaining men in close and whispered instructions. "All right, Bolton, it's on you now. We ride," he yelled.

Hawkins and his posse wheeled their horses near the edge of the rim to ensure that the sound of clattering hooves would carry into the gulch before they galloped off to the north.

Max waited a full minute before he called out, "All right, Bolton, it's your turn."

Tom Bolton peered cautiously out from the overhanging rock at the bottom of the gulch and, detecting no signs of the armed posse, scrambled to his feet. "Blake, I'm on my way," he called before starting up the narrow game trail.

"You come ahead. I'll be here."

A moment later, Bolton's dusty Stetson appeared at the top of the rim, and he peered cautiously from the edge and saw Max Blake sitting astride Buck, twenty yards or more away, casually watching, his arms folded across his chest. Bolton nodded and said, "I've been waitin' a long time fer this."

Max shrugged. "No more waiting, then."

As Bolton started to press forward, rubbing his hands together in anticipation, McGill and Haugen lunged from behind the boulders and knocked the former deputy to the ground. Bolton cursed loudly and fought wildly, but he was quickly subdued. McGill fired his revolver twice into the air to signal Hawkins, and Max swung down from Buck and walked slowly toward Bolton and his two captors.

Bolton continued to struggle, and he looked up and glared at Max. "Yer nothing but a coward, Blake – a yella-belly," he hissed. "You had to git help from these two and, hell, dirty tricks to git me. But I'll git you yet, dammit. It ain't done yet."

Max watched without emotion, and Bolton thrashed wildly again in an effort to get his arms free as Hawkins and his men thundered in once more.

Hawkins beamed as he pulled his horse to a halt next to Max. "Thanks, Marshal Blake," he said simply before adding for his men, "Good work, boys."

"Yer both yella cowards," Bolton cried. "And I ain't done with you, Blake – not by a long shot."

"You should appreciate the fact that you are still alive," Hawkins said.

"What do you know?" Bolton shot back. "When I git done with Blake, I'll git you too fer good measure."

McGill, a seasoned freighter with rock-hard fists and an easy smile, laughed loudly. "What you been feeding that man in your jail cell, sheriff?" he asked.

"It's funny how Max Blake seems to rile up a man," Haugen offered.

"I'll show you riled," Bolton said, and he shoved hard at Gary Haugen, catching him off balance. He toppled backward, pulling Bolton with him, and the one-time deputy rolled and elbowed the man viciously, wrestling the gun from Haugen's grasp.

Bolton twisted on the ground, trying to align Haugen's revolver, when Max Blake's Colt Peacemaker barked twice – before McGill or Stebner or Hawkins or even Bolton could fire. The first bullet caught Bolton in the right shoulder, snapping his collar bone with a thud. The second shattered the barrel of the revolver, splintering the weapon into shards of hot metal.

Bolton cried out, clutching his hand and writhing on the ground – his face twisted in pain, his eyes flashing with frustration – and he was quickly covered again by McGill and Frosty Bell and then an angry Gary Haugen.

Max waited until he was certain that Bolton was no longer a threat before he flicked his Colt back into its holster with a well-practiced motion and looked across at John Hawkins.

"It's over," he said simply, tipping the brim of his Stetson.

"I ain't finished with you, Blake," Bolton cried, his voice stung with rage and pain and the shattered dream of a planned revenge gone sour.

"Not by a long shot."

But Max ignored Bolton's cries and swung up into the saddle, scratching at Buck's ear for a moment.

"Time to go, boy," he said, and he nodded once more toward Hawkins and nudged Buck forward on the trail without looking back.

Epilogue

A Hollow Resolution

In the searing days that returned Max Blake from the edge of the territory to Twin Forks and home, it seemed that nothing had changed – and that everything had changed.

Joey Gray, the young stables boy, yelled a vigorous greeting when he saw Max and Buck appear at the edge of town, and he ran into the dusty street to meet them, a wide smile on his beaming face.

Lon Barbers, the livery owner who tried to appear indifferent to the comings and goings of the town's federal marshals, nodded casually when Max climbed down from his chestnut gelding and handed Buck's reins to Joey. The boy already had fired a dozen questions at his friend with the tin star and wasn't finished.

"I generally don't take much notice, but it's good to see you back, marshal," Barbers said, talking over Joey's non-stop barrage. "The dog'll be excited, I reckon."

Max nodded his thanks and turned to Joey. "It's good to see you, son. You grew another foot. How does your mother keep you in clothes?"

They talked for a moment, the three of them – the federal marshal, the stables owner, and the young boy who tended the stock – but it was clear that Max Blake had something else on his mind.

"I'll tell you all about it later, Joey. Take good care of Buck now," he said at last. "And tell your mother I'd be pleased to come for dinner, if that invitation's still good."

"Do you mean it, Max? Really? I'm gonna run home right now and tell her. Honest. You just wait."

Max smiled at the boy's enthusiasm and moved resolutely up the street, a vigilant observer of the ebb and flow of life on the dusty streets of Twin Forks.

The patrons of Mad Dog's steakhouse were ravenous and impatient as Max passed by. Jim Madden, the long-suffering owner, was indifferent.

"If you don't keep yer mouth shut and stop pestering me, Jim Guyor, I'm gonna give yer steak to the next man," Madden called to a rowdy cowboy as he worked over sizzling chunks of meat in the smoke-filled corner that contained his makeshift kitchen. "You hear me?"

"Come on, Dog, ease up some," Guyor protested. "I'm hungry is all, and I ..."

"That's it. I warned you and got no never mind," Madden snapped. "You can sit and wait awhile longer. Maybe that'll teach you to come to my place and keep a'jabberin' at me."

He looked around the room and yelled, "And that goes fer the rest of you, too," ignoring Guyor's calls of complaint.

At Radford's Saloon, the men who stood shoulder to shoulder, fighting for the attention of three busy whiskey-slingers working the long bar, were in a raucous and festive mood. A hanging hours earlier had energized the town; it was the first in more than a month, and people from a hundred-mile swath rode horses, arrived in buggies, or simply walked into town to celebrate the event.

The saloon owned by the town's famous judge always did a stellar business. Patrons knew that the judge himself often put in an appearance and sometimes could be persuaded to offer opinions about the merits of a case.

The latest outlaw to find his moment of justice in Judge Radford's courthouse before swinging from the end of a rope was a crook of little consequence and minor reputation named Hughes. But his public death still caused a stir.

"He weren't nothing more'n a horse thief – and not much of one at that," one of the patrons complained. But the occasion was memorable because everyone agreed that the hanging of even a second-rate outlaw was better than no hangings at all – and because it was rumored that the judge himself was scheduled for a visit within the hour.

"I got it on good authority – from the judge hisself," Clem Carson, one of the bartenders, said with certainty. "And one thing you can trust in Twin Forks is the word of Judge Radford."

A small roar went up, and another round of drinks was ordered.

Farther down the street, Doc Strand was involved in a card game with two regulars, Big Boy Pygon and Milt Milton, at The Watering Hole saloon. Doc was behind by a few dollars and recognized that a good hand was becoming increasingly difficult to acquire.

At the courthouse, Judge Thomas Radford was sequestered in his office, his reading glasses perched on his ponderous nose, a law book grasped firmly in his thick hands and held close to his face – his mind, too, on more pressing matters.

The arrival of Max Blake was noticed by a handful of townsfolk who happened along Twin Fork's dusty main street as the federal marshal rode in from the territory, stopped at the stables, and eventually made his way to the courthouse. He walked with the assured confidence of a man who feared no one, nodded as he passed Matt Grill, the bailiff, and knocked quietly on the judge's second-floor office door.

"Come in, Marshal Blake. I've been expecting you."

Max eased himself inside and stared at the judge, who placed the law book he was examining down on his desk, took off his wire-framed reading glasses, and began cleaning the lenses with a white handkerchief that he pulled from his back pocket.

"I received the wire from Sheriff Hawkins in Whiskey Bend, of course – and the one from your friend Sheriff Clark in Twisted Junction," he said after a moment. "Won't you take a seat, please?"

"No thanks," Max said simply, shifting his weight from one foot to the other, his face devoid of emotion, his hands at his sides.

"I see. Back to that already, are we?"

When Max made no reply, the judge looked past him, as though he had spotted something interesting on the far wall.

"Sheriff Hawkins noted the gallant effort you made to bring in the recalcitrant outlaw sheriff from Aguante, Marshal Blake, and the bad luck you all ran into with this fellow Walker. Yes, one Reno Walker Rentfro, as I remember it." He paused momentarily, smiling at his recall, before launching in again. "The court recognizes that effort. Something extra will be in your paycheck as a result, Marshal Blake, even though a criminal of known reputation again escaped the noose and his rightful due in my court."

He looked into Max's eyes at this point, expecting a response, but Max merely stared back, his face empty. "Understand, Marshal Blake, that I full well recognize why you didn't deliver the man to my courtroom. It's just disappointing on many levels – that's all I meant to say."

Max nodded, holding the judge's eyes, saying nothing.

"And the reason you didn't bring this Tom Bolton character back with you?"

"Sheriff Clark has a claim on Bolton for a killing in his jurisdiction."

"I see," the judge said and thought about this for a moment, his eyes wandering around his spacious office. He folded his hands and set them on the desk, flicking his right thumb casually in the air, again and again, unaware of the movement. His eyes came to rest on a series of telegrams stacked on the corner of the desk, and he picked them up now and examined them, as though for the first time, slipping on his reading glasses and nodding his head at various points, as though reaffirming facts in his mind.

"I also received a wire from a Lt. Col. Michael Corbin, commending you for your actions on behalf of the U.S. Army," the judge continued after a moment, scanning the papers as he spoke. "And I am in receipt of still another wire, this one from a Lt. Gen. Gary Mitchell, who was equally effusive, Marshal Blake – perhaps even more so."

The judged looked directly at Max, adjusting his reading glasses on the bridge of his hawk-shaped nose. "You seem to be making friends in high places. This fellow Corbin, as I understand it, has something of a reputation in political circles. Apparently he is well-connected back east."

Max shrugged indifferently. "Anything else?" he asked.

"A strange wire came in a day ago from a man called – wait, let me find it here," the judge said as he shuffled through the papers – "yes, here it is, from one Rufus Baxter. He indicates that he is doing well in Tombstone and that someone named Berger is resting comfortably. Does that make sense to you, Marshal Blake?"

Max smiled briefly. "Any word on the renegades?" he asked, ignoring the judge's question.

"Yes, the matter of the renegades, of course: There's a line in this fellow Mitchell's wire that Corbin and his men were continuing the pursuit of the band farther to the south; apparently some of the Confederates escaped and headed toward Mexico. Corbin himself makes no mention of it, however."

"And the gold?

"There is no mention from anyone about the gold," the judge said. "I even wired the Army personally. They told me, essentially, to mind my own business. Imagine."

Max's gray eyes flickered with amusement for an instant. "I'll complete my report by noon tomorrow," he said, and he walked out without waiting for a reply.

"We'll continue this conversation tomorrow then," the judge called after him.

Thomas Radford looked at the door for a long time before he picked up his law book, shaking his head, suddenly uncertain of the future that stretched before him.

Joey Gray was approaching as Max stepped out of the courthouse and turned down the street again. A big smile widened Joey's little boy's face, and he said breathlessly: "I talked with Ma, Max. It's all set. But I got to get back to the stables right now and finish with Buck or Mr. Barbers will shoot me – and maybe you, too. Stop by and I'll tell you all about it." He laughed aloud, clapping his hands, and ran off again.

Doc Strand peered over the edges of his playing cards at Milt and Big Boy, ignoring the incessant chatter, trying to read their faces for a clue about the hands they held. He looked up automatically when the batwing doors swung open and followed Max Blake with his eyes as the federal marshal cautiously entered The Watering Hole.

"Well, Marshal Blake, how nice to see you again," Doc called with a wave.

Max's eyes adjusted quickly to the dim light inside, and he nodded. "Hey, Doc, hoped to find you here. Got a minute?"

"Sure, marshal. These are doing me precious little good." He tossed the cards on the table and said to his playing partners, "You cleaned me out, boys. I'm all done."

Strand ignored the protests from Milt and Big Boy and joined Max at the bar, where the marshal had just ordered a tall beer. "What are you drinking, Doc?" he asked.

"I'll join you in a beer, marshal," he said. "Whiskey is for killing, and water is for cooling down after a good fight. Beer is just the thing for drinking, though."

John Lindley, the Watering Hole's nighttime bartender, poured a second beer and slid the frothy glass across the bar to Doc Strand. "It's on the house, gentlemen," he said. Max nodded his thanks but slid a silver coin back across the bar. "That's for you, then, John," he said.

"Hey, you fellas should meet Cliff Corn," Lindley added, pointing toward the man who was cleaning glasses with a bar towel a few feet away. "Cliff, say hello to Doc Strand and the famous Max Blake."

Corn turned, extending his hand first to Doc and then to Max. "Pleased to meet the both of you," he said.

"Corn is joining us here after a lot of years up north," Lindley said. Max nodded. "Adobe Flats."

"That's right, marshal," Corn said as Lindley added, "I'm breaking him in here the next few days till he gets the hang of the place."

"We heard about the Adobe Flats disaster, of course," Doc offered.

"A pity."

"That's one way to put it, I guess."

"So what made you decide to seek your fortune here, Mr. Corn?" Doc asked.

"Adobe Flats is gone," he said, looking from one man to the next as he buffed the same glass. "Only a handful survived the massacre. Them still living decided to let it go – pack up and move out. The whole place'll be nothing but a distant memory in time – a spot on the map that came and went. We'll all be lucky if we don't end up the same."

He turned his lanky frame toward Max and added: "Listen, Marshal Blake, I'm carrying a message fer you from a man lives up that way – been waiting fer your return."

Max waited, but Corn shook his head. "Now ain't the best time – gotta finish the glasses. Maybe before you leave tonight you can give me a minute?"

Max nodded, although he looked hard at the man, trying to determine what he might know and the importance of the information. *Whatever it is can wait,* he thought.

"It's nice meeting you boys," Corn said.

"Likewise, Mr. Corn," Doc Strand replied.

"They call me Col. Corn," the new bartender added as he moved away, collecting another glass.

"A witticism," Doc said with a chuckle. "That's a rare commodity in these parts."

Doc took a long drink from his glass and delicately wiped his mouth at the corners. "So what's the occasion, marshal?" he asked. "Or is there an occasion?"

Max tasted his beer and set the glass down again, turning sideways to face Doc. "Thought I'd ask for some advice, I guess," he said softly. Lindley was leaning in, doing his best to overhear the conversation, and Max nodded toward an empty table across the way and snared his glass again.

As Doc followed after the federal marshal, he called, "Bring us two more beers if you would, John." Then he muttered, "I've got a feeling we're going to need them."

Max ignored the looks of the men and the percentage girls in the saloon as he made his way across to the far table. He hooked a chair leg with the toe of his boot, pulled it out, and sat with his back to the wall so that he could see every movement of every person in The Watering Hole. And he nodded toward Big Boy and Milt as the two called across to him with silly grins, holding up their glasses in an informal salute.

Doc dropped into the chair next to Max with a thump. "You missed a hanging earlier," he said.

"Good for me," Max said. "Who was the offending party?"

"Can't recall his name. He wasn't famous – like the Morgan boys or Hoss Johnson, or the equally deadly and dead Reno Walker." He smiled at Max then and waved his hand as though he were swatting flies: "Yes, yes, I heard; half the town already knows about your success in Aguante."

Max looked at Doc Strand intently. "The men you mentioned never made it back to the courthouse – or the gallows," Max said. "The judge wasn't pleased at the time and still isn't."

Doc Strand rubbed his hands together with enthusiasm, a wide grin breaking out on the corners of his mouth, his eyes twinkling in the soft light. "Exactly, Marshal Blake. It's exactly the reason I brought it up – just to see if all was right with the world. I can see that it's not, however, which pleases me immensely."

He paused, and when Max offered nothing in return, Doc said: "Forgive my impertinence, marshal. It's just my little way of staying in the game. It's important for a man of my age and status to stay in the game. It keeps me even.

"So tell me, is this medical advice you are seeking out today, or something of a different nature, perhaps?"

John Lindley arrived at that moment with two additional beers and a wet bar towel, which he used to wipe the top of the table, lingering for as long as he could, hoping to pick up a snippet of conversation. Doc pulled a coin from his pocket and slid it across the table as Lindley fussed with an imaginary spot.

"Give it up, John," he said. "This conversation is of a ... private nature."

"Of course it is," Lindley said amiably. He finished with the table, looked first at Max Blake and then at Doc Strand, and added with an exaggerated smile, "If you gentlemen need me at any point, I am at your service – as always."

When Lindley strolled away, twice looking over his shoulder, Max leaned in closer to Doc and asked, "You have any advice on tending after a woman?"

Strand could hardly conceal the surprise that lit up his eyes. "A woman?" he asked incredulously, his voice loud enough to attract stares from across the room. "Any particular woman?"

Max's face turned a shade of red, and he indicated with his hands for

317

Doc to keep his voice down. "Does it matter?" he muttered.

"Does it matter? Of course it matters," Doc whispered in a conspiratorial tone. "Different women need to be pursued in different ways. You wouldn't approach a saloon girl in the same way you would approach, well, a woman who might actually seek courting, or a woman who – "

Without finishing the thought, Doc Strand pulled his six-gun in a fluid motion and fired twice at a man who was charging toward the table from no more than ten feet away, pointing two revolvers in his general direction.

But Doc's bullets were the third and fourth that barked in the saloon. Max Blake's Colt Peacemaker already was blazing from two shots that he had fired at the same man an instant before.

All four bullets found their mark, and the attacker's body twisted grotesquely as it was slammed backward into a chair that fronted an empty table. The chair spun sideways as the body toppled over, and the table splintered under the dead weight and collapsed and shattered into shards.

Smoke from the six-guns wafted through the now deadly quiet saloon.

Despite the advantage of surprise, the stranger had not been quick enough to fire his revolvers.

Max was on his feet, and he moved cautiously across to the body that was sprawled in a heap on the dirty wooden floor. Doc was at his side an instant later, and they stared briefly at the dead man and then at each other.

"You know this fella?" Doc asked.

Max nodded. "His name was Wilcox – a freighter from Whiskey Bend."

"You know why this … happened?" Doc asked.

"Payment for a good deed, I guess," Max said simply.

Doc Strand waited for a better explanation. When it didn't come, he stepped around Max, bent down, and felt for a pulse. He shook his head for an instant. "Nothing," he said, standing again. "I'd like to think this balances something out, but I'm damned if I know what it might be."

Max stepped over the body and headed for the door.

"Marshal?" Doc called after him.

Max stopped and turned once more. He reached inside his collar and removed the federal marshal's star that was pinned to his shirt. He looked at it once, then tossed it to Doc. "Would you give that to the judge for me?" he asked.

Strand looked first at the badge and then at his friend Max Blake, his face registering a thousand questions, his mind fastened on a single word. "Why?"

Max shrugged. "I'll be late for dinner with a pretty lady if I give it to him myself," he said and turned again toward the door. He moved warily, and he could sense every eye in the saloon fastened directly on him.

He pushed his way through the batwing doors and was moving briskly across the wooden planks toward the street when he heard a voice from behind. "Marshal Blake?"

Max turned quickly, his gun hand hovering on the grip of his Colt, and fastened his eyes on Cliff Corn, The Watering Hole's new bartender.

"I'm sorry that man came after you tonight," Corn said, nervously watching Max's right hand while he spoke.

Max nodded but said nothing, his face unreadable in the fading light. "Listen, marshal, about that fella from Adobe Flats ..."

"Sure. A message ..."

"Well sir, I wouldn't bother you after that shooting and all, but I think it's important. It's from a man calls himself Jack Sloan. Sloan is a prospector working a claim in the mountains north of Adobe Flats – what used to be Adobe Flats. Seems a decent enough galoot, though a hard drinker when the mood is on him, and it often is."

Two men burst out of the saloon at that moment and ran toward the courthouse, their eyes wide as they caught sight of Max, but he ignored them and nodded at Corn.

"Anyways, he asked me to deliver this message, and I wanted to git it exact in my head. He told me this: 'When you see Max Blake, tell him I'm sorry. Tell him I'm tired of running and hiding and pretending to be somebody I ain't.' He said it just like that."

"All right," Max shrugged, "but what does it mean?"

"Well sir, he said his name really weren't Sloan a'tall, marshal. He told me his name's really Reyelts – Paul Reyelts. He had me repeat it to him more'n once so's I'd remember it well enough – said you'd understand when you heard it."

The name struck Max like a body blow. "After all this time," he murmured. He looked puzzled and shook his head, trying to clear the confusion from his mind. It took him a moment to find Corn's eyes again. "Anything else?"

"He went up to the hills, marshal – said he'd be waiting for you."

Max's eyes were wide and unblinking. "That's all?"

Corn ran the image of Jack Sloan through his mind once more and frowned. "It was nothing he told me, but I got the feeling he knew bad things were coming his way."

Max nodded, his face drained of color and expression.

"You all right, marshal?"

"Mr. Corn – thanks," Max said after a minute. "I appreciate your finding me."

"Are you going after Sloan … I mean Reyelts, marshal?"

Max turned, still shaking his head, his mind racing.

"I'm going to dinner, Mr. Corn," he said softly as he walked away, his words hanging gently in the crisp desert air. "I'm going to dinner." And he moved with a purpose down the street, his eyes fixed on the livery stable ahead of him.

In the distance, the sun was fastened low in the western sky and a long-eared owl called from the safety of a solitary pine.

About The Author

William Florence is a former newspaper reporter and editor who teaches journalism at a college in Salem, Oregon. He worked at newspapers in Michigan, Washington, D.C., South Dakota, Indiana, and Oregon for almost 25 years before heading the Chemeketa journalism department in 1993.

He has written newspaper articles, features, columns, editorials, and has been published widely in individual newspapers and on wire services throughout the country. He has won writing awards in four states. His work has been published nationally in such widely read industry magazines as The Bulletin for the American Society of Newspaper Editors and APME NEWS for the Associated Press Managing Editors group.

As well as living in the West, Mr. Florence has traveled extensively throughout the Western states and has a good feel for the land and the people. He studies Western lore, is knowledgeable about the customs and history of the times, and is especially well-versed in the guns that were used during this period. In his spare time, he writes Western novels.

He attended colleges in Michigan and Ireland. He is a voracious reader (particularly of Western novels from all periods) and a movie buff (with Westerns again a favorite genre). He is married and has two adult children, along with three cats and a big mortgage. His wife, Linda, a high school administrator and former English teacher, is his toughest critic as well as his best friend.

Printed in the United States
79785LV00005B/45